Muddy Messy Love

EMME SPIRE

NINE LIGHT PRESS

First published in 2024 by
Nine Light Press
PO Box 1042
Golden Grove, South Australia 5125
Australia

www.ninelightpress.com

Print ISBN: 978-0-6459642-0-2
E-book ISBN: 978-0-6459642-1-9

A catalogue record for this book is available from the National Library of Australia

To my husband,
For loving all my messy parts and trusting me with yours.

Dear Reader,
This story uses Australian English spelling.

One

Can cops smell fear? I'm damn sure they can. At least, the chronic glut of mine.

I clench the ratty front seat and eye the side mirror. Smoke from Slade's cigarette fogs the car, clouding the reflection, but a gunmetal sedan still tails us through the night. Smooth like a shark stalking its prey. Black aerials in lieu of fins.

"Is that the coppers?" Liam yells from the back over Slade's thumping EDM. We're a rave party on wheels. All that's missing are strobing lights, but not for long. Slade hits the blinker to turn down a side street, and sure enough, as we round the corner, covert lights flash red and blue. *Shit.* This was not part of the plan. Then again, none of tonight was.

"Fuck," Liam drones. "Dude, I knew this would happen."

I snap my eyes to Slade, expecting his foot to jump pedals and the brakes to grind, but he shows no sign of stopping. Rather, trees whiz by in a murky blur, street lights ribbon, and sirens start to scream.

Say something, you idiot.

I hesitate, choked by my hammering heart and Slade's mere presence, but Jen squeezes my shoulder from behind, hard enough for her polka-dot nails to pinch my skin. South of the red line isn't her jam. She's here because of me. She and Liam both.

I gulp. "Pull over."

Slade cocks a brow and sizes me up, apparently surprised I dared to speak, but my body takes his velvet gaze in a totally different way, setting my skin abuzz until I squirm. A devious smirk tugs at his lips then, and my tongue darts out to lick my own, the taste of him still fresh. "Now where would be the fun in that?" he asks, eyes glinting with mischief.

My mouth falls open, and his smile grows.

He can't be serious.

He kills the music, stubs out his cigarette in the old ashtray, then shakes his head. "C'mon, Avery, live a little."

"Aves," Jen hisses, prompting me to turn around. Backlit by the lights closing in, her fiery curls glow, and her panicky frown begs me to do something—to reason with Slade.

Liam squeezes her knee, then clears his throat. "Come on, man. Whatcha gonna do? Get us in a high-speed chase? In *my* car? That shit ain't happening."

Slade locks eyes with him in the rear-view mirror. Liam's as placid as they come, but mess with his car—*his baby*—and God help you.

Slade's jaw ticks. "Fuck me," he grumbles before jerking the wheel towards the kerb. The dilapidated sedan jolts to a halt. "Maybe you shoulda driven, then, instead of playing footsies in the back bloody seat."

"I will next time, pie-fucker," Liam says under his breath.

I peer down at my feet and curse. The sugar-skull-decorated laptop Slade stole from my ex-housemate, Mia, sits neatly in my footwell. I take a deep breath and kick it back with my heel, hoping to hide it under the seat, but Mia's laptop refuses to budge more than an inch. It's as maddening as she is, yet smearing it with fingerprints isn't an option.

Fuck.

Car doors slam shut behind us, and my belly flips. "What are we going to do?" I ask Slade.

"Stay fucking cool. That's what we do." His eyes narrow on me, pupils eclipsing the hazel surrounds, and he leans in closer. "And remember, snitches get stitches." I furrow my brows at the thinly veiled threat, but he softens his words with a distracting smile that always steals reason from thought.

We stare at the mirrors in arctic silence as two officers approach, flanking each side of Liam's car with footsteps that crunch and thud. Jen whimpers, and her distress knots in my chest. We haven't been stopped by police since she and I were twelve and rollerblading without helmets. That was funny. *This?* Not so much. But still, that new feeling simmers low in my belly beneath the bitter warning. It spirals up my spine and poises for what's to come, craving adrenaline and turmoil—the chaos it knows.

Slade winds down his window and plasters on a charismatic smile. Each flash of colour illuminates his tan skin, and the red, in particular, does beautiful things to his complexion. *Heavenly* things. Tribal tattoos wind up the back of his neck through dark buzz-cut hair. A titanium stud shimmers in his left ear, and his eyes gleam with the promise of trouble. My stomach flutters.

God, he's beautiful.

"Good evening, Officer. Sorry, I didn't know all that was for us. What can I do for you?" Slade says in his most eloquent voice, never mind it being midnight.

The officer narrows his eyes. "Driver's licence, please?"

Slade makes a show of slapping his empty pockets, then rummages through the centre console. "Sorry, Officer, I seem to have left it at home."

"Is this your vehicle?"

"It's mine, sir," Liam says, poking his head through the gap between the front seats.

The officer shines his torch around the inside of the car, clocking every detail and illuminating us one by one. I squint against the sting of light while he holds aim longer than necessary, seeming to find fun in my discomfort.

Arsehole.

Blinking away the spots in my vision, I take a deep breath, still hoping this is merely a routine licence check. However, part of me knows the timing is too perfect. Especially when he spies the laptop at my feet.

Double fuck.

His jaw ticks, and he steps back, throwing a sharp nod to his partner. "All of you, exit the vehicle with your hands in the air." His tone is short, leaving no room for argument. He is pure authority, well executed in steel-cap boots and standard-issue midnight blue.

I fumble with the door handle, then trip straight over the kerb. Gravel bites my knees through the rips in my cuffed jeans, and my palms sting, but I scramble to my feet and raise my hands, praying Slade didn't see and that no bullets fly.

"Are you okay?" Jen asks ventriloquist-style. The chilly breeze rustles her baby-doll dress as she stands trembling on a grassy patch one metre away. Liam stands next to her, mimicking the trees with his lanky arms as his glasses reflect the disco of lights.

"I'm fine," I whisper, but it's a total lie. There is nothing fine about this.

Taking his sweet time, Slade climbs out of the driver's seat with no visible alarm in his gait. I catch his eye, and he winks at me, his pearly whites glistening in the night.

God, that smile.

"Keep your hands in the air," one officer barks, manhandling Slade as we're placed in a line and patted down. More lights flash, and tyres screech. A paddy wagon jerks to an angled halt in front of Liam's car, blocking it in.

Liam lets out a strangled groan. "Dude, could you park any closer?"

The once quiet suburban street soaks up the impressive light show. Curtains shift in windows, and curious eyes peer out, staring as two more cops exit the paddy wagon and amble towards us with a superior air.

The obvious top dog halts in front of Slade to eye him up and down. "Mr. Pearson, fancy seeing you here."

My jaw drops. *He knows Slade by name?*

"Sergeant Nile," Slade says, "lovely night for a drive, don't ya think?"

The sergeant's eyes glimmer with fleeting amusement. "Indeed." He clasps his hands behind his back and strolls past Liam, then stops at me and Jen, examining us over the generous hook of his nose. "Right. You two girls, come with me."

With a jerk of his chin, he stalks off down the leafy street, and reluctantly we follow with his partner hot on our tails. My chest clamps tighter with each step, so I rub my fist against the ache. Reality smothers me like a weighted blanket, leaving only panic room to breathe. *Stay fucking cool.* Slade's words of warning whisper in my ear, and I repeat them like a mantra over and over. The last thing I want now is a full-blown panic attack. I'd look ridiculous.

We come to a stop around the corner where Sergeant Nile points to Jen. "Name and age?"

"Jennifer," she says, fumbling a curl behind her ear. "I'm eighteen."

"Surname, Jennifer?"

Jen's head drops, and her cheeks bloom pink. "L . . . Lawrence, sir."

The sergeant's eyes flare with irritation, while his partner lowers her chin, fighting a smile. "As amusing as you think you are, Jennifer Lawrence, do you know I can arrest you for failing to provide your real name?"

Jen sways on her feet, and her heart-shaped face pales. Gone is her usual fiery spunk. Her wit died back at Mia's. I clear my throat of nerves and attempt to fill her boots. "It's her real name, sir. Just a coincidence."

His attention snaps to me, and I fight not to cower under his glare. "And you are?"

"Avery Masters." I hold his stare with wilting defiance. I remember the police being a lot less intimidating—nice even. What the hell happened?

Burglary happened, Avery. Burglary.

"And your age?"

"Seventeen," I reply.

He points a blunt finger in my face. "In that case, you're the one who'll tell me what happened."

I slouch as Jen is escorted away. Their strategy is clear—divide and conquer—find the weakest link to crack. And in this case, it's the youngest. Lucky me.

Sergeant Nile steps forth, towering over me like an ominous alleyway building. "Thirty minutes ago, an incident was reported on Vallen Street. Coincidentally, the vehicle you occupied fits the description, and the laptop found inside matches the one allegedly stolen. So tell me, Avery, who took it?"

I stare at the sergeant with wide eyes and no words as my blood drains to my feet. His razor gaze scans my face, compelling the truth to fly from my mouth, but I resist. He narrows his eyes at my silence, and when he speaks again, his tone is formidable. "I'll count down from twenty. If you don't tell me who took the laptop by the time I get to one—I'll arrest *all* of you."

I flash my gaze to Jen in the distance. She cradles herself as the officer speaks, her shoulders jolting under the weight of her sobs, and I wince. This is my fault. No one is arresting Jen. The only thing she's guilty of is terrible taste in best friends.

The countdown starts. "Twenty . . . Nineteen . . ."

And I silently curse. Chaotic thoughts spin as I struggle to invent a plausible story—one that sets us all free. Slade took it from a table. I saw him clear as day, but I can't snitch; he'll never speak to me again.

"Fifteen . . . Fourteen . . ."

I can't let Liam suffer either. *Damn, Mia.* If she'd done the right thing, none of this would be happening. You don't bail on your housemate the minute the bills are due.

"Twelve . . . Eleven . . ."

And since when is an enclosed front porch a proper part of a house? That unlocked door was meant to lead us to Mia's front door, not straight into her lounge. I only went there to ask for my money, albeit late. But it's Saturday, Mia's a night owl, and I didn't know Slade would steal anything. Maybe I should take the fall. I'm not eighteen yet. At twenty, he'd be in way more trouble.

"Seven . . . Six . . ."

No, I can't do that. But snitches get stitches, remember? My heart thumps so loud I can't hear myself think. I'm not a good liar—never have been—but I take a deep breath, close my eyes, and prepare to do just that. God, I hope Slade still wants me when this is all over.

"Three . . . Two . . ."

"Okay, stop! I'll tell you." The countdown halts, and I slump over, resting my hands on my knees, panting as though I've run the City to Sea. I tilt my head up and meet the sergeant's glare. "I took it, okay? I stole the laptop." My stomach somersaults in protest, and the sergeant frowns.

"Where were the others?"

"In the car. I went in alone." I will my traitorous cheeks to remain pale, hoping the biting chill of barely morning helps. Jen and Liam did stay in the car, so it's mostly true.

The sergeant searches my face, clenching his jaw. "Stay right here."

He leaves to confer with his partner, and they speak in hushed tones. He retrieves his phone, and I kick at the grass verge while I wait, staining the tips of my pink Chuck Taylors green. If I kick hard enough, the ground might open up and swallow me whole, banishing me to the fiery pits of hell where I belong.

Sergeant Nile finishes his call, then strides towards me, removing handcuffs from his duty belt. As chrome glimmers in his meaty fist, I brace for the inevitable words to come. "Avery Masters, I am arresting you for suspected burglary." The sergeant spins me around and binds each wrist behind my back with cold, hard steel. He reads out my rights, and I find refuge in a dream-like daze, refusing to process this cataclysmic fuck-up.

Footsteps echo up the street as Jen sprints towards us, her officer in pursuit. "No!" she yells. She halts toe to toe with the sergeant, catching her breath. "Sir, Avery stole nothing. I told the truth. Slade did it. Why are you arresting her? You can't do this." Her words grow more frantic as she speaks, and I shake my head.

"Jen, it's okay. You don't need to cover for me." I say the words slowly, imploring her to play along, but she's having none of it.

"No, you can't do this. I won't let you take the fall for him. He doesn't even love you. Can't you see?"

Her words hit point-blank, and my heart explodes like tempered glass knocked one too many times. My tears sting, and Jen winces. "I'm sorry," she says. "I didn't mean it. But tell them the truth. *Please*, Aves."

"I already did," I grit through clenched teeth.

The officer eyes me with scepticism, then pulls Jen aside. "Jennifer, even if your story is true—Avery entered the building with Mr. Pearson and apparent intent. Whether she took the laptop is irrelevant. It's still burglary."

"What?" Jen says. "But that's not fair. What intent?"

That minor fact is news to me too but only solidifies my decision. I was going down anyway. Why should two of us suffer? And I guess they would assume intent if my beef with Mia is known. Jen might've told them—Mia could've too.

"That's the law, I'm afraid."

"Well, it sucks." Jen pouts, then slaps a hand across her mouth. "Oh my God, I snitched on my best friend. Shit, I'm so sorry."

I roll my eyes, willing her silence. She's ruining everything.

"Enough," Sergeant Nile says, nudging me forward. "Let's go."

Sniffling follows me up the street, testing my anger. My instinct is to comfort Jen, but her words still sting. How would she know how Slade feels about me? Her sobs increase until I can bear it no more. I glance over my shoulder to the girl who's stood by my side through everything, and her splotchy cheeks and kicked-puppy eyes shatter my resolve in seconds. I sigh. "Please don't cry. Everything will be okay."

She wipes her nose with the sleeve of her denim jacket. "I'm so sorry."

I grimace. "I'm the one who's sorry."

She peeks at my cuffed wrists and stifles another sob. "What happens to us now?"

Sergeant Nile speaks. "We'd like you to accompany us to the station for further questioning, Jennifer."

Jen's shoulders slump, and her gaze drops to her cherry-red Doc Martens. "I'm so dead. My Dad's going to kill me. *Creatively.*"

I squeeze my eyes shut and look away. She's right. She'll be grounded, threatened with therapy, subjected to an exorcism . . . who the hell knows? The possibilities are endless. I never should have dragged her into this.

As we round the corner, I search for Slade, only to spot him standing handcuffed against the paddy wagon with an officer's palm pressed to his back. My heart plummets, and my grand plan to save him crumbles to dust. "Why did you arrest him?" I ask the sergeant. "I told you. He was in the car. I stole it."

The sergeant huffs, and sharp eyes meet mine. "A word of advice, Miss Masters—rethink the company you keep. Slade Pearson is bad news. Don't expect to see him for a while, irrespective of whether you keep up this little charade."

"He's going to jail anyway?"

"Almost certainly."

Dread pretzels my stomach. "Why?"

"I'm not at liberty to say."

My breath hitches, and tears slide down my cheeks, causing the sergeant's face to soften. I shake away his pity. I'm not some stupid girl he needs to feel sorry for.

I search for Liam and find him sitting on the kerb's edge, head hung and solemn but cuff-free. Jen tries to run to him, but the officer stops her. I call out to Slade, cringing at the desperation in my voice, but he turns his head, and our eyes lock. His gaze flickers to where my hands hide, and his mouth tugs into a smile. When he winks at me, his eyes sparkle like a rippling moonlit lake, and my shoulders relax, the twisted mess inside my chest unfurling ever so slightly.

He shucks away the officer's palm with an expletive-ridden claim of backache, then takes a dramatic breath before launching into song—as only he would in this situation. With terrible pitch but enviable passion, he belts out the intro to "Bohemian Rhapsody." The officer yanks him away from the paddy wagon, opens the back door, and shoves him inside, shaking his head as the door slams shut.

Slade's performance continues, albeit quieter, from the confines of his mobile cell, and a sad smile kisses my lips. The officers might well kill him before they reach the station, but that's okay. I'll be dead too when my sister finds out about tonight. We can be dead together, roaming the earth as ghosts with no rules, consequences, or shitty ex-housemates. And what's more, his girlfriend won't be there.

And that sounds like *heaven*.

"Beth, where are we going?" The turnoff to my apartment passes by in a stream of lights, and I look at my sister. "What, you're ignoring me now?"

She purses her lips tighter, narrowing her eyes to slits that burn through the windscreen. Ah. The dreaded Silent Treatment. Second tier on the Bethany Masters Scale of Anger and prelude to Armageddon. Right now, she's analysing my transgressions, polishing each point she wants to make with gleaming precision, and compacting her emotions into one almighty fireball. At some point, when the pressure grows too great, she'll take aim and fire. But that could take days, and God knows I'd rather it be over now.

I glance at her from the corner of my eye and brace myself. "Real mature," I mutter.

The air immediately charges with static, and Beth's nostrils flare as she saps the car of oxygen, her face blooming red like a constipated toddler. "Mature? How dare you, Avery! What do I say, huh? I get a phone call at two in the damn morning asking me to accompany my little sister at the police station for an interview. Post *bail* for you. *Aggravated burglary*? That's a major indictable offence. What on earth were you thinking?" Her shoulders heave, and her periodic glares scorch my skin. "Well?"

I shrink into the soft leather seat, knowing anything I do and say will be used against me from this point forth. That's the downside of having a lawyer for a sister. "Mia owed me money." My voice comes out squeaky, and Beth snorts.

"Someone owes you money, so you steal their laptop. Is that reasonable behaviour, Avery?"

"I didn't technically steal it, *Beth*."

She scoffs. "Yeah, you're totally innocent, clearly. Tell me, did you know Mia was home when you walked straight into her house?"

I feel so dumb. Not even Beth will believe that was accidental. "I left after five seconds," I say instead. "We didn't even see her."

"Like that matters! And don't get me started on the fact you lied to the police. You're lucky they didn't charge you for that too."

I clench my jaw. It was two against one in the end. Jen and Liam's version of events against my own. And, as Sergeant Nile pointed out at the station, Slade's fingerprints will be on the laptop without mine. I should have thought of that earlier.

"Next time, stay silent. You have that right. Name and address—that's all you need to give them." She shakes her head. "What am I saying? There better not be a next time.

"And *Slade*, Avery? I thought things ended when you found out about his girlfriend?"

I shrink further into the seat and swallow my shame. "He's going to break up with her. He's just waiting for the right time."

"You don't honestly believe that, do you?"

I shrug. *Maybe*. I did at first. I'm sure as hell still hoping he will. Does that count?

Beth rolls her eyes. "You know, for someone so smart, you're incredibly naïve."

My gaze falls to my lap, and I pick at my short fingernails, chipping away the lilac polish. Personal insults are typically Mum's MO—not Beth's.

As we hug Melbourne's city fringe, I watch out the window in silence. The usual bumper-to-bumper traffic is at home asleep, leaving a surreal empty-movie-set calm. Skyscrapers cut through the night sky with sharp edges and neon lights, then shrink to obscurity as we leave them behind.

We cross into the affluent inner east, and I clear my throat. "So I'm going to your house, then?"

Beth flips on a blinker and takes the corner too fast, making her tyres chirp in protest. Her eyes flicker to mine, the coldness in them unfamiliar. "I can't trust you, and it's my money on the line."

Her words punch me in the stomach. *She can't trust me?* What, does she think I'll skip town and cost her a fortune? I would never do that. Blinking back tears, I shake my head. "Are you done now?"

She pulls up her driveway and cuts the engine with a sigh. "That depends. Do you understand how serious this is, or is it a game to you?"

"A game?" I clench my molars. "Beth, in the last twenty-four hours, I've been evicted, charged, and my boyfriend's gone to jail— of course it's not a game. I fucked up, okay? I get it, and I'm miserable. Are you happy?" I dry my cheeks with the back of my hand, and Beth's eyes saucer.

"You were *evicted?*"

I nod, sniffling like the pathetic human I am. "He gave me notice yesterday. That's why I went to Mia's. I thought if I could get my money, I could change Old Frankie's mind."

Beth drops her head to the steering wheel and bangs it three times. "For heaven's sake, Avery. Mum pulled all kinds of strings to get you that place."

"Yeah, I know. It was her final motherly gesture before relinquishing her duties once and for all."

Beth snaps her gaze to mine. "Is that what triggered all this? Mum leaving?"

I stare out my window, skimming the topiary shrubs and grey ren-

dered facade of Beth's narrow two-storey house. She'll never understand the relationship I have with Mum. It comes down to one criti-
cal difference really—Mum actually likes Beth.

I love you because I have to, Avery Lee, but I don't like you. Not at all.
Beth sighs. "You guys clashed anyway. You should be enjoying
your new life away from the conflict, not mourning her absence."

Beth's right, but presenting logic to a wounded heart is like reasoning with a two-year-old—utterly futile. I know it's stupid to feel
abandoned at my age—I'm seventeen, not seven—but I counted on
having a home. Somewhere to stay until I could stand it no more. *I
was meant to leave, not her.* Besides, much of the conflict didn't go
with Mum. Most remains stuck inside me, festering like an infected
wound.

Beth eyes me as if hearing my thoughts. "I know things weren't
easy after I moved out. I know Mum was difficult. But you need to
let it go. For your own sake."

Let it go. And how the hell do I do that? Beth makes it sound like
a simple choice. As if I can snap my fingers and the junk twisted
through me will disappear forevermore. It won't. I've fucking tried.
I've snapped my fingers until they bleed.

"What about your savings?" Beth asks.

I forage through my worn-out canvas satchel in search of a tissue
to blow my nose and muffle my reply. "Gone." It turns out school art
competitions aren't all that lucrative, even when you usually win.

Beth's lips press firm, and she shakes her head.

"I'm sorry, okay. I know I screwed up, but I can't deal with you
hating me too."

Her face softens, and in that moment, Armageddon ends. "I could
never hate you, Aves, you know that. I just feel like I don't know you
anymore. Where's my sweet little sister? The one with clay-smeared
hands and big dreams?" She squeezes my knee, and my eyes fall shut.
That feels like forever ago.

"You know, I expected you'd run a little wild the first time on your own—but *burglary*? What happened to you?" She tucks a pale lock of shoulder-length hair behind my ear, and her clear blue eyes—our one common feature—search my own. I want to give her answers, if only to prolong her tenderness, but my head's a jumbled mess—a thousand-piece puzzle with no box to follow.

Beth sighs, rubbing her forehead as though in pain. "Look, you can stay here with me. Until you find your feet."

My mouth falls open. "Seriously?"

"On three conditions."

"Name them."

She holds up an elegant finger. "One. No more illegal activity, and you must show up at court."

Sounds fair.

"Two. Slade isn't to set foot inside my house."

My shoulders slump. "He's in jail anyway, so that won't be a problem."

"He'll be out at some point. I'm thinking ahead."

My heart squeezes. *Not soon enough.*

"And three, I want you to seriously consider the quality of people you surround yourself with. Life is hard enough without chaining yourself to anchors."

I frown. "Not all people who break the law are bad. If you got to know Slade, I'm sure you'd like him. He has this contagious zest for life, and he's funny too. You appreciate a good sense of humour, right?"

Beth squares her dainty shoulders and arches a dark, manicured brow. "Avery, the guy is trouble, and that contagious zest you speak of probably means he's high. I appreciate humour, sure, but I don't find it funny when someone screws around on my little sister or helps her break the law. Don't ask me to condone your relationship because I won't."

I mash my lips together, grinding my teeth. Anyone would think she's Mother Teresa, casting all those stones.

"Well, do you accept my terms?"

What choice do I have? I take a deep breath, rally my manners, then look up. "Yeah. And I appreciate it. Thanks."

Beth smiles a tight smile. "That's settled, then."

She climbs out of the car, stifling a yawn, and I follow her to the front door in silence. We step into the lofty foyer—or *gallery*, as she calls it. Colourful artworks hang on stark white walls, and that new-house smell still fills the air. Her high heels echo on the porcelain tiles as she throws her handbag on the table and heads to her bedroom.

Stilettos at five a.m. Typical Beth.

"Goodnight. You know the way." She half-heartedly waves without looking back, omitting her usual affection.

"Um, Beth?"

Weariness mars her pretty pixie face as she halts in the doorway with a sigh. She'll be at work soon, weekend be damned, on little sleep thanks to me. Gulping down guilt, I summon a breath. "Thanks for coming to get me. I'm sorry I dragged you into this."

The inadequacy of my words hangs between us like stench on a still day, and Beth stares at me in silence. Her disappointment weighs more than her anger ever could, but as her shoulders sag, it wavers. "We all make mistakes," she concedes, shaking her head. "Just don't do it again. You're better than this."

"I won't. I promise. And you're right, I am."

That earns me a nod and a tight whisper of a smile that I cling to as Beth lowers her chin and shuts her door.

I trudge through the gallery and into the open-plan living room, skimming my fingertips across the cold kitchen granite. Specks of quartz shimmer through the misty swirls, and gold handles line each white shaker door. A grand brass pendant hovers above the island with abstract arms and glass ball ends, while pops of pastel colours, blue velvet sofas, and chunky-knit rugs fill the lounge.

I pass a wall of windows, hidden by crisp blinds, then climb the steps to the plush mezzanine and flop onto its queen bed, staring at the roof windows sloped above.

The pillow top hugs me, and the dam breaks, destroyed by that smidge of affection. I cry into the quilt until its waffle pattern lines my face and the pain of Slade's remand dulls from jagged knives to mallets. I sob until the loss of my apartment, full of thrift shop finds and penniless charm, no longer burns my heart, and Mum's indifference stops gnawing at my chest. I weep at the prospect of going to juvie and visualise every horror. And then I drown myself in guilt for tangling those I love in my stupidity because that's what a good person would do, and boy, do I long to be that. Only then does the storm pass, leaving soft breaths and an eerie calm. Numbness, my phony friend.

Dawn soon swallows the night, casting a surreal haze through the room that urges me from bed. I mosey to the window and drop my forehead against the cold glass, staring at the terrace roof a few feet below. My apartment, though shoddy and stacked with fifty more, has a balcony out front, three storeys up. And at night, if you look past the messy yard and rowdy neighbours, stars blanket the sky over the field next door and long grass sways in the moonlit breeze. It's a glimpse of heaven in an otherwise turbulent world, and my refuge from chaos. It's what I'll miss the most.

Frigid air hits my damp cheeks as I slide open the glass and mount the window sill.

What have I got to lose?

The storm-grey sheets crack as I land, and I bum shuffle down the slope, careful not to rip my jeans on the screws. Lying back on crossed arms, I settle in to watch the stars fade.

If only I'd kept my big mouth shut about Mia.

Birds faintly chirp as the sun climbs, and the sound of traffic slowly grows. My phone buzzes in my pocket, and Jen's smiling face greets me. She's alive—her dad didn't kill her. That's something, at least. I open her message.

> **Jen:**
> Remember when you wore those
> patchwork flares for a month, hoping
> to inspire a fashion revival?

I roll my eyes and hit reply. Sadly, that was only two years ago and not my first thrift shop fail.

> **Me:**
> Yeah, unfortunately.

> **Jen:**
> Well, I know you're hurting, but this
> whole situation? Still not as bad as that.

Fresh tears sting, and I shake my head with a smile. Jen's nuts—the best kind of nuts. If only she were right too.

<h1 style="text-align:center">Two</h1>

iam drags the last box from the rusty hire trailer, and flecks of orange paint scatter across Beth's driveway like fluorescent confetti. The old thing sheds more than a chinchilla cat, courtesy of the backyard spray job, but it's all I could afford.

"No offence, but that place is a shithole. It's good you're outta there," Liam says.

Wiping sweat from my brow, I step back from the box pyramid stacked in the garage and sigh. "I know. But it was my shithole, you know? My first shot at independence, and I failed. Miserably." My chest twists. "Wait until my mum finds out."

One day I won't be here anymore, Avery Lee. Then you'll be sorry.

Liam hikes up the driveway, the tall box bulging at the bottom and cording his gangly forearms. Backlit by the late afternoon sun, the frames of his glasses glow lime green. He must own a dozen pairs, because they're a different colour every day. He halts in front of me with a raised brow, his messy blond hair pointing in all directions. "Will she care?"

I shake my head. "Gloat, more likely."

Pity flashes across his face, and I look away. "Where do you want this?" he asks, nudging the box higher and effectively changing the subject. Liam isn't one to pry, which is a whole lot of good for a very different reason.

"What's it say?"

"Nothing." He shrugs. "Another blank."

Strange. I swear I labelled everything. "Dump it there, and I'll go through it later." I gesture to my vintage dining table standing against the wall. It looks lonely already. The red laminate top seems duller—sadder somehow—and the funky chrome legs wobble as Liam sets down the box. They never wobbled at my apartment. After seventy years of service, it might finally be falling apart. Caving under the demands of the world. *Like me.*

Sighing, I amble to Beth's timber workbench and hoist myself up to sit off the edge. My dangling feet throb, and my bed calls my name from the mezzanine. I've spent so much time up there the past two weeks, swinging between numbness and tears, it's getting hard to leave, and Beth is worried. I can tell.

Liam wanders over to sit next to me, swiping up his bottle of water. A drizzle of sweat runs down his temple as he drinks. While late June, it's uncharacteristically warm, but that figures. Trust Mother Nature to taunt me with sun three weeks into winter and kill the only excuse I have to live as a hermit. I wish I was grounded like Jen. It would be a relief rather than punishment.

Liam uses his ratty *Star Wars* tee to dry his face. "At least now I can enjoy what's left of my day off."

I flash him a sympathetic smile. "Thanks for your help. I really appreciate it."

"Like I had a choice. Gotta keep the boss happy."

He throws me a wink, and I nudge him with my knee. Liam would help me even if he weren't dating Jen. He's that kind of guy. One of the good ones.

Chuckling, he retrieves his phone from his back pocket and glances down to check the screen. His mouth tilts into a goofy grin—*the Jen grin*. So while he's distracted, I summon a breath and work up the courage to ask the question that's pestered me all day: *Has he heard anything?*

"Hey, Liam?"

He looks up from the screen, brows high, and my gaze sinks to my feet. I kick my heel against the chunky bench leg, counting each strike. Asking this question will break a cardinal rule—*my rule*—and breach the silent understanding we have. We don't talk about Slade. Period. And one simple question might rip open Pandora's box, cursing me with details I needn't hear. I shake my head. Too risky. "Never mind."

Curiosity lingers in his gaze, but he lets it go. "I'll see you tomorrow night, yeah? Jen's finally outta quarantine." Excitement fills his voice, but I take a moment to understand, and when I do, my eyes fall shut. Ah, Comet Park. The colourful land of crazy rides and suffocating crowds. I promised Jen we'd celebrate her first night free, but that was before. Before sunlight became my nemesis. Before my limbs turned to lead. Before my bed became my best friend. All I want to do is hide. Hide and sleep. But I've already let Jen down enough.

With a resolved breath, I glance up. "Guess I'll see you then."

Liam swings off the bench, drops to his feet, and manages to lob his empty water bottle into a bin three metres away. "Score!" he bellows. "The man's a legend." He fist-pumps, then slides keys from his pocket and saunters down the driveway with extra swagger. Smirking, I follow him. He's such a dork.

He shuts the trailer's tailgate and opens his car door, then stands his tall frame at attention and salutes me. I straighten my back and return the gesture with the optimal dose of sincerity. We do this often, in tribute to Jen's drill-sergeant dad. Poor Jen. She may as well be eight for all the freedom eighteen affords her.

Liam climbs into his seat and shuts the door. The window rattles as he winds it down, and the engine buzzes to life, casting white smoke through the front yard. It hits my lungs, and I cough, swatting it away. "Damn it, Liam. That thing will kill someone."

He grins at me, then turns back to the steering wheel, patting and stroking it with affection. "Don't listen to her, Betsy. You can't fix stupid."

"You'd know," I quip back.

Groaning, Liam clutches his chest as if hit by an arrow, then slumps dead over the steering wheel, pausing for effect, before making a miraculous recovery. Sheesh, he should be a drama major, not a carpenter.

Following him out, I trek along the driveway's edge. The trailer jolts over the kerb, clanking and clattering like it might fall apart, and again over every bump up Beth's street. Liam turns the corner with two chirps of his horn, and I sag with a heavy sigh. It's over. My independence. All self-respect. Happy fucking Friday.

I dawdle back up the driveway, swipe the box cutter from my back pocket, and approach the mystery box with a stepladder. A familiar earthy scent fills the air once I slice the tape, and my stomach rolls as if it knows something I don't. Frowning, I open the cardboard flaps but then stiffen.

Oh. Of course.

Herein lies my first love. Abandoned like a sick puppy after Christmas. Untouched since I first moved out.

Clear plastic tubs, full of studio treasures, sit stacked with modelling tools loose on top. Half-empty bags of terracotta clay lie slumped at the bottom, mouldy by now, no doubt. And my hardcover sketchbook stands tucked down one side. Everything is quiet and still, like a ghost town devoid of the life and meaning it once had.

Butterflies circle my belly as I slide out the book. Tools tumble into the nooks and crannies. I climb down the ladder, clutching it under one arm, and then lay it on the table. The front cover is decorated with hand-cut birds perched in trees and cherry blossoms made of silk, and as I run my fingertips down the trunk, Mrs. Donovan's impassioned words return. *You, my love, have the makings of a great. You're the prodigy every art teacher dreams to find. Promise me you'll never stop.*

I swallow. This book once held every spark of my soul, so I flip through it tentatively, daring to hope I'll feel . . . something. *Anything*. But the drawings of sculptures are foreign. The concepts dead. Inspiration doesn't devour me like it would have just last year. There's no frantic need to grab a pencil. No desire to feel wet clay slide under my fingers. To push and pull—to mould and create. It's gone.

Like Mum. Like Dad. Like Slade.

Grimacing, I slam the cover shut. I never thought clay was just a high school fling. I thought it was my oxygen—my future—something I couldn't live without, but how fast things can change. How fast *I've* changed.

"Avery Lee Masters?" A deep voice echoes through the garage, and I spin around with a gasp, clutching my chest. A police officer looms at the threshold, his hands hidden behind his back, face shadowed by the rim of his hat.

Oh no.

I hoped I'd be forgotten—simply vanish from the pile of paperwork at the station, never to be seen again. But as a large yellow envelope appears from behind his back, that hope splinters and nausea takes its place.

"Yes?" My voice comes wrapped in cotton, and heavy footsteps charge towards me.

Halting, he holds out the envelope. "You have been summonsed."

His droopy face is blank, his voice monotone—bored—as if he's delivered a hundred envelopes today. I take it with trembling hands, and he nods once before stalking back to his car.

"Wait. That's it?" I call out, chasing after him. No instructions or pep talk—a shoulder squeeze or "Don't worry, you'll be okay, love"?

Stray gravel grinds under his boots as he turns back to face me. "The details are outlined in the documents." He talks like I imagine a zombie might. If he ever had excitement for his profession, it died many moons ago.

As he climbs into his neon-chequered car, I grumble my thanks to the grass, then watch as he disappears around the corner, swallowing before brushing my fingers over the perfect print of my name. This is really happening. It wasn't a bad dream after all.

My body floats back to the garage while my head spins a manic web of doom. The panel door squeals against the tracks as it shudders to the ground, and my legs carry me to the kitchen island. I stare at the envelope, trying to evoke telekinetic flames. If it burns to ash, did it ever exist? But when that fails, I hold my breath, rip open one end, and free the papers.

I dart my eyes around the page, collecting random words, and my knees weaken. This is a mistake. It has to be. Shaking my head, I read it again, but the details don't change. My court date is set for July 14.

July 14.

My eighteenth fucking birthday.

Someone must be screwing with me. A court clerk with a sadistic sense of humour. Or Sergeant Nile as payback for the lies I told. Eighteenth birthdays should be marked with pride, not shame.

The kitchen air thickens to syrup, and my lungs scramble to work. I fist the front of my T-shirt, rubbing my chest as my breaths grow shallow. Dropping the summons to the island, I race to the sink and brace my hands on either side, hunching my shoulders as tears join the chaos. Death grips me, and terrifying thoughts spin until one crushes me in its giant fist, allowing no escape.

In three short weeks, I'm going to jail.

And with that, I spill the contents of my stomach into Beth's designer sink, heaving like a rabid dog choking on a bone while my dignity circles the drain, bright yellow and acidic.

The second I physically can, I drag myself upstairs, crawl under the covers like I've longed to all day, and sob into my pillow until the room grows dark and keys jingle at the front door.

Beth's heels click against the gallery tiles, growing louder as she nears, before ending in two thuds. The fridge door clatters, followed by the unmistakable chink of a long-stemmed glass settling on granite. One generous serve of sauvignon blanc is Beth's nightly ritual and as sure as she is smart. Papers rustle, silence follows, then light footsteps hike the stairs. "Aves?" Beth flips the light, and I shield my face with the covers and groan. The mattress dips next to my knees. "Are you okay?"

I lift the quilt without showing my face. "I'm going to jail on my birthday. I can feel it in my bones."

She squeezes my calf and tsks. "We've been over this. That's unlikely. This is your first offence."

The word *unlikely* replays in my head. Not impossible, but *unlikely*. It was unlikely Mum would disappear interstate. It was unlikely a pandemic would hijack half my teens. A strangled sob escapes my throat, and Beth tugs at the covers. "Oh, honey, come here."

I surrender my grip but avoid her stare, and she pulls me into her tiny embrace. She smells of Chanel and success, and I sob on her shoulder, ruining her perfection—soiling her silk blouse with snot, mascara, and tears.

"You had another one, didn't you?" she asks.

I hate that I'm so weak, and I hate that these humiliating attacks broadcast that fact. Beth sighs when I nod against her shoulder. "I'm sorry," I say, but she shakes her head.

"Don't apologise. That's all you've done for two long weeks."

I sniffle in a ragged breath. "Does that mean I'm finally forgiven?"

Beth pulls back to meet my gaze, and her glistening pools of pity reflect the disaster I've become. "I don't hold grudges, Aves, you know that, and I think you've been suffering more than enough." She strokes away the strands of damp hair stuck to my forehead and smiles at me like most mothers would their child. "Listen, I won't let anything bad happen to you. I'll call in some favours at work. Find someone to represent you. We'll make sure this goes away."

I frown. "You can't be my lawyer?"

"I don't specialise in criminal law, but I'll find someone who does. Someone good, I promise. Trust me, okay?"

I trust her more than I trust myself, but Beth is an eternal optimist and drama tends to leave her be. She walks her path with hard work but little resistance, whereas I'm knocked on my arse at every left turn. Dad is the exception though, I suppose. That knocked us both, but we never talk about that because it turns out time *doesn't* heal all wounds.

Beth squeezes my shoulders. "Does that sound like a plan?" Bunching the quilt against my sternum, I nod. "Good. That's settled, then." She raises my chin, forcing my eyes to hers. "You're not alone, Aves. Know that."

Why is it, then, I always feel precisely that?

Three

Yesterday, Comet Park sounded like torture. Today it sounds like death. But Jen quashed my attempt to bail using every weapon she owns. Rows of praying emojis. Selfies of pleading eyes and pouty bottom lips. Declarations of love. *The threat of kidnap*. Then came this: "You can't hide in that house forever, and what true friend would let you?"

She has a point, so here I am. Face puffy from last night's mess, nerves frazzled, skin paler than my hair. But I do what I do best. I cage the swamp monster and mask up. "You can do this," I tell the mirror before practising a smile. It doesn't twinkle across my empty stare, but most people wouldn't notice. Slade included.

His smirk flickers through my mind, and I whimper. I wish I could talk to him, visit him, know when he'll be back. But that's not how we work. He contacts me. He visits me, and that's the way it's been since the day we first met—the day he boarded my near-empty train and flashed that magic smile. It took months of odd behaviour to discover why, but by then it was too late. My heart was his, and Slade's velvet words and hypnotic promises were everything it longed to hear.

The distinct purr of Liam's car sails up to the mezzanine. I close the lid of my mascara, shove strawberry lip gloss into my satchel, then ram my feet into black high-tops. I grab my fake leather biker jacket—one of my better thrift shop finds—and plod downstairs, hitching it on and over the cropped purple turtleneck I found at the same Salvos store.

Beth glances up from her book and smiles. Her jade cable-knit jumper drapes off one delicate shoulder as she sits curled up on the velvet sofa. She owns exactly one outfit for relaxing, because that's all she needs. One evening a week requires no more.

"Have fun," she says. Last night's worry has vanished from her brow. The hermit is leaving the building for the second consecutive day, and she's pleased. I wish I felt the same way.

Leaning down, I plant a kiss on her cheek. "I'll try."

I climb into Liam's back seat, holding my breath against the acrid fumes, and once sealed inside, plaster on *the smile*. Liam and Jen turn in their seats. "Hey, Aves." They speak in unison, then giggle like love-drunk fools. Their gooey eyes meet, and the sinking sun beams through the windscreen, silhouetting their profiles in a poster image of young love.

Wincing, I avert my gaze, allowing them their moment while I wrestle with the vintage seatbelt and tell my needy heart to shut the fuck up. I secure the belt on my third attempt with a frustrated shove, then look up to meet Liam's goofy grin.

"You ready for Shooters? It's tie-breaker time." He adjusts his glasses, pushing them up the bridge of his nose in that adorable nerdy way. They're red tonight—green yesterday. Maybe he picks a colour for every mood.

I wink. "You should be scared. Quaking in your boots."

He shakes his head. "Not a chance, little lady. I'm not even wearing boots." Facing the front, he hits the blinker, then leaves the kerb. "I'm a loyal Vans man."

Jen's gaze remains on me, narrowing ever so slightly. "Are you okay?" Her scarlet hair flows in vintage waves, a relaxed version of her usual ringlets, while red lips and winged eyeliner pop against her pale skin. She's Jessica Rabbit, grunge edition. Bold and equally beautiful.

"I'm okay."

She looks at me knowingly. "We'll have fun, I promise."

My shoulders loosen. She's right, we will. We always do. When cops aren't involved, that is. I nudge my chin towards her with a half smile. "You look hot as hell."

She grins, fluffing her hair. "I know, right?" She blows me a kiss, then turns to face the front, nestling into her seat. Liam rests a hand on her denim-clad thigh, and she squeezes it. His thumb strokes her pinkie, and I drop my gaze to fiddle with the rip in my jeans. I wish Slade were here too. Only, even if he could be, he never would. Comet Park is a public place, and I'm a dirty secret. A side piece waiting to claim first place. I squeeze my eyes shut.

What the hell am I doing?

Across the road from where we park, rusty marquee letters rise from the earth, spelling "Comet Park," and carnival rides peak over the perimeter walls, ripping screams from the brave. The scent of hot cinnamon doughnuts rides the sea breeze, and my reluctance to be here fades.

As I stand huddled with Jen, we watch Liam clamp a red lock over his steering wheel, then circle his car thrice. I lean in. "Is he serious right now?"

Jen smirks. "He checks once for common sense, twice to double check, and three times to hex away thieves."

I bite back a laugh, and Liam snaps his head towards us. "What?"

We feign innocence. "Nothing," Jen says.

"I told you, babe. She's a classic—a collector's item. Dudes cream their dacks over Betsy." Liam shakes his head, then stalks towards the entry, mumbling profanities.

Jen and I frown at the rusty blue sedan. Duct tape bandages the side mirror, and the makeshift aerial resembles a wonky star. It's amazing this *classic* wasn't defected the night we were stopped, or yesterday for that matter. "It can tow a trailer." I shrug.

Our eyes meet, glinting with mirth, and we erupt in a fit of giggles. As we follow Liam's steps, mine lighten, and I plant a kiss on Jen's cheek. "Thanks for dragging me here."

"You're welcome," she says with a smile.

We conquer ride after terrifying ride, the dodgem cars, and fried food served on sticks. Lights dazzle against the black sky amongst a vibrant ensemble of laughter, music, and the whirr of thrill-purposed machinery.

Jen snuggles into Liam's shoulder as we stroll past the carousel. He drapes his arm around her, kissing the top of her head, and she peers up at him with a secret smile. They converse with sparkly eyes in a silent world of their own, and I battle the dark feelings a best friend should never have, regardless of where her boyfriend is. Still, if I could experience their kind of love, my world would be magic, and I would be whole.

When we get to Shooters, I discover there's nothing like shooting the crap out of tin-plate silhouettes to release heartache. It must improve my accuracy too, because with laser focus and the skill of a professional marksman, I desecrate Liam's hopes and dreams of reigning trifecta champion.

I drop my rifle to the bench, cackle an evil laugh, then shake my butt in a dorky dance. "Victory is mine."

Jen laughs, but Liam hangs his head in melodramatic disgrace. I hip-check him. "Aw, c'mon, Liam. No space for sore losers here."

He arches a scruffy brow. "That's because your big-arse head takes up all the room."

I poke out my tongue, and he flips me the bird.

Jen's mouth falls open. "Liam James Harrington, don't flip off Avery. Apologise immediately."

Liam's face falls solemn. "Sorry," he grumbles.

I poke out my tongue again, and Jen rolls her eyes. "Children. That's what you are. Bratty children."

Liam and I laugh, and the attendant holds up two prizes—a plastic whistle and a hot-pink lollipop ring. I choose the latter and hand it to Liam with a wink. "Here, a sucker for a loser."

He snatches the ring with a scowl and rips off the wrapper, dropping to one knee at Jen's feet. He peers up at her with love-struck eyes framed with red.

Love. Red must mean love.

"Jennifer Lawrence, you are lovelier than any Hollywood starlet. Will you be my girl for the next five years, so then I can ask you to marry me?"

Bouncing on her rubber soles, Jen clasps her cheeks. "Yes! I will."

Liam beams as he slips the candy ring onto her outstretched hand. Smiling strangers slow to watch, and I grin. Across the lane, however, is a girl who's not smiling at all. Rather, she glares at me through narrowed eyes, clenching her hands into fists. My gaze drifts over her pale skin and purple-streaked ponytail, her tight black jeans and dark boots, in search of recognition, but none comes. Two other girls stand with her, mimicking her sour look with their arms crossed. I whistle under my breath. "Okay, then."

Liam follows my line of sight and stiffens. He drops Jen back to her feet and looks at me with a flash of panic. "Let's go."

"Do you know them?" I frown. He coaxes us to walk, leaving my question hovering unanswered. I arch a brow at Jen, but she shrugs. "Who are they?" I press.

Liam's jaw ticks, but his gaze remains fixed ahead. "No one."

His tone lacks conviction, and dread prickles my stomach. I walk faster to match his pace, but footsteps echo from behind, and pressure hits my shoulder, ripping me from Liam's side. The force spins me around, and I stumble, coming face to face with the girl and her scorn, her dark eyes throwing daggers as if they might kill.

I straighten my jacket and match her scowl. "What the hell?"

Her friends catch up and resume their prior stance. "Are you Avery Masters?" she asks.

"Yeah, why?"

Liam steps between us. "Zoe, leave her the fuck alone."

Jen pinches my arm, and I meet her panicked face with a frown. She mouths something, but I can't make out her words.

The girl runs a hand down the length of her dark ponytail with a smirk. "Don't worry, Liam, I'm not here to make trouble. Why not introduce me to your little friend?"

Her honeyed tone shivers up my spine, and Liam hesitates a beat before stepping back with a sigh. He runs his hand through his scruffy hair and gestures between us. "Zoe, this is Avery. Avery, Zoe."

Our eyes lock, Zoe's a dance of joy-edged spite, and I swallow the lump in my throat. She steps towards me, offering her hand out to shake, and I frown at her black-painted fingers and studded bracelets.

It couldn't be, could it?

Jen tugs at my jacket. "Aves, we should go. *Seriously*."

I ignore Jen's plea, but it tells me enough, and the penny drops along with my heart. I know who this girl is. She's a censored part of my reality with a name I never wished to know. My gaze drifts up the creamy white skin of her arm, past her elegant neck, and settles on perfect symmetry painted black. I had hoped she'd be ugly—a heinous witch with a wart on her nose—but she's not. Rather, she's painfully beautiful, even while layered in death.

I wipe my hand on my jeans before tentatively holding it out. This could end badly, I know, but the universe can decide my fate. Deep down, I know what I deserve. Part of me even craves it.

Zoe's nostrils flare as our hands connect. "Nice to meet you, *Avery*. I believe you're fucking my man." Her lips wrinkle like a dried-up plum, and her grip turns murderous. I try to retrieve my hand, but I'm locked in place, and the second I realise, her other fist flies. Pain explodes through my face like I've snorted a grenade, and I hit the ground. Hard.

Liam lunges for Zoe while Jen scrambles to my side. "Aves!"

My heart pumps a deafening assault, and the surrounding lights swim, but there's a peace that comes amid the chaos. For once, the pain on the outside matches what's in, and that brings clarity—balance. Hope that karma's paid.

Whiteness smothers my vision, and the carnival racket fades. Jen's cries grow faint, and then the world disappears.

"Aves, wake up." Jen's voice meanders through my semi-lucid state. "Please wake up."

The soft shaking of my shoulder causes my gut to churn, and pain flares with every heartbeat, hailing me back to the land of the living. I try to open my eyes and groan. One accomplishes the task, but the other is pinned shut. Bitumen bites the back of my head, so I try to sit up.

Jen dives in to help, cradling my back. "Shit. Are you okay?" She gently swipes the hair from my face, and I nod, immediately regretting the action. The surrounding insanity swoops back into awareness, alerting me to my whereabouts.

God, it's loud.

"Aves, are you with me?"

I don't answer Jen, because speaking is too hard. Instead, I stare past her shoulder to the blurry scene playing out front. My head bobbles like a buoy on rough seas, but the image soon clears. Zoe thrashes under the weight of Liam's knee as he pins her stomach to the ground. He twists her arm higher against her spine, and she whimpers. "Let me go."

"Not a chance," Liam grits out with anger I didn't think him capable of. "I don't care what that cock-swab does to me. That was bullshit, Zoe."

"She had it coming. What kind of dumb slut dates someone else's boyfriend? *Months*, Liam. They've been together for months. Did you know this whole fucking time?" Her eyes plead with him, and guilt smothers me. I preferred her angry and vile, not vulnerable and hurt. Before tonight, she was a faceless inconvenience I could pretend didn't exist. One that would soon be gone. Like Slade promised.

Liam winces. "Not even Aves knew. You should talk to Slade."

"Well, I fucking can't, can I? He's locked up because of her."

Her words freeze my blood, and Jen squeezes my shoulder. "Ignore her."

"She's right though." I meet Jen's frown. "About everything."

Jen shakes her head. "It's not that simple, and you know it."

Two security guards approach, one barking orders into his walkie-talkie as they push through the crowd. I scan the circle of spectators, the eclectic mix of worry and wonder. We're an amusement to them, a live action show, and one Zoe's friends didn't care to see finish. The fact they've fled should bring satisfaction, but pity swells instead.

Liam relinquishes Zoe to the guards and rushes to my side. As they guide her away, she glances back over her shoulder, her glossy eyes finding mine over kohl-stained cheeks. The image twists my insides, and I tear my gaze away. Her face will haunt me enough as it is.

Liam squats to eye level, lifting my chin. "Fuck, are you okay?"

"I think so."

Jen glares at him. "That was dumb. You should have warned us. And why the hell introduce them?"

The colour drains from his face. "I didn't know she'd deck her. I didn't want to upset everyone, and it all happened so fast."

Jen's lips mash together, and Liam looks at me. "I'm sorry. I knew she was pissed, but I didn't expect this. She never hit no one at school." He grips the back of his neck and shakes his head. "I fucked up..."

His words knock around my head, inflaming already tender points, and I raise my hand to silence him. "Not your fault."

He stills with a sigh, and I peer up at Jen. I won't let them fight because of me. "Kiss and make up. Please." She'd grant my every wish in this state, and I'm not above milking it for a good cause.

She grumbles at the ground like a toddler, "I'm sorry. I didn't mean it."

Relieved, Liam strokes her cheek with that soft Jen-only smile, then drops his hand and frowns at me. "Can you make it to the car?"

"I think so."

They help me up, slinging my arms over their shoulders. My head whooshes, but they keep me steady. A park attendant steps in, asking if we need help, but Liam assures him we have it handled.

People detour past with curious stares as we navigate our way towards the exit. A little girl stops to gawk in our path, her tiny lips shaped like an *O*, before her blushing mother tugs her away, apologising.

With each careful step, Zoe grows more vivid in my mind. Images of her and Slade together, in various sordid positions, violently flicker like an antique film full of heart-hollowing torment. I swallow down bile. "She's *very* pretty."

"Not as pretty as you," Jen says.

I roll my head towards her. "That still the case? Because my face feels like a bowling ball." Jen cringes, and I huff. "That bad, huh?"

"Let's just get you to ice. I'm sorry she hurt you."

"Like she said, I had it coming."

"Only one person deserves a smack in the head, Aves, and that's Slade. I should go tell that bitch a few home truths."

The protective growl in Jen's soft voice makes me smile, then flinch. "Please don't. I don't want you hurt too."

She huffs. "Thanks for the vote of confidence." She squares her delicate shoulders under the weight of my arm, but we both know it's true. She and I, we aren't overly short, but we aren't built for fighting either. Not in temperament nor frame.

In another few steps, I sigh. "*Zoe and Slade.*" My heart squeezes as their names dance together in the air.

Jen snorts. "They sound shit together, if you ask me."

The good side of my face tugs into a smile, but Jen drops her gaze to the ground with a sharp inhale. "You know, I wanted to tell you her name. I wanted to blab everything Liam told me, but that's not what you needed. It was hard enough already."

I stare at her cherry-red boots, and they blur. "I know."

I didn't want details. I didn't want any truth Jen delivered that day with sombre eyes and careful words as she sat there cradling my hands.

Riddle me this: What were the odds of Jen finding a boyfriend who knows mine? One who would recognise Slade's name and swear he's already taken? And tell me—what were the odds of being told this the day after losing my virginity?

Liam clears his throat, and his shoulders stiffen. I sense what's coming, but it doesn't matter now anyway. Pandora's box has been ripped to shreds. "I don't know Zoe well. We never hung out or nothing. Slade was a mate at school before he dropped out, but I only put up with him now 'cause of you. You get that, right?"

I look up at him, stunned. Guys are so strange. They can despise each other, and you'd never know until they tell you or fists fly. And even then, they can talk like nothing happened. "But . . . you let him drive your car."

Liam shrugs. "I was hammered. He wasn't."

No, Slade wasn't drunk; he was tripping balls. Beth wasn't wrong on that front, but I won't tell Liam that.

We make it out of Comet Park, and Liam's car is safe, precisely where he left it—Zoe, nowhere to be seen.

"You take the front seat," Jen says as Liam climbs behind the wheel.

Jen helps me in, but the second she shuts my door, I lower the sun visor and freeze. "Holy shit," I whisper to the mirror. My heart pounds, and I slowly reach towards my face. My eye socket bulges like a pop-eyed fish's, my lid sealed shut and stretched, and angry smears of purple and pink mar my right side. I'm a swollen, shiny mess. Unrecognisable, in fact. My throat closes, and tears spring. "*Fuck.*"

Liam's a fountain of pity as he silently stares, and Jen squeezes my shoulder from the back. "It's okay. You'll heal. Let's just get you to a doctor."

I meet her reflection with a horrified expression, two seconds from losing my shit. I'm not sure what I expected, but Zoe really fucked me up. And as the gravity of the situation sinks in, I choke out the last decipherable words I can manage. "Please call Beth. I need my sister."

Four

Some people are arseholes their whole lives and never pay, yet I try it on for five minutes and get pummelled by the universe. How is that fair?

Perhaps I'm more awful than I know. Maybe Mum's right about that. Perhaps I'm merely ungrateful—a glass-half-empty kind of girl. So many have it unimaginably worse, but I'll use that knowledge to breed guilt, and that guilt to self-inflict further pain. Because no matter my awareness, I can't seem to fucking stop. In any event, I don't want to play anymore. I've fucked up my life seconds out the gate, and in three weeks I might be in jail.

Me. *In jail.* I won't last a night.

With the untarnished side of my face buried in the pillow, I forage the bedside table for Advil, popping two from the blister pack before dragging myself upright and downing them dry. I press my bare feet into the carpet, watching as they sink into the grey plush pile, then drop my head into my hands.

It's been three days, and Zoe's fury still pulses inside my skull, snippets of that night replaying whenever I close my eyes. Then

Beth's question returns—the one that came after she rescued me again—circling like a whirlwind of rubbish in a grimy car park.

Are you done with him now?

It's a question I don't want to consider, but it plagues me regardless.

Beth wanted me to press charges too, but the prospect of more police, courts, and drama is one I can't fathom. Everyone has a breaking point, and I'm walking the tightrope of mine as flames nip my heels. Pursuing a charge against Zoe would be akin to cutting the rope. Besides, I deserved it.

One day, someone will finally teach you a lesson, Avery Lee, and the angels will sing.

I stagger from my bed to the dresser, gaze firmly fixed on the floor. They warned me the bruising would get worse before better, and I have no desire to see it. Beth's eyes tell me enough in the time they linger and the angle of her brows as they do.

"Good afternoon, sleepyhead." Speak of the devil. Her chipper voice floats up from the kitchen as she hums a flowery tune. Time off seems to agree with her, even if it was by force. The doctor said I needed monitoring.

I lean against the balustrade. "What's so good about it?"

She shrugs. "Well, it's raining, for one."

My gaze drifts to the wall of glass in the kitchen, eyeing the drops as they trickle down the pane. The deck is a vibrant glossy brown, the potted succulents plump from moisture. That *is* good. If it were another sunny winter day, I'd scream at the sheer injustice. I need the sky to cry with me.

"How are you feeling?"

"About as good as I look." I pad downstairs, nodding at the coffee pot Beth holds up in silent question. She slides the mug across the granite as I perch on a stool, and I cup it in my hands, relishing the warmth. Taking a sip, I moan. Coffee livens the deadest of souls.

Beth smiles as I drink, leaning against the island with a glint in her eye. I glance at my coffee and back to her, gaze narrowing. "What, did you poison it?" Given recent events, my sister turning into a murderous psychopath would be just my luck.

She chuckles. "No, but I do have a surprise for you."

I tilt my head, willing excitement to spark. It doesn't. "What is it?"

Her grin widens. "Come with me, and I'll show you."

She flitters down the hall, and I force myself to follow, halting outside the spare room, where she spins to face me. "Close your eyes." She fans the air in front of my face, and I do as she says. The door faintly creaks, and the air freshens with a familiar trace. Hands land on my waist, and Beth guides me forward, stopping several paces ahead. "Now open."

My gaze darts around the room from point to point like a pinball ricocheting around a machine. Tight knots tangle in my chest, and I meet her smile with one wide eye. "Beth," I whisper.

What has she done?

She nods me forward, encouraging me to explore, and I take a deep breath, channelling calm. I drift towards the rustic timber bench spanning one wall—the same one I sat on in the garage last week—then finger my collection of clay tools laid out in perfect order. Crimped metal letters hang above, spelling out "STUDIO," and below, tubs of colourful glazes line the shelf, straight and proud as though saluting. Fresh bags of clay rest underneath, and a familiar book, graced with cherry blossoms and filled with dreams, leans against the wall. Across the room, wire, pliers, snips, and my soldering equipment hang on a pegboard, adjacent empty racks of shelves ready to be filled.

"Oh," Beth says, "there's a kiln in the garage too."

I spin towards her, my mouth agape. I've never owned a kiln. School always had one I could use. My throat tightens, and I resist the urge to knuckle my chest. "I don't know what to say."

Thanks, this is incredible, but something's changed; I'm not ready and won't ever be again?

I can't hurt her like that. The work involved. The attention to detail. *The cost.* She's considered everything down to a sweet little Bluetooth speaker in the corner. Music while working is as essential as light. My stomach cramps, the concrete lump inside reaffirming its presence and the creativity it crushed.

Beth raises her hand. "Before you say anything, I didn't do this to pressure you. I know you haven't worked since school, but I think having an outlet might help. You have a gift, Aves. Your teachers knew it—everyone did. I figured if it's all set up, it might be easier to start again, but it's entirely up to you."

Sure, no pressure at all.

Near the speaker sits a photo of Jen and me with bright grins and linked arms, uniforms chequered and short. I pick up the gilded frame, and memories of high school rush in. The dusty blue floors in the art room where I spent my free time, and the grimy windows that still radiated perfect light. Mrs. Donovan's kind eyes and enthusiasm. My first, second, and subsequent art competitions. Why do seven months feel like a lifetime ago?

Prize ribbons flicker in the light window breeze, pinned in a row under a shelf full of my early work. I rest the photo back down and move closer, skimming my fingers over the rough, grainy finishes. These pieces once spurred uncontainable pride—excitement and passion. But now they evoke . . . nothing. They're juvenile at best, devoid of depth, and I am no longer that girl. Life has seen to that.

I turn to face Beth, and she stands fiddling with the cuff of her sleeve, smile now nervous and tight. Infused with as much gratitude as I can muster, I pull her into a hug. "Thank you. This is amazing."

Her slight frame relaxes as she sighs. "I'm so glad you like it. I worried I was overstepping, but I saw your sketchbook in the garage—that big open box—and I couldn't resist. It was so hard doing this quietly too." A giggle escapes her throat, the glimmer of youth softening her eloquent force. I don't think a more beautiful sister exists. But a curious thought lingers, and I frown over her shoulder.

"This all seems kind of . . . permanent. I'm only here for now."

Beth pulls away, holding my shoulders out at arm's length. "I said you can stay here until you find your feet, and I meant it. That could take months or more. Until then, this is your home, and it should feel like it, okay?" She shrugs. "Besides, I enjoy having you around."

Her words soothe a worry I didn't know was there, and my lips pull into a smile. But reality soon whispers in my ear, like it always does. "But what if . . ." My voice trails off, and I look at my toes as they press against the vinyl-lined floor. She's overlooking one glaring possibility. In a few short weeks, my residence might be among a mass of delinquent teens. A shudder rolls up my spine. How many more black eyes will I cop, or worse?

"That won't happen." Beth lifts my chin, forcing my gaze to hers. "I didn't want to bring this up so soon after . . ." Her eyes flicker to my injury, and her brows descend. "Well—you know—everything. But I got a call yesterday. One I never dreamt of. The stars are aligning for you, Aves, I can feel it. You'll have the best representation possible, and I filled him in on everything, so don't worry."

My brows furrow. "You found me a lawyer?"

Her smile glows luminous like the moon. "Did I ever. And he's from a better firm than mine. Sometimes favours pay off in the strangest ways."

I shake my head. "Thank you."

"You're welcome." With a satisfied grin and a twirl of her hand, Beth turns on her heel. "I'll leave you to explore."

And like that, I'm alone, surrounded by lost dreams, with hope sparking my heart. I wander the room with renewed purpose, willing the dead to rise in a whirlwind of glitter and light. But it soon proves a lost cause. There will be no miracles today. Guilt gnaws harder with every step, with each drawer opened and detail discovered. Fuck. She went to so much trouble and all for nothing. My eyes fall shut, but there's zilch I can do. Love is never forced—it flows easy like the breeze. With a last glance and belly full of regret, quietly I slip from the room.

I eye the studio as if it might bite. Whether passing by or staring at the door, fighting the push to enter—the pull to not. While Beth's said nothing, her hope radiates whenever I walk down the hall and spirals to disappointment when I bypass the studio to merely shower or wash our clothes.

As the garage door shudders down and the sound of Beth's car fades, I can finally breathe, or so I think. My phone blasts the Wicked Witch's theme from *The Wizard of Oz*, and Mum's name lights up the screen. I smile and roll my eyes at the ceiling. *Hilarious, Jen.* But the humour is fleeting, and a sour taste grows in my mouth. Beth wouldn't have mentioned the assault nor my arrest, since I asked her not to. But Mum hasn't called once since leaving all those months ago. Why now?

Dropping my legs down from the back of the sofa, I sit up and bring the phone to my ear. "Hello?"

"Avery." Mum's voice comes through the line, wired and breathless. "Can you do me a favour?"

My stomach hardens. "Hi, Mum, how are you? Long time, no speak."

"Avery Lee, I don't have time for attitude right now. I need to speak to Bethany, but she's not answering her phone, and her office line goes straight to voicemail. It's a matter of urgency."

My grip tightens. "Why? What's going on?"

"Nothing you need to worry about, but I need to speak with her. Can you please go to her office and deliver my message?"

"But, Mum, that's a ninety-minute round trip by tram. How long have you been trying?"

"Since this morning."

I shake my head. It's barely 8:00 a.m. "She's on her way to work. How about I try calling her?"

"I told you. She isn't answering."

"Yes, but she will eventually." *She might for me.* "Is everything okay?"

"Forget it," she grumbles. "I'll keep trying from here. Thanks for nothing."

The line falls dead, and I stare at the phone. A normal child would worry. But a normal child is the product of a normal mother, and unfortunately, neither of us fits the bill. Knowing Mum, there's probably a sale she can't get to or a question she needs answered. Everything is a matter of urgency where she's concerned.

I shoot Beth a text, warning her what's coming, and lie back down, hugging a golden scatter cushion to my chest. My heart hammers, and my stomach twists into infinity knots, but I expected as much. It happens every time. Mum's a hit of adrenaline that throws me into flight mode with nowhere to run.

She could have asked how I was, or at least pretended to care.

The thought burrows me further into the sofa, and I rub my sternum and groan. This icky feeling—the acid ball of nerves, the vice inside my throat, dark mind forever spawning doom. I'm so fucking sick of it. I want to rip it from my body with sharp claws and shred it into oblivion. Only then might I be normal.

I launch the cushion across the lounge room and stand. On autopilot, I amble to the studio and find myself staring at the bags of clay. R.E.M.—one of my dad's favourite bands—floats through the speaker, telling me everybody hurts, and in that moment, I'm a little less alone.

Lifting the heavy bag closer, I grab a box cutter and slice open the plastic, then shimmy it down the sides. Burnt orange stains my hands, and the scent of damp earth tingles through my nose. With fishing line, I slice off a generous piece and slam it down on the bench, then glare at it while pressure builds in my chest. It climbs up my throat and rips free as a guttural roar. My fists fly, and I pound the helpless clay until my shoulders heave from exertion and my screams turn to sobs. And then I collapse to the stool and purge every plaguing thought, every toxic feeling, and let my hands do whatever it is they will.

The sun sets beyond the plantation shutters, casting the room in a terracotta glow. I drop the modelling tool to the bench and roll back on my stool, staring in silence. In front of me lies a girl crushed to the ground, her abstract face contorted in anguish. She's long given up trying to move, the weight pinning her far too great.

I tilt my head to the side and admire her. It's like she came from somewhere else, or from another's hand. But as I examine my fingers and clay-smeared yoga pants, all evidence points to that not being true.

A smile finds my lips as I bow my head. The impossible has materialised, and time away seems to have only marinated my talent. Allowed it to rest and strengthen—acquire depth and flavour like Beth's fine cellared wine. I only pray this isn't a one-off. A cruel glimpse of what could be but won't. The tap could seize again, or in ten days . . . be jailed.

Shoving that thought aside, I wander to the pegboard and unhook the nest of copper wire and snips before resuming my seat. I know exactly what will pin her down.

The weight of the fucking world.

Five

While the Children's Court isn't the historic Gotham-style building from my nightmares, the sleek, modernist hub radiates something equally daunting—the promise of merciless process. Cold like the aluminium beams slicing the sky and hard like the cantilevered concrete shadowing me from above.

With a deep breath, I brush off the non-existent dust from Beth's pencil skirt and blouse for the fifth time, noting the subtle green tint of the glazed entry makes me look as sick as I feel. Karma has me cornered, and despite Beth's assurances, freedom feels as remote as the Everest summit. I look skyward but refrain from praying. Hope opted to stay in the studio, gathering dust in the dark with a collection part done.

With a whimper, I check my hands for stray remnants of clay. The fact we'd just found each other again is bittersweet. But maybe there's a kiln in juvie. Maybe I'll find fame as a delinquent jailhouse potter. Dark and edgy. Deep and troubled. Knowing this fucked-up world, that might fly.

The door swings open, casting my reflection into nearby shrubs, and a tailored woman exits with a black roller bag in tow. She holds the door open and arches a brow. "Are you going in?"

Nerves strangle my throat, and I emit a sound somewhere between a choke and growl. I bobble my head, miming the lost words, and her forehead furrows. She probably suspects a seizure of some sort. And maybe she's right. That's how it feels. Every cell in my body jiggles like slime, rendering my limbs loose and ineffective. And heels? What the hell was I thinking? I can't walk in these damn things at the best times.

Stumbling forward with a tight smile, I rescue the door from her grip and step into the foyer to face a barricade of armed security and metal detectors. My eyes flicker to the guards, and my cheeks heat. I've never so much as touched a gun, yet the paranoia one somehow crept into my borrowed handbag is real. Alarms will scream, and I'll have no choice but to lunge for my weapon, shoot my way to freedom, and achieve nothing but what I fear most.

Captivity.

Abuse while in captivity.

I'd rather be dead.

I inhale through my nose and avert my gaze. Why the hell does my brain do this? As I step through, no sirens sound, but I power forward in case they change their mind.

Random suits stride with purpose across the shiny floor, and police officers exit the concrete staircase, chatting and smiling as if it's just another day—as if my world isn't about to end. Waves of gleaming steel form bench seating too beautiful for bottoms, but I choose one that circles a square column and take a seat regardless. My phone vibrates in my blazer pocket, so I slide it out.

> **Jen:**
> Happy birthday, bitch. Welcome to adulthood.
> Now let's end this shit-fuckery.

I gasp, and my thumbs fly over the keyboard.

Me:
Since when are you such a hardcore potty
mouth?

Jen:
I'm trying to empower you in a way you
understand. Since when do you say potty
mouth? What have they done to you?

A smile tugs at my lips. There isn't a situation in the world Jen couldn't lighten.

Me:
Nothing yet. Waiting for my lawyer.

Jen:
You'll be fine. Say it.

Me:
You'll be fine. Happy?

Jen:
You're infuriating, you know that? Lucky
I still love you. See you soon. Bitch.

I shake my head, smile lingering, and my phone lights up again.

Beth:
Breathe, okay?
In, two, three, four.
Out, two, three, four.
Then repeat.

I follow her words while cursing the court case that's kept her away. Lawyers can't simply skip hearings, even if they are representing schmucks. I guess that's good news for me, at least.

Me:
Wish you were here.

Beth:
I know. Me too, but I'll see you tonight.
Thai Five. 6 p.m.

Oh crap, my mandatory birthday dinner. I'd completely forgotten. Thai Five may as well reside on the Everest summit, tucked away inside my freedom. I switch my phone to silent, hide it in my bag, take another Beth breath, and straighten my shoulders. I can do this. *Cole Benedict. He'll find me. He has my photo on file.* I repeat Beth's instructions from this morning and search the foyer. What if he doesn't find me though? What if I miss my hearing? What if I'm in the wrong building entirely?

My hands grow clammy, and I eye every suit who passes, skimming over a young couple sitting slouched against the far wall. The guy's knees sit spread like he might give birth, the crotch of his baggy stonewashed jeans pulled taut midway down his thighs. The girl chews gum like a horse would toffee, her hands clasping his shoulder where a figurative chip throbs red and angry. I look away but not fast enough, and she sneers, nudging up her chin. "What the fuck are you lookin' at?"

Her words bounce across the vast space and smack me in the stomach. I scramble for my phone like it will somehow protect me and bury my face, scrolling the screen in an absent frenzy while praying they leave me alone—praying my lawyer hurries the fuck up. If I can't survive the foyer, how will I survive juvie? The thought hammers through me, and an invisible python winds itself around my chest, threatening to squeeze.

Not here. Not now. Please.

Those kids are a different breed. I'm not like them at all. Yet that's bullshit because here I am. I crossed the same red line after flirting with it for months, savouring its wicked charm as it sparkled in the dark. I chose the same path, and that split-second decision has carved my eighteenth birthday into a slab of shame and rendered the thousand rules I did follow—the years of *As* and obedience—*worthless*.

If it were anyone but Slade, I would have said, "What are you doing? Don't steal that." And the words were there, tingling my lips and gathering power. Only, before they took flight, Slade leant in and stole them too. His warm mouth devoured every trace while Mia's laptop glimmered under his arm and frost on her front lawn climbed the bottoms of our jeans. He broke the kiss with sparkling eyes and shallow breaths and stared at me like I was *everything*. Like in that moment, Zoe's fate was sealed. I'd finally paid my dues and passed his test. I was, at last, Slade-worthy.

Fuck, I really am my mother—sacrificing all sense to impress a guy. *Was he worth it?* A snarky voice sounds in my head, and heat swells in the pit of my stomach, creeping up the side of my neck. Hot tears fill my eyes, and I swipe them away with the back of my hand, tensing as I touch the eye Zoe hurt, despite it having finally healed. Slade's smirk materialises in my head, tainting the shame with a pathetic longing, and I sigh. I wish my heart would make up its goddamn mind.

Pushing away his image, I glance up from the corner of my eye while keeping my head hung low. They've gone. Thank fuck. My shoulders slump on an exhale. I need to pull myself together, and fast. Distraction needed *stat*.

I type Cole Benedict into Google and hit search. It would help to know what he looks like. The law firm Benedict Kane pings as the first result, and I click the link to land on a home page built for kings and queens—the upper crust of society. Golden letters adorn a montage of hands shaking, the scales of justice, and white smiles in designer suits. Claims of innovation, success, and the latest legal news follow beneath, along with the history of Benedict Kane's inception.

Cole Benedict isn't the head honcho, despite his surname. That privilege belongs to the firm founder and managing partner—a gentleman named Gerard—who has coiffed silver hair with enviable volume. Cole is probably his brother or son. The relative who hangs from the coattails of family success, taking the glory of the name while only being competent enough to fetch coffee and watch cat videos. I mean, he's helping me for free. Even if Beth seemed thrilled, how much can I expect? You get what you pay for in this life. *Except in thrift shops.* They are a treasure trove of limitless potential where paupers can live like royalty with enough skill and taste.

Stumbling across Cole's name listed as one of two senior partners has me eating my words, and when I click into his profile, my mouth falls open.

Distraction wanted. Distraction granted.

I bring the phone closer and stare into green eyes that pierce the screen with an ethereal beauty. His pale irises are ringed in black, fanned by dark lashes, and guarded by straight brows. And he has hair the colour of dark rum, with sharp, angular features that should be immortalised in bronze. I find myself fiddling with the top button of my blouse. He's so young too. Why didn't Beth warn me?

Slade's face appears in my mind, and pain jabs the back of my throat. I shouldn't be ogling another man. *Why? It's not like Slade is the beacon of loyalty.* The little voice returns, and my forehead furrows. Who is she? And why choose today of all days to be heard?

I shake my head and exit Cole's profile, expelling the unease tingling in my stomach. Instead, I scroll through the remaining staff. There are fifty at least. Benedict Kane isn't small or boutique, dressing up mediocrity in fancy clothes—no, it's big, bold, and shiny. Every staff member wears confidence like a uniform. An accomplished smile. A chin held high. These people have mastered life and fit their skin in a way I never will.

Tucked away at the bottom of the list is a link entitled "Staff Summer Retreat," and I click through to find a series of group photos set amongst glistening gum trees and dry amber dirt. Men and women climb ropes, hike, and soar through the treetops on zip lines, with hard hats, sweat-sheened skin, and exhilarated grins.

But it's the tug of war, three rows down, that stops my breath. Cole Benedict stands shirtless and smeared in mud, yanking one end of a blue rope as it circles his low-slung shorts. His virile frame is lean and toned. Skin, smooth and olive. Determination strains his face and rips through his body, defining every single muscle, while colourful ink swirls the length of one arm. Since when do high-class lawyers have tattoos?

That is him, isn't it? I zoom in closer and bite my bottom lip.

Oh my.

"Miss Avery Masters?" A deep voice jolts me, and my phone jumps from my hand, plummeting to the ground with a crack.

"Fuck." I scramble to pick it up, and dust off the shattered screen on my skirt, overplaying my distress to garner the precious seconds needed for composure. If his photo twists me in knots, what will a flesh encounter do? And shit, I can't believe I just fucking swore. I squeeze my eyes shut. Maybe he didn't hear me. Maybe it wasn't as loud as I thought. Maybe the snaps are photoshopped to unrealistic perfection, and he is a mere mortal after all.

A throat clears above me. "Language, Miss Masters."

I fall still, staring at his long, polished shoes and sharp hems while the reprimand slides down my shoulders like warm, fragrant oil.

Double fuck.

With a deep breath, I drag my gaze up the deliberate crease in his charcoal pants—past the briefcase clenched in his fist, and the long fingers resting over the buttons of his blazer—to meet eyes that sparkle like shattered quartz. Light stubble graces his jaw and circles his mouth, worshipping lips too pretty for the intense stare dissecting mine.

I close my mouth and swallow. "I . . . I'm sorry. My screen broke."

His gaze softens and drops to my phone, but then he stiffens with a frown, one vertical line pressing deep between his brows.

I follow his line of sight, and my heart stops. His half-naked image decorates my screen like I cropped him from the photo and made him my wallpaper. My ears burn hot enough to brand cattle, and I shove the phone inside my handbag quicker than Zoe's left hook, clutching the leather sack in a death grip against my chest.

God, please kill me. I know you want to. *It's so freaking obvious.*

"I needed to know what you look like," I say to my bare knees. The resulting silence flames my skin while the weight of his stare prickles the back of my neck.

He clears his throat. "If it's any consolation, I had a heart attack when I saw that photo too. The tech guys enjoy pressing my buttons." I ease my grip and chance meeting his eyes, discovering a sparkle of mirth. He extends a broad hand with a tight smile, and I eye the rim of his sleeve. Gold cuff links, clean skin, and a dusting of dark hair show. No one would suspect he's a living colourful canvas underneath. "Cole Benedict. I'll be representing you."

I stand, willing my knees to lock and my voice to work. "Avery Masters, Beth's sister. Thanks for helping me."

His strong hand dwarfs mine in a warm, tingling grip, and his scent circles me in a swirl of sandalwood, oak, and the faintest hint of rose. It's subtle and sophisticated, miles away from the cigarette smoke and cheap body spray I'm accustomed to.

He tilts his head. "Your sister has friends in high places." His eyes search mine, and my cheeks flush. I look away, reclaiming my privacy and hand before slinging my bag over my shoulder and clutching the strap.

"Nervous?" he asks.

"Terrified."

He shakes his head. "You'll be fine."

"So people keep telling me," I mumble.

The side of his mouth twitches. "It's true, Miss Masters. Follow me, and I'll explain more."

Unease mingles in my chest, and I clear my throat. "Call me Avery. Please." It's a lame attempt at self-preservation, and as effective as throwing a foam cup at a charging lion, but it's all I have. If he utters Miss Masters once more in that resonant voice, my knees might rescind on our agreement.

He steps back, pausing to examine me, before motioning to a wide hall speckled with doors down one side and glass the other. A leafless courtyard lies beyond the window wall where shrubs stand in army formation. "Shall we?"

I nod, and he turns on his heel with long, confident strides. Determined not to cause further humiliation, I follow with every ounce of concentration on my feet and the four-inch sticks poking my heels. It's like balancing saucers on rods. I don't know why Beth wears these stupid things. As if life isn't hard enough.

"Do you have insurance?"

My gaze darts up to his back, and I ignore the way the fabric shifts across his broad shoulders, the slight out turn of his feet at each step, his long legs, solid thighs, and how his free hand clenches into a fist several times.

"Sorry?"

"Your phone. Any insurance?"

I shake my head. "Sadly, no." Who can afford insurance?

He stops at a frosted-glass-and-aluminium door and pushes it open, turning to face me. "After you, Avery. Take a seat."

My stupid heart flutters again. Perhaps it would be safer if he re-

ferred to me as *you*, or *it*—or refrained from addressing me alto-
gether.

The small room sits barren of charm and sparsely furnished amid
grey sisal carpet and sterile white walls. High windows steal light
from the hall, and downlights supplement the shortfall, drenching
the space in eye-burning glare.

I roll out the mesh office chair and sit, placing my handbag on the
laminate table in front. Cole's briefcase thuds as it lands opposite,
and the gold latches click. He removes a blue marbled folder and sets
it down before taking a seat facing me.

He flips open the folder, and I gasp, slapping a hand over my
mouth to muffle the sound. My mugshot lies clipped to the top, left
corner, where I stand against a height marker facing a firing squad of
contempt. My hair is wild. Mascara smudged. Eyes bloodshot from
tears. And the fluorescent station lights stress every single flaw. It's
like a criminal-edition photo filter—one that adds an air of drug-ad-
dicted dishevelment—only not pretend or amusing.

My cheeks burn, and I pull my handbag closer, hugging it to my
chest. If that's the photo he referenced, I'm horrified he recognised
me. Fuck, I hope Slade never sees it.

"I believe a happy birthday is in order."

I meet his pale gaze, ignoring the way my insides tingle. I could
deal with any other attractive feature and still find coherency, but
those eyes? They look through me, zeroing in on the crux of who I
am. They see things even I hide from, and it's too much. I swallow.
Hard. "Yes."

"That's unfortunate." He shakes his head and slips a gold pen from
inside the breast of his jacket. The chair creaks as he leans back,
stretching his long legs out front and tapping the ballpoint against
the table. "Someone must be screwing with you."

My eyes widen as he parrots my first suspicion. "Exactly," I say.

He tilts his head. "Or fate could be making a point. Teaching you a lesson." The corner of his mouth twitches with a smile. Another one he seems to restrain in favour of indifference, but his eyes betray him.

He seems . . . nice.

"You believe in fate?" He doesn't appear the type—too refined and grounded for such whimsical bullshit. Unlike me.

"At times. But I take issue with the idea everything is preset. That choice is an illusion." His gaze flickers to the inside of his briefcase, then back to me, and his jaw tenses. "Especially when you consider the horrors some inflict."

"Maybe it's a mix of both." I shrug. "Choice that leads to various paths and destinies."

He considers my words, his face softening. "Like a Choose Your Own Adventure novel?"

"Yeah." I nod. "Only with infinite choice." The memory prompts me to grin. "Those books were the highlight of grade three."

"Mine too," he says, and this time he doesn't fight his smile. Straight teeth gleam white, and a lone dimple puckers one cheek. Tingles shoot through me, exploding like popping candy—the *hot* kind. His smile is breathtaking but disappears too fast. Rubbing the stubble of his chin, he schools his expression. "So have you learnt your lesson?"

There's levity in his tone, but my grin slips away. "Have I ever."

He searches my face through a beat of silence, and I look down at the table, blinking away my tears before they start.

"Good. Magistrates like genuine remorse, and we need to give her every reason to help you." He sits forward, adjusting the chair, and scans the papers. "Do you have a job?"

I shake my head. "I did. Sort of. Before I moved in with Beth." I was the resident babysitter. The go-to girl for the myriad single mums. "I haven't thought it wise to find another under the circumstances." How does one explain to a prospective employer the impending possibility of jail?

"The circumstances being . . . ?" He looks up, raising a brow, and I frown.

Isn't it obvious?

"The fact I might go to jail." The words leave my mouth, reeking of melodrama, and Cole's eyes sparkle with amusement. With burning cheeks, I size up the space underneath the table, wondering if I'd fit and if so, how well it would hide me. It's not my fault I catastrophise everything. I'm wired this way.

Forcing solemnity, Cole lowers his chin. "Assuming your freedom, do you intend to find work?"

"Yes," I say, but the answer terrifies me. I hadn't thought past today. It would have only tempted fate to punish me further. Will I have the energy for a real job? I suppose that's irrelevant. Life doesn't care if it's too hard to move.

A faint charge pulses high in my stomach, spurring a memory to life, and my old plan pokes its head out of the studio box, checking it's safe to return. With Beth's generosity, everything changed. My hands move. The muse shows up, and I have a home until I find my feet. *For as long as I need.* Why didn't I think of this until now?

Meeting Cole's eyes, I straighten my spine. "I'm meant to start uni next year. I deferred this year."

He scrolls his pen across the page in looping cursive. "Melbourne?"

I nod.

"What will you be studying?"

"Fine arts."

He glances up with a raised brow. "Sculpture?"

"How did you know?"

He nods to the papers. "School reports. Your art teacher was . . . enamoured."

He read my school reports?

My chest tightens, and I pick at a frayed leather seam on my bag. Mrs. Donovan wasn't just a teacher; she was my friend. A friend who'd be so disappointed if she could see me now. Brushing away the thought, I tuck a lock of hair behind my ear. "I can find a job in the interim," I say, watching him read.

"How long have you known Slade Pearson?" He speaks without looking up, and the question jolts me. He says Slade's name aloud as though it doesn't stab my heart.

"Five months," I say.

He glimpses up. "Are you in a relationship with him?"

My cheeks burn. "How is that relevant?"

Cole's eyes narrow. "I'm on your side, Avery. The more information I have, the better."

Shoulders slumping, I stare at my lap. "I think so. Well, I was." I look up and shake my head. "I don't know anymore."

He taps his pen on the table while he studies me, then drops his gaze. As he lifts another page, his eyes return. "An aspiring sculptor with an ATAR of 98.2."

It's a statement, not a question, but I answer anyway. "I worked really hard," I say, and it's the truth. I even skipped year ten and graduated early. Mum tried to stop me, but I fought back. Why be in school longer than necessary? I never understood her logic.

The vertical line reappears between his brows, and he tilts his head. "So how'd you end up here?"

My chin drops to my chest. "Book smarts don't negate stupidity, I guess."

Shifting back in my chair, I close my eyes and recall the lonely nights at my apartment before Slade came along, Mum's announced departure at my graduation dinner two measly weeks before Christmas, and the swift shove into adulthood when the earth fell away.

Teardrops bead on my skirt before melting into the fabric, and I wring my hands in my lap. Gone is the colourful nail polish I typically wear, demure nude pink in its place. "I lost myself," I say, but the moment the words are free, I know it's a lie. How can you lose something you never found?

Silence darkens the room, and I wipe away my tears with Beth's blazer sleeve.

Cole retrieves a document from the file and slides it towards me. "I've spoken with the police prosecutor. Given the circumstances—the true lack of intent, your potential right of claim, and other facts—he's agreed to downgrade your charges to one count of trespass."

My eyes widen, and hope tingles my stomach. "Is that good?"

"Very good. If you agree and plead guilty. It will be a summary offence versus an indictable. As I'm sure your sister told you, detention was already highly unlikely, but this deal makes it impossible."

I stare at him. It's the word I've longed to hear. *Impossible*. Impossible leaves no room for worry. It deprives the spark of oxygen, snuffing out any chance of fire.

"I'd have a second chance." The words ghost my lips, and Cole's stare intensifies.

He looks at me like he knows me. "You deserve a second chance, Avery."

Do I? The prospect places responsibility for my future squarely back in my palms, and I don't quite trust myself not to fuck it up again.

"The prosecutor also agreed to no conviction being recorded and a six-month good behaviour bond as recommended punishment. We'll request the magistrate hear sentencing submissions today. Should she accept our request, you'll be free to get on with your life. Naturally, we still need to present you as favourably as possible, since she will make the final call."

I nod. "I'll do anything."

Cole considers me for a moment before sliding a document forward. "I'll need you to sign here."

Our fingertips brush as I take the pen from his hand. Fluorescent sticky notes show me where to sign, and my belly flutters more with each letter inked. "Thank you," I say, returning his pen, unable to stop my smile.

He slips it inside his jacket, then squares the documents against the table. "Don't thank me yet. We still have the magistrate to convince." He returns them to the folder and closes the cover, hiding that awful mugshot. Hopefully, he burns it.

"A good behaviour bond requires you to adhere to set conditions. If you breach those, the bond can be revoked, and a harsher penalty may apply. Not to mention potential fresh charges in respect of the breach. You're legally an adult now, Avery. This is no longer child's play. Do you understand?"

"Yes. I would sooner sell a kidney than break the law again." I'd have more chance of surviving the former.

"Good," he says, "I'll let the court know we're ready."

Cole rolls out his chair, stands, and refastens the button of his suit jacket before returning my file to his case and tossing a thin rubber band across the table towards me.

I frown and pick it up. "What's this?"

He remains focused on his case, arranging the satin-lined lid. "I suggest you tie your hair back before your appearance."

"Why?" I ask.

His eyes flash to mine, darker somehow, and it does funny things to my insides. "Because you need to appear as innocent as possible."

"What's wrong with beach waves?" Emma Stone pulls them off with the precise elegance and maturity I thought perfect for today. And she always looks smoking hot, which never hurts.

The case clicks shut, and he arches a brow. "Apart from us not being at the beach, you mean?"

Shrinking in my seat, I push away the image of Cole in Speedos and gulp. I suppose he has a point.

He lifts his briefcase from the table and turns for the door, glancing back over his shoulder. "You should be fine to wait here."

"Okay, thanks," I say while twisting the rubber band in my fingers and cursing my stupidity. Beach hair for court. What was I thinking?

He rubs the back of his neck as though he wants to say more, but instead offers me a tight smile. "See you soon."

The room feels bigger when he leaves, and I deflate against the backrest, skimming a palm down the length of my hair. Begrudgingly, I dig my phone out from the depths of my bag, wincing at the shattered screen. It's a pocket reminder of humiliation to carry with me always, and one I can't afford to fix. Cole's ripped physique pops up the moment I swipe, and I squeeze my eyes shut, mashing my finger against the go-the-fuck-away button. With the front camera active, I balance it against my purse, tie my hair back into a low ponytail, and then sigh. Cole's right. I look five years younger—as innocent as a tween. Perhaps he should have given me two rubber bands. Pigtails would elevate my virtue to pre-school level, and the magistrate might only send me to the naughty corner then.

I toss my phone back inside my bag. At least I managed intelligible English. And I didn't fall over, snort-cry, or dissolve into panic. Beth would be proud, but I'm still going to kill her. Looks like that don't go unmentioned. No. They evoke giggles, girly whispers, flushed cheeks, and tingly nether regions. In different circumstances, of course. Mine are far too dire. And I have Slade. Wherever the fuck he is.

The police prosecutor turns to look at me, and fresh nerves crawl through my chest. He is a small man—wide, thin-lipped mouth, eyes pink and beady like a carnivorous lizard—and seated right side of a table spanning half the courtroom. A dainty microphone swans towards his mouth, ready to pluck words, and he blinks at me once, emotionless, before looking away.

Clenching the cold metal frame of my chair, I resume staring at Cole's broad back and the razor-cut line of his hair. He sits at the same table, left of the central lectern, suitcase standing at attention next to his leather shoes.

The scent of jail lingers as if oozing from the walls, and my stomach rolls over that spark of hope. Instinctively, my eyes drift to the hulky sheriff guarding the double doors. He's built for strength rather than speed, but his vastness blocks the exit, ensuring no room to run.

A knock sounds at the front of the room, and the clerk lifts from her chair. "All rise."

My hands wring as I stand, and the magistrate enters a hidden door behind the oak bench, a black robe wafting in her wake. She bows before taking her seat, and we return the courtesy from three feet below.

"Please be seated. Matter of Avery Lee Masters." The clerk passes a folder to the magistrate before resuming her seat, and my name circles the room with uncomfortable clarity. Thankfully, the rows of chairs behind me stand empty. Any member of the public could have chosen to witness this debacle, but none have. Mia could have been here, but I guess her police report was enough.

"Mr. Benedict, I looked twice when I saw your name on this case." The magistrate casts her gaze over the brim of her wire spectacles, golden curls brushing the curve of her chin.

Cole stands. "Good morning, Your Honour. Always a pleasure."

The smile shines in his voice, and my belly flutters. She knows him. That has to be good, right?

"My condolences regarding your uncle. Gerard was an exemplary lawyer."

"Thank you, Your Honour," Cole says, but his shoulders stiffen.

"How are you finding the helm?"

My frown deepens. *The helm?*

"Challenging, Your Honour." His response comes raw and dipped in pain, and I find myself irritated with the magistrate's insensitivity. The loss must be fresh. That much is clear. Not even the website has been updated.

She purses her feathered lips. "Challenge is where we thrive, Mr. Benedict. I'm sure you'll do fine."

"Thank you, Your Honour." Cole glances at his papers, taking a moment before clearing his throat, and my heart aches for him. "I'm representing Avery Lee Masters today, Your Honour, who sits behind me. Avery lives with her elder sister, Bethany Masters, a fellow lawyer who is presenting a case before the County Court today and, regretfully, cannot be here."

The magistrate nods and looks to the police prosecutor, who then rises too. "Good morning, Your Honour. Senior Constable Greening prosecuting today." His voice comes high and gargled like a bubble is trapped in his throat. Or maybe it's a fly—the snack of choice for lizards.

"Good morning, everyone." The magistrate looks at her notes before settling her attention on Cole. "What's happening today, Mr. Benedict?"

"The matter is resolved, Your Honour. My client has entered into a plea agreement with the prosecution. As such, the original charge of aggravated burglary has been downgraded to trespass. We are satisfied with this outcome and request the new charge be substituted for the old. We rely on the facts set out in the apprehension report, bar the allegation of intent."

"Is that accepted by the prosecution?" she asks.

Senior Constable Greening nods. "Yes, Your Honour. We believe the new charge more accurately reflects the alleged conduct of the accused. We have amended the information in this matter and do not object to the charge being substituted."

"Very well." The magistrate's eyes find mine, tugging me upright in my chair. The urge to stand is strong, but I was told to do so only when asked. "Avery Lee Masters, you are being charged with one count of trespass. How do you plead?"

My heart hammers. This is all moving so fast. In movies, trials drag on for days. And somehow the weeks spent dreading today feel dishonoured by the haste.

Summoned by my silence, Cole turns towards me, and his pale eyes lock on mine, speaking soundless words. He dips his chin in a nod, bestowing me enough certainty to answer, and my chest unfurls ever so slightly.

Inhaling a Beth breath, I look back up. "Guilty, Your Honour."

Again, Cole nods, and I savour his approval like the first sun of spring. He resumes facing the front. "Your Honour, I'm ready to make sentencing submissions. I understand the prosecution isn't opposed, if Your Honour has the time."

"I'll hear it," she says, and the clerk descends from the cubicle adjacent, collecting papers from Cole, before handing them to the magistrate and resuming her post.

Cole starts his submission detailing my lack of criminal history and post-incident exemplary behaviour but then ploughs into the muddied depths of my family tree. At the mention of Mum and Dad, my defences flare. A mental barricade forms around me like a rust-laden cone of silence, and I fight back Cole's words.

"Emotional and financial stress—"

I squeeze harder.

"Under the influence of a new acquaintance known to police—"

Nooo.

"Top three of her class—"

How far I've fallen.

"Bethany has provided a character statement in support—"

I inch the barricade down, sensing the worst is over, but tune back in with caution.

"Furthermore, my client will attend the University of Melbourne next year, and until such time, has an offer of full-time work at Benedict Kane."

His words jolt me like defibrillation pads shock back life.

What did he just say?

"Are you to accept this offer of work?" The magistrate's gaze pins me, and my eyes widen, my mouth opens, but no words come out.

I look to Cole for help—clarity—*a fucking explanation*, but he remains facing the magistrate, who is fast losing patience. Squirming in my chair, I clear my throat. "Ah . . . Yes, Your Honour."

What else can I say?

She tends to her notes, and I frown at Cole's back.

What the hell was that?

His perfect voice refills the room. "While sentencing is a matter of discretion for Your Honour, I understand the prosecution isn't opposed to this matter being dealt with without conviction, and I'd argue an appropriate sentence in this case is a six-month good behaviour bond."

"Senior Constable Greening, are you opposed to a bond in this matter?"

"No, Your Honour. We agree that's appropriate given the personal circumstances of the defendant and circumstances of the offence."

The magistrate's eyes find mine. "Stand, please."

My heels wobble as I rise, and I squeeze my hands until they ache.

"Avery, I've read through the facts of this case and the supporting documents you provided, and I'm satisfied this incident was isolated and uncharacteristic. I accept the incident occurred at a troubled time but strongly advise you to exercise wisdom when choosing acquaintances. Considering your employment and education prospects, I believe you deserve a second chance and the opportunity to proceed with life, record untarnished. Therefore, I agree that no conviction will be recorded in this matter. I will, however, be placing you on a good behaviour bond for a period of six months. Please be seated."

"Thank you, Your Honour," I whisper on wobbly knees. Giddiness swamps my head, and I drop to the chair with limp arms as dread floats free from my bones. Tears prick my eyes, and glitter twirls through my tummy. I have a second chance.

You deserve a second chance, Avery.

Gently, I smile at the ground.

The clerk's order to stand pierces my daze, and I rise like a feather riding the breeze, swaying on my feet, light and free. The magistrate disappears through her hidden door, and Cole turns to face me. Our eyes lock—his wary—and slowly, I crinkle my brows.

"You cornered me," I say.

With a shake of his head, he plucks his briefcase from the floor and rests it on the table. "A simple thank-you will suffice."

Latches sound, and my frown deepens. I'm more thankful than ever, but pride and curiosity prevail. "Why?"

He returns the folder and snaps the case shut. "Instinct. You only provided one reference, and I sensed six months spent twiddling your thumbs wouldn't bode well in the magistrate's eyes."

I cross my arms. "Twiddling my thumbs?"

He stares at me, head tilted, and that adorable crease resurfaces between his brows. "I only made the offer, Avery. You accepted it."

My gaze drops to the carpet, and air fills my chest easier than it has in months. He's right. I could have said no and braved the consequences, but I didn't, and now it's time to grow up and live with my choices. Besides, it's temporary. A chance to save for uni.

A chance to see him again.

I squash that thought faster than it came and close my eyes. This is good—an opportunity for a fresh start. I'll force my limbs to work if need be.

Unfolding my arms, I grip my wrist and look up. "Thank you."

He slides his briefcase from the table, and his face softens. "You're welcome." He slips a hand inside the breast of his jacket and returns a white card embossed with black and gold. "Be here eight a.m. Monday. Check in at reception and ask for me."

I nod and take it from his fingertips, fighting the urge to ask the dozen questions circling my head. "See you then."

His eyes glimmer, and the lone dimple reappears. "Happy birthday, Avery." Tucking one hand inside his pants pocket, he turns and strides from the courtroom without looking back.

The gift of freedom. What better present is there?

A smile spreads across my face, and I stare at the door long after he leaves, processing everything that's him. Eyes soon burn into my awareness, and my gaze shifts to the brawny sheriff standing a foot to the left. He frowns at me, and I flinch. *What the—?* Then it hits me. He thinks I'm staring in wonder at *him*.

Turning my back and swallowing hard, I shove Cole's business card inside my purse and find my phone. With a downcast gaze, I rush through the door, keeping a wide berth. I hold my breath past the security guards and choke in fresh air as I hit the footpath. Everest is conquered, and tonight we celebrate. Life starts here, and I won't let anything bring me down. Not even the message from Mum on my phone.

Mum:
Happy birthday, Avery Lee. Busy today. Talk soon.

 Six

The rich scent of roasted chicken and vegetables saturates the crisp evening air, and the metallic letters of "Benedict Kane" flash white and gold as they catch and shun the dwindling light. I tilt the card back and forth, reading his name over and over.

Cole Benedict.

Cole Benedict.

Cole Benedict.

"What are you doing out here?"

I snap my head towards the voice. Beth stands at the mezzanine window, her dark hair hanging limp against her pale skin. The jade jumper is back, artfully draped off one shoulder, and she's home early, but after last night, who can blame her?

"Waiting for the stars," I say, patting the corrugated iron. "Come and sit. It's beautiful up here."

Beth shakes her head. "I'll take your word for it." She leans against the sill with her arms crossed, fingers tapping a beat against the glossy white paint. "Aves, we need to talk."

My stomach flips, but I cock a brow and smirk regardless. "About the fact your eighteen-year-old sister drank you under the table last night?"

She rolls her eyes but grins. "You're proud of that?"

I'm proud I went out at all. "Beats using the toilet seat as a pillow all morning. Tell me, was the porcelain upgrade worth it?" I tap a thoughtful finger against my chin, and she shakes her head.

"You'll keep, missy."

My chuckle floats away on the breeze, and I tilt my head. There's no use postponing the inevitable. "What did you want to talk about?"

Beth's clear blue eyes sparkle. "Well, I have some news." She glances down, and her smile grows. "The senior partners have asked me to oversee the opening of our new Sydney office, and I suspect this may be a test of sorts. If I do well, my dream of making senior partner by thirty might become a reality. So yeah"—she shrugs—"it's a pretty big deal."

"That's amazing," I say.

"It is?"

"Of course it is. How long will you be gone?"

"Five months," she says, fiddling with the cuff of her jumper. "Until the new year, basically."

My smile falters. "That's a long time."

She nods, silently watching me, and I look away. My index finger circles the cold hex head of a screw, building speed in line with my thoughts. Beth deserves every success. God knows she's worked hard for it. But *five months*? Do I need to find another place to live? And what if she doesn't return? My stomach lurches, and a little voice creeps in, twisting my chest with long, sabre-tipped fingers.

She's leaving too. See, no one can stand you. Not once they know *you.*

My breath hitches, and I rub my forehead with the heel of my hand.

"Aves, look at me. What's going through that head of yours?"

Beth's brows are drawn together, and I swallow back the question

I really want to ask in favour of those more acceptable. "Will you come back?"

"Absolutely. I'll fly back every other month and be home for good in five. I have no desire to move permanently."

"And what if the promotion depends on you staying?"

She inhales a deep breath. "Like I said, I have no desire to move forever. I just finished building this place, and my family is here."

The hideous fingers ease their grip. She means *I'm* here. That's the glorious extent of our family in Victoria.

"When do you leave?" I ask.

"If I accept, three weeks."

"You haven't said yes yet?"

"Not without talking to you first. I'd need you to stay here while I'm gone. I don't want this place empty." My shoulders loosen as another fear falls flat, and Beth continues. "And I'm not leaving unless I know you'll be okay. The timing is bad. You've been through a lot and only just—"

Her words sink in, and I halt her with my hand. "You'd say no for me? I mean that much?"

She holds my gaze. "Yes, Aves, you do." But I don't miss the stiff line of her lips or the flicker of fear in her eyes. She's worried I'd ask that of her—I never would.

Coming to a kneel, I shove Cole's card and my phone inside my back pocket and crawl up the wavy tin. Beth steps back as I mount the sill and climb through with practised ease, landing on the carpet with a thud.

I rest my palms on her shoulders and grin. "Congratulations."

Her shoulders fall on a sigh, and she wrenches me in for a hug. "Thank you."

Pulling back, I arch a brow. "You sure you trust me alone in your house?"

My jest is clear, but she searches my eyes with seriousness as though it's been well considered. "I trust you. You wouldn't break our agreement."

I shake my head. "I won't. I promise." Slade won't set foot inside this house. An ache hits my chest. With each passing day, Slade's feeling further and further away—like he's slipping through my fingers and there's nothing I can do.

"I figure at worst I'll come home to sculptures everywhere. Promise me you'll leave the house and talk to *real* people."

Mirroring her crooked grin, I hand Beth the business card from my back pocket. "I don't think you'll need to worry about that."

She takes it and scans the card. "What's this?"

"My new job. I start Monday."

Her mouth falls open. "Why didn't you tell me last night?"

"I wanted to enjoy my birthday dinner, and . . . I hadn't thought about it yet."

Lie. It's all I could think about.

"What's there to think about?"

Nothing. Everything. I nibble my bottom lip. "He just . . . he makes me uncomfortable. That's all."

Beth huffs out a laugh. "From what I hear, Cole Benedict makes everyone uncomfortable, but don't let pretty wrapping intimidate you."

Or intelligence, the voice of a god, and all-seeing eyes.

I swallow. "I guess."

Beth returns the card. "Besides, you'll probably never see him. I imagine he's busier than me."

"Is that even possible?" I tease, sliding the card back into my pocket. Beth's a work machine, but it can't be healthy. I've never even known her to date.

"Afraid so," she says. "I'm guessing eighty-hour weeks."

I shake my head. "That's crazy."

"That's passion." Beth tilts her head with a smile. "You've spent that in the studio the past two weeks. I know you have."

"That's different." It's not work if you can wear pyjamas and curl up on the floor when your arms grow heavy and tears start.

"Is it?" she asks.

I shake away her question, and my gaze drifts over her shoulder towards my bed, where a small box sits tied with string. "What's that?"

Beth turns. "Oh, it was on the doorstep when I got home."

"For me?"

"That's what it says."

My breath bottles in my chest. "Mum?"

Beth sighs. "I don't think so, hon." Her words are gentle, like a soft caress, and she nudges me with her shoulder. "Open it."

In the glow of the bedside lamp, the quaint silver box shimmers gold. It's light in my hands, and the zigzag-trimmed tag says only my name and address. It can't be from Jen or Liam—they gave me gifts last night—but if not them, then who?

I look up at Beth. "Can parcels be sent from jail?" Hope squeezes my heart, but I'm not sure Slade even knows my birthday, let alone where I live.

Beth mashes her lips together and folds her arms. "I don't know."

The brown string loosens with a sharp tug, and I whip off the lid. A beautiful black phone shines like a grand piano nestled on a bed of scrunched-up tissue paper. I pick it up and study all sides, admiring the sleek lines and pretty purple. It looks brand-new, minus the box. The tissue paper rustles as I rummage through in search of a note—a card—any clue who it's from. But only a charge cable and tiny SIM pin appear.

Beth and I frown at each other, and she nudges her chin. "Turn it on."

An Android logo lights up the glass, and Beth and I watch, waiting while it loads. "So pretty," she says when the vivid home screen appears, nudging me with her elbow. "But who would—" The phone chimes, severing Beth's question as a text alert flashes, donning a strikingly familiar name. My heart does a Riverdance, and I immediately turn away to hide and process, but Beth climbs to her tippy-toes and peers over my shoulder. "Spill, sissy. Who is it?" Beth never calls me sissy except for the rare occasion she's the one who wants something. She grips my shoulders and manually spins me to face her, raising her brows all stern and matron-like. "Well?"

I gulp, certain the name I saw was a product of my crazy imagination. "Um, it appears to be from . . . Cole." Beth stares at me blankly as if we weren't just talking about him. "Benedict," I clarify, and her pale eyes saucer. She snatches the phone from my grip. "Hey!" I squeal, lunging for it, but I'm too slow, and Beth opens the message, then gives me her back. This time, I peer over *her* shoulder, panting tiny, panicked breaths.

> **Cole Benedict:**
> Compensation for yesterday.
> Temporary SIM installed.
> Enjoy.
> —C

Frozen, we stare in silence, my head scrambling thoughts like eggs, until Beth speaks. "Avery Masters, why did Cole Benedict send you a flashy new phone?" She turns to face me, and the cat-got-the-cream smile on her face incinerates my own.

I snatch my phone back and shrug, feigning indifference terribly. "My screen broke yesterday. He was there. That's all." I won't tell her how it happened or why. That humiliation I'll take to my grave.

Seemingly unsatisfied, Beth considers me through narrowed eyes, and to be honest, I don't blame her. Why did Cole Benedict send me a flashy new phone?

My brain screams out answers like overzealous high school nerds.

He's being nice! Welcoming you to the team.

Nah, he pities your sorry arse, loser.

That man is flirting. Look at that presentation. And why not wait until Monday? He likes you.

At that, I scoff. Why the hell would he? Unless, of course, he has a fetish for criminals.

With pursed lips, Beth perfectly arches one brow. "That explains nothing, dear sister." Then she shakes her head with a smirk and turns for the stairs with a twirl of her hand. "But have fun with that."

Her footsteps fade as she descends, and I stare back at the phone, perplexed. Nibbling my bottom lip, I read his message a dozen times and stare at the keyboard, typing and deleting strings of words in reply as I pace.

> **Me:**
> Thanks!

Nope. Not grateful enough. Delete.

> **Me:**
> Thank you so much! I love it.

Gah. Delete. Too peppy, hollow, and familiar.

> **Me:**
> Mr. Benedict, ordinary words cannot
> express my gratitude for the awesome
> phone, but the following Haiku poem might:

What the fuck are you doing, Avery?

On and on this goes for thirty solid minutes until I'm delirious and writing the most ridiculous replies while giggling like an idiot. A still slightly drunk idiot who decides to try on bravery like a pair of bejewelled Louboutin sneakers. Ones I have no intention of buying but want to revel in the fantasy of owning for one glorious minute. I type the response I'd send if I was everything I'm not— bold, brave, and worthy.

Like him.

> **Me:**
> Thank you for the lovely gift, Mr. Benedict. I
> would love to show you my appreciation . . .
> in person.

I add a smiling devil emoji to the end of the text and snicker under my breath. Rolling my eyes, I drum the delete button. But something happens. The message jumps up the screen in a sent grey bubble, and my deleting does nothing but slam the cursor against an empty white wall.

"Oh my God," I gasp. "No, no, no, no." My decibels climb with every word, and I stamp my foot on the floor, pleading with the ceiling. "I didn't press it. I didn't even press it!" The ceiling doesn't respond to my flailing-armed cries, and I drop to sit on the edge of my bed with a whimper. "Please tell me this isn't happening." But it is, goddamn it. So, under duress and holding my breath, I type another message and hit send.

> **Me:**
> Oh my God. I'm so sorry. That was not
> meant to send.

And when that does nothing to alleviate the suffering, I send another.

Me:
It was a joke. I was being stupid. I intended
to delete the last part. Please disregard.

And another.

Me:
I'm sorry. I have no desire to show you my
appreciation. At least not in that way. Thank
you for the phone. If you don't want me to
come in on Monday, I completely understand.

I curse my stupidity every time, but I'm possessed. The demon of panic muddles my thoughts and controls my will.

Me:
I can return the phone too. If you want.
Fuck, I'm so sorry.

Regret drowns me, and I fall back on my bed, tucking my head under the pillow to muffle the wails. They don't come from me but rather the mortally wounded heifer dying by my side. My new spirit animal.

How could I be so freaking stupid?

A dull chime sounds, and I toss the pillow aside and reach for the phone. With one eye screwed shut and the other barely cracked, I open the new message and read.

Cole Benedict:
Language, Miss Masters.

I jolt upright, staring at his reply while heat and tingles rush through my body at the imaginary sound of his deep velvet voice. Holy moly. What is it about those three words that hits me right between my thighs and makes debauched scenarios play on a loop in my head? And how do I respond? Do I consider myself fired before I even start? I needn't wonder for long because another message pops up.

Cole Benedict:
I hope your birthday finished better than it started.

An olive branch. Thank God. I reply within seconds.

Me:
It did, thank you! And I remember every minute, unlike my sister. But let's just say Beth now has a bond with her toilet more solid than most marriages.

I hit send with immediate regret. Oh shit. A toilet, really? That was probably more information than he needed or that Beth wants divulged to the head of a rival firm, but my fingers and brain seem to be operating without my permission, in collusion with this traitorous tech I swear pressed send on its own.

My heart stutters when the next message arrives. I'm expecting Cole to gracefully exit this conversation as fast as he can. But he doesn't.

Cole Benedict:
Lol. That contradicts every rumour I've heard about Bethany Masters. Is it wise to assume you corrupted her?

I smirk, remembering how Jen, Liam, and I all thumped the restaurant's bar, yelling "Skull" at poor Beth, who actually wore her fancy lawyer suit out on a Friday night, essentially painting a target on her back.

> **Me:**
> Well, I am the naughty one, though I can't
> take full credit. I had two accomplices. How
> about you? Do anything special last night?

Alarm bells scream. *The naughty one?* I literally facepalm. Did I really just send that? *For fuck's sake, Avery, slow down and think. You're talking to your boss here.* But he doesn't feel like my boss right now, and I'm high on panic and uncharacteristically chatty.

> **Cole Benedict:**
> Me? No. I'd like to say working until 2 a.m. is
> special, but it's not. That's normal for me.

> **Me:**
> Another workaholic. Must be a hazard of
> the trade. Does it ever get lonely?

I crunch my molars. From silliness to inappropriate prying in two seconds flat. Don't worry, I'll kill myself later.

> **Cole Benedict:**
> Actually, it gets peaceful. Alone is my
> favourite time to be at work.

Peaceful. Now *that* I understand.

I reread his words, feeling like he's shown me a warm glimmer of the man beneath the suit. Why? I don't know—the fact he's even texting me is mind-boggling—but it appears Mr. Benedict might be an introvert like me. A thoughtful, open one who doesn't shy away from inappropriate questions about his emotional state from some strange girl he met yesterday. Maybe I *can* fix this.

I take a deep breath to conjure calm and this time think hard before hitting send.

Me:
I really am sorry about that text. And I'm
truly grateful for the phone. Thank you. I
won't say you shouldn't have because no
one means that anyway.

Then I hold my breath and wait.

Cole Benedict:
Don't worry, and you're welcome.
See you Monday. 8 a.m.
Don't be late . . . Naughty One.

Seven

The home of Benedict Kane is heritage sleek and five storeys high with arched colonial windows and snow-white corbels. It's a serene piece of yesteryear amid modern city chaos and a thirty-minute tram ride away.

I cut through the flow of mindless pedestrians to stop at the foot of six bullnose steps and brass letters spelling "Benedict Kane" on black marble. As I stare up, my stomach is in knots, and my heart pounds loud enough to drown out the peak-hour traffic. The thought of corporate nine-to-five makes me ill, and the prospect of photocopying, filing, and fetching coffee all day suffocates my soul. However, it's a small price to pay for a clean slate.

With a deep breath, I climb the steps, push against the heavy brass doors, and enter a foyer that oozes sophistication. One where timeless elegance meets the contemporary in a seamless transition. Black-and-white terrazzo chequers the vast floor, rustic brick walls add an edge, and gold accents dazzle.

I approach a long desk behind which sits a woman in her twenties. Her nails are unnaturally long, yet she types at speed, somehow conquering the keys, then scoots away from her screen and lifts her gaze to mine. "Good morning." She offers a polite smile. "Welcome to Benedict Kane. How may I help you?"

I glance at her name badge—Chantel—then clear the nervous sludge from my throat. "I'm here to see Cole Benedict."

"Do you have an appointment, Ms.—?"

"Masters." I clench the strap of my handbag tighter. "He told me to ask for him."

"One moment, please." Chantel picks up the phone and singsongs into the handset, "I have a Ms. Masters here for Mr. Benedict." Pausing, she looks back at me and smiles. "Certainly." She hangs up and motions to a regal lounge area dressed in burgundy and deep-buttoned leather. "If you'll take a seat behind you, Mr. Benedict will be down shortly."

"Thank you," I say before following her instructions.

The back of my knee bounces against the cold, hard cushion. This is a bad idea. I can feel it in my bones. I don't belong amongst elegance, suits, or stilettos. I belong in clay-smeared yoga pants, locked in a creative trance on my studio floor, but damn if that will pay the bills or impress a judge.

I scan my surroundings, trying to diffuse my panic and repress the memory of that super-dumb text. At least today no one's here to swear at me or knock me out. And even if they were, the six tiny surveillance cameras I've so far spotted just might be a deterrent.

"Avery." The familiar deep voice whips my heart back into a gallop, and I snap my head up to find Cole striding across the foyer in another impeccably tailored suit. Inwardly, I sigh. That man fits this place like a queen fits her castle, carrying grace with a confident ease. He looks me up and down as I stand to greet him, but the resulting clench of his jaw sends my stomach into free fall. My shoulder-length hair hangs straight—after all, it's not the beach—and I'm wearing another of Beth's skirts with a pinstripe blouse, blazer, and heels. But . . . did I dress wrong?

I feel the blood drain from my cheeks and let my eyes fall shut. How presumptuous to assume I'd qualify for office duties. *What was I thinking?*

He halts in front of me, and again I sigh. "I'm the new janitor, aren't I?"

Cole's brows jump, but amusement tweaks one corner of his mouth. "What were you expecting?"

Perhaps I should have asked, like a normal person.

I shake my head. "I can go home and change."

"Not necessary. Though you may want to wear something easier to move in tomorrow. Something that can get dirty."

The way he says that last word adds a confusing layer of crackling heat to my humiliation, and I toy with the idea of running back through the doors, jumping on the first airport bus, and flying to Jamaica. But I don't have a passport—or money—or a desire to see Jamaica. All in all, it's a terrible plan.

"Christ, don't look so scared," Cole says. "We don't bite. Not on this floor, at least."

That's a shame, I find myself thinking as I stare at those straight teeth and perfect Cupid's-bow lips. I drag my gaze up to meet his. "But the other floors? You bite there?"

A dark flash crosses his eyes. It only lasts a millisecond but is enough for the last two words of his final text to rumble between my legs.

Naughty one.

I suppress a shiver and squeeze my thighs together.

"Only on the good days," he says. "But don't worry, you'll be down here."

Again, I scan my surroundings. He said this was a full-time job. And while I mightn't be the fastest cleaner in the world, there's no way this will take eight hours every day unless it's with a toothbrush.

Oh crap. Is it with a toothbrush?

I frown at the maze of grout lines until Cole clears his throat. *Shit.* He probably earns ten dollars a minute, and I've just wasted one of them staring at the floor, trying to decide what cleanser would work best with said toothbrush. Still, he doesn't seem to mind. In fact, Cole appears mildly entertained, but I can only assume it's the flavour of entertainment one gets when they visit a foreign zoo—more of a fascinated bewilderment. After all, going by this place, he rarely mixes with people like me.

He tilts his head in the direction from which he came. "Come. Follow me."

So I do. I follow him like a lost puppy on trembling knees and four-inch sticks for the second time in a week, the discomfort I told Beth about running rife in my chest. Maybe I should have downed a few shots this morning too. I could've been a drunk but far less awkward janitor.

Cole rounds the corner and halts outside a golden elevator, turning to face me while he adjusts the cuff of his sleeve. "Do you like kids, Avery?"

"Kids?" Immediately, I blush because for a nanosecond, my wild imagination has the audacity to think Cole might be asking for himself—that I'm a viable breeding candidate. I mentally slap the thought away. "How is that relevant?"

"It's not only relevant—it's vital. Didn't you complete child studies in your final year?" His brows rise hopefully.

God, what else does he know? "Sure. I love kids," I concede.

"Good. Then I think you'll be pleased." Palm side up, Cole raises his hand, motioning over my shoulder with a dip of his chin, and I turn to find a clear glass wall, beyond which lie toys of every colour, size, and shape—filling polka-dot boxes, lining royal-blue shelves. Space-themed mobiles and handmade sea creatures dangle from the ceiling, and a cartoon bumblebee flies across the back wall, spelling out "Mini-Bees" in a dashed and dotted trail. Three tiny humans, ranging in size, speckle the large space, and a white bassinet stands in one corner, draped in netting.

I spin back to face Cole with butterflies twirling around my heart. "So I'm not the new janitor?"

With a glittering, lopsided smirk, he shakes his head, rocking back on his heels with pocketed hands. "Afraid not. Bernie prefers to work alone."

I itch to playfully punch his arm for messing with me, but I'm so damn excited and relieved I can't move. "I don't know what to say." This is perfect, and I'm guessing my goofy smile conveys as much, because Cole is staring at me with one of his own.

God, those eyes. That dimple.

We stay like that a smidge too long until Cole seems to catch himself with a tiny shake of his head. His smile fades away, and he removes his hands from his pockets to adjust the knot of his tie. The transformation from soft to hard—from open to closed—takes mere seconds, but what's left standing before me now is most definitely Managing Partner Cole. Professional. *Impenetrable*.

"Shall we?" he asks, and even his voice has changed from wearing wool to armour. It's subtle, but I'm wired to notice subtleties. The bad ones, anyway.

I frown a little but nod, feeling like someone just stole my cosy blanket on a frosty morning. But we are in a workplace—a fancy law firm, no less—and he is the big boss and I an employee.

Cole steps past me to the door, swipes his fob across the sensor, then holds it open for me to enter. I pass him, stepping into a magical wonderland with star-spangled carpet and joy braided through the air. A brunette beauty approaches us with a warm, homely smile. She'd be a few years my senior and wears lilac skinny jeans with shoes resembling Chucks. My feet rejoice from their squished confines, and my eyes literally glass with gratitude.

Thank you, universe.

"Avery, this is Hannah Beaufort," Cole says. "Hannah, Avery Masters. Avery is the new Marla."

"Nice to meet you, Avery. Welcome to the madhouse." Hannah offers me her hand, which I shake.

"Thank you. Nice to meet you too."

"You'll answer to Hannah. She'll fill you in on the hours and expectations."

Cole's tone is fit for a courtroom. Still, I meet his gaze with a smile that could burst. "Thank you."

His armour vanishes for a beat, and it's like hitting the warm, gooey centre of a chocolate lava cake, but then he looks away, nods once, and marches for the door. "Good day, ladies."

"Bye, Cole," Hannah calls out—almost tauntingly.

Interesting.

Turning back to me, she rolls her eyes. "Don't mind him. Sometimes he's as warm as a snowman."

So it seems. I much prefer Sunshine Cole to Snowman Cole, that's for sure, but I chuckle all the same and scan the room. One little girl is playing dress-ups. A boy is mastering a puzzle. And a second girl is hiding under a desk, covering her eyes with her hands to aid invisibility.

"We only have a few here now. This group will triple as it approaches nine, and you'll meet Tej soon. He's the other full-timer. The kids love him."

Hannah takes me around to each play- and workstation, summarising all the procedures before showing me where to leave my bag and store food.

As we reach the bassinet, her voice softens to a whisper. A tiny baby in pastel green lies asleep on his back, his hands resting either side of his head. Gently, I reach in, pressing my index finger into his teeny palm, and his little fingers curl around it in a grip ten times his size. "This is Jack, our latest addition. Only seven weeks old," Hannah says, and my stomach flutters. He's the youngest baby I've ever met and smells like talcum powder and promise.

"He's beautiful," I whisper, wrestling my finger out to meet Hannah's smile.

She leads me to the craft area next. Eccentric fish and cellophane seaweed hang from the ceiling, and a small weight barrels into my thighs, knocking me unsteady. Catching my balance, I look down at the precious little girl wrapped around my knee. Caramel pigtails curl either side of a perfect part, and pale denim overalls cover her puffed-sleeved shirt. She was the one hiding. "Hi, there." I smile at her, and she smiles back with chubby, dimpled cheeks and big green eyes.

"Avery, this is Ella. Ella, this is Avery," Hannah says, untangling her from my leg. "Come here, cookie." She lifts Ella onto her hip and kisses her temple. "This is my daughter. She's a girl of few words."

"She's adorable," I say.

"That she is, but don't let her silence fool you. She can be very opinionated when it suits her." Hannah winks, and I laugh. "Your hours will be Monday to Friday, eight until six. I'm here at seven for the early birds, and we stagger our one-hour lunch breaks to maintain ratios. Think you can handle that?"

"Sure." I nod.

"Well then," she says, "guess I'll leave you to it. Feel free to introduce yourself to the parents and kids as they arrive."

Hannah wanders over to the costume corner, so I head to the opposite one, taking a seat on a mini chair at an equally small table next to a boy named Alex, who's almost four. "Hey buddy, what are you doing?"

"A farm puzzle," he replies with articulate words and intelligent eyes.

"You're doing a great job. Can I help?"

Alex nods and hands me a timber chicken. Exaggerating difficulty,

I try to squeeze the piece into the spot meant for the pig, and Alex grins at my idiocy, shaking his little head. "That's not where it goes!"

"Oh, it's not?" I frown.

His giggle fills the air as he grabs the piece from my hand and puts it in the correct place. "There you go, silly."

"Well, aren't you clever?" I ruffle his hair, and pride beams from his cherubic face, squeezing my heart and shooting warmth through my chest.

If I can't spend my days covered in clay—paint, soggy food, and kiddie germs are by far the next best thing.

When I return from lunch ten minutes early like always, twangs of acoustic guitar are floating through Mini-Bees. Tej croons a smoky rendition of "Brahms' Lullaby" to his gathering of fun-size fans, who all sit with their mouths hanging open like carnival clowns. I mosey over to Hannah's side and glance her way. "Um . . . is he hypnotising the kids?"

I catch her staring at Ella with a glimmer of melancholy in her expression, but it's gone in a flash, replaced by one of her serene smiles. "Oh yeah. That's Tej's superpower."

"A man of many talents." I chuckle. "Tell me, why's he working here with a voice like that?"

Hannah stares at Tej as if she, too, is entranced. She shrugs. "It's one of life's great mysteries."

My gaze lingers on her for a beat. She's striking today. Wavy tendrils of cinnamon-brown hair frame her rosy cheeks, and her flowy blouse matches her sky-blue eyes. Hannah's like the first day of real spring: warm, cheery, and filled with all the beginnings of life. But at times, her mind seems to live in a land far from nice. I guess it's not easy being a young mum.

Finishing the final bar, Tej plucks the last tranquil note, then opens his eyes, flashing a white grin that pops against his light-brown skin and floppy jet-black hair. "Okay, my loyal munchkins, what shall I play for you next?" Little arms fly into the air, and high-pitched voices whimper to be chosen. "Ella," Tej says, winking up at Hannah. "What would you like to sing?"

Hannah grins at her daughter but leans in towards me. "The Wiggles. 'Rock-a-Bye Your Bear,'" she whispers behind a cupped hand.

"Umm." Deep in thought, Ella rubs her little lips. "Rocky bear, please."

"Good choice, and good manners," Tej says before rising from his chair and sliding it aside with his boot. The children follow his lead and stand, jumping and bopping in anticipation. "Now, remember, if you don't know the actions, just make them up." Tej strums the first notes on his guitar, and the lullaby calm is chased out of the room by a burst of high-energy rock. The children buzz. Little arms and legs flail, flap, and bounce in all directions, and they're so damn cute—so untainted and free—I dissolve into laughter.

Ella rocks an imaginary bear in her arms with such gusto she loses her balance with each jumbo swing. Giggling, Hannah shrugs up her hands. "What can I say? Clearly, she's the next Maddie Ziegler."

We watch the pandemonium for another hilarious minute before Hannah frowns as if she's heard something. "I think we've woken up Jack. I'll be back."

I glance up at the clock, remembering the reason I return early from lunch, and then eye the elevator. Like clockwork, a minute later it dings, boosting my heartbeat to the tempo of the song. The golden doors slide open, and Cole's glimmering eyes meet mine. He's alone, like always. And offers me a nod, like always. Politely, I smile, ignoring my traitorous cheeks as their heat travels south, sparking everything to life.

If working at Mini-Bees is a sumptuous red velvet cake—1:35 p.m. is the decadent cream cheese frosting.

Typically, I behave during these encounters, but today when Cole steps out of that softly lit cabin, time stands still, and my gaze drifts down the length of his body as if controlled by another force. I admire every nuance of his frame. The skim of that V-neck vest across his broad chest. The emerald tie that dips behind it. His relaxed hands-in-pockets stride, and the way those black suit pants gently hug his lean yet solid legs.

Our eyes meet again as he skirts the great glass wall of Mini-Bees, but this time his are darker—harder—and I flinch awake.

Uh-oh. *Busted.*

Severing contact, I stare at my dirty pink Chucks as Tej's guitar and the song roll back into my awareness like they've returned from outer space.

God, what's wrong with me?

Yes, we exchanged some flirty texts. And yes, he bought me a phone. But ever since I set foot inside Mini-Bees twelve days ago, Cole has been nothing but professional.

I should be doing something constructive. Cleaning. Restocking the nappy bay. Dyeing the macaroni for Monday's jewellery making session. Maybe that's why he stares. He's paying me to work, yet I stand here every day like a perverted slacker, toying with the notion a man like him could ever be interested in little lost me.

You have no substance, Avery Lee. You're just a shiny, empty tin.

I grind the tip of my shoe into a trio of carpet stars. It's just . . . *I felt something.*

The door to Mini-Bees unlatches, and I look up to find Cole walking in. My breath hitches. He never comes in. Shit, am I in trouble? If covering my eyes could make me magically vanish, I'd do it this very second, but unfortunately toddler logic isn't particularly sound.

Cole strolls over and halts at my side, bringing with him that soft sandalwood-rose scent. Resisting the urge to sniff the man, I force a trembling smile that probably appears creepy. "Hi," I say with a regrettable dorky wave in case he didn't hear me over the music.

Cole returns the smile, but his isn't creepy at all. It's a smooth and sexy smirk that tilts up to the left and triggers *that* dimple. "Hi," he half yells, returning his hands to his pockets. That one baritone word runs through my veins like warm maple syrup. "How are you?"

"Good." I nod, too eagerly, like an overenthusiastic bobble head. "Yourself?"

"Good," he says before falling silent.

We watch Tej, and I pretend to be engrossed by the next lively Wiggles song, but Cole's in my peripheral, and I'm hyperaware of his every breath and minuscule movement. His fingers tap away inside his right pocket, but they're triple speed to the beat and only seem to escalate the jittery, electric tension I'm certain hums between us.

Fuck, this is awkward. I don't have functional pockets, so my hands just wring and mangle each other. Am I in trouble or not? I last another thirty seconds before I bite the bullet and lean in to speak. God, he smells phenomenal. "I should be working, not just standing here. I think the nappy bay's calling my name." I offer another dorky wave to say goodbye, but Cole frowns as I turn to leave, and a warm hand locks around my wrist to stop me. Tingles explode through me like a confetti cannon.

"Avery, wait." I turn back to face him and catch him swallowing. My gaze darts to my wrist and back up again, which alerts Cole to the fact he's yet to let go. Abruptly, he remedies that situation and instead rubs his jaw. "Um, I was wondering," he starts, and the number of ways I'd love him to finish that sentence swirl through my mind, "if I ordered some air-dry clay, how would you feel about running weekly lessons for the kids?"

Oh wow. That idea is gold. "I would *love* that," I beam, but the music cuts out, leaving my words booming across the room. The little ones all turn to gawk up at me, as does Tej, and Ella's face lights up as she eagerly waves hello. My cheeks are on fire, but I wave back. So does Cole, which is nice.

Again, he does that annoyingly sexy smirk but this time studies me like I'm simultaneously the most endearing and tragic human on the planet. Heat pools between my legs regardless, but if I was a turtle, I'd slam inside my shell.

"Good," he says, "I'll make the arrangements. Enjoy the rest of your day." Then, turning on his heel, he heads for the door.

I watch until he disappears into the foyer before exhaling, my shoulders slumping as I catch Tej's curious gaze. He looks away, redirecting his attention back to the children as Hannah approaches with Jack nestled in her arms. "Was that Cole?" she asks, tilting Jack's bottle of breast milk higher as it nears empty.

"Um, yeah," I reply, tucking my hair behind my ears.

She frowns. "What did he want?"

"Um, he suggested I teach the kids sculpting once a week." I wave a dismissive hand. "I think he was just on his way to lunch."

Hannah crinkles her button nose. "He never used to leave for lunch. Not sure what the recent appeal is." She discards Jack's empty bottle on a shelf and rests him upright against her shoulder, patting his back. "So sculpting is your thing?"

"Yeah." I smile. "It's my thing."

"What do you make?"

"People mainly." I shrug. "Nudes. Masks. Busts. All from clay, but most have metalwork too."

"Nudes, hey?" Hannah waggles her brows, and I roll my eyes.

"What are you—twelve?"

She chuckles, then hip-checks me. "Give or take nine years." A small burp erupts from Jack, and Hannah returns him to a cradle position. "I'd love to see pics sometime."

I stiffen. If sharing photos of my work didn't feel like publishing my secret journal, I might agree. "Maybe one day. They're works in progress for now."

"Fair enough," Hannah says, grabbing the empty bottle from the shelf. "It's nappy time. Say bye-bye, Avery." Jack's little eyes boggle in my direction as she waves his tiny hand. I wave back, even though he'd only see me as a giant grey blur. Fitting, since that's how I often feel. Like a clump of grey fog blemishing an otherwise crisp and elegant scene.

Hannah winks before heading to the nappy bay, and the second she turns away, I scan the hall outside, counting down the seconds until Cole's return. God, look at me.

You're pathetic, Avery Lee. Quit now before you embarrass yourself.

I clench my jaw. I think it's too late for that, but I can still do something about it. I can stop this obsessive childish nonsense. This is my job, after all—my means of paying for uni—and I won't jeopardise it. I can vow to epitomise professionalism and evict all racy thoughts of Cole Benedict.

The dramatic damsel in my head falls to the ground in protest. "But, but, but . . . ," she cries, draped in flowing white robes. "There's something special about Cole. He's different. We're different *with* him."

I huff. Yeah. I'm sure my mother tells herself that before every doomed fling. Hell, I thought the same about Slade and look how that's turned out.

I sigh. *Oh, Slade.*

Sitting back up, the damsel crosses her arms and mutters, "No, you didn't."

But I choose to ignore her.

Eight

Holy shit.

My mouth hangs open as I process my bank balance, and then I squeal, drumming my feet against the mattress before leaping from bed to race downstairs.

When I peek through Beth's bedroom door, I spot her asleep in a nest of chocolate-brown hair, her face half-covered by the chenille comforter.

Perfect.

On tiptoes, I creep to the foot of her bed and then throw myself on top of her, screaming, "I'm rich!"

Beth lets out a mighty groan. "What are you doing? Get off me!"

Not a morning person, obviously.

"Beth, look, I'm rich." I shove my phone into her screwed-up face, and she blinks against the onslaught of blue light.

"Is that your pay?"

I nod.

"For the fortnight?"

I nod again.

She looks at me, then back to the screen, shaking her head with a sleepy smile. "Well, that's—wow. Congratulations. Nice to know if this law caper doesn't work out, I could try my luck at Mini-Bees."

I huff out a laugh. She's being kind. Beth rakes in the big bucks, as she well should. She closes her eyes again, so I snuggle up next to her, inhaling her honey-vanilla scent before blowing the hair from my face with a contented sigh. By the year's end, I'll have enough money to support myself through my first year of uni.

"You know what," I say, kicking her awake a few minutes later, "I finally feel like everything is coming together. Like I'll be able to master this whole adult thing after all."

"Of course you will. Never doubted you for a minute," Beth mumbles dryly. I meet her sly smirk with narrowed eyes, and she chuckles. "Okay, maybe I did. For a few, at least." I swing a gold tasselled pillow towards her face, but she blocks it with her forearm. "Hey! Can you blame me?"

No, I can't. Not even a bit.

"You should go out and celebrate," she suggests, and I stare at her, waiting for that familiar dread to wrap around my chest—for my limbs to double in weight at the mere thought—but they don't, and my smile brightens.

I plant sloppy kisses all over Beth's face and ignore her cat slaps and pleas to stop until she's suffered enough. Then, after declaring her the best sister in the world, I flop to my back and text Jen.

Me:
Hey, are you and Liam free tonight?

Jen:
Yeah, why?

Me:
We're going out.

Jen:
Who is this, and what have you done with Avery?

Me:
Funny. I'm crying with laughter.

Jen:
I'm dead serious, but I guess it doesn't matter.
I'll party with anyone. Where are we going?

Me:
You choose. I'm happy with music and vodka.

Jen:
There's a band playing the Bellcat at eight.
Meet you out front?

Me:
Sounds like a plan. See you then.

Jen:
Can I at least grab your name?

Me:
Fuck off.

Jen:
Oh, it is you. My bad.

"Look at you." Jen whistles as I approach, walking down the quaint cobblestone lane in my short grey sweater dress and trusty faux-leather jacket. Cast-iron lantern lights dot the way, and their warm yellow glow shines Jen's cheeks like a pair of leather shoes.

She drops her gaze to my new pewter eight-hole boots and gasps. "Are they real?"

With a lopsided grin, I nod. "And crazy expensive." Thirty-five bucks a hole, but Beth insisted I treat myself.

"Worth every cent," Jen says, but I'm not so sure. Had I waited twelve months, they might have shown up at a thrift shop for twenty bucks. Bruised perhaps—maybe a size too big—but with ample miles left in them.

I pull Jen in for a hug and then twirl her around with one hand like we're dancing. "You look beautiful." Her tweed pinny dress has love hearts on each pocket and pearlescent buttons down the front.

She shrugs. "Half-price at Myer."

"Worth every cent." I wink before smiling at Liam. "Hey, Liam. Nice glasses."

Jen groans. "He looks like a clown."

"I do not," Liam says, pushing the giant yellow frames further up his nose.

I press my lips together, fighting a smile. Jen has a point.

"You do," Jen says. "Even your nose is red."

Liam narrows his eyes on her. "It's cold, if you haven't noticed."

She pokes out her tongue, then flashes him a sparkling, sassy grin, and Liam pounces. He locks his long arms around her waist and rubs his icy nose all over her neck. Jen squeals and giggles, batting at his arms, begging him to let go. He concedes eventually, plonking her back to her feet before turning to me. "I hear tonight's on you, Aves. In that case, I'll have doubles of their finest scotch."

I shake my head with a smirk. Liam wouldn't know fine scotch if it smacked him in the face. He'll stomach four, maybe five, beers at most, by which time he'll be jumping around the dance floor like a lunatic. "Anything you wish, sir." I offer him a small bow, and he puffs out his chest like a pigeon.

Jen chuckles and hooks her arm through his. "C'mon, let's get this clown inside before people drop coins at his feet and expect him to perform."

My laugh echoes down the lane as I follow them inside the Victorian building, seeking comfort in their shadow. Nerves flare, but I swallow them down. This is what people my age do. They go out, get drunk, and have fun amongst other real-life humans more than twice a year.

Speaking of people my age . . . what if Zoe is here? My sparkly boots halt in their tracks, and I inhale through my nose, pacifying the paranoid little voice that now accompanies me everywhere. If she's here, I'll hide or run. Simple. It won't be the brave thing to do nor dignified, but it's resolution enough to keep my feet moving across the dinged-up wooden floors.

The Bellcat is clean and trendy with low-hanging pendant lights and walls of abstract art dangling from picture rails like sumptuous fruit on a tree. The scent of alcohol taints the air, and people linger with drinks in hand, chatting and laughing at the bar, where colourful spirits line a mirrored wall and wine glasses hang upside down, glistening like raindrops in the sun. Tall, scattered tables lead to a dance floor, and a carpet block stage sits stacked at the end. Zoe is notably absent, and my shoulders relax. Our early arrival affords us a candy-striped booth seat with a clear stage view, and Liam slides in to rest against the end wall, encouraging Jen to sit between his legs.

Slipping my debit card from my pocket, I halt next to the table. "What do you guys want to drink?"

"We're not actually letting you pay, you know that, right?" Jen asks.

"But I want to. Please. It's the least I can do." The mental tally of IOUs has grown too big to recite, so I offer my best version of Jen's famous puppy-dog eyes.

She sighs. "That's unfair. You can't use my own weapon against me."

"Cosmo?" I ask, adding prayer hands. Her reluctant smirk says yes, as does the roll of her eyes, so I glance at Liam. "A double Glenfiddich on the rocks?"

"Corona, thanks." He throws me a wink, and I grin. I knew it.

"I'll be back."

Prickling stares follow me back from the bar, causing my steps to grow awkward as I navigate the maze of cocktail tables, juggling three drinks. From the corner of my eye, I scan the room, determined to prove it paranoia, but alas, it's not. My gaze locks with several others, and smiles flicker, eyes darken. Some subtly—a flash and they're gone—but others lock on like radar-guided missiles, following my every move. My face burns, and I stare at the hardwood floor. *Sheesh*.

"What kind of place *is* this?" I ask as I set the drinks down on the table and slide into the seat opposite.

Jen smirks. "Attracting attention, are we?"

I frown. "Is there crap on my face or something?" It's happened before. I once walked through Bourke Street Mall completely unaware of the grease smeared on my cheek. Not to mention the perils of clay—I find that in the strangest places.

"It's those baby blues, long legs, and platinum bed hair," she declares.

"*Beach hair*," I correct, then take a sip, choking as vodka burns the back of my throat. I never should have told her about Cole. She reads far too much into things.

"If you say so," Jen singsongs, jiggling her brows. "But seriously, they're staring because you're the hottest girl here."

Liam clears his throat. "Second hottest."

Jen grins up at him and strokes his cheek. "Aw, you're the sweetest."

He nods across the room. "The chick at the bar is definitely the first."

Jen bucks from his embrace and signals a waiter. "Cheque, please."

But Liam lowers her hand and regathers her in his arms, turning her face to his. "I'm joking, baby. You leave everyone for dead. No offence, Aves."

I raise my hands. "None taken."

Liam places a soft kiss on Jen's pouting lips, and not three seconds later, she climbs over his lap, straddling him. Their hands fumble, their breaths grow frantic, and I quietly curse. "Ahem. Guys . . . Hello? Awkward third wheel, right here."

They break apart, sniggering like naughty children, and Liam drops his head back against the wall with a dopey smile. He's love-struck. Smitten. Pussy-whipped.

All of the above.

"Sorry, Aves." Jen dabs her lips with a green serviette, and I crinkle my nose.

"You guys are so gross."

"Aw, you're just jealous," she jokes, but my smile turns awkward.

Staring at my lap, I take a deep breath and coach myself to abstain from all thoughts of Slade tonight. *And* Cole.

Jen leans across the table to squeeze my hand. "I didn't mean to upset you."

I shake my head. "You didn't. I'm being stupid, and you're right— I am a little jealous. Who wouldn't want what you guys have?"

Liam finishes his last swig of beer and belches, then drops the glass bottle to the table, wiping his mouth with the back of his hand. "Where is Slade tonight, anyway?"

My heart stutters, and Jen snaps her attention his way. Our booth falls silent, and I frown. "What do you mean?"

Liam's eyes widen, and he looks at Jen before dropping his gaze to the table. "Shit."

"Shit, what?" Jen asks, growing taller in the booth while Liam shrinks.

"You don't know," he says, flickering his eyes to mine.

My stomach sinks. "Know what?"

"Oh boy," he says under his breath with a whistle. He sighs, carving a hand through his messy hair. "He's out."

"Slade?" I feel my blood drain.

Liam nods, and Jen hisses, "Why didn't you tell me?"

"Because I'm not meant to talk about him, remember?" His reply comes through clenched teeth, and he winces at his empty beer. "Look what happens when I do."

Jen whacks his arm. "To Avery, not me!"

"When?" I ask, gripping Jen's wrist to quiet her.

Liam sighs. "Two weeks ago."

"Two weeks ago?" I swallow the lump in my throat. *Two whole weeks?* "Why so soon?"

"Good behaviour and overcrowding, apparently."

"And you didn't know?" My gaze darts back to Jen. She's said as much, but I need the reassurance.

Vehemently, she shakes her head. "No way. I would have told you. You know that. My boyfriend here apparently doesn't know how to communicate."

Liam winces. "Sorry, Aves. I thought you knew. Hell, I thought he'd be here. I was psyching myself up all day to deal with the cunt-nugget."

My frown deepens. When would Slade ever come to a place like this with me?

Liam dips his mouth to Jen's ear. "Sorry, baby. I should have said something." Jen's shoulders relax when he kisses her cheek, but her eyes remain locked on mine, wary and waiting.

The news tumbles around my head, punching my heart, and I take a few deep breaths, trying to make sense of it all. Two weeks and he hasn't contacted me. *Two fucking weeks.* My chest tightens, and the pub air grows stuffy and warm. *Too warm.* I yank at the collar of my jacket, willing my lungs to work. The decision's been made for me, evidently. Slade's done. After *everything*. That night. The blame I tried to take. Zoe and her iron fist. My . . . *virginity*.

I squeeze my eyes shut as my sense of self deflates like a balloon blown up and let go before being tied. It lands in a dark corner with dust bunnies and dirt. Small, saggy, and used. "Did he ask about me?" I brace for Liam's answer.

"I only saw him at Maccas. We didn't talk long. Sorry, Aves." Pity rasps his voice, and my eyes glass.

Leaning across the table, Jen grabs my limp hands in hers. "You don't want him, okay? He's an arsehole."

She's right. Slade is an arsehole, and damn it, I don't want him. Or more aptly, I don't *want* to want him. Not anymore. My chest heaves against the invisible weight crushing it, and Beth's voice counts in my head. In, two, three, four . . .

It takes every ounce of strength to wrestle my panic into mere anger, but I manage it. Just. And as I'm trying, out of nowhere, Cole's face appears in my mind, soft and luminous. His knowing eyes and smile loosen the shackles across my chest so I can breathe—breathe and purge my anger so as not to explode.

Slade and his bat-shit-crazy girlfriend can go to hell. He thinks *he's* done—well, fuck that—he has no idea how done *I* am.

There. I feel better.

I return from the land of spinning thoughts like I've stepped out from a dark fog of battle. As Liam and Jen watch me in careful silence, I lift my cosmo to my lips with shaky hands, down it in one shot, then slide from the booth, forcing a smile. If one thing's for sure, Slade Pearson is not ruining my night. "I'll get us some more drinks," I say before heading to the bar. And this time, I don't give a fuck who's watching.

Three sorrow-numbing cosmos, two flattering pick-up attempts, and one hour later, the deafening screech of an amplifier jolts the pub to silence. I cover my ears, and everyone's attention darts to the stage where Riot of the Ruby Soul are setting up their equipment.

The bassist leans into the mic with a charismatic smirk. "Sorry about that, folks." Stepping back, he strums a few notes and adjusts the dials some more.

"These guys are so good," Jen says. "You should hear the lead singer. He's like an Indian Ed Sheeran."

Looking back to the stage, I narrow in on a familiar face and squint through my cosmo haze to ensure I'm seeing right. I am. It's him. "Um, Jen. That lead singer—I know him. That's Tej Patil. He works at Mini-Bees."

Her glossy lips drop open. "No way."

"Way. He sings to the kids. Never knew he was in a band though."

She slaps her hand down over mine. "You have to introduce us."

"It would be weird if I didn't say hello, I guess. Later though. They're about to start."

Tej steps up to the mic, raking fingers through his tousled hair. He's all Green Day grunge with black-rimmed eyes, a red tartan suit jacket, and skinny black jeans. "Good evening, dear patrons of this amazing establishment. Thanks for coming out tonight. As you might know, we are Riot of the Ruby Soul." Cheers and whistles erupt across the crowd. "Thank you." Tej smiles. "We have a pretty special show planned tonight. Hope you like it."

Tej swings his guitar into position, adjusting the strap over his shoulder, and with a nod, the drummer taps his sticks together three times. The medley of instruments boom through the speakers, charging the air and swallowing the room, and bass thumps through the seats, rattling our glasses on the table. Tej delivers the first line with a dark, gritty voice, and I arch a brow at Jen. "How does *he* remind you of Ed Sheeran?" Don't get me wrong, I love Ed, but Tej is edgier. More intense. Angrier.

She leans across the table. "He writes his own songs too. And just look at that cheeky smile. Don't you want to pinch those chubby cheeks?"

I'm not convinced we're watching the same man, but one thing's for sure: Tej is an epic showman—a grunge god who commands the stage with charisma and skill, luring the crowd into his orbit and leading them on a journey through his soul.

Jen pulls me from the booth and drags me to the dance floor, and two hours pass as if they were twenty minutes. The music and movement finish what the cosmos started, purging the last scraps of pain from my cells and freeing my mind from looping torture.

Wiping dampness from my brow, I guzzle down a bottle of water. Bodies gyrate around me, and sweat stifles the air. Riot of the Ruby Soul ascends into the climax of their encore, and Liam bounces around the dance floor, flailing his arms like the kids at Mini-Bees. Jen shakes her head, and I laugh. Beer number five never ceases to entertain.

As the final song ends, Tej's guitar cuts through the air with a vibrato-filled power chord that lingers. Then the music cuts out, and the crowd goes wild. Tej frees his guitar and leans into the mic. "Thank you very much," he says, Elvis-style with a wink.

We cheer, clap, and whistle our thanks, and slowly the bodies disperse. Top-forty music hijacks the speakers, coaxing some to stay and dance, but many head for the bar or out the door.

"Introduce us, introduce us!" Jen says.

"Okay, okay. Follow me." I push through the remaining crowd, liquid courage fuelling my nerve, and halt stage side, fiddling with my hands, flanked by Jen and Liam. "Tej?"

He snaps his head towards me, and a smile lights up his face. "Avery?" Standing up, he leans his guitar against the amp and walks over. "Hey, what a surprise. Did you see the show?"

I nod. "You were incredible. I had no idea—well, I mean I did—at work you're great, but on stage you're something else." My voice comes jittery and high like a fangirl half my age, and I cringe.

"Thanks," Tej says, his grin sparkling. He shoves his hands inside the front pockets of his jeans, and his straight white teeth glisten under the dim stage lights.

A petite hand pincers my waist, and I clear my throat. "Oh, I'd like to introduce you to my friends. This is Jen and her boyfriend, Liam. Jen's a huge fan."

Tej leans down, fist-bumping Liam. "It's great to meet you both. Thanks for coming to the show." He offers his hand out to Jen, and she grips it with both of hers, jumping up and down.

"No. Thank you!" she says. "You're awesome. I love you." She freezes as her words sink in and then flushes beetroot. Liam grumbles unintelligibly, but Tej throws his head back and laughs.

"Thanks, Jen. We love our fans too." Prying his hand from her grasp as politely as possible, he turns to me. "I don't suppose you guys have time for a drink?"

I shrug and smile, ignoring the muffled squeal circling Jen's throat. "Sounds great."

Tej grins. "Give me ten to finish up here, and I'll come find you."

As he heads off, Jen squeezes my shoulders, still bouncing. "Holy shit. We get to *drink* with him."

Liam rolls his eyes. "C'mon, crazy girl. Let's wait for him at the bar." He wraps his arms around Jen's waist from behind and picks her up. Protesting, she surrenders her grip on me, then pouts as she's carried away.

As promised, Tej soon finds us, and his charisma doesn't stop on stage. Our conversation flows like Van Gogh. We discuss everything from Benedict Kane to existential ponderings to memories of our respective school years, and I take every opportunity to rile Jen in her inebriated, smitten state.

She smacks her hand down on the bar and points to me. "You can talk, Little Miss Perfect. Remember when you got a C-plus on your science test and sobbed like the world was ending?"

I do. Vividly. I narrow my eyes on her. "How about you? I seem to remember steam pouring out your ears when Mr. Curnow gave you a 'good job' on your rabbit presentation."

Her eyes grow wide. "That's because it was epic. How many other kids got live, detailed footage of their rabbits mating?"

"Half of us were only nine." I laugh. "Mr. Curnow's head almost exploded, and tiny Trent Sparrow didn't stop humping furniture all year."

Liam and Tej crack up, and Jen pulls her mouth into a devious smirk. "Trent Sparrow soon graduated from furniture."

He sure did. It's all anyone could talk about for an entire semester.

Liam's curious eyes question Jen, and she surrenders her hands to the air. "Not me, babe. He humped the choir teacher's leg and got suspended."

Tej barks out a bellowing laugh, and I nudge Jen. "See, you corrupted him."

She waves me away. "That kid was doomed from the start. We all knew it."

She's not wrong.

Liam lays an arm around Jen's shoulders and leans in towards her ear. "Maybe you could corrupt me later."

His whisper is anything but quiet, and I look at Tej. "Don't mind them. Trent Sparrow isn't the only one with a humping problem."

"Hey," Jen says, muffled against Liam's lips.

Tej grins. "Young love, raw and new. To be one of the lucky few."

His words float around us, soft and pretty like delicate flakes of snow, and I raise a brow. "Wow, you should write songs."

His grin turns lopsided. "Suppose I should join a band too?"

"You should totally do that." I wink, and Tej quietly chuckles.

As if lost in thought, his gaze drifts to the spirit-lined shelves behind the bar, but then he returns and checks his phone. "Hell, it's nearly two already." He downs the last of his beer, then slides the empty glass towards the bartender. "How are you guys getting home?"

"Uber," Jen says, coming up for air.

"Same." I shrug.

"Together?"

I shake my head. "Nah, they live on the other side of the city."

"We can't all afford to live in *Glen Iris* like Aves does." Jen nudges me with her knee, and I roll my eyes. I can't afford it either. Beth charges me a pittance.

"Glen Iris?" Tej asks. "That's on my way. Want to rideshare?" When I hesitate, he half shrugs. "Seems dumb paying twice."

"Sure." I smile. Why the hell not?

Tej grabs his guitar with Gibson scrolled across the case and fist-bumps a few friends before yelling goodbye to the pretty bartender.

Our warm breaths create plumes of frost in the chilly night air as we traverse the cobblestone lane. Jen and Liam stagger arm in arm ahead. We pass a closed café and an art gallery I didn't notice earlier with colourful pottery lining the window sill. Quirky dogs and cats with boggled eyes and toothy grins. Polka-dot flamingos with wire legs. Price tags in the *hundreds*.

A pang of longing hits my chest. Talent is nothing without drive, but neither saves you without bravery—the balls to step into the spotlight and tell the world "here I am." Unfortunately, I'm balls deficient.

"Two-minute ETA," Jen says, severing my thoughts.

Tej checks his phone. "Ours is still six minutes away."

We come to a standstill on the main street, and revellers gather a few shops down, swarming a late-night kebab bar like seagulls to hot chips. Moans of ecstasy leave their lips as they bite into the greasy goodness, cradling the wraps in their hands.

My stomach grumbles as Jen pulls me into a wobbly hug. "Thanks for a great night, chicky." Her words are slurred but sweet, and Liam joins in, throwing his arms around us both.

"Yeah, thanks, Aves." His annunciation is no better. "You're the best. Slade is *so* stupid for letting you go."

My eyes fall shut, bracing for impact, but Liam's loose words dissolve in my alcohol-soaked blood like a body in acid. I only hope Tej didn't hear.

"Babe," Jen says. "Don't talk about him."

"Shit," he groans, facepalming. "Sorry."

I worm from their embrace, needing fresh air, and Jen finds a new target. "So nice to meet you, Tej." She stretches her open arms towards him. "I can tell you need a hug too."

"Yeah, bro love," Liam says. "You're all right, man." They capture Tej and his guitar in a bear hug with mumbled words, and I wince, mouthing "Sorry" to him behind their backs.

Tej laughs, hugging them the best he can without dropping his case. "Nice to meet you too."

A shiny Mazda pulls up to the kerb, and Jen frees Tej and claps her hands. "Oh," she says, turning back to me. "If anyone asks, I'm staying at yours tonight, okay?"

I shake my head. It's moments like these I'm thankful for the distinct lack of parental concern in my life. "They know you're eighteen, right? As an adult, you should be able to sleep at your boyfriend's house."

Jen looks at me like I've recited Satan's curse. "You try telling them that. I dare you."

I wouldn't have the courage. Her Dad is Scottish and built like a bulldog. His accent alone rods my spine and makes my voice squeak. Jen harrumphs, satisfied she's made her point.

"Since when do they let you stay at my house, anyway?" I call out as Liam climbs into the back seat. Our slumber parties promptly ended when I first moved out.

Jen rests one foot on the chassis and leans atop the open door with a proud grin. "Since I told them you live with Beth, work full-time, and are done with your stupid phase." As she climbs in, my cheeks burn. The thought of Tej knowing my dirty little secret stirs fear. Winding down the window, Jen pokes out her head and winks. "I told them the old Avery is back."

The *old* Avery. Who is that, anyway? The naïve Goody Two-shoes who thought perfect grades could make her mother proud? What a fat waste of time that was.

Their Uber indicates, then pulls into a stream of cars, all spectating us revellers as if on safari tour. Liam seizes the opportunity to press a giant blowfish against the back windscreen, and Jen topples over in a fit of giggles. We stand on the footpath, laughing, until Liam's tonsils fade from view.

"Wow. They're some glasses, hey?" Tej remarks.

I chuckle. "Liam's special."

"So I noticed."

"They're nutjobs, but I love them," I say with a grin, but my gaze drifts over Tej's shoulder, locking onto a familiar frame in the distance, walking towards us. As I frown, Tej turns to follow my line of sight.

"Of all the places to see boss man," he says, and butterflies swarm my stomach.

What is he doing here?

Tej answers me as if I spoke aloud. "Knowing him, he's probably just left work. Oh no," he whistles under his breath, "looks like he's on a hot date."

My brows jump, and I zoom in on Cole as he stops to allow his female companion time to catch up. She's wrapped in sapphire-blue satin from breast to knee, her earlobes sparkling as they catch street lights and neon signs. I rake my gaze down her long legs to stiletto heels—long ago mastered—then fixate on my new boots. They glitter in the headlights of passing cars but are comparably unsexy all the same.

"Mr. B, how's it going?" Tej says, and I look up to find Cole standing mere feet away with his eyes locked on mine.

I force a small smile and wave. "Hi." Hell knows why I keep waving at the man whenever I say hello. It's so dumb, but I can't seem to stop.

The vertical line is back between his brows, and his date watches on with a polite but empty smile, barely disguising her boredom. She must be freezing. Or cold-blooded.

"Tej, Avery," Cole says with a nod. "I trust you're having a pleasant night."

"You bet, Mr. B. We're just waiting for our ride home." Tej slaps Cole's shoulder in a friendly man-to-man gesture, but Cole stiffens and hardens his eyes on mine. He opens his mouth to speak, but Tej beats him to it. "Ah, here it is now." I drag my gaze away from Cole's to find a white sedan hovering at the kerb. "See ya, man. Monday morning." Tej salutes with a grin, then dips his head towards the lady in blue. "Madame."

She smiles at Tej, but the sparkle leaves when she looks at me. She drags her gaze over me from head to toe like a trawler searching for treasure on the ocean floor, and when she finds none, satisfaction floods her tight smile. I've been classified as no threat, and I barely refrain from withering.

Why do successful men like Cole need hollow, etiquette-trained arm candy to reaffirm their superiority? And why can't I be like that, goddamn it? I clench my jaw, and Cole's eyes narrow on me.

I nudge my chin higher. "See you Monday, Mr. B." I throw in the last part knowing he disliked the moniker, and his annoyance radiates in blistering waves. Climbing into the sedan next to Tej, I don't look back. I'm not sure what it is about that woman, but I don't like her. And I'm annoyed too. At Cole. Only, I'm not sure why.

"Well, that was strange," Tej says as we turn onto King Street.

I look at him. "How so?"

"Mr. B stopping to chat. Thought we'd get a nod at most."

"Do you always call him that?"

Tej winks. "Just to make him feel old."

I smile and shake my head. "You're evil."

Tej shrugs. "Someone needs to keep him grounded."

Speaking of age, I school my expression and conjure indifference. "How old is he, anyway? Do you know?" Google doesn't seem to, and who isn't on social media these days? Cole Benedict. That's who.

Tej tilts his head to the side and considers me. "Why's that, Aves? You interested?"

I scoff too loudly. "No. Of course not. He's old. And . . . weird. Yeah, *so* weird." I mentally facepalm. *Weird?* Cole is anything but weird.

Tej arches a brow, his teasing smile morphing to smug. "Twenty-seven."

My eyes widen. "Twenty-seven? That's all?" He's younger than Beth, and only nine years older than me. What's nine years, really?

Tej nods. "Twenty-seven. Three measly years older than yours truly and a hundred times more successful." The shine fades from Tej's smile, and he stares at his guitar case leaning next to him in the footwell.

My shoulders slump. Cole's in a league of his own, and everyone knows it. "At least your talent will take you somewhere." Unlike mashing mud.

"You think so?" Tej asks, rubbing his knee.

I scrunch my brows. "You serious right now?" He doesn't answer me, rather drops his gaze to the empty seat between us, playing with the seatbelt buckle. "Oh my God." I elbow his arm. "Despite hundreds of screaming fans, you don't know how good you are."

He shrugs. "Figure if we're that good, we'd be signed by now. At least, that's what Papa reckons."

I shake my head. "It's a matter of time. In three years, I won't be surprised if everyone knows your name."

"Thanks," he says. "Sometimes, I need to hear that."

Nine

s. Masters." Chantel rises from her chair as I enter Benedict Kane early Monday morning.

Curiously, I approach her desk. "Morning, Chantel."

"Good morning," she says, resuming her seat with a small sigh. "Mr. Benedict would like to see you in his office."

"He does?"

She nods. "Immediately. Take the elevator to level four. You'll see his assistant on exiting."

I search her expression for clues as to the reason, but Chantel only stiffens, tightening her smile like she's in pain. All signs indicate Cole's not summoning me for an early promotion or declaration of lust, nor to discuss the qualities of air-dry clay. So what's this about? I've been punctual. Polite. Great with the kids, friendly to the parents, and pleasant to my colleagues. I haven't done anything wrong. Unless . . . it's about my case. Did something happen? Did the magistrate change her mind? Am I going to juvie after all?

A middle-aged woman waits at the elevator as I approach with a thumping heart. When the golden doors slide open, I slip in before Hannah or the children spot me. My companion smells like old money, and when the elevator bypasses her floor, ascending straight to level four, she's less than impressed. She eyes me up and down, her raw silk ensemble shimmering as large gold hoops wilt her earlobes. By comparison, I'm a hobo who's stumbled in from Collins Street lost, or at the very least, unworthy of level four. But she needn't worry. I'm well aware.

With a deep breath, I exit the elevator. Unlike the foyer, the top floor is minimalist and modern with crisp white walls, steel instead of brass, and pale chevron timber floors. Cole's assistant is a round woman with salted curls and kind eyes who smiles as I approach her desk. "Go straight in, Ms. Masters." She motions to a hallway of frosted glass that reflects the triptych of tall paintings hanging opposite. "First door to the left."

Thanking her, I advance to the hallway and halt outside Cole's door. His name is see-through on the glass, the letters like small islands floating in a frozen lake. I knock twice.

"Enter." Cole's voice has that icy snowman edge, but I obey, clicking the door shut behind me. With the posture of an aristocrat, he sits in wingback leather, regarding me with steepled hands. Gone is the sparkle of mirth in his eyes. Back is that vertical crease between his brows. "Take a seat," he says, motioning to the twin chairs facing his desk.

To my left, a view of Collins Street looms. A skyscraper stands beyond the colonial windows, but now doesn't feel like the time to admire. I offer a timid smile as I drop to the chair, but Cole's gaze remains hard, knotting my stomach.

"Did you have a good weekend?" His sullen tone doesn't match the sentiment, but I respond to his words alone.

"Yes, actually. You?" Memories of his dazzling lady friend surface, and my teeth clench. I'll bet he had a *great* weekend. But rather than answer me, Cole presses his mouth into a firm line, and his nostrils subtly flare. *Shit*. "Is this about my case?" I ask, wringing my hands.

He shakes his head. "Provided you don't breach your bond, your case is done."

I loosen my grip, but Cole doesn't continue, so I cock a brow and add a cheeky smile, trying for levity. "Are you promoting me already?"

That earns me a wince as Cole retrieves a chunky white binder from his drawer that thumps to the desk. "Have you read Benedict Kane's company policy manual?"

"I didn't know you had one."

"Well, we do. Copies are available in every section, Mini-Bees included. Hannah should have told you."

"I'm sorry." I swallow. "I'll read it as soon as possible."

Cole's mint gaze pins me, swirling with a dozen indecipherable things, and my insides twist and tingle. Gifting transcendent eyes to a mere mortal really isn't fair. I itch to rub that crease from his brow with my thumb. The weight of the world seems to live in that line. "Um . . . was that all?" My voice is pitchy, this whole scenario strange, and Cole hesitates a beat as if warring with himself before sliding the binder to me.

"Turn to section three, page eighty-seven, and read."

I fumble through the pages with a frown that only deepens when number eighty-seven appears. I glance up. "Staff fraternisation policy . . . ? I'm not sure I understand."

Cole plants his elbows on the desk, re-steepling his fingers under his chin. "I think you understand perfectly. Turn to item 3.1."

I look down, flip the page, then read, "Sexual and/or romantic relationships between staff are forbidden." The accusation drops like acid rain, heating my cheeks and scorching Tej's face into the zigzag timber floor. Saturday night. Us together. Sharing a ride home. How it must have looked. But surely Cole wouldn't assume— I snap my eyes back to his. "I'm afraid you have this all wrong."

"I doubt that. I'm rarely wrong. Were you, or were you not, in the company of Tej Patil on Saturday night?"

"Well, yes, but it wasn't—"

"And did you ride home together?"

The son of a bitch is interrogating me. Squaring my shoulders, I calmly inhale. "Yes, but we—"

"The yes will suffice. Consider this your first warning. If you value your job, you'll stay away from Tej Patil. Work together, and that's it."

My mouth opens and closes wordlessly like a goldfish. Arguing with Snowman Cole seems tantamount to fighting a grizzly bear. But a warning? For bumping into a colleague outside work and sharing a ride home? I had no idea employment came with such control. It feels like . . . jail.

Tears prick my eyes as humiliation sets in, and the air thickens to glue, but a foreign urge sparks high in my stomach too. One that steels my spine and urges me to fight this ridiculous injustice. After all, I'm an adult now, and I decide what treatment I will and won't tolerate, hierarchy be damned.

I drop my gaze to the binder and skim my fingernail across the laminated words as I stand, searing each one into my brain.

"What are you doing?" Cole asks.

I hold up a finger, shushing him, and finish the section, scanning the contents page before meeting his gaze with clenched fists and hot pride burning away my fear. "Nowhere in that section does it forbid platonic friendships between staff. In fact, your core values and history of trust-building retreats encourage it. But despite that, firing someone for screwing a consenting parity colleague outside work hours screams unfair dismissal to me, and I doubt this policy would stand up in court. In fact, I bet you know it won't. It's merely a deterrent, costing promotions at most.

"And, finally, what kind of brilliant lawyer jumps to rash conclusions instead of first gathering the facts? Facts like Tej and I live three suburbs apart, and it's cheaper to rideshare. Facts like men and women can be just friends. Facts like most guys don't carry a guitar around on a date night. And facts like I don't sleep with people I just met!" My chest heaves, my breaths coming fast and shallow, like I've conquered Kilimanjaro. Hell knows his ego seems akin. But beyond the sound of blood rushing in my ears, there's silence.

Stunned. Silence.

Cole leans back in his chair and rubs his clean-shaven chin. "Have you ever considered law school?"

I scrunch up my face. "Are you fucking kidding me right now?"

His lips twitch with amusement. "Language, Miss Masters."

But the usual effect those three words have is lost in my fury. "What is all this? Do you regret hiring me, is that it? Do you want me gone? If so, I'll go. I'm not staying somewhere I'm not wanted." Not anymore. I've spent half my life living that way.

While it's my job to raise you, Avery Lee, it's not my pleasure. It's not uncommon for women to regret having children, they just rarely admit it.

"Sit, Avery. Tantrums aren't becoming."

My mouth slackens as my face flames.

He deems my defence a tantrum?

My fingernails dig crescents into my palms, but I clench them harder, working my jaw. "Did you just tell me to sit? Like a dog?"

Cole chokes on the accusation with a half laugh, half cough. "Not my intended implication," he claims, but the fact he's amused at all right now pisses me right off. Fuck this—I should be at home in my studio, covered in clay. Cole mumbles a string of words under his breath, but I only catch the last one. "Feisty."

My brows hit my hairline. "Did you just call me . . . feisty? What, like some little woman who dares to voice her warranted rage and look unpretty for five whole minutes? God!" I cackle a deranged laugh and throw my hands in the air. "I never realised Millennials could still be chauvinists. And to think I wasted weeks pining after you!"

The words slip out before I can think, and my hand slaps over my mouth before I can stop it. Why is this man my anti-filter? And why are my emotions magnified by ten when I merely think of him? And where is doormat Aves when I need her? The one who could barely talk to Slade.

"You've been . . . pining after me?" The vertical crease returns, and damn if it isn't one of the sexiest things about him.

I mash my lips shut, lower my hand, and drag air in through my nostrils. "That's not what I meant."

It's exactly what I meant.

"So you were . . . lying for dramatic effect?"

Oh boy. I must be due for my period, because every word coming out of this man's mouth feels like a hot poker up my butt. I try to conjure calm, but it's the creepy kind of calm. The fleeting transition between angry and bat-shit crazy. I need out of this situation pronto or it won't end well. "That's it. We're done here. Thanks for your help, but I quit. This is feeling a lot like jail." I frown. "A weird, confusing jail." Then I turn on my heel and storm for the door, already wondering how this escalated so fast and why I'm so triggered. Blades of regret dice my heart. I don't want to leave. I adore my job. The kids. Hannah. What have I done? And to top it off, I've loved my two weeks of secret pining—of Cole consuming every second thought.

"Avery, wait."

Oh, thank God. Please stop me, and erase everything you said from my brain; otherwise, I can't guarantee I'll back down.

"Please," he adds desperately.

I halt at the door, tears tumbling, and when I turn around, Cole's pacing towards me. He stops a foot away, carving fingers through his brandied waves. He clenches his jaw and searches my eyes with an intensity that makes me shiver. He smells like he did the first day we met. Like sandalwood, oak, and the faintest hint of rose, but this time, there's more. A scent I know well.

Panic.

"I'm sorry," he says. "Your job is safe. Don't go." The vulnerability in his voice—his expression—is something I never thought a force like him could feel, and I study him as something invisible between us locks into place—a deep familiarity—an instinctive knowing. The same glimmer of lonely pain.

Cole rests a hand on the door frame above my head and leans in. "Please stay."

His rough voice rumbles between my legs as I inhale his peppermint breath. "Why? What was all that?"

Sighing, he looks at the ground. "You don't understand."

Try me.

"I was . . . well . . ." He grimaces like the words hurt. "I was out of line. I jumped to conclusions, and I'm sorry." He's holding back, but his sincerity bleeds, and it's not lost on me how lucky I am. Few employees would survive saying what I did and have their boss apologise, but alas, I'm still miffed. Anger doesn't have an off switch. It takes time to cool.

"What about the warning?"

"What warning?" His dimple glimmers shyly, and my ego slowly deflates.

"Okay," I whisper.

Cole's shoulders sag in relief, as does my heart, but then he slowly reaches up to cup my face. My breath hitches, the contact triggering a flurry of sparks and electric warmth that rolls down my back and cocoons me from head to toe. A tender smile plays on his lips as he dries my tears with his thumb, and I nuzzle into his palm, closing my eyes. It's as though my body not only recognises his touch but has spent a lifetime craving the reunion.

"You're so beautiful," he rasps, and my lips part. I stare into the depths of his striking jade eyes while he trails his thumb lower, skating the rough pad over my bottom lip while he watches intently. "I can't stop thinking about you."

My brows furrow, mirroring his, as I wrestle with the feelings that admission stirs—the sparkly ones, the confused ones, the downright suspicious ones—because despite my childish fantasies, none of this makes sense.

My voice comes choked, barely there, and I regret the words before I even finish. "Section four. Sexual harassment. I suggest you read it."

Cole drops his hand like I stung him and steps away, and losing his touch is akin to being doused with a bucket of ice.

He rubs the back of his neck, frowning at the floor. "Christ, I'm sorry. That was highly inappropriate." He walks away and halts, facing the city view. "Please accept my apology. For everything."

I stare at his back, envious of the jacket that hugs him, fighting the urge to reconnect—to touch him—to apologise. Fuck section three and four. Fuck everything. But I stop myself. Enough damage has been done, and I'm lucky to be leaving with my job.

So without words, I slip through the door, closing it on my way out. I rush past his assistant, avoiding eye contact, and smash my palm against the elevator button, willing it to hurry. I notice a memorial portrait of Gerard Benedict hanging above. "Your nephew's a hypocrite," I whisper but then immediately feel bad. "Sorry," I mumble as the elevator dings. When the doors glide shut, I slump against the mirrored wall with a sigh.

What just happened?

A war rages inside me. Irritation strong enough to bend steel but also white-hot heat, blistering enough to melt it. And then there's the tingling, the confusion, the butterflies pirouetting through my belly. Ickiness at the way things were left. It's all too much.

I think back to that silent moment when my heart and pain recognised his in some mystical energetic fusion. I shudder.

He's too much.

Arriving at the foyer restroom, I lean against the vanity and stare at the mirror. My skin is blotchy. Eyes wild and smudged with mascara. Lips still buzzing from his touch. I trace the feeling with my fingertips, and my eyes darken as less innocent images descend. Need aches between my legs. I want more. I want *him*. Growling, I pluck a tissue from the box and clear the smears from under my eyes.

I'm so screwed.

The fact I'm late seems to have gone unnoticed when I arrive at Mini-Bees. A curvy woman I've never met is settling in the newest arrivals, and Hannah feeds Jack while Ella stands guard.

"Where's Tej?" I ask, scanning the room.

"Sick. Probably the man flu, but don't worry, I called for reinforcement." Hannah kicks her chin towards the grey-haired stranger. "That's Marla. Your predecessor. Retired now, but still magical."

Marla smiles at me, and I offer her a friendly wave, but Tej's absence sits like concrete in my stomach. Did Cole reprimand him too, or is he actually sick? For his sake, I hope it's the latter. I sign in and approach the art corner.

What if Cole fired him?

Shaking away the thought, I halt next to the bank of miniature easels.

No, surely not.

Young Alex, Lily, and Max stand in puffy smocks, painting modern masterpieces, so I resolve to focus on work. However, the scene upstairs replays on loop, and my mind feeds on it like a frenzy of fish at dusk.

I don't get it. Cole defends me for free, then gives me a job. Buys me a phone, flirts, turns cold, then reprimands me. *Threatens* me, then begs me not to leave. He caresses my face, touches my heart, then walks away with regret. Albeit after I threatened him with harassment.

Fuck. Why did I *do* that?

"Avery. Avery."

I snap from my daze to find Alex tugging on my sleeve, his little hands drenched in blue paint. "What is it, short stuff?"

"I'm finished." Alex points towards his easel. "Look, it's you."

I crack a smile as I examine the portrait. I look more sun than human with arms as ears and insanely long legs, but I'd never tell Alex that. "Wow, that's amazing! It looks just like me." Alex beams. "Let's get you clean." Acknowledging my paint-smeared sleeve with a grimace, I guide Alex to the wash trough.

"I like painting my hands," he says, grinning up at me.

"I can see that."

When Alex no longer looks like he murdered a Smurf, I start work on my once light-grey sleeve. I expected stains, only I hoped it would take longer than two days. Damn you, Cole. It's all your fault.

Lathering the soap, I scrub away but soon toss the bar aside to begrudgingly accept fate. Perching my hands on the trough, I stare at the wall and drift away. He said I was beautiful. And with such . . . reverence. I shiver at the memory.

"If you soak that now, you might save it."

Knocked from my trance, I turn to see Hannah standing beside me, staring curiously. "Sorry, what did you say?"

She tilts her head to the side. "Are you okay?"

"I'm fine." I try to smile reassuringly, but Hannah looks sceptical. "I'm feeling a little off," I sigh.

"Do you need to go home?"

"I'll be fine."

She studies my face. "Take lunch first today, okay?"

God, she's a gem.

Fumes taint Collins Street's frosty air as grey clouds loom overhead, dusting Melbourne in a fine mist of rain. I look left and right through the city bustle, determining which direction to flee. Lunch times are still reserved for finding cheap eats nearby. After this morning, a stiff drink beckons, though I'm sure that's prohibited too.

"Aves." My name comes muffled and trodden by the crowds, but I'm certain I hear it. I scan the street with a frown. Maybe not.

"Aves." It comes again. This time clearer, closer, and from behind, with a tap on my shoulder. I turn around and bump face first into a taught, muscular chest. A very familiar one. Hands grip my shoulders, and my blood drains south. It's like seeing a ghost. A smiling, tan ghost with tribal tattoos and a naughty gleam in his hazel eyes. "Slade. What are you doing here?"

He drags his gaze up my body with a lazy, lopsided grin, frowning when he sees my blue sleeve, but he continues his perusal, licking his lips before meeting my eyes. "Waiting for you, duh."

"Why?" I ask, scrunching up my sleeves despite the cold. I spent the better part of my weekend stripping Slade from my brain, yet his smirk comes dipped in sin, and my knees wobble. Stupid muscle memory.

With exaggerated disbelief, he shakes his head. "You're my girl. Why else?"

My chin hits the footpath with a thud. "Your . . . girl?" Never in our fucked-up relationship has Slade declared I'm his. But now . . . *now* I'm his girl? I grind my molars. "How'd you know I was here?"

"I messaged Liam. He told me."

"He *did?*" Jen will have his balls.

"When I told him my intentions, yeah. Nice joint, by the way. *Fancy*." He looks up at Benedict Kane, and my protective instincts flare.

Crossing my arms, I arch a brow. "Intentions?"

He releases a hefty sigh. Jesus, was he always this dramatic? "Like I said. You're my girl."

There it is again. I can't believe it. Did I somehow teleport to the 1950s? I shake my head and huff a laugh. "I'm not your girl, Slade. Not sure I ever was." Nudging past his chest, I start up Collins Street. I don't know where I'm going but refuse to deal with more crazy today. It must be a full moon.

Slade chases me, sidestep bouncing down the footpath like an athlete warming up. "What are you talking about?"

After months of pining for this guy and all the tears that fell, I could've sworn I'd fall back into his arms should they ever reopen. But now—with my nerves already frayed and temper still warm from this morning—anger strikes me like lightning, and I'm *pissed*. At him. At myself. For all the months I wasted in limbo, waiting for his late-night visits. All the trouble I stupidly found cool. For letting him use me as a convenient piece of arse.

For giving him what I never should have.

He hurt me. In all kinds of ways. And I let him.

Stopping dead, I turn to face him, prodding his chest with my finger. "What am I talking about? Zoe. How about we discuss Zoe? You know, your *girlfriend*. The one who knocked me out."

Slade cringes. "That's over. I'm not with her anymore. I love *you*."

Love? Now I cringe. Never have I heard the word delivered so emptily. "Bullshit." I turn to walk away, but Slade grabs my bicep.

"No shit. I dumped Zoe when I found out she hurt you."

Unlike the *L* word, this part rings true. His eyes plead as rain sheens his skin and dots his T-shirt with tiny crystal beads. Those words are everything I've longed to hear but now sorely inadequate. Too little, too late. My bones ache at the realisation and tears return.

Why did he have to wait so damn long?

I shuck from his grip and wipe my eyes, regretting wearing make-up at all today. "It's been two fucking weeks since you got out."

"I'm sorry," he says, stepping into my space. "I was busy." He pulls me into a hug, and I let him. Sniffling all over his tight black tee. Relishing his soothing strokes of my hair. He's bulked up since I last saw him. His embrace is strong and warm. It's a shame he so seldom offered it.

"Gimme another chance, Aves. I'll text you back. We can go out together—like to the movies and shit—and I'll come see you all the time. It'll be a vibe."

He lifts my chin to meet his gaze, and I search his face for everything I idolised, awaiting old feelings to stir. But my belly doesn't flutter. My heart doesn't skip. And my mind mocks me for ever wanting more. All that remains is lust. Shallow. Empty. Lust.

Slade licks his lips, and I fight the temptation to taste him. One nibble might bring back everything else, but as he lowers his mouth towards mine, reality smacks me awake. "I tried to take the fall for you that night at Mia's. Did you know that?"

Slade halts and straightens back up, his jaw ticking. "Well, it didn't work, so what's it matter?"

I frown. "And if it had? Would you have let me?" I stare at him as one . . . two . . . three seconds tick by, then let my eyes fall shut. "God, I'm an idiot." I buck from his embrace and try to walk away, but he grabs my wrist.

"C'mon, babe. Of course I wouldn't've let ya. But a slap on the wrist is all you woulda got anyway."

"Not the point," I say, turning to face him, jerking back my hand. "You made me an accomplice and then threatened me too."

"*Threatened* you?"

"Yeah. Snitches get stitches, remember?"

Slade rolls his eyes, letting his head roll with them. "Well, I never meant it. You know I was trippin'. But who'd wanna be a rat, anyway?"

I scoff, but then Slade sneers. "You act all innocent and shit, Aves, but you're the one that wanted to go there, remember? Mia owed you money, and you came to *me*."

I stiffen. What is he implying? That I *wanted* him to swipe her laptop? I didn't even know he was capable of that. I shake my head. "I only wanted a lift there. I was surprised you even followed me to her door."

The sly smirk returns. "But you never tried to stop me, hey?"

"I was nervous and about to be homeless. I felt safer with you there. I never thought you'd steal anything, let alone stroll right into her house. You opened that door so casually I assumed it was her porch."

He hitches a shoulder. "Well, it was unlocked, and you wanted your money, right?"

Loudly, I sigh at the pavement. It's like we're speaking different languages, but he is right about one thing. I didn't try to stop him. Not when he followed me—not when he stole it—not afterwards either. In fact, I let him kiss me instead, right there on Mia's ratty lawn. I was totally smitten and obviously brain-dead too.

Slade steps in and lifts my chin. "I was trying to help you, Aves. Don't forget that part. I didn't want you homeless neither."

A spear of guilt hits my stomach. Sadly, I think that's true. Sadder still is the fact this is our first *real* conversation. "I'm sorry," he says again. "It was a dumb thing to do." But I grit my teeth. I might not have seen us clearly before, but I sure as hell do now.

"It's not enough," I say, hugging my elbows. "It's never been enough."

Slade drops his hand and kicks up his chin. "What's that meant to mean?"

I search his face one last time and then drag in a breath. "I mean it's over, and we're done."

Slade huffs, but a spark of amusement still twinkles. "Are you for real?"

He's not taking me seriously, but I guess he never did. Retrieving a sleeve to dry my cheeks, I firm my voice. "I'm sorry."

The glint leaves his eyes, and that faint, ever-present smile disappears. Leaning in, I softly peck his cheek, hovering longer than necessary to tuck away his memory like a childhood keepsake. "Goodbye, Slade."

I'd be proud of my strength—my dignity—if it wasn't immediately ruined. On my third step backwards as Slade watches without words, I hit another wall of muscle. Frazzled, I turn to apologise to the person, only to meet another pair of familiar eyes. "Cole."

Cole glares over my shoulder, his angular jaw tight, and the rain falls heavier, as if invoked by his presence. "Is everything okay here?"

My head dizzies. "Everything's fine. I was just saying goodbye to a friend."

His laser-sharp eyes stay locked on target, but his words are mine. "Care to accompany me to lunch?"

My brows jump. "L . . . Lunch?"

"Yes. Lunch," he says, offering me a quick glance as though the notion isn't out of this fucking world.

I glimpse over my shoulder to see Slade standing with his chest puffed, eyes narrowed, and hands balled into fists. It's a standoff between strangers for reasons unbeknownst to me, but one I should end all the same.

I grip Cole's wrist, ignoring the warm tingles it sparks through my hand. "Sure. Let's go. Lunch sounds *grand*."

As I coax him away from Slade, east down Collins, Cole's reluctance soon turns to powerful strides, each spanning two of mine. I let my grip fall away, but the intimacy warms my skin, as does the knowledge he didn't pull away.

"Have a nice life, Aves." Slade's words hit the centre of my back like an arrow, and I flinch.

Brakes squeal, and cars honk. Buskers perform hooked up to amplifiers, and people chatter away huddled under awnings. But Cole seems lost in his own silent world, until his throat clears. "Slade Pearson," he sneers.

My eyes widen, and I look up at him. "How . . . how do you—"

"Mugshot. Unlike you, he resembles his."

My cheeks burn at the reminder, and I drop my gaze to the glittering footpath blemished with grease and gum. Cole's footsteps are solid next to mine, and his black leather shoes shine with polish and scattered raindrops.

"I ended it," I say. I'm not sure why I tell him. I'm not certain he cares in any way that matters, but the wintry air softens around his silence as we continue walking. If I weren't so drained, my brain would dissect this interaction like a dead frog in science class, but even mine has its limits—and this, whatever this is, feels easy when not much does.

The Italian café we find is half-empty, yet to be devoured by the lunchtime rush. The scent of tomato and basil soaks the air, wafting past the coffee counter and circling the red-and-white chequered cloths draped over every table.

Cole leads us to a quiet corner, where he slides out my chair and tugs off his jacket to hang over the back of his. Taking a seat, he leans against the wall, then stretches out his long legs, crossing them at the ankles. His white shirt glows against his pale-caramel skin, and silver marbles through those forest eyes. They're luminous mandalas ringed in black, like full moons circled by night. They're also locked on me. Fiercely.

"We need to talk," he says.

My stomach backflips. My earlier words have had time to brew—percolate and spread through his veins like poison. Who goes on a tirade, calls their boss a chauvinist, and gets away with it? "I'm sorry about this morning. I was angry."

Cole narrows his eyes. "I hadn't noticed."

"You belittled me," I fire back.

"And you served me my bullshit on a sterling-silver platter."

I search his eyes. Amusement glitters, but his mouth remains pressed in a hard line. "I did?"

He nods once, the hint of a smile breaking through. "Brilliantly."

The compliment lands, and an imaginary cheer squad erupts. Pom-poms shake, high kicks fly, and bodies tumble in perfect formations. I hide a smile behind my hand and rally composure. "I am sorry though."

"Don't apologise for being assertive, Avery."

Assertive is sugar-coating—minimising—wrapping shit in a shiny bow, but I'll take it.

"Well, I am sorry for slapping you with section four. That was harsh."

Cole's intake of breath is sharp. "You were right."

Nothing about it felt right.

"No." Lowering my gaze, I pluck a red serviette from the small silver stand and twist at its corners, tearing off little pieces. "To be honest, it wasn't unwanted, just . . . unbelievable."

The truth comes as news to my ears too—a succinct summary of the sticky mess still churning inside me. And again, I'm not sure why I tell him or when I grew so brave, but something about Cole feels safe. Like I can give him my secrets and he'll guard them like jewels. He won't use them as weapons or soft targets.

His gaze holds mine, filled with a disarming amount of tenderness, maybe even hope, but then he winces. "Yet it was inappropriate. Especially given my position." His shoulders rise and fall on a sigh. "Can we start again? Wipe the proverbial slate clean?"

I half smile. "That depends. Can you banish my mugshot from your brain?"

A deep laugh escapes his throat, and the dimple puckers his cheek. "I can promise I'll try."

God, he's handsome.

I stare at him, stuck in his magnetism, entranced by the quiet power he emits.

"So tell me something real," he says, resting one forearm on the table while he traces little circles on the cloth with his finger.

"Real?"

He nods. "About you."

I swallow. If that isn't the scariest request he could make, I don't know what is. "Well . . . I'm finding the fact we're having lunch incredibly surreal."

He examines me with complete seriousness. "Why?"

I squirm in my seat, the serviette now mangled in my hands. "I just don't understand why you're wasting your time with me."

The concern etched on Cole's face makes me wither. "I'm not wasting anything," he says with a gentle firmness that makes me feel contained—*protected*.

I glance around the café as people pour in through the accordion doors. "Why are we here, then?"

"Why do you think?" Cole's voice is softer, his expression imploring.

"I don't know." But I think I do. This pull between us is undeniable, and Cole Benedict, for whatever crazy reason, can't stop thinking about me, just like he said. Despite Miss Blue Satin Sparkles being clearly more his class.

Men have two brains, Avery Lee, and fortunately, women like us activate the most profitable one. Use it to your advantage.

I cringe. God, I hope he isn't that shallow, but what else could Cole see?

"Do you always blush when you lie?"

His knowing smirk is devilish, and blood surges to my cheeks with a vengeance, but I push aside the remnants of my serviette, then interlock my hands on the table, tilting my chin like a shrink. "Does your ability to psychoanalyse people make you feel superior?"

Cole huffs a laugh as if I knocked the air from his chest. "I deserved that."

But I wince. *Duct tape*. That's what my snarky mouth needs around this man. If he didn't appear to enjoy it, that is.

With impeccable timing, a server appears. I order a latte and polenta fries from their smudged blackboard menu, while Cole settles on a cappuccino, focaccia, and table water.

His eyes glimmer, but I wish he'd stop looking at me like that. As though I'm a golden equation worth solving. I'm not that deep or complex—just damaged and flawed.

"How are you finding Mini-Bees?" he asks, and my shoulders loosen. At last, a reprieve.

"Great. The kids are so special. And Hannah—well, she's amazing." I don't mention Tej, his mad talent or affinity with the kids, nor the fact it would have broken my heart had Cole let me quit.

"I'm pleased," he says. "You seem like a natural."

Sunshine fills me up. "Children inspire me. Especially the little ones." That's why two clay toddlers already sit on my studio bench.

"How so?" Cole asks.

"Well, they're brutally honest for one, which is refreshing. They're not afraid to tell you what they want and don't. They know who they are and have so much trust in people—in the world. It's amazing and horrifying all at the same time." With a shrug, I tuck my rain-damp hair behind my ear, an action Cole seems to carefully watch. "Sometimes I wonder if I used to be that . . . whole. If I knew who I was and what I wanted but somehow forgot along the way."

Cole's forehead furrows, and the vertical line makes yet another appearance. I twist my lips into a secret smile, and he searches my face. "What?"

"You have a WTF line."

He frowns more, and I chuckle.

"A *what*?"

"This frown line that appears right here"—I trace the spot on my forehead—"whenever you seem confused or deep in thought. I've coined it your WTF line." His face lights up as he presumably deciphers the acronym, and I shrug. "That's what it looks like you're thinking."

Cole's smile grows, then his shoulders shake with laughter, triggering my own. The resonant and pure sound tickles my heart and glides over my skin like silk, leaving goosebumps. He looks younger when he laughs—when he lets in the light.

The server returns with our drinks, setting them down in front of us. We thank her, and Cole fills our glasses with water before resting an elbow on the table. He rubs his chin, skating his fingers around the edge of an impish smile. "So what's with the blue warpaint?"

"Huh?" I ask, emptying a packet of raw sugar into my latte.

Cole flickers his gaze across my face, and I stiffen. "Oh my God. Where?" I rub at my flaming cheeks, forehead, and chin with the heel of my hand, while Cole watches on with a smirk so smug and endearing at once I want to strangle *and* kiss him. I check my hands for paint. Other than lavender nail polish, there is none, so I unravel my sleeve, but it's already dry. Goddamn it, why do things like this always happen to me? "Has it gone?"

Rather than answer, Cole quakes with laughter and watches me drown, throwing no lifebuoy. The café grows stuffy, and I growl. The lady's room it is. "Excuse me." My chair screeches against the dimpled tiled floor as I push back, but then he finally speaks.

"Wait." Cole grabs a serviette and dips one gathered end into his water, then leans across the table, beckoning me closer. When I hesitate, he cocks a brow. "I won't beg."

I flash him a lopsided grin. "Why? Wouldn't be the first time today. *Please, Avery. Don't go*," I grovel in my best Cole voice.

Cole shakes his head, but his cheeks pinken. "For Christ's sake, woman, come here."

The word *woman* isn't lost on me. It flutters through my chest like a happy butterfly unaware of its incredibly short lifespan. Tucking my chair back in, I meet him halfway across the table and eye the ceiling. "Please kill me," I grumble.

Cole chuckles and gently wipes across my right cheekbone, then the left.

"Both sides? Really?" *Fuck me.*

"There. As beautiful as a Parisian sunset."

We stay too close together, hovering over the table as the bustle in the café fades away. That's the second time he's called me beautiful today, and nothing about it feels shallow. I search his face as he does mine, like we're unearthing each other's secrets—discovering each other's truth. There's something achingly soothing about Cole whenever the tizzy he triggers in me calms. A solidity—a steadiness—that my internal chaos craves.

My gaze dips to his perfect Cupid's-bow lips that look smooth, full, and utterly kissable, but then I shift back in my chair and re-scrunch up my sleeves, shutting down all wonder about how they might taste or feel against my own.

Looking conflicted, Cole shifts back too, rubbing the nape of his neck. So much for a clean slate, but to break the awkward, I fold my arms, nudge up my chin, and badly fake annoyance. "You could have told me sooner."

Cole's mouth tilts, then he throws me a wink that turns said arms to jelly. "Consider us even. Oh, and one more thing . . . I accept your apology." He lifts his coffee towards his lips, arching a brow. "Regarding section four."

Ten

Without replying, I toss my phone into my bag where it dangles from my designated hook, then hang my jacket over the top. It's the fifth message Slade's sent since yesterday's encounter, and the most phone contact he's ever bestowed.

"So who is he?"

I snap my gaze to Hannah and knit my brows. "Sorry, what?"

Highlighter shimmers at the tops of her cheekbones, and mischief glints in her ocean eyes. "I haven't seen you in anything but jeans and sneakers since your first day. Now here you are in paisley print and ballet flats. *Who is he?*"

Warmth creeps up my neck, and I stare at her, speechless, before looking down at my new dress. The hemline could be an inch longer if I'm honest, but at least I'm wearing tights. "No one. And I take offence to your anti-feminist accusation."

Hannah twists her lips into a smile. "You're a terrible liar. Do you know that?"

Yes, I do. And so will Cole when he sees me. I'm so full of shit I should be a septic tank.

She leans in conspiratorially. "Is he one of the dads?"

"Hell no," I say, fumbling through my bag in search of Narnia. But that requires a wardrobe, not a Vinnies vinyl tote.

"Huh." Her ruby mouth tilts into a smirk as her sunflower scent tangles me in her web. "So there is someone. I knew it."

With a sigh, I abandon my search efforts and face her. "You're crazy."

"Perhaps. But I'm also right." She plops a hand on her hip and cocks a brow, forcing my eyes to roll, but behind her, Tej enters Mini-Bees, and an invisible weight lifts off my shoulders. He's here—employed—alive and early. Thank fuck.

He approaches with a spring in his step, a tan satchel slung across his torso, his black Nirvana tee ragged at the collar. "Hey, Aves. Hannah. What's shakin'?"

"Are you feeling better?" I ask.

"Much. Must have been a twenty-four-hour bug thing."

Hannah folds her arms. "That just happened to give you a long weekend. *Convenient*." She taps her foot against the speckled vinyl floor and narrows her eyes, but humour lingers.

Tej elbows her. "Shush, mamma bear. We aren't all immune to germs like you are." He turns to me. "Hey, listen, I had a really great time the other night."

Hannah's wide eyes jump to mine, and I shake her off with a scowl before offering Tej an awkward smile. "Me too."

Tej hangs his satchel on the hook next to mine before tucking his hands in his pockets. "We're playing the Calantas this Saturday. If you want to come watch again, you'd be welcome."

Under Hannah's scrutiny, my cheeks flush. She's got this all wrong. And despite Cole's apology—our lunch, the lingering smiles, and newfound rapport—his warning rings in my ears. "Actually, I already have plans. Thanks, though, for offering."

"No drama," he says. "Maybe another time." There's no disappointment in his voice, and my shoulders loosen. Throwing Hannah a quick wink, he ambles to the costume corner, pretending to be shot by a pint-sized cowboy on the way.

Meeting Hannah's smirk, I shake my head. "Don't even. I'm not into Tej, okay? We're just friends."

Through a narrowed gaze, she appraises me. "Hmm, I believe you. But there is someone. I can tell." With a satisfied harrumph, she turns on her heel.

"Hannah, wait." Spinning back, she raises a brow. "Do you have the company policy manual here?"

She tilts her head. "Yeah, I think so. Why?"

"Can I please see it?"

Her nose scrunches. "If you really want to. You know no one ever reads it though, right?" That's not how Cole portrayed it yesterday, but I shrug. "Company rules are comedy in this place," she says.

"How do you mean?"

"Put it this way"—lowering her voice, she strolls back to me—"have you ever seen *The Bold and the Beautiful*?"

"I have." Liam Spencer forever, thank you very much.

"Well, there's more scandal here than at Forrester International, and no policy would ever stop it. Lawyers have quite the appetite, if you know what I mean. Just don't tell the boss."

I do know what she means. They're fucking like Jen's late rabbits. *Fraternising*. The very thing I was drilled for yesterday. *Huh*. My nostrils flare. Why is there one set of rules for me and a different one for everyone else?

Why do you think?

Cole's words from yesterday douse one fire but spark another. One far too indecent for work.

"I'll dig it up sometime today," Hannah says, making an oof sound as Ella barrels into her legs. She picks her up and strokes her pigtails, curling them around her finger.

"Thanks," I say, but my mind is already lost in the land of aventurine eyes.

"Look, cookie," Hannah says. "Tej is about to sing. Should we go and sit?" Ella squeals and claps her pudgy hands. "C'mon, Aves." Hannah nudges my shoulder. "Plenty of time to daydream about Boob Boy later."

I choke on a gasp. "Boob Boy?"

Her gaze flashes to my cleavage, and her smirk grows. "Uh-huh. Apparently so."

Perched on a stool in the corner of Mini-Bees, I peruse the thick binder and nibble my sandwich while my eyelids fill with sand. It's official. *The Benedict Kane Company Policy Manual* should be mandatory bedtime reading for insomniacs. And Hannah's not wrong. I'm sure the only person who's read this monstrosity is the schmuck who wrote it. And maybe Cole.

Stretching my spine, I roll my shoulders and knead the stiffness from my neck. The elevator dings, and I glance at my phone—1:05 p.m. Too early for Cole, but as the doors glide open, there he stands regardless. My heart whips to a gallop, and his gaze zeroes in on mine before flickering to my chest for a nanosecond and back up again. I don't miss his flinch, nor the unmistakable heat flaring in his eyes.

Thank you, plunging neckline.

Rallying every crumb of confidence, I offer a flirty smile, which he returns. Only, his comes coated in sex and shimmer, surrounded by dark one-day stubble, and finished with a dimple. A dimple that, when pressed, makes his eyes sparkle even more.

God, those eyes.

Swooning, I grip the edge of my stool and stare as he reaches his arm out to the side.

God, that arm.

But my dreamy daze shatters when his hand comes to rest on the lower back of a young woman standing next to him. Her shiny chestnut hair is swept into a French twist, her sharp suit skims elegant curves, and her long, familiar legs befit a Paris runway.

I feel the colour drain from my face and gulp. Cole's gaze leaves mine, and he smiles down at her as they step from the elevator. He guides her to the foyer, whispering close to her ear. And all I can do is watch as a knife twists in my gut and irritation simmers under my skin. The same irritation I had outside the Bellcat on Saturday night the first time she appeared from nowhere to ruin a perfect scene. Only then, her presence could be dismissed as an anomaly. A one-off. Now she's visiting Cole at work. *Who is she?*

Shutting the stupid manual, I check the time. Twenty minutes left of my lunch hour. I slide from the stool and trudge to the bathroom, then lean against the vanity, blowing the wayward strands from my face. My expression screams jealousy. There's no denying it, but at least I have time to walk up Collins Street and exorcise this awful feeling.

Cuddling my jacket, I rush through the foyer, looking down at my feet, feeling an inch tall and covered in grime. That shiny, pristine woman is Cole's female equivalent and everything I'll never be, but for a moment there, I forgot.

God, I'm dumb.

"Whoa, easy there," a deep voice says as firm hands halt my steps and squeeze my biceps. The buzzing through my arms confirms who stands before me, and I glance up into serene silver-green, then back to the ground with a sigh. *Shit.*

Cole holds me out at arm's length. "I must say, green is definitely your colour."

I snap my gaze to his, and his eyes twinkle with humour, a lopsided smirk pulling at his lips. My cheeks smoulder, and I look away. *Please kill me. Really, how many times does a girl have to ask?*

His warm fingertips find the underside of my chin and guide my attention back to his annoyingly perfect face. He cocks his head along with one brow. "I'm talking about your dress. Did you think I meant something else?"

Bastard.

I shake my head, ridding his touch with immediate regret. "Of course not," I say while yanking at my hem, willing it to grow in length but only revealing more of my chest.

His gaze skates the thin fabric with hesitant admiration rather than sleaze. "Did you wear it for me?" His voice is a low rasp, but my mouth falls open.

"What?"

"You heard me."

"No." I shake my head vehemently.

This amuses him. Leaning in, he whispers, "The flush creeping up your neck and rapid little breaths say otherwise. Tell me the truth. Was I considered?" His warm breath feathers my neck and heats my skin, urging complete honesty. Dragging my eyes up from where our shoes stand facing each other—my synthetic suede to his polished leather—locked in a conversation of their own, I meet his challenging gaze.

Oh, fuck it. "Okay," I concede. "Maybe you were. But I bought it for *me*." There. Girl power lives on. *Barely.*

Cole smiles a warm but wicked smile. "You look lovely," he says before releasing me. Then he steps from my path and strides away, calling out over his shoulder as he turns the corner, "She's just a client, Avery."

Damn him. How can he read me so easily?

"Hot date this weekend?" Hannah looks me up and down, grinning at my fourth dress of the week. I do like them for work. I only wish this revelation came four weeks from now, in spring.

"Nope," I reply. "You?"

Hannah chuckles. "Definitely not."

I skim Hannah's left hand. She never wears a ring, but that doesn't mean much this century. "Well, have a good weekend. See you Monday," I say, grabbing my bag.

"You too, Aves."

I return her smile, then head for the door, admiring the colourful macaroni monsters we made this week strung from the ceiling. The air-dry clay Cole ordered made for perfect monster heads, and the kids were ecstatic. And more so, I loved teaching them. It's never something I'd considered before.

"Aves?"

Halting at the door, I turn to see Hannah walking over. "Yeah?"

"Just wanted to say you're doing a great job. We're lucky to have you."

Her words warm my heart. "Thanks, Hannah. That means a lot." So much I want to hug her, but that would be inappropriate. She returns my sappy grin with one of her own and throws me a wink before wandering back to the staffroom.

The foyer is deserted. Even Chantel has gone home for the day. I was starting to wonder if she slept upright at her desk. With no audience, I lift my chin and straighten my back, pretending I'm one of the female lawyers that come and go. They stride across the terrazzo with purpose and pride, their hips in a perfect sway. Time is of the essence, and their time is more valuable than most. Respect finds them from every glance, so for one tiny moment, I imagine I'm that capable and bask in the feeling.

The brass doors click as I swipe my fob across the sensor, but when I push one open, the icy night slaps me in the face and diagonal rain pelts my shins. Crap, I forgot my jacket. Catching the door before it locks, I scramble back inside and head for Mini-Bees. I only hope Hannah hasn't already locked up, or I'm destined to freeze on the tram ride home.

As I turn the corner, I sag in relief. Mini-Bees remains alight in the distance. Hannah stands in the middle of the playroom with her back facing me, arm in arm with a tailored man who's holding Ella. Ella's chubby little arms are locked around his neck. *So cute.* It seems Hannah does have someone—and a suit to boot. I'm eager to meet the guy, but as I get closer, my steps slow and then completely stop. His build is too familiar, his hair the same walnut colour in my dreams, and I'm certain if he turns around, his eyes will pierce me with green. He squeezes Hannah into his side and kisses the top of her head, then turns his attention back to Ella, smacking kisses all over her sweet face.

Ella giggles, and I die inside. They're together. Cole and Hannah . . . and Ella. A vision of Ella's pale-green eyes pops into my head, and the resemblance hits me like a freight train. Oh my God. I never picked it. I'm such a fucking idiot. My vision turns blurry behind tears, and my breaths turn rapid and shallow. As if sensing my presence, Cole and Hannah turn to face me. Hannah brightens when she spots me through the glass, but Cole's initial surprise morphs to a deeper frown the longer he stares, his WTF line slicing his brow.

I have to get out of here, and fast. Screw the jacket.

With an awkward wave, I leg it across the foyer as fast as I can without losing a shoe—no Cinderella delusions here. Not anymore. Fumbling with my fob, I push the door open, stumble out into the rain, and run for the tram stop like a madwoman. Tears stream down my cheeks, and I know I'm way more upset than I should be. Only, I don't know why. Maybe because I fell for it again. Maybe because I'm way more infatuated with Mr. Cole Benedict and his perfect fucking tailoring and pompous law firm than I'm ready to admit. Maybe because every time I think I'm crazy, he does something that shows me I'm not.

That arsehole. How dare he flirt with me when he's clearly taken. He was flirting, right? I haven't made it all up in my head, have I? No. Not at all.

And to do that to Hannah, and innocent Ella. What the fuck is wrong with men? Isn't one woman ever enough? It wasn't for Slade. And what is it about *me*? Do I have "mistress material" stamped on my forehead?

Scanning my Myki Pass, I ignore the stares as I board the tram. The shivering drowned-rat look I'm rocking perfectly depicts my emotional state. Keeping my eyes on the mud-streaked floor, I find a seat and rest my head against the cold window, hugging my goose-bumped arms.

I've been pining after Hannah's man. *Flirting* with Hannah's man. *Dreaming* about Hannah's man. And I won't admit to what else I've done—or *tried* to do. Alone. At night. Between sateen sheets I can't afford.

Shame and embarrassment smother me, and my chest grows hollower the more it hurts. I'm such a goddamn fool.

My saturated dress splats to the penny-tile bathroom floor, and I hop from side to side, rubbing my arms, trying to generate heat while I wait for the bathtub to fill halfway.

The water burns my frozen toes as I step in, and I curse, clenching my teeth until the sting subsides. Stupid ballet flats. Stupid flimsy dress. This never would have happened if I'd stuck to my trusty jeans and Docs—perhaps invested in an umbrella. And what was I thinking, buying ballet flats in the first place? I'm not the ballet flat type.

Why am I changing myself for him? That's exactly what Mum would do.

I ease myself into the free-standing tub, then lie back and sigh. Warmth cocoons me, but pain twists through my chest like the charred branches of a dead tree, and there's no way to escape it. I eye the razor, lying innocently in the marble niche. Not one I'm ready to commit, anyway. But the thought is there, living in the shadows, waiting to taunt me whenever I'm weak.

You'd need a sturdier razor.

Thanks for that, brain. You can't imagine the solace it brings, you always having my back.

God. I've known Cole for three measly weeks, yet now I feel . . . empty—like my only joy was the hope of having him. Why does separation feel like death? And why do I crave his touch and company so badly? What the hell is wrong with me?

Everything, Avery Lee. Everything is wrong with you.

My phone chimes. It's Slade. Again. I roll my eyes and groan again but this time hesitate before dismissing it. Desperation to alleviate this horrible feeling claws at my rib cage, so I swipe in my passcode and read.

> **Slade:**
> Aves, don't ignore me. Read this. Please.
> When the sun comes up, I think of you.
> In the beam of light. The golden hue.
> I long to hold you until I lose me.
> Only then do I ever feel free.
> I love you, Aves. See me tomorrow night.
> Please. I can pick you up at six.

My lips twitch with a faint smile. This is very un-Slade-like. He's obsessed with EDM and purports anything mainstream as commercialised crap. Yet here he is reciting Bellamy Ford love-song lyrics by text. Written evidence of his corruption left at my disposal. Shocking. And a little endearing, if I'm honest.

I stare at his message while the bath bubbles melt into a milky ocean. I'm no longer his fool. I know the deal, and I know to never sacrifice myself for him again. Surely I can mess around—have a little fun—keep things on *my* terms without getting reattached. God knows, I could use the distraction.

The idea lightens me, and it's the small reprieve I desperately need. Against my greater judgement, I send Slade my address and then leave the bath in preference of my studio, refusing to acknowledge what I've done or the shame thickening inside me. Rather, I bury it with clay and set to work, transforming this clusterfuck of a day into solid form. And come midnight, the lump of terracotta resembles a woman on her knees, her heart bleeding in her outstretched hands as she begs someone to take it. As she begs *me* to take it. But I can't help her. No one can.

Eleven

"Y ou look nice," Beth says as she strolls into the kitchen the following evening, her billowy blouse untucked, toes webbed by nude stockings.

I eye the time on my phone. Had she arrived ten minutes from now, she might have encountered Slade, and what a shitshow that would have been. "I thought you had farewell drinks."

"I do," she says, plucking the front of her blouse. "I spilt coffee and needed to change. Where are you off to?"

"Dinner with friends from work." I flash her a small smile, then avert my gaze. I don't like lying, but I'd rather not ruin her night or endure a lecture. Besides, Slade won't set foot inside her house. That was the deal.

"Anyone I know?" Beth eyes me with a smirk that heats my cheeks. She still hasn't let the whole phone gift go. But the fact I squirm whenever she alludes to Cole doesn't deter her either. I shake my head, hoping she drops it.

"We still good for a movie night tomorrow?"

"Like I'd miss it," I reply. It's her last night here for five long months. The thought curdles my stomach. What seemed tolerable yesterday now threatens to unravel me.

"Just making sure you didn't get a better offer." Beth waggles her eyebrows, and I release a heavy sigh. Time to end this nonsense.

"Cole has a girlfriend. And a daughter. So you can stop with the teasing, okay?"

Beth's smile fades. "Oh. I didn't know that."

"Makes two of us," I grumble to the island bench, tracing the shimmering swirls with my fingertip.

She eyes me curiously, then turns to open a cupboard door. "You sound disappointed." There's control in her voice. The perfect balance of calm and cool. She's fishing. Trying for subtlety but failing miserably.

I use a shrug to feign indifference. "Don't be silly. I know what I am, Beth."

"Oh yeah?" She sets a crystal wine glass on the granite and opens the fridge, retrieving the near-empty bottle of sauvignon blanc. "And what's that?"

Inhaling through my nose, I stare at her baby blues, trying to formulate a response that says it all. "A fucking mess."

Beth's eyes widen, and she opens her mouth to speak, only to be cut off by the drawn-out blast of a horn.

Slade.

Early for once in his life, but at least he didn't come to the door. I never expected he would. Sliding my bag from the island, I peck Beth on the cheek. "Gotta go. Don't wait up."

The front door slams behind me as I rush to the long silver sedan hovering at the kerb. The windows are black mirrors, which eases my worry. Even if Beth peers out her bedroom window, she won't see who it is. The car is unfamiliar, but as I hesitate, the passenger door pushes open, and I spot Slade leaning across the seat, a dark Adidas hoodie cloaking his head. Grin flashing.

I climb in, latch my seatbelt, then force a smile. "Hi. We should go."

Slade whips back his hood. "Well, someone's keen," he says, sliding his gaze over my slinky white top, then down the length of my jeans. "Killer boots."

I soften my smile but rein in all giddiness. "Thanks."

"Killer place too." He whistles under his breath, eyeballing Beth's house and then the surrounding residences. My protective instincts flare again. Like they did outside Benedict's. "My girl's come up in the world," he says, winking as he puts the car in gear. A cheeky smirk sparkles in his hazel eyes. Baggy track pants bunch against his glowing white Nikes. And that titanium stud glimmers in the lingering sun. His hair has grown long enough to hide the scalp tats, but he still looks badass. And hot. So fucking hot that I quietly sigh. At least I had the foresight to wear cartoon-bunny-print knickers. No man is ever seeing those.

The engine rumbles as Slade leaves the kerb, and I rub my hand over the velour seat, taking in my surroundings. There's an abundance of red. The seats. The carpet. The vinyl-lined doors and steering wheel. *The fucking seatbelts.* Someone could be murdered in here and you wouldn't see blood. "When did you get this car?" I ask.

Slade shakes his head. "Not mine. It's my cousin's. He owed me a solid. Let me have it for the night to take out my chicky-babe."

His girl. His chicky-babe. Wow, I really have come up in the world.

"Didn't know you were a Bellamy Ford fan, by the way." I grin, and Slade's neck blooms pink up to his cheek. It's the first time I've seen him blush, and I bite back my amusement.

He recovers quickly. "You know damn well I'm not. Had to get your attention somehow, and chicks love that mushy shit."

I roll my eyes. He shouldn't have spoken. He killed it.

Slade looks at me, noticing I'm unimpressed. "Aw, c'mon, babe, don't be like that. I meant every word." He squeezes my thigh before returning his eyes to the road, and I stare at him, perplexed. The "bullshit" sign flashes violently in my head, but it needn't bother. I already know. What I'm wondering is if he's always been this transparent? Or did his skills deteriorate in jail? In any event, staying detached will be easier than I thought.

"Where are we going?" I ask.

"The boys are hanging at Razz's. Thought we could swing by. Introduce you."

Once upon a time, meeting his tribe would have made my life. Now I'm wondering why he bothered asking me out if he wants to smoke weed and play Xbox with his mates. Cole jumps to mind then, stirring my stomach. I'll bet he's at home playing with Ella. Or cosied up with Hannah on the couch. What I wouldn't give for that placid life. The white picket fence. Stability. A soft place to fall amid the scent of freshly baked cookies. Hannah strikes me as the type who'd bake.

My stomach grumbles, but I blame it on a hunger easily fixed. "Think we could grab food first?"

Slade nods once, then cranks the music. More hammering EDM. I open the window an inch to rid the stale ashtray stench and watch everyone go about their business trapped in their own little worlds. I don't like deceiving Beth. It feels awful. I should have told her the truth and dealt with her ire. After everything she's done, it's the least I could do.

You're rotten, Avery Lee, and everyone can smell it.

The quaint sandstone shopping centre has a chemist, delicatessen, hairdresser, and fish-and-chip shop, all lined up under a grapevine-lavished bullnose verandah. It's deserted considering the time, yet Slade parks down an adjacent street rather than the car park.

He cuts the engine and looks at me. "Fish and chips it is. I'll grab some for the lads too. They'll have the munchies."

We climb out the car, and Slade tucks my hand in his as we walk.

The public display of affection shocks me. Other than that night at Mia's and last Monday's hug, it's never happened. Too risky. Someone might have seen, and Zoe might have found out. I can't say it doesn't feel nice either, because it does. His hand is warm. Skin pleasantly rough. But it doesn't fit mine like I imagined, and it's sad we never did this before fucking.

Across the car park, tyres screech, gravel spits, and the air electrifies. Slade and I freeze, gaping at a black coupe that jerks to a stop five metres away, chrome rings looped across its grille. Wheels like golden starbursts.

"What the fuck?" Slade says as the driver's door flies open.

A figure surges from the seat, and my blood drains into my boots. "C . . . Cole?" His shoulders are rigid. Fists clenched. WTF line trebled in fury. But his glare isn't pointed at me—rather, Slade.

What the hell?

Slade looks down at me and tugs the side of his mouth into a smirk. "Aw, you got a jealous boyfriend, Aves? You shoulda told me."

Dropping Slade's hand with a brusque shake of my head, I intercept Cole's charge and stop him. His chest burns against my palms, and a current tingles through my arms, but I've come to expect as much when we touch. It's like our energy melds in some delicious way. "Why are you here?" I hiss.

He rips his eyes away from Slade and meets mine. The anger in them softens, but his chest heaves with flustered breaths. "Get in my car, Avery." He refixes his gaze on Slade, and his nostrils flare, but I stiffen.

"What? No. Why would I do that?"

"Avery," he growls, this time without sparing me a glance. "Get. In. My. Car." He steps around me and charges for Slade. He grips him by his hooded collar, twisting the fleece in his fist, and my mouth gapes.

Cole leans into Slade's face, towering over him a good three inches. His body is lean and muscular—elegant—compared to Slade's jailhouse bulk. "You're a piece of shit. You know that?" Cole spits.

"That right, pretty boy?" Slade smirks in classic Slade style. "If you'd kindly remove your hands, I'm sure we can settle this like gentlemen."

Cole growls. "She could go to prison if she's caught in that hot car of yours. Do you know that? Do you even care?"

My heart trembles, and my stomach splats to the ground. I look at Slade as my head grows dizzy. "You . . . You stole it?" The question comes strangled and high, and Slade presses his mouth into a hard line, darting his gaze to the ground.

Oh my God.

My body sways.

I was in a stolen car.

And I'm on a bond.

I could go to jail.

I could go to jail!

I can't breathe—the air's too thick.

"Avery, please go. Now!" Cole says, but this time I listen.

My heart pounds triple the speed of my frantic steps, and I watch my feet scurry across the rough bitumen in an oxygen-deprived daze. I climb into Cole's passenger seat and grip the piped edges. My vision glows white, so I drop my head to my knees. I know the drill, and I know what comes next if I don't.

How could Slade do this?

I vaguely hear the driver's side door slam shut moments later and the engine roar to life. Cole spins out of the car park in much the same manner he arrived, so I brace my forearms against the glove box, my head still down, as he starts a winding ascent.

"I . . . didn't . . . know." I say each word in a separate breath. "I swear." Tears drip from the tip of my nose, and I cough and splutter, praying I don't vomit on Cole's spotless ebony floor.

"I know," Cole says, then finds my back, rubbing firm circles with his hand. The motion shoots warmth through my veins, neutralising the adrenaline and unlocking my chest.

The car soon pulls over, and his hand disappears. The engine cuts out, leaving a silence that drowns me with shame. Panic attacks are worse than hell—no red devils or molten lakes could eclipse the mind's ability to torture. But add an audience, and you have something even worse: a mirror reflecting the mess you truly are.

Wiping away my tears, I sit up and glimpse Cole's way. His crystal eyes burn wild with worry. His breaths come jacked and rough. He's probably never witnessed such a ridiculous display. I've probably scared him half to death. My gaze sinks to my lap. I can't believe that happened in front of him.

Of all people.

But a second later, I'm crushed to his chest. His strong arms cocoon me, and he clutches my head with one broad hand while his other resumes circling my back, around and around. I melt into his warmth as my worries crumble, gripping his blue dress shirt like I might float away. He smells so fucking good. Like safety and hope and peace. And his chest is the perfect mix of soft skin and hard muscle. Goldilocks would lose her ever-loving mind.

"You're okay. I'm right here." His deep voice vibrates through his chest, sending shivers through my body, and I have to pull away. If I don't, I never will. Cole should run—kick me from his car before I infect him with crazy—not comfort me. But he is, and he has no idea what that does to me.

I take a deep breath and look at him, wanting to apologise but frowning as reality returns. "I'm going to jail. My fingerprints—" I choke on the thought and clench my eyes shut. "—my fingerprints are in that car. They won't believe I didn't know."

Cole shakes his head. "You're not going anywhere. I'll fix it."

Unlatching his seatbelt, he slides his phone from his pants pocket, retrieves a contact, then brings it to his ear. "I need a favour," he says, low and gritty.

The words spin through my belly, and I stare out my window, beyond the wallaby grass swaying down the hill, to the view of Melbourne's skyline peaking above the bushes and trees. The buildings stand hazed by distance, and scattered lights twinkle as twilight bathes the sky. But the attempt to distract myself fails. What is Cole doing? And what does "I'll fix it" mean?

The air hardens around a beat of silence, and Cole's throat bobs. He seems nervous, which inspires little trust. "There's a silver seventy-nine Fairlane next to Brookby Shopping Centre. I need it gone. ASAP."

A murmur drifts from the earpiece, and Cole drops his chin, pinching the bridge of his nose. "Thanks. I owe you one." He ends the call and tosses his phone into the centre console, then stares at me and I at him, while tension hums between us.

"What was that?" I ask.

He eyes me from beneath the ridge of his brow. "You build connections in my line of work. I'm not in the habit of exploiting them, but this situation is . . . unique." His tone comes measured, and he watches me, but dumbfounded, I just stare.

Connections?

Every mob movie I've seen parades through my mind. I wonder if Beth has those types of connections. I doubt it. But then again, she's in contract law, not criminal. But Cole—strait-laced, tailored Cole—breaking the law he vowed to uphold . . . *for me?*

"What will they do?" I ask.

"What they do best. You don't need to worry. It's done."

That might be so, but for every thought I shove aside, three appear in its place. "The car won't be there. Slade would have taken it."

"He won't touch it now. Trust me. Or come near you, for that matter."

His possessiveness stirs low in my pelvis, but as that worry dies, a monster grows. I clench the seat. "Oh my God, surveillance cameras. Someone will have us on tape." Angry Zoes in orange jumpsuits charge through my mind, and I trace my cheekbone, recalling the damage.

"The police don't track surveillance on every stolen car."

I snap my head towards Cole. "Are you sure? Isn't that their job?"

"Unless it's connected to something more serious."

"And what if it is?"

Cole huffs. "It's not."

"But how do you know that?" No amount of reassurance will be enough. Getting pinched for this will be the fresh fear I take to bed every night for eternity. I'm certain of it. And now there's a cover-up. And Cole's involved. I've dragged him into my mess like I did Jen and Liam. *What the fuck is wrong with me?*

Cole rakes his fingers through his hair, then pins me with that gaze. "Stolen cars are Slade's MO. Murder and kidnapping aren't."

I flinch. "He . . . he's done this before?" Pity swamps Cole's eyes, and I look at my lap, shaking my head. "I'm such an idiot."

He squeezes my shoulder, and some of my self-loathing melts under his touch. "No, you're not. You just don't know what you don't know."

His words circle my head and hollow out my chest. I look up at him. "That's an extremely unsettling truth."

His mouth twitches with a smile. "The fact we're all going to die wins out for me."

Now I smile. "Fair point." We stare at each other while our souls silently converse, but my paranoia soon kills the moment. I must look like my mugshot.

Snatching my bag from the footwell, I scrounge for a tissue, but Cole catches my wrist. "You couldn't look bad if you tried," he says, ending my pursuit. I glance up at him, knowing I never said a word. Is he a mind reader now too?

Reaching out, he tucks a lock of hair behind my ear, slowly, as if he's savouring every second. The tingles return and blanket my skin. My eyes drop to his lips for a sweet second, but then reality thumps me on the head. "How did you know where I was?"

Cole stiffens, and a million thoughts flash across his face, but he remains silent.

I frown. "Are you spying on me?"

He clears his throat. "I've had the firm's PI keep tabs on Slade since his release."

My mouth falls open. "Why?"

"I don't trust him, and I need you safe."

My face screws up. "But I'm not your responsibility."

"Well, someone needs to look out for you, clearly," he says, raising his palm to imply my predicament.

I clench my teeth because I hate that he's right. Still, to track Slade . . . ? What the actual fuck? As my mind reels, a puzzle piece slots into place as if young Alex set it there himself. "The other day, outside work. It wasn't a coincidence, was it? You knew Slade was there." His eyes tell me I'm right, and my nostrils flare. "And me? Are you keeping tabs on me too?"

He shakes his head. "I wouldn't invade your privacy like that."

I scoff. But my ex? That's a different story?

"Please don't make this a bigger deal than it is. Slade is trouble, and you're a magnet to him. I don't want him near you or Benedict's."

I crinkle my brows, unsure how to feel about this. The "bullshit" sign pulses in my brain, but it's dim—uncertain—like me. The man wants to protect his business. Well within his rights. But why me? The whole thing borders on creepy, despite what the squealing tween in my brain thinks. But maybe in the glitzy legal world with a PI at your disposal, this kind of thing is no big deal. Maybe I'm catastrophising again.

Crossing my arms, I narrow my eyes. "How did you know the car was stolen?"

"A simple database search and a hunch. Didn't you notice he had no keys?"

No. No, I didn't. *Good one, Avery.*

My cheeks flush, but I smother my embarrassment with annoyance. "Who exactly do you think you are?"

Cole hardens his jaw, and I hate that I imagine skimming my lips across the stubble. "A simple thank-you will suffice." His sharp tone cuts, and I flinch. He notices, then looks down with a sigh, gripping the steering wheel with one hand, bleeding his knuckles white. "I care about you, okay? Way more than I should."

Elation rushes me in a tsunami of liquid gold, and I fight the urge to climb into his lap, burrow in, and stay there forever. Safe. Cared for. Maybe even one day, loved.

You're like a vine, Avery Lee. A vine that slowly creeps up and strangles people.

I wilt at that thought but manage to speak. "Stop following Slade. Promise me."

Cole sighs but agrees. His pale gaze finds mine, but the vulnerability in it wrenches my heart. "I thought you broke up with him."

The hurt in his voice stuns me. "I did. I . . . Well, I—" And then it all comes flooding back. Mini-Bees. Hannah. Ella. Him. Their trifecta of perfect love. I grind my molars. "Where is Hannah, anyway?"

Cole frowns. "Probably at home with Ella. Why?"

"Shouldn't you be there with them—at home with your daughter rather than stalking me?"

Cole's brows shoot up. "Excuse me?"

"What? Is it so common for you to gallivant around with other women no one's ever questioned you?"

The confusion on Cole's face settles into a smug smile. Throwing his head back, he laughs, and the sound booms through the car. "Oh, green really *is* your colour."

"I'm not jealous," I grit out. "I'm angry. How can you do this to Hannah? Not to mention Ella. How can you mess with that sweet little girl's life?"

Cole folds his arms, tilting his chin. "What exactly have I done?"

I meet his cocky gaze, the slight twist of his full lips, and my cheeks burn. Only a naïve twit like me would think a platonic lunch and a few flirty comments are anything of consequence. But here we sit at a picturesque fucking lookout after he swept in and saved my butt. That's got to mean something, right?

"Oh, you're jealous all right," Cole says. "Jealous of my sister and niece."

"Wait . . . what?" I whisper.

"Hannah is my sister, not my lover. And Ella is my niece."

I stare at his glittering smirk. He's loving every damn minute of this. "But she has your eyes."

"She does." He nods. "The same eyes as her uncle. And grandfather, for that matter," he adds blackly. "Family resemblance, nothing more."

I look away, shrinking into the supple leather seat, willing it to swallow me whole. No word adequately describes my humiliation, but at the same time, oh, the relief.

"Is that why you ran off on Friday?"

I don't answer him. Rather, I stare at my lap, squeezing my hands.

"I thought Hannah would have mentioned it by now."

"Well, she didn't," I say, picking at my fingernails.

Cole's hand comes down over mine to still them, and I brave looking up. His intense gaze studies me, and he narrows his eyes. "So you were upset at my perceived betrayal. Is that why you went out with Slade?"

Am I that transparent? Fuck my life.

"Well?" he asks.

Looking away, I nod once.

Cole tuts. "Silly girl."

The words sting, and I tense. Silly girl. He's just confirmed everything I feared. In comparison to Miss Blue Satin Sparkles and the refined women he's surrounded by daily, I'm nothing but a silly girl.

"Hey," he says, lifting my chin to make me look at him. My vision is blurry with unshed tears, and Cole frowns. One escapes, sliding down my cheek, and he swipes it with his thumb, staring at me with eyes that seem to read *everything*. "Christ, you're gorgeous," he whispers, then drops his gaze to my lips. "Like a broken angel."

Those last words end me, forcing my eyes to close as they swim dreamily around my heart, and it's heaven for five whole seconds until more confusion rears, and the car grows stifling. I open my door and climb out, cradling my arms against the chill as I drag in fresh air and fight a barrage of thoughts. It's all too much. *He's* too much.

Cole follows me, scrubbing the back of his neck as he stands to shut his door. He looks equally confused, but so he damn well should. What is he doing here, and what does he want?

"Avery," he says, coming around the front of the car to join me on the footpath. "Did I—"

I cut him off. "You can't say things like that to me."

His steps halt. "Why?" Long grass and trees sway and rustle behind him, but Cole stands atop the hill, backlit by muted grey and twinkling lights, like he's the only solid form on earth.

"Because when you do . . ." I shake my head, feeling pent-up and supremely flustered. "When you do, I want . . ."

"What do you want?" His voice is low and heavy, and he takes one step closer, clenching his hands at his sides.

I swallow but then fixate on his lips. *"This."*

I rush towards him and press my mouth to his. If I can keep one taste forever, I'll die content. I slide my fingers through his hair and skate my tongue across his top lip, pulling it between mine to suck and gently nip. He tastes divine, and I breathe him in, relishing the scratch of his stubble, worried he'll push me away. But he doesn't push me away. Rather, Cole groans the kind of deep, hungry groan that rumbles through my cells and yanks me harder against his mouth.

He finds my hips and hitches me onto the bonnet of his car, then settles between my legs, and the cold metal bleeds through my jeans in a heady contrast to the fire burning between us.

I moan as he kisses up my neck, his hot breath sending a cascade of shivers down my back as he reaches my ear. "I'm going to hell," he says, but then he reclaims my mouth and kisses me like I've never been kissed. With ferocity. Fervour. Need I can feel in my bones. And it's then I decide, if this is hell, then I'm definitely coming too.

Twelve

don't like to work sitting on a stool at a bench facing a wall. Rather, I prefer to plonk down on the floor right in the centre of my studio, cross-legged on a jumbo patchwork cushion, at the base of my spinning stand as if in worship. Or on my knees, scuttling from side to side, dancing with the piece as it comes to life. The classroom prevented that freedom, and it's one I now cherish. Inspiration flows, creating its physical form before my eyes. Creativity is divine. It doesn't come from me, rather through me from something infinitely more creative. Source energy. The universe. Whatever the fuck you believe in. All I know is I'm lucky, and when it stopped, my insides felt dead. But right now, they're anything but dead. They're tickly and squirmy. Hot and restless. I haven't yet slept, and last night loops through my head on repeat. Was it even real?

Christ, you're gorgeous.

The memory makes me giddy. Not even my imagination could fake such exquisite detail. Cole's scorching-hot mouth. His fingers knotted in my hair. The press of his hardness against my jeans, and the rough, hungry sounds he made. It was real, all right. And my bunny-print knickers are the main reason I have any self-respect left. That and the fact just talking to Cole felt as magical as kissing him.

Like a broken angel.

A goofy smile finds my lips as I press my fingers into the wet clay and hum along with Coldplay's love of shining stars. Adding one final detail, I smooth it over with my thumb. Hours disappear to dust when I sculpt. Time is lost, and what feels like an hour is usually four. So it's no surprise when the sunset blazes through the studio window, wishing adieu in iridescent glory. The day has gone, but in its place sits what could be my best work yet.

Terracotta covers my hands, smears extending up my arms. My clothes are an artwork unto themselves, and so is my face, judging by the tight feeling across my cheeks and chin, but I wouldn't have it any other way. I revel in the mess.

Flopping my legs out front, I toss the modelling tool next to the others and lean back on my hands. If I touch it even once more, I might ruin it. Rarely do I manage to replicate exactly what I envisage, but this time I have, and fast. My first duet—two lovers entwined—immersed in each other. The composition is balanced. The texture rich. Lines modern. It's intimate and erotic, unlike anything I've ever done, but not in a raunchy, red-light way. A man holds a woman, his muscular forearm running up her back. He knots his hand in her hair and drags his other one down the middle of her bare chest. She's arching back as her slender calf wraps around his thigh. And with her eyes closed, she stretches out her arms as though she can fly. Once complete, their scrolled-wire hearts will interconnect and circle them in swirls of copper. I only pray it survives the kiln.

I stare for a while and then snap a photo with my phone. A gentle knock sounds on the door. "Aves?"

"Just a sec." I rocket to my feet, grab a pink bedsheet from the shelf, and sweep it up and over the lovers.

Beth's soft voice reminds me how close I came last night to screwing everything up. How easily I broke our agreement even if I didn't know. I thought about coming clean and concluded she'd forgive me post-Armageddon. But Beth leaves at dawn, and blighting her plans now would be a dick move, especially when there's nothing more to fear. I'm well and truly done with Slade. That's my new solemn vow, and it will have to do. I take a resolved breath, but it doesn't quash the awareness I'm still a total jerk. "Come in."

The door cracks open, and Beth peeks in. Grinning, she opens it further and steps inside. She scans my muddy clothes and then the lumpy pink ghost standing next to me. "New piece?"

I nod, and she ambles to where the others sit. Until now, she's respected my privacy but made it clear she'd like to see my work before leaving, and I can't deny her that. She stares at the girl crushed to the ground, but the longer she does, the more I itch to make excuses. "They're not done yet. They still need firing, glaze, and metalwork. Usually copper or steel. Sometimes scraps, metal clay, or household items morphed into what I need."

Beth acknowledges me with a silent nod, then steps over to the next piece: a bust of a man losing his mind. "There'll be metal fragments circling his head when finished," I explain.

A minute later she moves on to the child who's cowered and blocking his ears—the third piece I made before court. When done, he'll have a tin butterfly perched on his head.

After considering him, Beth moves on to the next two: the Alex and Ella wannabes, each sitting off the side of Beth's bench, their faces alight with mischief. "They'll both have rainbow hair," I say.

Beth nods again, then moves on to the last piece: the woman on her knees, holding out her anatomically correct bleeding heart, begging someone to take it. I lift the clear plastic it's drying under so Beth can better see.

She turns to me. "Do you take commissions?"

"Commissions?" I gulp, recovering it.

"Yeah." She taps a finger against her chin. "I think I'd like an Avery Masters original in my gallery."

I huff out a laugh. "Real cute, Beth."

"What?" she says. "I'm serious."

I flop my arms over her shoulders from behind and kiss her cheek. "I appreciate the support, but you don't need to do that."

She unhooks my hands to turn around. "Is that a no?" She arches a brow, and I laugh again.

"My work won't fit in with your Hesters and Boyds."

Beth gathers my hands in hers. "It will when it's done. Even I can see that." Over her shoulder, she regards them again. "What are you planning to do with them all, anyway?"

Blank-faced, I just stare. That's a question I hadn't considered. "Um, nothing?"

"Nothing?" Beth says incredulously.

"This is therapy more than anything else. You know that."

"But they're so good. It would be a waste not to share them." She squeezes my hands, and I scrunch up my nose.

"Who would want to see them?"

"Who wouldn't?"

Freeing my hands, I step away. "You're biased."

"Maybe so, but these are something else. Surely you can see that?"

I stare at the six pieces all lined up in a row. They're next level for me, but by professional standards I'm not sure they'd even rate. In any event, the thought of showing them feels akin to posting my naked photos online or publishing my darkest secrets for all to read. I'm not ready for that and doubt I'll ever be.

"Just think about it, please?" Beth says.

I nod purely to appease her, then gather up my tools from the floor to lay them on the bench. Murky water spills over the side of the bowl as I set it down adjacent. My stomach growls for the twentieth time, sick of being ignored, but this time it registers. "Is dinner here yet?"

"Fifteen minutes. Enough time for you to shower and clean your-self up."

"What are we watching?" I ask, blotting up the mess with a rag.

"*Dirty Dancing*."

I grin. "Classic."

Beth nods. "Especially on VHS."

"Can we do the end dance?" I ask.

Beth smiles. "Do we ever not?"

The addition of a human aeroplane ride instead of the famous lift is our best modification. And balancing Beth on my feet while she pretends to fly is the most fitting send-off ever.

"I see you have a new fascination with elevator doors."

I snap my gaze away to meet Hannah's smirk. There's no point denying it. What started as a glance whenever they dinged yesterday has progressed to checking them every ten seconds, desperately will-ing Cole's presence. Add that to the fact I'm doing the same with my phone and you have a beautiful concoction of pathetic. I'm my fuck-ing mother, but not knowing where he is or where I stand is torture.

"He'll be back Thursday night."

My heart stutters. "Who?"

The smuggest smile in history peels across Hannah's face. "Cole."

I see it now, the resemblance. Hannah has the same Cupid's-bow lips, the same twist to her smile and glint of delight in her eye when she teases. My breath quivers. "You know?"

She laughs and clasps her hands together as if relishing the news. "Oh yes. You thought I was shagging my *brother*. I might be single and a smidge desperate, but come on." She does the vomit sign, de-livering it with the appropriate noise, before tilting her head to further savour my mortification. Lured by her mother's theatrics, Ella approaches.

I can't believe he told her.

Well, maybe you're not a dirty secret this time.

The thought flutters around my belly. "Did he tell you anything else?"

Like how he found me in a stolen car with a criminal? Or how he broke the law to save my arse?

Hannah perches Ella on her hip, then looks at the ceiling, rubbing her chin like she's deep in thought. Ella copies her mum and mimics the same cheeky grin. God, it runs in the family. "Hmm, not really. Apart from him slobbering all over you inside his car."

I feel my face flame red. "He told you that?" *In* his car—*on* his car—both are true. I look around the room, ensuring Tej is out of earshot, and Hannah laughs.

"No, but you just did. Jeez, you guys are easy to crack. I knew you both had it for someone, and after you dashed away on Friday, it wasn't hard to do the maths."

"You're not . . . upset?" *Baffled. Bewildered?*

"Upset?" She frowns. "Why would I be? You're both consenting adults. I only ever want my brother to be happy."

Her openness to the idea puzzles me. I can't say no eyebrow would rise if Beth hooked up with a mailroom clerk nine years her junior, but I'll take it.

And she thinks I could make Cole happy?

Out of habit, I glance back at the elevator, then feel Hannah's smirk return. Rolling my eyes, I sigh and meet her amusement. "Please don't tell him how stupid I am."

She chuckles and pats the top of my head. "Don't worry. Your secret's safe with me."

Cole:
I hear you've taken up elevator watching.
Intriguing hobby.

Oh my God, I'll kill her. I sink to the edge of my bed, staring at Cole's text in horror, but at least he's reached out.

Me:
Your sister sucks. No offence.

Cole:
Is it true? Have you been waiting for me?

Shaking my head, I bite my top lip with a smile. "Obsessively pining" might be a better description. "Wondering what I did wrong" another. In fact, when he disappeared on Monday, I started to wonder if I made it all up. Concocted a delusional Cole fantasy while sitting catatonic in a psych ward somewhere. That's how unreal and magical this all feels. That's how mind-blowing *he* felt.

Me:
Maybe.

Cole:
You could have called, you know. I wouldn't
have minded.

The million knots in my shoulders untie, and my heart swells.

Me:
You might not realise this, but my generation
doesn't call people. That's just plain creepy.

> **Cole:**
> Ha-ha. I object to the inference a nine-year
> age gap is a generation, but like I said, if you
> ever need anything, I'm here.

He's here. He did say that. At the lookout after I told him Beth was leaving. Only, I thought he meant if I needed something—not simply him.

> **Me:**
> I appreciate that.

> **Cole:**
> I haven't stopped thinking about you. About
> the other night.

Tell me about it. I shiver at the memory.

> **Me:**
> In a good way or with soul-crushing regret?

> **Cole:**
> Definitely the latter, hence why I'm texting
> you. Obviously.

I laugh at that.

> **Me:**
> Wow. Sarcasm and use of the word hence
> without a trace of geek. I'm impressed.

But then I second guess myself.

> **Me:**
> You were being sarcastic, right?

Cole:
What do you think?

Me:
I think about everything. All the time. The good,
the bad, and the horrible. It's one of my worst
traits, hence why I asked.

Cole:
You're definitely the loudest thinker I've met,
but it's probably because you're smart, and
personally, I find it cute. Especially when
your mouth does that crooked little scowl.
But yes, Avery, I've been thinking about you
in the best way.

The best way. I pinch my wrist to make sure I'm awake. He could
be onto something too. I mean, I doubt dumb people spend their
time overthinking. And he finds it cute? *Me* . . . cute? Grinning, I read
the message again, feeling like I'm toffee melting in the sun. But I
don't scowl, do I? Before I can deny the claim, another message pops
up.

Cole:
Also, now I'm impressed. I've just discovered
receiving a casual hence is oddly hot.

I giggle—*literally* giggle—and squeeze my thighs together.

Me:
How hot exactly?

I stare at the screen, waiting for a response, bouncing one knee,
but this time Cole's taking a while. Shit. Did I go too far with the

flirt? Just as I'm ready to dive under my pillow and scream, a photo pops up, and immediately, I blush. It's a close-up of Cole—*the* close-up of Cole—shirtless and smeared in mud, yanking one end of a blue rope as it circles his low-slung shorts. I cringe. I'd hoped he'd forgotten about that, but instead he's tormenting me with it. Secretly, I'm delighted.

Cole:

This hot. Or so I gather ;-)
Goodnight, Naughty One. Sweet dreams.

Me:

They will be now ;-)

Image saved.

Thirteen

A crisp breeze wafts through my gauzy bedroom curtains, beckoning me outside. The roof is nearly dry from the dinner downpour, so I tuck my phone into the front pocket of my fuzzy hoodie, jam my feet into unlaced Chucks, and hitch myself up and out the anodised window.

When I lie down, I cross my arms into a cosy pillow under my head and leave my phone resting on my stomach so Ed Sheeran can sing to the stars. The night sky is clean. A huddle of clouds circle the moon in a glowing dome of light. I love it up here. Alone. Looking up into the vast unknown. It confirms my insignificance and shrinks my woes to specks of stardust.

As the cold air cleanses my lungs, I smile. I can't remember ever feeling this peaceful—like chaos went to sleep—but I know who to thank for that.

I close my eyes and picture Cole. His intense, pretty stare. The way he tasted last weekend. My skin tingles at the memory like I'm bathing in champagne, and I sink into the blissful feeling . . . until my phone scares me shitless with a deafening ring.

It slips off my waist as I jolt, hitting the tin with a clunk before sliding down a valley. Lurching forward, I slap my hand down to stop it, but my foot loses traction, sliding on shoelaces like a puck on ice. It all happens in a blink, and I scramble through my descent down the roof, sending prayers to the moon, only finding purchase at the very last second by grasping the flimsy gutter. My feet dangle six feet in the air as my phone finishes its trip, plonking into the gutter mush next to my hand. I sigh. I guess that's something, at least.

Looking down, I assess the drop. Concrete will break my fall, but without Wonder Woman's strength or ability to fly, what choice do I have? Inhaling, I count to three through gritted teeth, let one hand go, snatch up my phone, then free-fall.

Down.

Down.

Ouch.

The pebbled concrete bites my tail bone, and the soles of my feet sting as I stare up at the battened eaves, panting and holding my ankle. I'm an idiot. Beth warned me, but I knew better. Thankfully, my phone seems to have survived unscathed, so I light up the screen to check who called. Mum. That'd be fucking right. Guilt made me change her ringtone back to the default, which I now regret. Jen's choice would have made me stiffen, potentially averting my fall. But even if it wouldn't have, tumbling off the roof to the Wicked Witch's theme song feels like an opportunity missed.

I kill the music and climb to my feet, then dust off my baggy pyjama pants and limp to the back French doors. My ankle hurts, but it could be worse. All I need is access and ice. As expected, the doors are locked, but a rustic clay urn stands nearby at half my height. I tilt it up with both hands, willing a spare key to appear underneath, but only a ring of dirt and scuttle of silverfish do. I check the rest of the potted succulents on the deck without success.

The sensor light flickers on, making the porch tiles sparkle as I limp to the front door. I check underneath the daisy-print doormat. Zilch. But that would be too obvious. I check under the ficus plants standing sentry at the twin pillars. Nada. I dial Beth, but she doesn't answer. After scanning the neighbouring houses, I deflate with a sigh. They're strangers. No way would they have a spare key.

The milky glass squeaks as I slide down the front door and lean back against it with my feet flopped out front. I should have added a unit of lock picking to my rebellious curriculum. That would have been handy right now. Or perhaps I should have tied my laces for a change. I pull the cuffs of my pants up my calves to compare ankles. It's a mild sprain at most, and I'm lucky—trams, toddlers, and busted ankles don't mix. But my gratitude soon fades along with the adrenaline, and the frosty night creeps into my bones.

I could call Liam, but phoning him out of the blue because I need something feels scummy. And Jen doesn't pick locks or stay awake past ten on weeknights, which is deplorable for a uni student. A locksmith could help, but how much do they cost? Fuck, Beth's been gone less than a week and I've already nearly killed myself.

You're hopeless, Avery Lee. Smart, but stupid in all the ways that count.

My chest clamps, and I wince.

After fifteen minutes of flipping my phone face up and down on the doormat, I take a deep breath, triple check it's definitely Thursday, then shoot a text to the only person left circling my brain. The one who never leaves. After all, Cole did say if I needed anything, right?

Me:
Hi there. You wouldn't happen to be in the area, would you?

It's a long shot, but his reply comes fast.

Cole:

No, but I am back at the office. Why's that?

Ten thirty p.m. and he's at work. No surprise there.

Me:

Never mind.

Cole:

Why, Avery?

Me:

It's stupid. I'm locked out, and Beth left on
Monday.

Cole:

I'll be there in thirty.

A sheepish grin blooms across my face, and I roll my eyes. Only the slimiest of slime would derive joy from someone's inconvenience, but apparently that's me.

True to his word, thirty minutes later, Cole rolls up to the kerb, climbs out of his flash car, then saunters up the driveway with a smirk. "Nice pants."

I look down at the turquoise smiley faces floating in a sea of purple flannelette, then back up to him. I love these pants. Usually. "Thanks. Made them myself." With a Salvos sewing machine, no less.

"A lady of many talents," he says, halting at the porch entrance, eyes twinkling like stars.

My cheeks warm along with my heart. He looks ten feet tall from down here. I smile up at him. "Whatever gave you the impression I'm a lady?"

Cole laughs. "Well, not your language, that's for sure. But your pinkie finger does lift whenever you drink."

"What?" I chuckle. "No, it doesn't."

"Ah, yes, it does. With water and coffee, anyway, so I'm guessing it's an all-beverage thing."

I tilt my head. "Is there anything you don't notice?" Leaning on my hands, I work my good foot under me and manage to stand, bearing minimal weight on the other.

Cole swoops in to clutch my waist as I find balance. "Well, I didn't notice you were hurt. Christ, what happened?"

"It's nothing." Beneath my hands, his biceps are solid, and I squeeze them a little. "Thanks for coming. I really appreciate it."

His frown softens, and he strokes my cheek with his thumb, his warm fingertips light on my neck. The gesture sends tingles down my spine. "I'm glad you messaged." He looks down at my feet where one shoe hovers, barely touching the ground. "So are you going to tell me?"

I'd rather he didn't know how clumsy I am, nor picture the absurd scene, but to hell with it. "I fell off the roof and tweaked my ankle. Locked myself out in the process."

Cole's eyes saucer. "You fell off the roof?" He grips me out at arm's length, scanning for further injury.

I squeeze his wrists, pressing his gold cuff links into my palms. "It sounds worse than it is. I'm fine, don't worry."

The line reappears centre of his frown. "What were you doing on the roof?"

"Stargazing. Listening to music." *Thinking about you.* "The usual."

Something flickers in his gaze, and he softens his voice. "There are safer places to do that."

"Yes, *Dad.*" I roll my eyes with a laugh, but then Cole steps in and kisses me, draining me of all sass. He glides his warm lips over mine, and I breathe him in with a sigh, tangling my fingers in his hair.

God, I missed this.

Pulling back, he stares at me. "Stay off the roof, okay?" His expression is pleading, so I simply nod. Releasing me, he eyes the ficus plants.

"There's nothing under them. I already checked."

With a nod, he continues to search before stopping at the pebbled garden bed lined with small lollipop trees. He picks up a palm-sized rock, and I hobble towards him. "No! Please don't smash a window. Beth will murder me."

"Not my intention," Cole says. He steps out of the garden bed and returns, holding the rock between us like a sacred offering. I look at him like he's mad, but his eyes glint, and he turns the rock upside down, revealing a smooth grey surface. He unlatches a plastic lid, then flips it open, exposing a hidden compartment and shiny silver key.

I frown. "What the hell?"

He holds the key up between his fingers. "I gather you didn't know?"

"I had no idea."

"Hmmm," he says, dragging out the sound while arching a brow, insinuation lingering in his smirk. My cheeks burn, and I drop my gaze to the large plastic rock in his hand. It's as fake as a blow-up doll and surely a beacon to prowling thieves. I'm surprised by Beth's naivety, but I've truly never seen it. Besides, who knew key-holding fake rocks were even a thing?

I narrow my eyes on him. "I didn't stage a lockout just to see you. If that's what you're thinking."

He stares at me, and that lone dimple shines like Sirius. "Never dreamt you would. Though, the ankle injury would have been a nice touch. Convincing," he adds.

Fighting a smile, I shake my head and pluck the key from his hand. It slides into the barrel, turns with an easy click, and my relief dances with the moths circling the light above. Pushing the front door open, I look back over my shoulder to Cole. Silence hovers. "Do you … want to come in?"

"I'd like that," he rasps. He shoves the rock inside his pants pocket, but the bulge makes me blush.

God, Avery. Are you twelve?

Cole studies me, then shakes his head with a huffed laugh and scoops me into his arms. I squeal and grip the lapel of his suit jacket, locking my other arm around his neck. "What are you doing?"

"You make fleece and emojis look incredibly alluring. Has anyone ever told you that?"

"They have now." I grin. Traces of his designer scent coil around me like incense, and his body heat melts away the cold. I love being in his arms, so much so I'd like to never leave, but that's not what I say. "I can walk. It's not that bad."

Ignoring me, Cole steps over the aluminium threshold, then kicks the heavy glazed door shut. He scans the gallery, the lofty raked ceilings, the paintings. "Which way to your room?"

I direct him through the kitchen and towards the mezzanine, and he glides up each step with ease, then gently rests me on my bed like I'm priceless antique glass. The soft glow of my bedside lamp paints his complexion gold and casts shadows across half his face. He's mesmerising. *And here.* In my bedroom.

He slips off my shoes and examines my ankle, asking me to wriggle my pink-painted toes. A tiny smudge of purple pools near my heel, but the swelling is minimal. "It's fine, really. A minor sprain."

Cole concurs with a nod. "Do you have any ice?"

"Downstairs. Left down the hall. Third door on the right. Freezer in the laundry."

He grabs a crocheted cushion and rests my foot on top before descending the stairs. I scrutinise my room. Thankfully, it's clean. The bed made. Dresser junk neatly arranged. No dirty knickers strewn across the carpet, bunny-print or otherwise. But when I scan myself, I cringe. Despite what Cole says, my outfit is woeful. Had I staged a lockout, I definitely wouldn't have worn this. I shuck off my hoodie, uncovering a black camisole trimmed with lace, but immediately shiver in the window's breeze.

Worth it, I tell myself.

Cole takes nearly ten minutes to return with a chequered tea towel balled at the bottom. His eyes flicker to my chest, and his throat bobs, his jaw ticking as he averts his gaze. Glancing down, I stiffen. I hadn't considered my frozen nipples might triple in length and poke through the slinky fabric like they're trying to escape. I tug the satin away from my skin, but it falls right back into place. I eye my jumper but can't bring myself to do it so instead choose ignorance. "Did you get lost?"

Cole takes a seat at the foot of my mattress. "I returned the key, but the rock is hidden in the left corner of the backyard now. Safer that way. You should probably let your sister know."

I reach for my phone to shoot Beth a text before I forget. "You've never met my sister, have you?"

Cole shakes his head. "No, but we've spoken on the phone. I know one of her colleagues well."

Lucky for me. "Done," I say after pressing send.

Cole holds up the ice. "You ready?"

I nod but still flinch when he presses it to my ankle. The ice bleeds through the woven fabric, needling my skin. To secure it, Cole double knots the wrinkled towel ends together.

"Thanks," I say.

He glances around my room, taking it all in. "I never picked you for the mirror on the ceiling type."

My gaze snaps up. Instead of the sky, the roof windows frame a reflection of the bed. And he's right. They're a perfect mirror, albeit tinted. I chuckle. "Beth isn't that creepy, I promise."

Our eyes meet above, and we stare at each other. Me at the foreignness of him in my room. Him at hell knows what. Despite our mismatched attire, we look good together.

"How was your trip?" I ask.

Cole immediately looks away, pinching the bridge of his nose. "Tiring and tedious."

"Sounds amazing," I tease. He flashes me a crooked smile, pinning me with those intense pale eyes, but I drop my chin and tangle the fringe of a throw cushion around my finger. "Where did you go?" I casually ask. Five nights ago we kissed, broke the law, bonded, and then he disappeared. While he doesn't owe me an explanation, I am curious. And I *was* worried.

"Canberra," he replies.

Canberra. I wonder what's in Canberra other than Parliament House?

"Client meetings, subzero temperatures, and politicians. A lethal trio," Cole adds as if reading my mind. A whisper of a smile tweaks his lips when I look up. "I'm sorry I didn't tell you," he says, but I shake away his words.

"You don't owe me anything."

He leans in closer and lifts my chin, compelling my eyes to his. "I'm sorry," he repeats as if rejecting my last response.

I frown a little. "Okay. Apology accepted."

He presses a kiss to my forehead, then stands to approach my dresser. His reflection fills its mirror, and I stare as he removes his jacket and lays it neatly in half over the back of my cushy armchair. I'm still processing the fact I'm worth an explanation and apology as he loosens the knot of his emerald tie, then looks at me apologetically. "Sorry. I hate wearing this noose any longer than necessary."

"It's fine," I say, swallowing hard.

He whips the tie over his head and drapes it over the jacket before undoing the first two buttons of his white shirt. Next, he removes his cuff links, sets them down on my dresser, and rolls up his sleeves. My eyes lock onto the rainbow ink swirling up his sinewy forearm, and my chest fizzes like it's full of Sunkist and sherbet. My fingers itch to touch and trace—to admire the tropical jungle and flowers up close—but I bite my top lip in restraint.

Control yourself, Avery. Jesus.

With a grin, Cole studies me. "What?"

I swallow again. "You look like a *Vogue* cover model."

Duct tape. Where is that fucking duct tape?

Cole's laugh is full and deep. "Really? Maybe that's fitting." He ambles to my window. "Most days it feels like I'm playing dress-ups." Poking his head outside, he surveys the roof, then turns to me, frowning. "That slope is a slide. Do you have a death wish?"

"Not most days."

Cole seems to catch my bleak undertone, and something flashes across his face. "Can I shut it?" He dips his eyes to my chest for a millisecond before scrunching them closed as if to stop himself. "It's pretty cold."

"Sure," I say, blushing and wriggling as I take stock of my naughty nipples. Heat immediately curls up from downstairs, but it's not beneficial. The chill is helping me keep my cool, which is supremely difficult when Mr. Vogue is this close to my bed and images of him naked in it are assaulting me.

Cole looks equally pained as he kneads the back of his neck. "Mind if I grab some water?"

I pounce on the opportunity to do anything but sit here and squirm. "Let me get it for you. I'm the host, and my ankle is fine. The ice has already helped."

The ice anklet holds as I swing my legs off the bed, and I manage to stand just fine as Cole rushes around towards me. I hold up my hand to stop him. "I'm fine. See?" I take a quick step with my good foot and flash him a triumphant smile, but when I take my next one, a sharp pinch of pain catches me off guard, and I buckle straight into his arms.

I stare at my hand clutching his colourful ink—my nails digging into that warm rainbow flesh—then slowly look up. Cole's pupils are huge. *Hungry*. And I feel them right in my core. "Avery," he gravels, so rough and low I shiver.

"Touch me," I whisper.

So he does.

His mouth and body crash to mine. Hands knot through my hair. I scratch my fingers up his back, over the fine cotton of his dress shirt, and moan into his mouth as he delves in with his tongue—lapping and tasting. *Devouring*.

He slips his thumbs under the hem of my camisole, bunching it against my waist, then meets my eyes, seeking silent permission. I lift my arms, and in one smooth sweep, he pulls the satin over my head and flings it to the floor.

Ravenous eyes roam my naked chest. The backs of his fingers graze down the sides of my breasts. "Christ," he whispers, ragged and breathy. He flickers his gaze to mine, then down again and slides his hands over the full mounds, circling each pointy pink nipple with his thumbs before pinching them. I gasp, but the shock of pain fires south, making my knees press together and squirm. "Lie back down," he says.

So I do. I settle across the width of my bed with my knees bent over the edge, while Cole sinks to his on the plush carpet at my feet. Gently, he unties my ice anklet, placing a kiss on the numb purple bruise. Then he hooks his fingers inside the waistband of my pants and meets my eyes again.

My heart jackhammers, but I lift my hips, allowing him access to slip them off. I'm bare underneath, as Cole fast discovers. "Avery," he says again, swallowing hard. And the gritty, hungry way he does sets my skin on fire. I'm naked—vulnerable—while he's still fully clothed, but he's witnessed my worst and so far rejected nothing.

He runs his strong hands slowly down my ribs and stomach, then out to massage my hips, littering goosebumps across my tingling skin. "You're gorgeous," he whispers as he drinks me in, sliding his hands down my thighs to dip between my knees. The mezzanine air buzzes. My pussy clenches around naught. And Cole searches my face, checking in. Ensuring I'm with him.

I think he's about to do what no man's done to me before—with a light on, no less—but I'm *so* with him. Well . . . 90 percent with him. The other ten churns my stomach and scrambles to ruin every-thing. *What if I taste bad? What if I stink? What if I'm . . . ugly down there?* The shower I had after dinner brings little comfort as the sound of blood rushes through my ears.

"Are you okay?" Cole asks.

"Yeah," I lie. No way I'm letting my fear kill this.

Cole parts my knees and falls still, rubbing two fingers over his bottom lip as he soaks up the view. "Christ," he rasps again before sliding his thumb over my clit and through my folds.

I gasp as warm sparks chase his touch, and a metallic ache throbs deep inside me. With a groan, Cole hitches my knee over his shoul-der, then dives in to lick me in one long sweep. My hips jump, but he clamps them down, plunging his tongue inside me. It's scorching hot, wickedly soft, and deeply intimate, but nothing more so than what he says next. "Watch us in the windows."

My gaze snaps to the ceiling, and I liquify. The naked, desperate siren, grasping hair and grinding against the face of this delicious man isn't me—she's another creature entirely. One ripe with need. In a trance of pleasure. Face flushed and slack with lust. And the suited god between her legs—devouring her like she's his last meal, sucking every morsel of delight, wringing every note of pleasure from her body like he's built for nothing else—is breathtaking.

As Cole moves, his muscles contract, tightening the thin cotton across his back. His fierce grip digs into my soft thighs, and his stubble grazes my most sensitive skin as he laps at my clit, driving me absolutely fucking wild. Thick fingers push inside me, and I moan. "Cole."

Holy fuck.

I melt into the mattress, and a euphoric wave hurls to life. It's insanely intense. Unlike anything I've ever felt. And that scares me to fucking death. "Stop," I gasp. Cole immediately listens as I breathlessly sit up. "Something's not right." The wave recedes over several heavy breaths, but I scoot back to sit against the headboard and hide behind my knees.

Was that what I think it was?

Cole shoots to his feet. "Are you okay?" His confusion ripples through the air and roots inside my bones. Clearly, that's not a reaction he's experienced before.

A heavy fog of shame smothers me. "I'm . . . I'm fine. Sorry." I squeeze my eyes shut and shake my head, wanting to disappear. "It's just . . ."

You're an idiot, Avery. What did you think might happen?

Nothing! Nothing ever happens.

Cole's frown deepens, but he drops to sit beside me, bringing a fluffy blanket from the end of the bed to drape over my shoulders. When he subtly wipes away my glisten from around his mouth, I shrink even more, but he lifts my chin, forcing my eyes to his. "Talk to me, Aves."

It's the first time he's used my nickname, and it washes over me like warm aloe balm. My mild yet strange, tangy scent floats from his lips. I've never felt more exposed—naked in every terrifying way possible. I almost lost control in front of him. Hell knows what he might have witnessed then.

Inhaling through my nose, I stare at the pointy part of his collar. "I'm sorry. It's just . . . that's never happened before. Even when . . . I've tried." My cheeks are lava, but the words still tumble free. "I thought something was wrong with me. You caught me by surprise, that's all. And I never imagined it would feel like so . . . much."

Cole blinks rapidly. "Are you a virgin?"

"No," I say, "but Slade never . . ." My words trail off, and I chance meeting his eyes, cringing. A million emotions flash through them—anger one of them.

Anger. I hope that's not for me.

Cole's jaw twitches, but he covers my hand with his. "He never made you come." His candour incinerates me, and I stare at the rumpled quilt. "Listen to me, nothing is wrong with you," he says, picking up my chin. His dark gaze bores into mine. "That's just what happens when you fuck boys instead of men."

The gritty yet eloquent way he says "fuck" does things to me. Dark, needy things. Fixating on his mouth, I lick my lips. I need to taste him—to swallow the words that claimed me unflawed before they disappear.

I lean in, and Cole captures my mouth, delivering a soft and searing kiss that pools between my legs. Knotting my fingers through his hair, I drag him on top of me and lay us down. He settles between my thighs, covering my body with his comforting weight. His arousal grinds against my core through the thin wool of his pants, and I roll my hips, making him groan against my mouth.

The intense ache returns, pulsing its hunger through my pelvis. Zingy and raw, my nerve endings fight to reclaim their peak and beg me to relinquish control—*to trust*. And soon enough, they win. "I need you inside me," I whisper. So badly I could scream.

Cole stops to look me square in the eye. "Are you sure?"

"Positive." I tug at his shirt, freeing it from his pants, and fumble to undo the small clear buttons. Cole helps me, then yanks it off and tosses it to the floor, crashing his bare chest skin to skin with mine. He feels warm and safe, like a suit of armour made of sunshine. My hands roam his chest—so smooth and deliciously hard—grazing over his tight tawny nipples. I run my mouth across his collarbone and kiss up the front of his neck. He tastes like warm salted caramel—smells earthy and clean, like a forest after rain—and I die a little inside.

"Let me show you how you should be loved," he whispers roughly in my ear before biting it hard enough to hurt.

The action floods me with heat. "Please," I breathe.

His belt buckle jangles as our greedy hands fumble to undo it, and when it finally frees, Cole flashes me a sweet, horny grin that I return. He evokes an ease I've never known—a pull to just be me—feelings of friendship and raging lust I never thought could mix.

I undo his button and zipper while he strokes the side of my face with his thumb. "I love these hyper-colour cheeks," he says. "They tell me more than you'd ever want me to know."

My cheeks burn hotter, and I cover them with my hands, cursing their traitorous ways. Sitting back on his knees, Cole laughs but tugs down my wrists. "Don't hide from me. I want to see everything you are." His hooded gaze strips me barer than I already am, and all that's left is surrender.

He slips off his shoes and black socks, then stands to rid his pants, retrieving his wallet and a condom before he does. The small silver square crackles softly in his hand while my heartbeat thumps in my ears.

My sculpture didn't do him justice. It lacks the sentient lustre of him in the flesh. The sheen silking his smooth olive skin. The ripple of light down his abs. The dusting of hair on his chest. The elegant brawn of his thighs. His calm yet commanding presence. *The angle of that lickable V.*

Cole's hardness strains against the fabric of his navy-blue trunks, prodding at the embossed waistband. He's long and thick—bigger than what I've known—and I bite my bottom lip.

"Close your eyes," he says.

So I do. With my head resting atop my soft pillow, I feel his stare trace the length of my body—blazing into my skin. One of my legs sits bent up at the knee but, with a nudge, topples out to the side. Cool air hits my wetness with a feathery kiss, letting me know just how exposed I am. The bed shifts, and I hear foil crinkle.

Cole covers me with his delectable weight and trails the head of his cock through my juices, causing us to groan. He pushes inside me, swallowing my gasp before releasing one of his own. "Aves," he says.

"Cole," I whimper.

No shyness remains, only an incessant drive to bathe in every sensation of him. My breasts heave towards him as he sucks a nipple into his hot mouth. He bites there too, delivering pain-edged bliss, and I moan.

He fucks into me with vigour while I watch the filthy scene above. I encircle his hips with my legs and dig my nails into his back. My feet bounce against his thighs with each smooth, delicious thrust.

The wave returns, filling me with liquid gold, and my breath hitches. "Oh my God." The intensity is too much, like I'll explode into another realm. Is this really how it's meant to be?

"That's it." Cole breathes against my neck. "Let go."

His words dissolve the last of my resistance, and my head digs into the pillow as my back arches off the bed. I crash over a cliff higher than Angel Falls, exploding like a glitter bomb. My pussy vices his cock, and Cole grumbles strangled words through several more thrusts before groaning his release against my neck. The primal sound vibrates through my body like it's branding every cell, and in that heavenly second, I'm forever his. Whether he wants me or not.

"Holy hell," I whisper, trying to catch my breath. "That's what I've been missing?" I get it now—the grand lure of sex. Why people obsess and covet—chase and idolise. Write songs, books, and movies about it. Create art. *Ruin lives.*

Cole's sweat-sheened forehead kisses mine as our rapid breaths mingle. "Aves," he whispers. He pulls back a little to stare at me, tucking away wisps of my hair. "That was . . ."

He searches for a word that doesn't exist, and I sink deep into his green eyes, drowning in every emotion swirling through them. "I know," I say, smiling gently.

Cole drops a tender kiss to my forehead, then slides himself out of me and sits back on his knees. He removes the condom, then climbs off the bed and picks up my melting bundle of ice. "How's your ankle?"

I'd forgotten. Sitting up, I wriggle my foot. "Barely a twinge." Jokingly, I arch a brow. "Can orgasms heal injuries?"

Cole chuckles. "Hospitals would be way more fun if they could." He holds up the ice bundle. "I'll be right back."

I watch as he descends the stairs and again when he returns, sans the condom and tea towel but with a bottle of water in one hand. He tips it towards me in a silent offer, but I shake my head and continue to stare, committing every nuance of his potent masculinity to memory.

The mattress dips as he takes a seat off the side to drink. The tattooed jungle flourishes all the way up to his shoulder with feathery leaves, rainbow birds, and more hibiscus flowers. But immersed in the middle, in the centre of his upper arm, stands the focal point of the piece—a stoic and serene tiger.

I shift closer and run my hand over it. The line work is clean. The shading smooth. Whoever did it has serious talent. "This is stunning. Did you design it?"

"My mother did," Cole says, recapping the bottle and setting it down. "It's a replica of the mural she painted on my bedroom wall as a kid. She was an artist." He flashes a sad smile over his shoulder. "Like you."

"Was?" I frown.

"Was," he confirms, looking at the floor. "She passed away."

"I'm so sorry," I whisper.

We're quiet for a long minute. I continue to rub his colourful shoulder, pressing in my thumb to ease the knots. I guess that means Hannah is motherless too. "My dad was a writer," I confess with immediate regret. *A writer and my favourite human.*

Cole searches my face, verifies what he already knows, then clenches his jaw. "I'm sorry too."

Quiet sombreness leaks from us both like oil into a pristine lake, so I scramble to change the subject. Fast. "Who is Miss Blue Satin Sparkles?" *Fuck.* Of all the things to blurt out.

Cole shifts to face me properly. "Who?"

"Never mind." I shudder.

Cole narrows his eyes. "Uh-uh. You're not backing out of that one." He gently nudges me with his elbow. "Spill."

I stare at my stripy quilt and cringe. "That woman outside the Bellcat. She was at work the other day too. You said she was just a client, but you were with her at two a.m."

"Miss Blue Satin Sparkles?" Cole's laugh vibrates through the bed, and he grins like a Cheshire cat before composing himself into *naked* Managing Partner Cole. "Vivian Beck is a client who asked me to attend her charity event to discuss business with prospective donors. And I promise you, that name is far too kind for her."

Still, my molars clench. "She has designs on you."

"Oh, I'm aware," Cole says, "but she also has claws, and she's as cold as a shark. But her father was a close friend of my uncle's, and they're a client we need to keep."

I trace small figure eights on the bedsheet between us. "Have you . . . slept with her?"

"Hell no." He climbs back under the covers, ushering me under with him. We lie face to face, his head resting atop a bent arm and turquoise pillow I'll never again wash. He brushes his fingertips up and down my shoulder and stares at me like I'm a miracle he's dreamt to life. "It's actually been a while since I've touched anyone. I work a lot, and since Gerard died, well, it's been the last thing on my mind. Until recently, that is." Cole's dirty, flirty smirk hits me right between my legs. "Vivian isn't my type either, so don't worry."

A hopeless sigh escapes me. Even her name is classy. "How is she not your type?"

Cole squiggles his brows. "Did you not catch the cold shark part?"

"Fair point," I concede with a rueful smile. I snuggle in closer, rejoining our naked skin, and Cole arranges my leg over his hip, pressing his knee up against my sex. My pelvis rolls of its own volition, and flames lick deep in his eyes.

"Do you want to know what I like, Angel?" he asks.

Angel.

I nod.

"I like deep, and soft, and honest. You don't often find that in my world. Smart is usually the limit, not the start."

God, those words. That low, raspy voice. This man could make me orgasm from them alone.

"I'm sorry," I say, crinkling my nose. "I killed our whole vibe. That question should have stayed locked inside my brain."

"Bollocks," Cole says. "We're involved. Ask me whatever you want."

"Involved?" I jiggle my brows and smirk.

"Very," he gruffs. "Besides, you're cute when you're jealous. I get to see that crooked little scowl." I open my mouth to protest, but he presses a finger to my lips. "And for the record, I'm the same with you, if you haven't noticed."

I'd kind of noticed. The whole Tej reprimand—the multiple standoffs with Slade. I just couldn't believe what I was seeing, let alone understand it. "You don't need to worry about me. I don't have attractive men falling at my feet, vying for my attention, like women do you."

He gives me a doubtful look. "Ah, yes, you do. Slade Pearson. Tej Patil. Mike Reynolds. Jed Holston. Should I continue?" The names are counted on different fingers and delivered with a hint of venom I quite like.

I perch up on my elbow, resting my head in my palm. "Mike Reynolds—Alex's dad? But he's married. And who the hell is Jed Holston?"

Cole's jaw tightens. "Mike is separated. Jed is Lily's dad and on the cusp of being fired. And yes, I've had to tell them multiple times to shut up about you and Hannah around the coffee machine in the mornings."

"Seriously?" My shock is real, but I can't stop a smile from peeling across my face. The revelation is . . . flattering. "I thought they were just being nice."

Cole scoffs. "Those two men are anything but nice."

"Well," I say, dragging a finger up his chest to bop his nose. "Slade is history. And you have the wrong take on Tej."

"We'll have to agree to disagree on that," he says, and the possessiveness in his voice twirls around my belly. It seems we're as bad as each other, which is comforting. His crazy might cancel out mine.

"Like I said, you have nothing to worry about." I drag the backs of my fingers across his stubble. "I'm actually a little obsessed with you." My admission is gentle and guarded, but all coyness disintegrates when Cole grabs my wrists and pins them to my pillow, mounting me in one swift move.

"I'll have to fix that," he says, playfully nibbling down my neck. I giggle. "Fix what?"

He continues his assault, peppering wet kisses all over my cheeks and chin. "A little obsessed won't cut it, I'm afraid. I want you consumed." *Kiss*. "Owned." *Kiss*. "Infatuated." He comes back up to meet my eyes, severity in his. "Like I am with you."

His confession sinks into my veins, delivering the bliss I imagine heroin might, and I search his face while a desperate need to keep him close bubbles up inside me. "Stay with me tonight?" My heart batters my ribs. Slade never stayed. He came and went while the night loomed like a nocturnal beast allergic to light.

But Cole's smile is warm and cosy—his kiss to my temple grateful. "I'd like that."

Fourteen

When I asked Cole to stay, it didn't occur to me we'd be going to work together this morning . . . like a proper couple . . . out in the open for anyone to see.

I scurry to keep pace with his long strides through the dim car park behind Benedict's. Petrol tinges the air, and my ankle pinches in protest. "Um . . . people will see us together," I point out. "Shouldn't I wait a few minutes and then follow you in?"

Cole stops, abruptly turns, then settles a hand on my shoulder. "Let them see. I've got nothing to hide."

I stare at him, bewildered. "But it's hypocritical. No one else can date."

Cole twists his mouth into a dark smile. "They all screw like college kids on ecstasy."

My eyes bug. "You *know*?"

"Of course I know. I'm not an idiot."

But panic still pings through my chest, and I drop my gaze to the sparkling concrete marred with tyre marks and dark splotches of unknown origin. "But think about it, what will people say? You're the boss—nine years my senior—and I work at . . . Mini-Bees."

"What's wrong with Mini-Bees?" Cole's knuckles whiten around the handle of his briefcase.

"Nothing," I quickly say. "It's just . . . you're out of my league. I mean, it's so obvious you can do better. Aren't you . . . embarrassed?" Hell, I'm embarrassed *for* him.

Cole's face pales. "Embarrassed? By *you*?"

"Yes," I hiss, and it takes strength not to roll my eyes at his deliberate obtuseness. He's smarter than this and usually more direct.

Cole studies me, his head tilted. Brow sliced by that line. "What league are you referring to? The make-believe one in your head?"

He brushes his thumb over my temple, but I sigh. "Social hierarchies and class systems are a fact of life. Don't pretend you're oblivious and haven't considered my place."

The muscle in his jaw ticks. "Aves, none of my colleagues could do what you and Hannah do all day. They would go mad by the week's end. And at your age, I wasn't a lawyer. I wasn't a managing partner or even a decent human. I'm here because of my uncle, and everybody knows it."

His admission jolts me, but he softens his voice as he continues. "I know who you are—what one day you could be—and I'm not, nor will I ever be, embarrassed by you. How could you think that?"

My shoulders slump. For a hundred reasons, and one more than most. "The way we met for a start." Swallowing, I frown at our shoes. My disco glitter boots to his sleek, sophisticated leather.

Cole steps one long foot between mine and brushes away loose strands of hair from my vision. "Don't let one mistake define you. If everyone did, we'd all be screwed."

My chest unknots a little, and with a half smile, I glance up. "Would you give that same advice to a murderer?"

He huffs. "You are not a murderer."

"I'll bet some ants and spiders would beg to differ," I singsong, and Cole's dimple flashes. "In any event, you could still get in trouble. We're not parity colleagues."

"I'd argue we're not colleagues at all. Mini-Bees is a separate business, and my role is . . . unofficial."

I cock a brow. "Yet Benedict's company policy manual still applies?"

He leans in closer to my ear. "That wasn't my finest moment, and we both know what fuelled it."

Oh yes. Irrationality. Jealousy. The endearing qualities we seem to share. "People will still talk." I shrug. "Judge and begrudge."

Cole knits his brows mirthfully. "You didn't consider all this before pouncing on me last weekend?"

My cheeks smoulder, but I can't help but smile. Considering anything beyond the taste of his lips wasn't a priority. And in fairness, I never dreamt we'd end up here. "Not my finest moment," I reply, recycling his words before biting the inside of my cheek.

"I disagree," Cole says, pressing his chest to mine. "I found it extremely fine." His deep voice settles between my legs, igniting memories of last night while his fingertips skate down my spine. "Listen, when my colleagues work eighty-hour weeks—pull in half the revenue—eat, sleep, control, and breathe Benedict's like I do, they, too, can do whatever they want. And I'll fire anyone who dares look at you the wrong way." He lifts my chin, and his eyes sparkle like dew-kissed spearmint leaves. "Okay?"

My gaze flickers to his mouth, and I lick my lips. "I don't think that's legal."

A smug smile peels across his face. "How about you let me worry about what's legal and not, hmm?"

I huff a soft laugh, and Cole drops a gentle kiss to my forehead, slowly, like he's bestowing wisdom. "Good. Now let's go. I'm late."

"It's seven-thirty."

"Exactly," he says, setting charge up the car park exit ramp.

Chantel eyes us as we enter the brass doors to Benedict's, but her expression remains neutral. "Good morning Mr. Benedict, Ms. Masters."

"Good morning, Chantel." Cole doesn't spare her a glance as he strides through the gleaming foyer. I, on the other hand, smile and wave like an awkward moron. The faint smell of disinfectant and the wet floor sign suggest Bernie's nearby. Usually, I get to say hello, but usually I arrive thirty minutes from now when he's packing up for the day.

We turn the corner, and Mini-Bees appears. The golden elevator stands opposite, mirroring the monochrome terrazzo sweeping down the hall. Hannah and Tej are there, along with two suits depositing their offspring. Hannah catches my eye with a smirk, then winks, while Cole merely glares ahead, game face on as he summons his inner snowman for the day.

"Well, I'll see you later," I say as I veer off towards the door, not wanting to interrupt his process. But a hand locks around my wrist.

"Wait," Cole says, tugging me back to face him. He glares hard over my shoulder towards Mini-Bees and then crashes his lips to mine, clutching the back of my head as he feasts on my mouth like no one in public should. My knees weaken, and my body melts against his. If he doesn't stop in precisely three seconds, I'll ride him right here in the hall.

Thankfully, Cole does stop, but then he whispers in my ear, "I'll be at your house tomorrow night. Say hello to Mike for me."

"What?" I ask as I gather my wits, but Cole's already tucked inside the elevator by then, his dark smirk glimmering as the doors glide shut.

Frowning, I turn to catch Hannah, Tej, and Mike Reynolds all staring before their gazes scatter like sprayed cockroaches. Hannah cups a giggle in her hand, and Tej's brows climb higher than Snoop Dogg.

But Mike's reaction is the best. His face shines beetroot as he squats to kiss Alex goodbye.

I feel my cheeks follow suit and gulp. *Cole.* That cheeky devil. Staking his claim for all to see. He could have bonked me on the head, hitched me over his shoulder, and paraded me around caveman-style and it would have been far more subtle. And . . . I adore him for it.

As the door to Mini-Bees clicks shut, Mike rushes past me, averting his eyes as he mumbles my name. I bite back a grin. Maybe Cole was right about him.

I rest the small soldering iron inside its coil, flick off the power, then roll back on my stool. My first five pieces survived bisque firing, but *High Heart Symphony*—what I've named the lovers—and *Girl, Take Me*—the bleeding-heart piece before that—aren't close to bone dry. And if they go into the kiln even slightly wet, they could explode, so I'll wait a couple weeks to be safe.

I've finished the metal- and wire work for all seven. Coils and nests of copper. Tin-plate fragments woven through a webbed canopy of fine silver. A delicate crimped-wing butterfly. Two wire-spun hearts. Nothing will be attached until after the glaze fire, but things are taking shape, and honestly, I'm excited. More so than I've ever been about my work. So much, in fact, I snap a photo of the copper hearts to send to Jen. Her reply is immediate.

Jen:
Hearts? You send me hearts?
I'm still waiting for that steamy pic of lover boy.

I laugh. I've only told Jen about that photo and our first magical kiss, but she's nearly as excited as me and now persistently curious.

Me:
Don't hold your breath.

Jen:
Rude. Sharing is caring, remember?

With perfect timing, a knock sounds at the front door.
Finally.

As I pad through the gallery, I double check my phone. Ten p.m. Cole wasn't lying about eighty-hour weeks. He pulls that easy.

"I was starting to think you weren't—"

I'm pushed up against the wall, the end of my sentence swallowed by Cole's mouth as soon as I open the door. The ripe heat of his kiss rushes through my veins, but it ends with a weary smile. "Hey, you," he says, stroking my cheek. He looks a little pale too.

"Hey, yourself. That was quite the welcome."

"Only for you." He winks.

Playfully, I frown. "You mean your other clients miss out? That's hardly fair."

Cole chuckles, and a spark of vitality seems to return. "They'll live." He catches my mouth again, and I run my hands over his shoulders and down his back, relishing the warmth still trapped in his suit thanks to the Audi's heated seats.

"What's that smell?" he asks, lifting his chin to better sniff the air.

"That's the sweet scent of metal fusion," I say before his quizzical look prompts me to clarify. "Soldering."

"What are you soldering?"

"My sculptures usually include metalwork," I say with a shrug.

His brows rise, and he gives my waist a quick squeeze. "Show me."

Stepping back, I shake my head. "Uh-uh. No way. I don't *show* people." Beth excluded, for unavoidable reasons. "And anyway, they're works in progress."

Cole considers me. "That sounds like a challenge."

But I dismiss him with a laugh and head for the kitchen. After shutting the front door, he follows. The metal stage of my work comes with the benefit of me not ending up covered in mud. So, for once, I'm clean enough for company.

Cole leans against the kitchen door frame, pocketing his hands so his navy jacket splays open in that business-chic cover-model way—one shiny black shoe crossed over the other. I hold up a frosty bottle of water from the fridge in a silent offer he accepts.

"I'm glad you got home safe," he says, taking it from my hand. "I don't like the idea of you on public transport at night alone."

My belly twirls. He's worried. *About me.*

"It's fine," I say, coming to lean against the island. "There are mostly the same commuters every night, and the tram stops right around the corner."

His throat bobs as he drinks. Capping the bottle, he shakes his head. "I still don't like it. I'll have to teach you to drive so you can license up."

I cock a brow. "How do you know I don't already have it?"

"Do you?"

"Well, no. But even if I did, I'd still catch the tram. City traffic is too nuts for me."

Cole comes closer, resting his water on the granite next to me. "Are you always this difficult?"

I swallow but look him square in the eye. "If you mean to control? Yeah. The whole freedom thing is pretty important to me, as you might imagine."

He cages me against the island, bracing his hands either side of my hips. His minty breath feathers my face, and his racy smile trembles my knees. "So much sass, young lady. I'm trying to protect you—not control you." He kisses the shell of my ear, sending shivers down my spine, then drags his nose up my neck. "Have you christened this bench yet?"

"I think you know the answer to that," I whisper.

Cole lifts my waist and plants me on the cold granite, then settles between my straddled legs. "Good."

The brass pendant light hovers just above my head, gilding his dark-rum-coloured hair, and his hardness presses against my crotch, sending flurries through my pelvis. I marvel at how perfectly we fit. How well standard kitchen benchtop height would accommodate sex. Is it deliberate? A tried and tested design choice? Eighty to a hundred centimetres will work, but ninety is optimal fucking height, so we'll go with that? Maybe. Or maybe at six foot one, Cole's the perfect height.

Yesterday morning returns to me, triggering a grin. "I never got to pass on your hello to Mike, by the way. Sorry about that."

Cole laughs at the ceiling and rubs the outsides of my thighs, generating heat through the stretchy fabric. "You should have seen his face. I'd forfeit my partnership to see that again."

His satisfaction is tangible, but I teasingly scold him. "Are you happy with yourself?"

"Very." He nods. "That was an efficient way to deliver a message Mike needed to hear." The green in Cole's eyes seems to intensify as his humour fades away. "You're mine, Aves."

Silence floats between us, and I fidget with his lapels. "Does that mean you're mine too? . . . Exclusively?" I have to ask. I've been burnt before, and I'm not setting myself up again.

"I don't share," Cole gently says, "and I wouldn't expect you to either."

I lean forward to press my lips to his, catching his top one between my teeth to gently bite and suck. I inhale his clean, earthy scent beneath the faded cologne and savour the scratch of his stubble—the pleasant taste of his mouth. He cups the back of my neck, dives in harder, and groans. I'll never tire of kissing him. Even decades from now.

Cole rests his forehead against mine, and I bite my bottom lip. "I still don't think the kids needed to witness that display."

He shakes with a quiet chuckle. "They were occupied. And besides, there's nothing wrong with a little kiss."

"A *little* kiss?" I laugh, but he trails his fingers up the inside of my thigh, brushing over my sex before dipping into the waistband of my yoga pants.

His eyes darken as he slips his hand inside my knickers, eliciting a gasp. My head tilts back, my breath hitching, as his fingers enter me—sliding in and out. Rubbing that swoon-worthy spot I love so much. Aftershocks of Thursday night have rippled through me ever since, and I'm wet. Really fucking wet. I yank his head towards mine and devour his mouth like he is life essence itself.

"That's it," he says, and the gruffness alone amps up my impending orgasm.

"Oh God." I'm a breathy, needy mess on the cusp of obliteration, and I'm dying to feel it again. To ensure it wasn't a fluke—a one-night-only event I'll never again know.

But Cole's movements slow just as I need him to keep pace, then his warm breath tickles my ear. "Will you show me your studio?"

"What?" I ask at the top of a gasping breath.

"You heard me."

Heat swirls through my body, and I moan. So close. If he could just—

"Answer me," he says.

I shake my head, finding a semblance of rational thought. "No."

But the second the breathy word leaves my lips, his fingers and body weight vanish. My eyes pop open as I leave the blissful fog, and I take in his stance. The slight tilt of his head. His calm yet defiant expression. That teasing, lopsided smirk.

"Are you serious?" I hiss. "You're blackmailing me?"

"Coercing at most," he corrects.

I blink a few times, processing, then stare at my thighs where they squish against the benchtop, twice their usual size. My face burns, and irritation spatters through my chest. I hop down from the island, my bare feet hitting the cold tiles with a slap, then push past Cole towards the bathroom. "You should go. I don't negotiate with terrorists."

He snorts a laugh. "Aves, come on." His footsteps follow me down the gallery hall. "Don't have a tantrum."

A tantrum? A fucking tantrum! *The nerve*.

I spin around and poke my finger into his hard chest, gritting my words. "I am not having a fucking tantrum."

Well, maybe I am. A little. And considering I deprived myself of the same thing forty-eight hours ago, I'm not handling this well. But that was before. Before I tasted inconceivable ecstasy. Before I knew what bodies could do. Before I experienced it with *him*. I'm so pent-up I could scream.

Cole smirks, but I itch to wipe it off his smug face. Why does he have to look so delicious while being so annoying? And why do a few orgasms grant him this much power? God, I need to buy a vibrator. *Stat*.

He raises his hands in an open-palm surrender. "I'm sorry, okay? I was just playing."

I frown. "You took me right to the brink and then left me with . . . nothing. That's so . . ." I shake my head, grinding my teeth. "Mean!" My bottom lip quivers, and I mentally facepalm. What the fuck is wrong with me?

With a chuckle, Cole steps in to kiss my forehead. "Christ. Remind me never to deny you an orgasm again. It's like I've killed your puppy." He kisses my lips, and to my annoyance, I melt into him. "Turn around and face the wall. I'll make it better." His promise dissolves my pride, so I comply. I'm on the brink of bursting with something, and it may as well be pleasure.

"I'm not showing you my studio," I whisper to the wall.

"Why?" Cole slides down my pants and knickers, kissing and biting my bum cheeks. Tracing my spine with his tongue on the way up. He sounds wounded, which wrenches my chest.

Because he'll see I really am obsessed. That I'm in free fall, like a skydiver without a chute. Because he'll see all my hurt—my love—my crazy. He'll see . . . *me*.

"Because." My voice cracks.

He must sense the onslaught of thoughts spinning through my head. "It's okay. You can show me whenever you're ready." He slides his mouth down the side of my neck, teeth grazing, tongue tasting. A warm hand slips up the front of my jumper, squeezing my breast, pinching my nipple. I hear the jangle of his belt—his zip opening. The sound of crinkling foil. "Place your hands up against the wall."

My purple fingernails shimmer against the stark white wall as a topless woman stares down at me from her golden canvas. Pulling my hips back towards him, Cole sinks into me, biting my shoulder and running his hot breath up my neck. "Better?" he rasps.

I rest my head back on his shoulder and moan. "Yes." The angle. The depth. The man. Pure. Heaven.

He slides his broad hand up the wall to cover mine and entwines our fingers as he thrusts into me. "You feel divine," he says, and the words dance through my mind, tango with arousal, and morph into everything.

The orgasm slams through me with double force, and I ride out the waves, cursing Cole's name.

"Turn around to face me." Cole pulls out, and I do as he says. He hitches up my knees and re-enters me, wrapping my legs around his hips, ramming me hard against the wall.

"Come home with me next Saturday," he breathes, grinding against my clit, conjuring a delicious second wave.

"I'd like that," I manage to say.

The canvas bangs against the plasterboard with every smooth thrust, and Cole stares into my eyes, bracing one forearm near my head, grazing my scalp with his thumb. Silent, tender words fill his gaze, connecting with the ones building inside me.

His breathing grows ragged. "Come with me."

And as though he's trained my body, I do. In perfect synchrony with him.

Fifteen

Cole navigates the narrow, windy road with ease as we ascend into the hills en route to his house. A luminous amber cliff soars up to our right, lined with metal mesh to control any rocks, while a death gully plunges down to the left, disguised with waxy leaves glistening in dappled sunlight.

I admire Cole's profile. The straight Roman line of his nose. The shadow of stubble darkening his jaw. The curve of his full lips. He grips the steering wheel at ten and two, and there's something beautiful about being at his mercy.

"You're staring at me," he says.

I wriggle in my heated seat. Warmth seeps through my jeans and puffer jacket like a big, cosy hug. "Yeah, and for once you can't dissect my thoughts with those pretty X-ray eyes."

He bats his dark lashes and spares me a quick glance. "You think they're pretty?"

"Ridiculously." I grin, and his dimple flashes.

Cole runs a hand down my thigh, giving it a quick squeeze. "Thanks for coming."

"Thanks for inviting me." Memories of that invite rush back in.

Beth's painting thudding against the wall. His splayed hands pinning mine. The feel of him inside me. I shiver.

Cole hits a blinker, then slows down to turn. Stacked bluestone walls sentry his driveway, holding open a rusty cast-iron gate. Gravel crunches under the tyres, and emerald trees canopy the trail with a glow of feathery leaves until we curve further up the grassy hill.

A sleek timber cabin comes into view, sitting at the crest. Glass spans its entire front wall, and a butterfly-winged roof sits lightly on top as if ready to fly. An elevated deck juts out the front. A pointy oversize eave shades a rattan suite, so I turn in my seat to admire its view. Misty, lush green hills. Endless trees. Tiny houses dotted across paddocks. I gawk up at Cole. "*This* is your house?" Only architects live in places like this.

Cole shrugs. "It's peaceful up here. The opposite of Benedict's."

The garage stands off to the right and lights up when the panel door shudders down behind us. Cole kills the engine and unlatches my seatbelt with a shy smile. "The stairs are right over there. Follow me."

We climb twelve reeded steps up to the jutting deck, and the view expands. Beyond the rolling pastures, in a faraway blue haze, the rugged Yarra Valley Ranges swallow the horizon, looking too glorious to be real.

Cole ushers me through the glass front door into a warm open room with polished concrete floors. A black elliptical fireplace hovers above the ground in the middle, diffusing a rich, smoky scent, and rumpled tan leather sofas—worn in like a beloved old book—slouch around it. A matte black kitchen runs across the far end wall, oozing masculinity, and cedar panels clad a soaring ceiling that Beth would simply adore. "Wow," I whisper.

The corner of Cole's mouth twitches with a smile. "I'm going to lose the suit. Make yourself at home." He heads towards a door that presumably leads to his bedroom, but rather than follow him, I amble to the fireplace and hover my hands over the top. Framed photographs hang on a narrow section of nearby wall. Black-and-white portraits of Hannah chuckling with ponytailed hair. Ella with a cheeky cookie-thief grin. A man I recognise as Cole's Uncle Gerard. And another lady—an older version of Hannah—with wavy dark hair and pale eyes that shine with wit. Their mother. She has to be. Hannah's resemblance is uncanny.

A low bookshelf stands near the sofas below three canvas paintings, so I mosey on over. Antique scales sit on top, balanced with brass weights, next to a world globe that I gently spin. Non-fiction books line the shelves. Law. History. Philosophy and art. Some old, some new, but all ordered by height and shelved by topic. The man is fastidious.

Cole returns dressed similar to me—dark jeans, knitted jumper, hardy boots, and a puffy black jacket. Not the sloppy home attire I typically choose, but he looks so fine my chest flutters. I nod towards the middle canvas. "That's a beautiful painting of Ella. Who did it?"

Cole's smile falters. "My mum."

My heart hiccups, and I look back to the painting. Ella isn't much younger than she is now. I shake my head. "I'm sorry. I didn't know it happened so recently." His mother and uncle—all in the space of what—a year? The poor guy.

Cole drops his gaze to the floor and buries his hands in his jacket pockets. He shakes his head. "It wasn't. Mum passed away twelve years ago. Ovarian cancer." The information spins around my head but fails to make sense, and a sad smile tugs at Cole's mouth. "When she was really ill, towards the end, a little girl kept visiting her dreams. Mum wanted to paint her, so I set up an easel across her bed, and this is what she painted. Hannah has two more."

My lips part, and I stare at him, speechless, then study the painting again. A lump balls in my throat. "That's the most beautiful thing I've ever heard," I say, glancing back to him.

He smiles at the ground, then meets my eyes. "While we have daylight, I'd love to show you the property. We'll need to scrounge up kindling too."

Rolling with the change of subject, I arch a brow. "Kindling?"

"For the bonfire."

My eyes widen. "We're having a bonfire?"

"Tonight." He shrugs. "If you want. Best way to stargaze. And safe," he adds with a wink.

I smile. I've never been to a bonfire. School camps always happened in summer amid bushfire restrictions and brown snake warnings. "Do you have marshmallows?"

He steps closer and squeezes my shoulders, quirking a brow. "Of course I have marshmallows."

I climb to my tiptoes and press my lips to his. "Let's go, then."

So far as anyone can own nature, Cole owns a forest. Or more aptly, hectares of bushland, sporting gum trees and other Australian natives of all shapes and sizes. The tall and sturdy. The twisted and wrangled. Smaller ones more twig than tree.

Sticks crack under our boots as we hike over bumpy roots and fallen branches. The scent of eucalyptus and damp winter soil soaks the fresh air, and I fill up my lungs, hoping to take some home. There's something magical about this place. A quiet peace and conscious presence. It's like the earth absorbs all worries and emits calm through the soles of your feet.

Cole stops to gather some thin branches and bundles them into a giant blue Ikea bag that could easily fit Alex and Ella. I pass him several more, then dust off my hands on the back of my jeans. In the distance, a black rope dangling from a tree catches my eye, so I squint to better see. "Is that a . . . zip line?"

"Um, yeah," Cole says with zero excitement. Counter to it, in fact.

"Does it work?"

His steps veer left, away from the contraption. "I presume so."

I follow him. "You've never used it?"

"Hannah has a few times."

"How long have you lived here again?"

"Three and a half years."

I halt and plant my hands on my hips. "Three *years* and you've never been so much as tempted?"

He stops and turns to face me. "Once. After too many bourbons, but thankfully, common sense prevailed."

I rub my hands together. "Oh, that's it. We have to try it."

"Oh, no we don't," he says.

"Sure, we do."

He tilts his head with a wry smile. "With all due respect, it's hard to trust the woman who thinks falling off a roof is no big deal."

"It *could* have been a big deal, but it *wasn't*," I clarify.

He stares at me with those eyes, and they burn with flames not yet lit.

A thought jumps into my head. "But wait—your staff retreat. You zip-lined there."

"Not me. I prefer to keep my feet on the ground." Cole narrows his eyes. "Exactly how many staff photos did you snoop through?"

My cheeks burn, but I shrug. "A few." Well, *all* the retreat ones. And the conferences. Award ceremonies. And I've revisited several times since, playing Where's Cole in lieu of Wally, to observe him in his natural habitat amongst fellow suits and polished shoes. That's what happens when someone refuses all social media, thereby blocking the opportunity to stalk. Slade was the same, but I guess he had more sinister reasons. Or an alias, come to think of it.

The corner of Cole's mouth inches up, and I pull out Jen's puppy-dog eyes and join my hands in prayer. "Please," I say, dragging out the word.

He laughs and shakes his head. "I have a sister. That bollocks doesn't work on me."

"Are you sure?" I poke out my bottom lip, completing Jen's technique.

He stares at me, and I watch his resolve evaporate like droplets of water on summer-scorched concrete. "Christ. At least let me grab a helmet."

Not fifteen minutes later, Cole stands atop a weathered timber platform built around the thick trunk of a gum tree, wearing a graphite-coloured helmet more aerodynamic than a futuristic plane. He clutches the zip-line rope above his head, face ashen, chest rising and falling as he grumbles under his breath.

"I can go first," I call up, but he shakes his head, keeping his eyes pinned ahead.

"If the line snaps, I don't want you hurt."

I gulp. Maybe this was a bad idea. Maybe he'll end up injured—*paralysed*. Maybe he'll . . . die, and it will be all my fault. My spine stiffens. "Wait—"

But Cole jumps off the platform, hooks his long legs around the discus seat, and soars through the trees. His shouts fade into the bushland, and I run down the hill, zigzagging my steps to avoid tripping up. My lungs burn by the time I meet him at the end. "Are you okay?"

Snapping the helmet clasp open, he turns to look at me with a brilliant white smile. "That was . . ." His eyes sparkle as he tries to find the word. "Awesome."

"Awesome?" I cock a brow. "I didn't know you knew that word."

"I didn't, until then." Cole lifts the helmet off his head and plonks it on top of mine. He clips it shut and tightens the straps, then bops the end of my nose with his fingertip. "It's your turn."

We hike back up the hill, dragging the zip-line rope behind us. "I'm glad you're here," Cole says, and his smile is incandescent.

"Me too." Then I nod towards the zip line. "Not for much longer, perhaps."

"*Now* she's nervous." He laughs and nudges me with his shoulder. "Don't worry, it felt solid, and I'll catch you at the bottom."

I wince. "Please watch out. I'm not known for coordination. With my luck, I'll accidentally knock you out or break something."

"I've noticed." He chuckles. "Your nerves hijack you."

I nod. "I know."

"It's cute."

His smitten grin flips my belly, and I look at my dirt-caked Docs, smiling. "I'm glad you think so."

We make it back to the towering gum, and Cole spots me as I climb the silvered wooden steps pinned to the trunk with nails that bleed rust. He swings the zip line towards me once I reach the platform, and I catch it, throwing my weight behind so I'm not dragged overboard. It's higher up here than it looks from the ground. Kookaburras sing, and sun-kissed treetops glimmer and rustle in the breeze like cheerleading pom-poms. I could so live here.

"Give me a two-minute head start," Cole says before jogging down the hill. There's life in his steps. A sprightly energy he rarely carries, and it's beautiful to see. He often seems so much older than twenty-seven, weighed down by responsibility and grief. But maybe that's why we're drawn to each other—our dark and broken parts fit.

I consciously breathe in the fresh air again until Cole's voice carries up the hill. At least if I die, I've experienced him. I count to three, then jump from the platform. My butt finds the small seat, and I angle my legs straight out like a Barbie doll. Cold wind whips through my hair and swooshes over my skin like jetted water. Branches barrel towards me with the illusion we'll collide, but I whizz by unscathed. Squeals leave my throat, and Cole grows bigger and bigger as I race towards him. I squeeze my eyes shut, bracing for impact, then feel padded arms lock around my waist, ripping me from the seat. We tumble to the bushland floor, and I land on top of him, panting around a fit of giggles, my nose an inch from his. "That was fucking wild."

Cole grins at me, and his joy curls through my chest, squeezing my heart. "Language, Miss Masters." He winks, and I play-punch his arm as he pulls me down for a kiss. The helmet objects. With a growl, Cole unclips and frisbees it away, then grips the nape of my neck and smashes my mouth to his.

Our noses are cold, our mouths soft and warm. The fresh forest air sinks into our skin. We dive into each other and roll around, gathering twigs in our hair and dirt on our clothes.

Cole stares at me when we part, and our eyes silently converse— confiding in each other. Sharing secrets yet to find words. "Thank you," I say.

He cups my cheeks. "For what?"

For sharing you. For liking me. For saving my butt and seeing past my crazy.

"For everything."

His eyes shine as they search mine, but I climb to my feet. If I stay any longer, I might say something that ruins everything.

Three hours later, flames curl and leap into the inky black sky, and the firewood cracks as sap boils and explodes. I lie on my back next to Cole under a thick quilt that smells like him on the daybed cushions we carried down from the deck. Dirty plates and mugs lie in the dirt nearby with an empty marshmallow packet, charred toasting sticks, and our scattered boots.

The clouds have thinned, and stars blanket the night like a million tiny portals to heaven. "There's no comparison," I say. "There's a gazillion more out here." My words frost in the winter air as I stare up, absorbing every ounce of awe. "It's humbling."

Cole shifts, and I feel the heat of his gaze on me. "That's my favourite look on you, you know." I turn my face to his, and he smiles softly, running his thumb across the rise of my cheek. "That spark of wonderment in your eyes when you find beauty in something. It's breathtaking."

My face heats, and my insides melt, but I flash him a lopsided grin. "I would have thought it was my orgasm face."

Cole laughs. "That's a very close second." He touches his mouth to mine. "And I'm lucky to be the only one who's seen it."

I press my knees together, and my body tingles like I'm filled with lemonade. Cole's words spark so much hope inside me. His reverence infects my blood and forges new pathways in my brain. One's lined with daisies and sunshine instead of oil slicks and broken glass. "How did you get to be you?" I whisper. "So strong and smart, yet kind and humble?"

Cole's smile melts away, and he turns to the stars. "I'm not perfect, Aves. There are things I regret—events I wish I could undo. You see only the good, but everyone has a shadow, including me."

Whoa. That turned dark fast. "So you suck at taking compliments too, I see."

A smile tugs at his lips. Again, he looks at me. "What do you love about sculpting?"

I exhale a heavy sigh and stare at the moon, trying to formulate words. "Clay is my armour. It siphons pain and creates beauty. Turns the invisible tangible. Makes the unbearable manageable."

There's a beat of silence. "Spoken like a true artist." A smile laces his voice. "So what do you do with everything you make?"

I've been asking myself that same question. At some point, the studio will be full, and then what? "That's the hard part. I don't know what to do. At school, every piece was put into local shows and amateur competitions. Some even sold, and I didn't care. In fact, I loved it. But now . . ." I inhale through my nose. "Now it all feels so much more personal. It's the real world, and I'm . . . scared."

"Of what?"

"Judgement. Exposure. Criticism. My work keeps me sane. For a while I stopped, and everything got worse. I can't afford to lose it, and if I step out into the world and it cuts me down, I might."

Crickets chirp, flames flicker, and I look up at Cole. He's frowning, that line pressed deep between his brows. I rub it away with my thumb like I've longed to so many times, and he grabs my wrist and kisses the heel of my palm. "Are you any good?" he asks.

With a nervous titter, I shrug. "Apparently. You read my school reports."

"I'm asking you." Cole's eyes bore into mine, summoning a foreign feeling that pulses in my solar plexus and fills me with gold.

"I'm *really* good."

He presses his palm to my heart. "Then people need to see it. If you love what you do—if it lightens life and helps you breathe—hold on to that when you step out. Do it only for you, then it won't matter what they say."

I love he didn't deny the danger, because it's inevitable. Not everyone will like my work, and art is always critiqued—artists are always exposed. Their hearts hang on gallery walls and bleed on busy floors at risk of being trampled, but that's just part of the job. I've been fighting that reality, willing it to be untrue as if resistance alone could change it. But that battle is futile, and it's time to find a better way.

"I needed to hear that," I say.

Cole plants a kiss on the tip of my cold nose, then whispers against my hair. "You won't crash, Angel. You'll fly."

My heart beats a crazy rhythm. Who is this man? And what did I do to deserve him? Little old fucked-up me? A sickly feeling crawls through my chest—the one that warns me none of this makes sense. The one that stirs unease and claims sanctuary as my intuition, but I'm not sure it is. "What about you?"

"What about me?" Cole asks.

"Are you happy at Benedict's?"

He inhales sharply, then sighs. "Honestly, before my uncle died, I was planning to leave."

"*Really?*"

Cole swallows. "I wanted out, but I didn't know how to tell him."

"Why?" My brows furrow.

"Something was just . . . missing. And I was tired. Really tired."

I ponder his words. "What about now?"

"Now I can't bring myself to dishonour his memory. I owe him more than I'll ever owe anyone."

"Even yourself?" I ask.

Cole falls silent for a pregnant beat, then glances at me, quirking a brow. "You should flip some of that wisdom onto yourself."

"True." I smile. "But it's so much easier to dish out."

A moment later, he speaks again. "Gerard was only fifty-five. Heart attack. It was sudden."

"I'm sorry," I whisper, and his jaw ticks.

"So am I. More than you could know."

Silence falls, but Cole's features remain tense. After a minute, he squeezes his eyes shut and shakes his head as if shucking off a thought.

"Do you have a big family?" I ask, but the air tightens like it's made of elastic.

"Hannah and Ella are my family." Cole's clipped tone knots my stomach.

"I shouldn't be so nosey. Sorry."

The quilt shifts, and Cole sighs. "Don't be. There are just certain things I don't like to discuss."

"Same," I admit. "My dad, for one. To a lesser extent, Mum." I shut down my dad's adoring smile and fuzzy beard the second they materialise. I can't go there tonight.

"Same," Cole says.

He wriggles an arm under me, then pulls us closer. Our padded jackets wisp against each other, and our denim legs entangle. I rest my head high on his chest. Maybe Cole's history is just that. Maybe mine could be too. Maybe it's right to leave the ugly in the past to die and only be judged on who we are now. It's an enticing thought, but the mood has already plummeted. Why do I always fuck things up?

"Aves, there is something I should tell you." Cole's sombre tone triggers that sickly feeling to return, and I don't want it, especially if it causes him pain.

I reach up and press my finger to his lips. "It's okay. I only need to know your now."

Ignoring the clench of his jaw, I snuggle back in and look away, letting nature soak into my bones until the silence returns to comfortable. Under the quilt, our body heat creates a sauna that offsets the chilly air.

"Do you want to sleep out here?" Cole eventually asks. "There's no rain forecast."

Water. The only element missing. I glance up at him. His skin glows amber, and that sprightliness rekindles in his eyes as flames dance in their reflection. I commit the image to memory. "Sounds perfect."

Beyoncé's velvety voice pines through the speaker as I step back from the studio bench, planting my hands on my hips with a sigh. It's been nearly two months of work, but completion is at last in sight and tickling my tongue like sweet popping candy.

I scan over the first five pieces, all finished with copper and steel and rainbow-glazed hair. Each is significant on its own, but together they're starting to tell a story. A story of depletion and futility—heartache and torment—innocence and beauty. *Hope*. They're a solid manifestation of my year to date, and when *High Heart Symphony* and *Girl, Take Me* are complete in a few short weeks, so will be the series.

I drop to the dusty vinyl floor, cross my legs, and stare some more as pride flourishes through my body and tugs at my lips. They're amazing.

Cole's advice from last night rings in my ears: *People need to see it. Do it only for you, and it won't matter what they say.* As I nibble my bottom lip, memories of Beth's optimism follow: *I think I'd like an Avery Masters original in my gallery.* Beth has expensive taste, and the more I recall her reaction that day—reanalyse her tone and micro-expressions—the more I believe her.

My stomach swirls but this time feels different. It's light and tickly and dancing around a deep-rooted sense of knowing, like tiny white butterflies circling a century-old tree. I climb to my knees and snatch my phone from the bench, then clean the camera lens on my stretchy pants. The natural afternoon light spears through the studio window and perfectly illuminates the bench. I take multiple snaps of each piece from varied angles, then plonk down on my jumbo patchwork cushion to edit the best ones. I draft up an eloquent email and attach the photos, research eight local galleries, and register a domain name and the corresponding social handles while I'm at it. Just in case. Then I do what I'm finally ready to do. I bulldoze my fear and hit send.

World, here I am. Do with me what you will.

"You're glowing," Hannah says as she wanders into the Mini-Bees staffroom early Monday. "I don't know whether to be happy for you or disgusted given it's my brother who undoubtably put that goofy look on your face."

She's mostly right. I hang my satchel on my designated hook and grin. "Disgusted, definitely. He did this thing where—"

"Oh God, please don't." Hannah plugs her ears and breaks into a horrible rendition of "Twinkle Twinkle Little Star."

Tugging down her hands, I chuckle. "I'm joking. A lady doesn't kiss and tell."

"Thank God for that," she says with an exaggerated sigh.

I shrug off my jacket and sling it over my bag, then adjust the fall of my floaty dress. Mother Nature has gifted us a glimpse of spring with luminous blue skies and fluffy clouds that make Melbourne sparkle. "Did you have a good weekend?" I ask.

Hannah shrugs a delicate shoulder. "The usual mum stuff. I played with Ella, cleaned my apartment, bought groceries, and watched Netflix." She strains a smile. "As you can see, I'm quite the party girl."

I study her for a beat, then lower my gaze, sensing I'm snooping through her private thoughts. There's sadness there, made all the more obvious by the jittery way she's wringing her hands, but I don't know what to say. I can't imagine being a single mum at our age. I can't even look after myself, let alone a tiny human. Especially one as precious as Ella. "You know, if you ever need a sitter, I'd be happy to help," I settle on. "You could hit the town. Get your single groove on." I waggle my eyebrows, but Hannah scoffs.

"Oh yeah. My brother would *love* that." Sarcasm drips from her silvery voice, and I frown.

"Cole doesn't like babysitting?" The thought saddens me more than it should. "Never mind, I'll do it alone."

"Oh, he likes babysitting just fine, but not so his little sister can go out to get her '*single groove*' on, as you put it." She makes air quotes around my words.

"Seriously?"

With a baby sigh, Hannah winces. "Cole's protective. He's done a lot for us. I don't want to disappoint him, and I get it. The world isn't always a great place, and I have Ella to think about. I'm not the meat market type, anyway. I'd rather a gushy book and quiet night in."

As I stare, silent screams radiate from her like a sonar signal, compelling me to ignore that elaborate justification and help. "Let me deal with Cole," I suggest. "Block out Saturday night in three weeks. That'll give me time to prime him." Red flags ripple at the thought of interfering, but Hannah's a sensible, grown-arse woman. She deserves freedom and to feel her age for once. What is it with her and Cole and their baby-boomer severity?

Her eyes twinkle. "You'd do that for me?"

"Of course."

The identical twin to Cole's dimple puckers her rosy cheek, and she squeezes me into a hug. "Thank you, Aves." Her sunflower scent intensifies, but before I can hug her back, she dashes out to the playroom as if spooked by her own affection. I watch through the glass as she sweeps Ella into a spin, then kisses her chubby cheeks. Regardless of what happens with Cole, I might've found a lifelong friend in Hannah.

Grinning, I dig my phone out from my satchel to see if there are any replies to my emails. Wishful thinking given it's barely 8:00 a.m., but a girl can hope. The tiny envelope is missing from the top of my screen, and still missing four hours later when I check again. But this time, I slouch and drop my phone back into my satchel with a sigh.

Patience, Avery. Give it time.

Tej finishes the last gentle strums on his petite guitar as I plod back into the playroom. Nine out of eleven Mini-Bees lie asleep on the floor in a maze of gym mats, little limbs, and blue frog blankets.

When the elevator dings, my chin snaps to the shiny doors. An elderly gent exits, hobbling on his walking frame, and my heart sinks but not from empathy like it should. I drop my gaze to the ballet flats I've bitterly befriended and fiddle with the hem of my dress. Is it normal to miss someone this much? To pine and obsess *every* minute of the day? It's been twenty-four hours, for fuck's sake.

You're a parasite, Avery Lee—hungry whenever you're alone.

An icky shudder rolls through me. "I'll be back in a sec," I tell Tej as he approaches with his guitar, "Taylor" glinting across the headstock in gold. "I'm just going to the bathroom."

An easy smile crinkles around his eyes. "No worries. I'll hold down the fort. Hannah will be back soon anyway."

I wander down the terrazzo hall feeling oddly flat, and I don't like it. My mood can't be dictated by when I see or hear from Cole. I had a taste of that with Slade, and it's not healthy, but my stupid head won't quit. It's consumed and jonesing for a Cole fix. I grit my teeth against the feeling. We all have our vices, I guess.

The unisex bathroom door opens with a falsetto creak, and I amble to the far end cubicle, lock the glossy black door, and slump on top of the toilet seat. I don't need to go. I just need a few minutes to talk some dignity into myself—to remember the sun is shining today.

The bathroom door sings again, and slow footsteps sound across the honeycomb tiles. I wait another minute and flush to keep up the facade, then make my way to the long concrete vanity to wash my hands.

A presence looms behind me, but the second it registers, my scream is muffled by a hand, and I'm yanked back into a hard body. My frantic eyes dart to the mirror.

"*Shhh*," he says. "It's only me."

I sag as the hot words tickle my ear and send shivers down my shoulder blades. *Only* him. How can it be *only* him when he is everything?

Cole's spearmint gaze glimmers, and I spin to face him with a galloping heart. "You scared the bejesus out of me."

"Bejesus?" He quirks a brow, gripping my hips with his warm hands. "I expected an obscenity at least."

"Eh." I shrug. "Thought I'd try it on for size."

"And how'd it feel?"

I crinkle my nose. "Fucking weird."

Cole chuckles with that devilish, sideways grin. "I don't actually mind your dirty mouth, Miss Masters." He leans into my ear and lowers his voice. "In fact, I quite liked it."

Liked. Past tense. And, yes, he certainly did. My cheeks flame at the reminder of what I did to him on that daybed cushion, but I also lick my lips. An action Cole seems to notice, according to his darkening stare and the way his nostrils flare. "I missed you," he says.

"Me too," I whisper. "I think I'm going mad."

The corner of his mouth twitches back up, and he wipes away my frown with the pad of his thumb like I did to him under the stars. The fact he remembered makes me smile and ache to kiss him, so I wind his tie around my fist and yank his mouth to mine as I climb to my tiptoes. Cole smirks but complies, pressing me against the vanity as he knots a hand through my hair. I run mine over his shoulders and hum against his lips. He tastes like home and smells like heaven—a starlit, foresty heaven in the hills.

"Christ, I want you," he whispers. He lifts me to sit off the vanity's edge. Wedged between my legs, he grinds his erection against my core, making me gasp as he groans. He bites and kisses his way down my throat, tracing the Queen Anne neckline of my dress with his tongue down to where it dips between my breasts. His breaths grow heavier—his mouth greedier—and I grip his shoulders like I might float away, bunching his cotton shirt in my fists. I itch to tear it off him—to feel his naked skin burn under the scrape of my fingernails—but now isn't the time.

Inhaling, Cole drags his nose up my neck. "You always smell so good. You have no idea."

"So do you," I breathe. "You're like a drug." I feel him smile against my jaw—the sandpaper scratch of his stubble.

"Is that so?" He trails his fingers up the inside of my thigh and tugs the crotch of my lace knickers to one side. "Are you wet for me, Aves?"

Blood charges through my veins and ignites every nerve ending. "Always."

His belt buckle jangles, but reality creeps back in. "Wait," I whisper. "Anyone could walk in."

Cole tears open a condom wrapper with his teeth, cocking a brow. "And?"

"They'll see us."

Rolling it on, he leans in. "*And*?" When my spine stiffens, Cole gently laughs. "Don't worry. I locked the door."

"But are there cameras in here too?" I ask.

"Hell no." I release a pent-up breath, but Cole cups my chin and lifts my eyes to his. "You think I'd let anyone see you like this?" His brows are furrowed. His green gaze, steel. "You're for my eyes only. Understand?"

The words tug at my heart and heat my pussy in equal measure. I nod, and that's all the permission Cole needs. He bites my bottom lip, then our tongues collide as groans whirl and mingle around us. In one powerful thrust, he pushes inside me, and my head falls back on a gasp that melts into a desperate moan. One of my ballet flats tumbles to the tiles with a smack, but he feels so fucking good I could do this forever.

My pleasure builds with every sound and grunt that grinds through his teeth. "Look at me," Cole says. "I want to watch you when you fall."

I meet his intense eyes, and they blaze with a primal possessiveness that strips me bare. As he stares into my soul, I have nowhere to hide. I'm completely exposed, and Cole reads everything. All my secret desires, my shame and regrets. All the muddy, messy parts I disown. It's too much, yet I can't look away, because I'm reading him too. I see his fierce lust, his need to protect, and all the tenderness behind it. And beneath that, I see the boy inside the accomplished man—his innocence, hurt, and hope. His need to be wanted. His need to be loved.

An orgasm charges up my spine and explodes through my body like a collision of shooting stars. Cole catches my cries with his mouth and cradles my back as I buck against his grip. With several deep thrusts, his own release comes, and he bites my shoulder to muffle his groans, then captures my lips again. This time softly—*reverently*—as he guides us down from the vicious high through a gentle descent of feathery breaths.

"Stay right here." Cole kisses my temple, then disappears inside a cubicle. I hear the thud of the sanitary bin's plastic lid. The sound of his zipper and belt. Then he returns to wash his hands, drying them on his pants as he drops down in front of me. He picks up my shoe from the floor, kisses my ankle, and gently slips it back onto my foot. My heart flutters, and the little girl inside me jumps up and down, clapping. My very own Cinderella moment, albeit a little filthier.

I smile down at him, and he rises from one knee, readjusts my knickers, then lifts me down from the vanity, pressing his soft lips to mine. "I've got a meeting in ten, but I'll see you soon, okay?"

I want to ask when, where, and how, but instead simply nod. "See you then."

Cole unlocks the door and disappears, and I head back into the cubicle to resume my earlier ruse. This time, however, the grin won't leave my face, and I'm officially screwed.

Sixteen

The tap dance of a key on glass echoes through the gallery, and my excitement bubbles. Slinging my satchel across my chest, I race to open the front door. Jen stands on the porch, smiling with scarlet lips, matching ringlets, and car keys jingling high in her hand. "Are you ready to pop some tags, biatch?"

I trap her in a bear hug and squeeze. She groans as if I've tackled her, but I can't help it; I've missed her. "It's so good to see you."

"Ditto," she says, hugging me back. "But it's been a month, not a year, and a girl needs to breathe."

Chuckling, I let her go. "It feels like forever. So much has happened."

She narrows her winged eyes. "Ah, yes, the elusive Cole. I'm starting to think he's a sexy hallucination. Guess I won't know until I finally get to meet him."

I smirk. "You'll meet him later if we time it right."

"Well, in that case, we will." Jen winks.

I pull the front door shut behind me, lock the deadbolt, then follow Jen to Liam's car. "I still can't believe they gave *you* a licence," I tease.

"I know, right?" Jen settles into the driver's seat and leans across to unlock my door. I climb in and fit my seatbelt, then watch as she checks her mirrors, wriggles the gearstick, and secures her own. Her trembling hands inspire little confidence as she struggles to slot in the key. Perhaps a racing harness might have been the safer option. Maybe even the bus.

"Gotta say, I'm gobsmacked Liam trusted you with Betsy."

Jen rolls her eyes as she cranks the ignition. "Oh boy. Don't even get me started. I had to beg to borrow it today. Literally. And I won't tell you the lengths I went to." A dirty glint sparkles in her eyes, and I cringe.

"Gross," I say.

Jen laughs, and the engine hums a wobbly groan as we shudder away from the kerb, smoke trailing. It never shudders when Liam drives, so I grab the oh-shit bar on instinct.

Jen hits the blinker to cut the corner of Beth's street. "He's sure this freaking car is a jackpot investment waiting to happen. He's also sure I'm going to crash. Nice to know the guy who's meant to love me has so little faith, huh?"

Jen floors it into a tiny gap between cars, but the old sedan shudders again and takes longer to move than she likely intended. Horns blast, brakes screech, and my muscles coil like springs, but Jen seems unfazed.

"It's insured, isn't it?" I ask, feigning support while praying the Grim Reaper stays the fuck away. My life is finally turning around. To die now would be a cruel twist of fate.

"Oh yeah," Jen says, changing gears and picking up speed. "But he claims the insurance company doesn't yet see the value. They're wrong, apparently."

Jen reaches over to mess with the stereo—the only new thing in here. A second later, Macklemore's "Thrift Shop" pumps through the speakers, and she bounces in her seat. "Where to first?" she yells.

Ducking into the footwell, I retrieve my long list of thrift shops, ordered from nearest to furthest—from new stomping ground to old—and point to number one. "Vinnies, Malvern."

Jen slides on her black cat-eye sunglasses. "Done."

The first twelve stores yield us a garbage bag full of clothes destined for the washing machine, a pop-art painting, two funky vases, and an ab roller. Yes, an ab roller. No thrift shop is complete without one. It was Jen's buy—not mine. And the grand total spent? A whopping thirty-six dollars. Pauper, meet queen.

"How's uni?" I ask once we climb back into Betsy with our bakery lunch.

"Good," she says, adjusting her meat pie higher in its crumpled paper bag. "I'm pretty sure I meet the criteria for half the mental disorders in the *DSM*, but apparently it's normal for psychology students to fear that."

I laugh. "Don't worry. You're the best kind of nuts."

Jen takes a bite, hums her appreciation, then swallows. "I tried to find a disorder my dad fits but couldn't, weirdly enough. I thought having the delusion your adult daughter is still a child who needs your control would fit something for sure."

"He hasn't mellowed out any, then?"

She shakes her head. "He thinks Liam's gay. That's the only reason I'm allowed near him."

I stifle a laugh before my mouthful of Cornish pastie can escape. "Sorry. I shouldn't laugh."

But Jen cracks a smile. "Oh, it's as funny as you imagine. Liam puts on quite the show for Dad. He's very convincing."

I grin. "What about your mum?"

"Mum's no dummy. She knows what's going on but can also keep a secret, thank God."

"I'm sorry," I say, catching Jen's gaze so she knows I mean it. Jokes aside, her dad's overprotectiveness has plagued her since puberty. My mum didn't care enough. Her dad cares too much. Both extremes suck. "I know it's hard for you."

Jen wipes away flakes of pastry from her lips. "I just thought it would get better when I turned eighteen. But hell, was I wrong."

Shoving the rest of the pie in her mouth, Jen screws up her empty bag. I take it from her grasp and dump it in the footwell with mine, then retrieve the hot cinnamon doughnut balls that have scented the whole car. The oily paper bag rustles as I wave them under Jen's nose. "Want one?"

She holds up a finger, making a show of swallowing that last bite. "Abso-fucking-lutely."

The warm crunchy dough outer gives way to fluffy goodness, and my eyes roll back in my head. I lick the crystals of cinnamon sugar from my lips and moan. "These should be illegal."

"Better than sex," Jen agrees.

I ponder the comparison. "Nah. Close though."

She chokes down a mouthful. "*Really*? Well then, do tell."

"A lady doesn't kiss and tell," I say, repeating the same words I told Hannah, but Jen scoffs.

"Cut the crap. You tell me everything, and I mean *everything*." She drags out the last word while jiggling her brows.

Cringing, I recall the intimate conversations we've had about Slade. But the thought of blabbing sordid details about Cole sits like a dumbbell in my chest. It would be a betrayal. To him. To us. I shake my head, pretend to zip my lips shut, then throw away the imaginary key.

Jen stares at me, and her heart-shaped face slackens. "Oh my God."

I frown at her. "What?"

"Oh. My. God," she repeats.

"Oh my God, what?" I wriggle in my vinyl seat, growing increasingly uncomfortable. What is she on about?

She covers my hand with hers and gives me gleeful doe eyes. "You love him."

I scoff. "I've known him for six weeks, and we've only been together for three. That's not even possible." But my stomach flips, my ears burn, and Jen cackles.

"Oh, babe. You're screwed." She grins, but I deflate.

"Totally," I agree.

Playfully, she slaps my knee. "Why do you look like I gave you a terminal diagnosis? This is a good thing, right?"

My brain spins. Is it? Am I not just setting myself up for heartbreak? I mean, Cole is successful. Smart. Virtually my boss. Nine years older—decades wiser. And hot. So damn hot he could have anyone. Slime creeps over my skin, and my stomach curdles. The higher you fly, the further to fall, and boy am I familiar with splatting to the ground. I've only just scraped myself back together from last time and don't think I could do it again.

"I'm terrified," I whisper, barely audible but loud enough to make it real.

Jen squeezes my hand. "That's understandable. Especially after Slade." She coughs into her other hand and mumbles, "Tosser."

"It's not only that," I say, fighting a smile I don't want.

Jen studies me, but her calm and thorough attention triggers some kind of stage fright. I avert my gaze and twist at the paper doughnut bag in my lap. "People leave me," I rasp. "Dad. Mum. Beth. It seems . . . inevitable."

I don't admit I think there's something horribly wrong with me deep inside—a fatal, unforgivable flaw. A repellent people only see when they get too close. After all, if your own mother doesn't like you or stay, who the hell ever could?

"I haven't left," Jen says.

The corner of my mouth tilts up dryly. "*Yet.*"

Her red brows furrow as she considers me. "I think you have an abandonment wound."

"An abandonment wound?"

She nods. "We've touched on it in class." Jen nibbles her bottom lip and seems to search her brain. "I think the thing to realise is that people didn't leave because of you—they left because of them—and it doesn't mean everyone in future will."

My chin falls to my chest. She's probably right. It sounds logical enough. But regardless, that same sick, dark feeling grips my solar plexus, screaming bullshit.

"I can't speak for your dad," Jen says. "I never met him, but I'm certain he adored you." The delicate way she talks about Dad does little to soften the instant ache inside my bones. "But your mum? I hate to say this, Aves, but she was nasty. I had to bite my tongue until it bled. I think it's good she left. I think the universe did you a favour even though it hurt. And Beth?" Jen tilts her head. "Well, she didn't leave like that or forever. She's just chasing her dreams in sexy sky-high stilettos." Jen winks, and I smile.

God, I miss Beth.

"In any event," Jen continues, nudging my arm. "Don't let fear captain your ship."

My grin is wide and instant—the out I desperately need. "Did you really just say that to me?"

Jen's nose crinkles. "I really just did. But please don't tell anyone I'm the Queen of Corn."

I laugh and launch a doughnut ball towards her mouth. She catches it and chomps away with a grin, then nudges her chin down the road. "I spy another thrifty calling our name."

"Lucky last," I say.

We park directly in front of the op-shop and lock Betsy before heading inside. A hideous orange couch stands off to our left with baby-pink ruffled cushions plumped in each corner. A shaggy green rug covers the floor at its feet with all the splendour of fake grass. Sometimes thrift shops nail their displays and work brilliantly with what they have. And sometimes they don't.

I caress the couch and squeeze, enjoying the silky texture under my fingers. "Quite the pinnacle of interior design, huh?"

Jen giggles. "Maybe for Austin Powers."

I meander to the next display but then stop dead with a gasp. Across the room, standing with the white goods, illuminated by a beam of light as if sent from heaven itself, is one thing I never thought I'd find. "Holy shit," I whisper, barely believing my eyes. I race towards it and drop to my knees, running my hands over its cold metal curves and sturdy legs.

Jen wanders over to halt beside me. "What is that?"

With my arms wrapped around it, I look up at her in disbelief. How can she not know? "It's a pottery wheel."

"Oh," she says.

"Just 'oh'? Do you have any idea what I could do with this?"

Her smile tugs up, and she arches a cheeky brow. "Have a filthy Swayze moment with Cole?"

What a stellar idea. I'll bookmark that for later. "I could expand my collection. Incorporate smaller thrown pieces. Vases, mugs, bowls. And fast too. This is exactly what I need."

I scan the wheel for a price tag and pray I can afford it. Professional wheels like this cost a bomb, and sometimes thrift shops assign near-retail prices. Especially when they look this new. Faint grey digits grace the small sticker on the bottom of one leg. "Two hundred dollars." It's not nothing but still a bargain.

"Can I help you, girls?"

I whip my head up to see an older woman in an apron with fluffy dark hair standing next to Jen. I return her smile. "Does this work?"

"Sure does. All our electrical items are tested before they hit the floor."

My heart tap-dances as I climb to my feet. Squealing, I grab Jen's elbows and jump up and down.

"You're mad. You know that?" she says.

"All artists are. But when you have talent, you're *eccentric*, not mentally unstable. It's the polite term." Grinning, I look back to the shopkeeper. "I'll take it." I itch to hug her but refrain.

Clearly amused, she nods towards the counter. "Follow me. Will you be taking it today?"

"Absolutely," I say, picturing where in my studio it will sit.

Jen tugs on my jacket sleeve. "Will it even fit in the car?"

"I'll make it fit," I throw over my shoulder.

But Jen groans. "Please don't get me killed."

"Trust me. Liam will never even know."

Then again . . . on second thoughts . . . he might. The wheel looked way smaller inside the store. "If we just angle it a little more to the . . ." The leg finally slips past the chassis, and we rest it upside down on Betsy's back seat. I release a breath. "There. It's in."

"Finally," Jen says. "You owe me a bowl for that. A big-arse one for my dresser. Preferably purple. With elephants."

I smile and slam the car door shut. "Done."

"Aves?"

The deep voice freezes my blood, and Jen and I exchange panicked looks before we turn towards it. "Slade," I bite out, stepping away from Betsy—away from him. "What are you doing here?"

Fidgety and beady-eyed, he smirks. "Saw Liam's car. Thought I'd say hello. Was expecting him, but I guess it's my lucky day."

Jen huffs. "No way he'd talk to you after what you did to Aves."

Slade jerks his chin towards Jen with a sneer. "Go fuck yourself, Jen."

I stiffen. "Don't talk to her like that."

"I don't wanna talk to her at all. I wanna talk to you."

I scan him up and down, taking in the tattered bottoms of his tracksuit pants, his sallow face, the dark rings under his eyes. He looks . . . sick, and that alluring spark has vanished. It's like I'm seeing him for the first time—beyond those tanned muscles and that sly, sexy smirk. There isn't superficial beauty potent enough to hide an ugly soul. Slade is poison, and the dismal future we would've had if my former dreams came true flashes through my mind like a horror film.

"I've got nothing to say to you." I give him my back and meet Jen's gaze, silently pleading she gets in the car and unlocks my door so we can go.

"Why? Does your fancy boyfriend forbid it?"

My brows furrow, but I don't take his bait. I keep my gaze fixed on the door handle and bite my lip.

"You think you're too good for me now? Is that it? Think you're fucking better than me, Avery *Lee*?" Slade says my name with venom, and my stomach sinks. I once told him how I hate being called Avery Lee. How only Mum calls me that.

I snap my eyes to his and inhale a deep breath, gathering every scrap of confidence I own. "No, Slade. I *know* I'm better than you. Stay the hell away from me. I never want to see you again." The passenger door finally clicks, and with trembling hands, I climb in and slam the door shut, smacking down the lock.

Jen starts the engine and hits reverse. Slade stands there, blocking our exit, but Jen refuses to stop. He steps aside at the last second, and we peel out of the car park, my heart sprinting.

"What a wanker," Jen says, checking her rear-view mirror as she stops at the traffic lights. She glances at me when I don't reply. "Are you okay?"

I slowly shake my head. "What did I ever see in him?"

"Trouble and tats?" She shrugs.

A revelation hardens in my mind. "I was completely delusional. Next time, tell me."

Jen's eyebrows twist like pretzels as puzzlement fills her face, and I hear the words she's too kind to say. She did try to tell me. Repeatedly. But I didn't want to hear. And what's worse, I dragged her into my mess. I'm lucky she's still here. I'm lucky *I'm* still here. I could be showering with thirty naked women right now, praying I don't look at one the wrong way. With a mental facepalm, I groan. "I'm so sorry."

"I forgive you," Jen says as the light turns green. "I just hope Cole's way better for you."

"He is," I say, and despite all my lingering fears, deep inside I know that's true.

Betsy's rear bumper hovers low to the ground on Beth's driveway but rises an inch when I hoist our garbage bag of clothes out of the boot and over one shoulder. I waddle my way to the laundry like I'm Santa. As expected, the vases look chic on my dresser, but I'll leave the painting unmounted to spare Beth's pristine wall.

"I'll have a six-pack in no time," Jen says when I return out front, patting her flat tummy as she admires her ab roller.

"My money's on you using it for a week, then never again."

"Ye of so little faith," she says, tilting her head to consider me. "You know, you have the pessimism of an old woman. I really don't think you need to worry about the age gap thing."

I shake my head with a laugh. I'm starting to learn that age is relative to the body with little bearing on the soul.

Up the street, Cole's car appears at the corner, then turns towards us. Butterflies dance in my stomach, and Jen follows my gaze. "That's him, isn't it? An Audi, seriously?" She whistles from high to low. "I can't believe you get the guy with the Audi, and I get the one with a hard-on for a rusty tin can."

My smile grows commensurate with Cole's proximity, and Jen sidles up next to me near the lollipop trees, linking our arms and bouncing up and down. "If he's real, I owe Liam twenty bucks, but I don't even care. This is so exciting."

I roll my eyes and elbow her. She's seen a G-rated headshot of Cole. She knows he's real. "Behave yourself, and please don't drool."

"I can't promise that," she says.

I don't blame her.

Cole's black coupe glides up to the kerb. He climbs out of the driver's seat and saunters towards us. The sun's golden rays halo his hair, his stubble glistens, and his dimple shines at full beam. Dark-grey jeans skim his strong legs, and the vivid jungle ink decorating his arm glows as if it can breathe. I swallow.

Jen tugs on my arm. "Are you freaking serious?" she asks through clenched teeth while smiling.

"Yup," I reply in the same manner.

"Lucky bitch."

That I am.

I detangle from Jen and move towards Cole. His grin widens as I near, quickening my steps. I throw my arms around his neck, and he sweeps me into a hug, then spins me around, eliciting a ridiculous squeal.

With a deep chuckle, he stills, then tenderly swipes the hair from my face and tucks it behind my ear. His pale forest eyes sparkle. "Hey, you," he says in that low husky voice reserved just for me.

"Hey, yourself."

His full lips tilt into a crooked smile. My favourite one of all. It comes soaked in humility with a dash of sarcasm and humour, a spark of intellect, and the promise of later.

God, that smile.

I press my lips to his. Sweet spearmint tinges his tongue, but the rest is all him. Warm and woodsy—soft and soothing. Like a new kind of cosy home.

A minute later, Jen coughs. Sheepishly, I wriggle back to my feet. "Sorry." But I'm not sorry at all. The number of times I've had to watch her sucky face with Liam is enough to make any girl weep.

Light glimmers in Jen's eyes like silver tinsel. As Cole nears, she holds out her hand. "If you're not Cole, we have a serious problem."

Cole shakes it. "You must be Jen. I've heard a lot about you."

"Likewise, although she won't give me any juicy stuff."

My face burns, and I whack Jen's arm as I halt at her side.

"Not sorry," she says. "Making you change colour like a mood ring is the best part of our friendship." At that, Cole's laugh bellows, and Jen looks at me. "I think I like him."

I roll my eyes at Cole. "You passed, apparently."

"Phew," he says, wiping invisible sweat from his brow. He winks at me, and my belly flips. Will that ever stop? I hope not.

Cole regards Liam's car where both back doors hang wide open like elephant ears. He wanders over, nodding to my pottery wheel. "You need a hand with this thing?"

Jen sniggers, and I plant my hands on my hips. "It's not a thing, thank you very much. It's a heaven-sent gift from the gods."

Cole arches an amused brow. "That needs to go . . . ?"

"In the entry," I say. "I'll help. You won't be able to lift it on—" Cole's biceps flex as he effortlessly pulls the wheel from the car. "Okay," I mumble, "maybe you will."

His dimple reappears as he strides past me and Jen. Cole suited up and carrying a briefcase is one thing, but Cole in dark denim and a soft grey tee carrying heavy machinery is an entirely different stratosphere of hot. Jen and I both sigh. "That man is doughnut balls dipped in chocolate sauce," she says. My eyes boggle, and Jen cringes like she's sucked on lemon. "That sounded worse than intended. Sorry."

I elbow her. "Behave yourself, or I'm dobbing on you."

She nods. "Fair enough."

I follow Cole inside. "Just dump it here," I say, pointing to the corner nearest the studio.

Gently, Cole sets it down, his forearms cording under the strain. I slink up next to him and bat my eyelashes. "What strong muscles you have." I drag my short scarlet nails over the flourish of leaves and birds on his skin.

He offers me a devilish grin. "All the better to sex you with." He winks, and we snicker like idiots.

I love us like this. Relaxed and playful and flirty. All sparkling eyes and secret smiles only for each other. The hollowness inside me has gone, filled by shooting stars and rainbows and all my other favourite things. My chest isn't twisting. My stomach isn't aching. And it's all because of him.

I push up onto my tiptoes to kiss his cheek. "Thanks for your help."

"Is there anything else?" he asks.

"Nope, that's it."

We stroll back out front. I close the car doors and boot, then look at Jen. "Would you like a coffee?"

She flashes a regrettable smile. "Can't. Liam said if I don't have Betsy home by two, he'll report her stolen."

I huff a laugh. "Are you serious?"

She shrugs. "I wouldn't test him. Put it that way."

"It's a great car," Cole says, and our heads snap to him in unison. He takes in our gaping expressions with a smirk, then leans against the chassis and taps the roof twice with his knuckles. "These are sought-after. Rotor-heads are a die-hard, loyal bunch."

I peruse the car, then look back at Cole with an arched brow. No fucking way.

"I'm not kidding," he says. "Even in this condition. It's a house deposit, at least."

"Oh my God." Jen's hand flies up to her mouth. "So he's not delusional? This whole time, I thought he was bonkers."

"He's not," Cole says.

"Well then, I guess I'll have to stop fantasising about Betsy's untimely demise in some freak accident." Jen makes air quotes around the word *accident*, then eyes Betsy with newfound admiration. She looks up a moment later. "It was nice to meet you, Cole."

"Likewise," he says.

Jen throws me a wink. "Talk later, babes."

"Thanks for today," I say.

Cole bear-hugs me from behind and walks us inside, his steps straddling mine. It's new and awkward but completely adorable. "Betsy?" he asks.

"Uh-huh. Liam is special. Let's just leave it at that."

"Jen seems nice."

"She's the best." I glance up at him over my shoulder as we step inside, then turn in his arms to face him, pushing the front door shut.

"So you guys had a fun day?" He searches my face with soft eyes, like he's committing every detail to memory or refining the last one he had.

"Apart from running into Slade, it was perfect."

Cole stiffens. "*What?*"

I shake my head, trying to downplay the situation, but his tension radiates like heat from a grill. "He saw Liam's car. It was no big deal. We told him where to go."

Releasing me, Cole steps away, carving fingers through his hair. "That son of a bitch. I warned him to stay away from you. You could be in prison because of him, and he approaches you like nothing happened?"

"Well, I'm not in prison, thanks to my knight in shining armour.

He and his shady snooping tendencies saved me." I wink, trying desperately to conjure levity. I knew mentioning this would mean trouble but keeping it a secret meant betrayal. Rock, meet hard place.

Cole's hands find his hips, and he shakes his head at the ground. "You should take out a restraining order."

"What? Are you serious?"

Sharp eyes meet mine. "Deadly. The guy's trouble. There are things about him I don't think you know."

"Like what?"

"Like his juvenile record reads a mile long. Like he pickpockets the elderly and sells drugs to children. And you know about the cars. Should I go on?"

Slade hurts children? Targets *grandmas*? My gut twists. That's a special kind of low. "How do you know all this?" Juvenile records are sealed, or so I thought.

"Connections."

I grow dizzy. Am I that crap a judge of character? My shoulders slump as I stare at my feet. How can I trust anything I feel when my intuition seems AWOL?

Cole winces, then ambles back to me and rests his hands on my shoulders, kneading out the knots. "Look, I'm sorry to push. I need you safe, is all."

From the first day we met, he's been saving me, protecting me, and keeping me close. If I weren't so deliciously cocooned in the cosiness that brings, I might ask why.

I look up to meet eyes that ache. "I told Slade to leave me alone. He won't bother me anymore, and I won't fall for it again. With or without you in my life."

Cole tucks me against his chest, cradling my head. "I'm sorry. I'm glad you told me. Really, I am."

My muscles unwind, and I pull back, choosing to smile and forget this ever happened. "Good. Now c'mon, I want to show you what I found today."

I hold out my hand, and with a resigned but playful sigh, Cole takes it. "Lead the way."

I grin and drag him through the gallery, but he stops in front of the pottery wheel. "I can't see you throwing pots in the entry. Are you sure there isn't someplace else you'd like me to put this?" There's an air of caution to his words.

So he does know what it is. I stare at him silently while I consider the question. Jen's corny advice twirls through my head. *Don't let fear captain your ship.* Huh. Easier said than done. If a picture's worth a thousand words, a sculpture's worth a million. It's showing someone the encyclopedia of my heart and the shadows of my mind, then still having to look them in the eye afterwards. But Cole's seen my worst, and he's still here. That's gotta count for something.

I imagine my studio through his fresh eyes, trying to gauge what he'll think. It's busy but tidy. The finished pieces all sit lined up across the bench on display along with *High Heart Symphony.* I refocus on Cole. "You're right. Do you mind moving it to my studio, please?"

"Sure," he says, his smile beaming brighter than a solar eclipse.

I open the door and step back, allowing him entry. "In the corner near the shelves would be great."

He positions the wheel facing the room diagonally, exactly as I pictured, then stands, dusting off his hands on his jeans.

I take a deep breath, willing my nerves to calm. "Well, this is my studio," I say with a showcasing wave and wobbly voice. "Feel free to explore."

He looks at me and faintly nods once, then wanders around the room slowly. Carefully. Taking in every detail in absolute silence. My stomach flutters as he approaches my new collection. He throws a glance towards me over his shoulder as if seeking permission. Wringing my hands, I nod a tight smile and hold my breath. I think I'm going to throw up. Every second feels like an hour as he steps from one piece to the next, contemplating each.

Still. Silent.

When he reaches *High Heart Symphony*, regret rushes through me with the force of a monster wave. What if he hates it? What if it scares him off? He gives me a ripple of affection, and I respond with a tsunami. Oh God, this was a mistake.

His continued silence amps up my panic. He's probably rehearsing his response and formulating lies so as not to hurt my feelings when he dashes out the front door. But just as I'm about to end this torture—usher him out, apologise, and declare this an epic mistake—he turns to face me. Wide eyes lock on mine. Full lips part. "Aves," he whispers.

He's . . . *horrified*.

My eyes glass and meet my feet. "I'm sorry. This is stupid. *I'm* stupid." The humiliation rivals the worst I've ever felt. It twists around every limb and muscle like a boa constrictor. Squeezing. Compressing. I can hardly breathe.

Cole charges towards me and lifts my chin. "Hey. Look at me."

Reluctantly, I comply.

He wipes away a tear from my cheek with his thumb. "What's wrong?"

I wince and close my eyes. "You're so quiet. You hate them, and I've scared you off."

He chokes out a huffed laugh. "I'm quiet because I never imagined how talented you are. I'm in awe. *Speechless*."

I peer open one eye at a time and see him shake his head, dark brows all twisted and furrowed. "They're . . . gripping," he says.

Gripping. That's a good word. A very good word.

The noose loosens around my neck, and I take a deep breath. Cole squeezes my shoulder, then walks back to *High Heart Symphony*. "When did you start this one?"

My heart splutters. He's not so arrogant to assume it's him but suspects it nonetheless. And rightly so.

Lowering my gaze, I shrug. Here goes nothing. "The day after I kissed you. It's not finished yet." I chance looking back up and watch his eyes flicker with a thousand thoughts.

"It's us," he says in wonder. Gently, he caresses the woman's hair, then traces his fingers over the copper-scrolled hearts I've temporarily positioned.

I step closer and rally courage. "What do you think?"

His eyes find mine. "I've never felt so humbled and honoured all at once. It's . . . breathtaking."

My face heats, but a smile kisses my lips. "I thought you'd flee."

Cole studies me, frowning, like what I said made him sad. "Don't you feel this?" he asks, motioning a hand between us. "The relief when we're finally together? The raging pull when we're not?"

God, this man.

I nod as I melt. "Every single day," I whisper. The evidence stands right before him. That's what scares me. I don't understand this connection we have, but maybe I don't need to.

Cole picks up my hands and brushes his thumbs over my knuckles, looking me dead in the eye. "I'm not going anywhere, Avery."

His words hit my heart like a Cupid's arrow and explode into fairy dust and glitter on impact. Those are sacred words to someone like me, and they came armoured in sincerity through honest eyes. I search for deceit, but a sense of calm pools in my belly.

I believe him.

Emotions blast through me as if freed with a magical key. They rip from their chains, potent and wild, and fill me with frenzied need. The need to taste him, to touch him—to hold and have him.

I press my mouth to his, knot my hands through his hair, and crush him hard against me. I want to fall into his soul and fill every fracture. I want our hearts to entwine like *High Heart Symphony*'s copper scrolls.

Cole meets me with equal passion—equal ferocity—and speaks one gritted breathless word against my lips. "Strip."

So I do.

Seventeen

As I'm on the edge of sleep, visions of last night mist through my dreams. Our encounter on the studio floor that left our naked bodies dusted in terracotta. In the steamy shower where we washed it off. At the top of the stairs on the plush carpet when we didn't quite make it to the bed. And finally, here, when we did.

My thighs clench together from the memories, sending ripples of bliss through my core. I roll over and snuggle up against Cole's naked back, then nuzzle my face into his neck and inhale. He smells like sex and sin. But rather than wake him again, with a content moan and new hope for life, I drift back off to sleep.

"Avery?"

"Hello? Anyone home?"

The familiar shrill works its way into my consciousness, and I bolt upright.

What the fuck?

I pinch my arm to see if I'm dreaming, then grab my phone from the bedside to check the time. Eight a.m. and five missed calls from Beth.

"Avery Lee?"

Oh shit. There it is again, followed by the sound of high heels clacking up the stairs. I'm definitely not dreaming.

"Mum?" I ask, bundling the quilt up to cover my breasts, ensuring Cole has the rest. *Please tell me this isn't happening.*

A blonde beehive rises from the landing like an unwanted sun, and I blink away the sting. "Mum. What are you doing here?"

She takes the final step up—adorned in pastel heels and a flowing yellow sundress speckled with tiny white flowers—then comes to stand near the end of my bed. Age is yet to conquer her pretty face but hasn't spared her fragile neck, nor her arms, which lie crossed as she taps one foot. A predatory smile flitters through her eyes like a luminous lick of black fire. "That's no way to greet your mother, Avery Lee."

As my name passes her lips, I flinch. My mother is razor wire wrapped in daisies, and "Avery Lee" is a weapon used against me, delivered with enough secret spite to make me bleed every single time.

Cole stirs next to me, blinking in a sleepy daze. I stare at him in horror. "My mum's here."

Alertness registers, followed by shock. He twists the covers tight around his waist and sits up with tan skin gleaming in the morning light, tattoo vibrant as ever. "Ah . . . hello . . . Mrs. Masters, is it?" It's the first time I've seen Cole nervous in front of anyone. Maybe except for me.

Mum slides her curious gaze over his naked form like a snake winding itself around a tree. Her blue eyes heat, causing me to grimace. "Unfortunately for me, it's Mrs. Wilson at the moment."

My face screws up. "You remarried . . . ? When?"

Her eyes snap away from Cole and back to me, sharpening on impact. With a wave of her pale slender hand, she dismisses my question. "I see you've found a way to combat the loneliness. He's a nice one too. Wherever did you find him?"

I clench my teeth. She speaks of Cole like he's a shiny, hollow object procured at a fair. One she can lock in her antique display cabinet with the rest of her prized trinkets. I drag in a breath through my nose. "Mum, can we please have some privacy? As you can see, I wasn't expecting guests."

"Well, maybe if you'd returned my phone call, you would've known I was coming."

"Phone call?" My temples throb in silent protest. Quiet, calm mornings are my best friend. Rude awakenings are not. Especially when last night was so . . . *perfect*. The contrast is cruel.

"I called you two and a half weeks ago, Avery Lee. You didn't answer."

I search my memory. Of course—the night I fell from the roof. With everything that happened, I forgot, and who can blame me? But to be honest, I probably wouldn't have returned her call anyway. Nothing good ever comes from the mix of Mum and me. We're an incompatible cocktail that leaves a putrid taste. "Does Beth know you're here?"

"How do you think I knew where to find the key?" The silver key shines in her French-manicured fingertips as she holds it up, and I deflate. That stupid fake rock. How fast a saviour can turn saboteur.

Defeated, I slump against the headboard and shoot Cole a silent sorry. Then, with a hefty inhale, I plead with the woman who birthed me. "Mum, some privacy? *Please*." I motion towards the stairs. "I'll be down in a minute."

Beneath her sweetheart neckline, Mum's dainty shoulders tighten, and her pink-painted lips press firm. She does not respond well to being dismissed. But after a hesitant beat, she turns for the stairs. "Well, don't be long. Bethany offered me her bedroom, but my luggage is still in the hall, since I don't know where that is."

As the beehive descends, I hold back a sigh. While Beth's house is ritzy—big it ain't. Mum would have seen Beth's room on her way in, but handling her own luggage is beneath her. I'm surprised it made it inside the house.

I scroll through Beth's missed calls. They're limited to this morning, indicating the notice was short. She would have warned me sooner otherwise, then I could have begged to stay at Cole's—hid in the toilet—caught a train to Adelaide—*anything*.

I curse the ceiling. Beth was probably railroaded into this, or simply told how it would be. For a ruthless lawyer, she caves like a shaken mine when it comes to our mother, but that's where infallible optimism gets you.

I look at Cole, and his amusement unknots my chest. "I'm sorry. I honestly had no idea she was coming. If I did, you could have evacuated for your own protection."

Cole laughs and catches my hand, circling his finger on the pulse point of my wrist. "Is she really that bad?"

"Yes," I hiss, but that's the question I wrestle with constantly. Sticks and stones, after all. I frown. "And no."

Cole's smile falters, and it occurs to me how horrible I must seem for feeling this way. He would give anything to have his mum back, and here I sit, ungrateful and bitter with mine. "I'm sorry," I sigh.

He cups my cheek. "Don't be. If I understand anything, it's anger towards a parent. In my experience, it's rarely unfounded."

Holding his gaze, I search his eyes, seeking everything he's yet to tell me about his father. There's a story there. Maybe even bigger than mine. But it will have to wait.

I drop a kiss to his cheek, drag my nose across his stubble, and breathe him in, then force myself out of bed to sling on a hoodie, yoga pants, and Ugg boots.

Mum sits on the blue velvet sofa, admiring her nails as I stomp down the steps. Swallowing my irritation, I force out a polite offer of tea.

"Yes, please. Strong with a dash of milk, one sugar. In a proper teacup, and let it brew well."

"Sure." I nod, holding back a "Yes, ma'am" and a salute as I make my way to the kitchen. If I let her, Mum would have me in eternal servitude. *Avery, can you pass me this? Avery, can you do me this favour? Avery, can you solve every problem I create and take the wrath of my un-happiness?*

Sure, Mum, sure. It never stops.

As I lean against the kitchen bench, my skin burns with scrutiny. I glance over my shoulder to find her eyeing me up and down over the rise of her nose, her posture stiff as a corpse. Ah, there it is. The infamous gaze of unfavourable judgement. It's a specialty blend of disgust, disappointment, and shame. And one that's had plenty of time to brew.

"You look very . . . comfortable," Mum says.

I shrug. "It's Sunday morning." Then turn back to stir her tea. The spoon chimes against the fine paisley china, and I will my invisible shield to erupt from the earth to keep me safe. But Mum is kryptonite to my defences in a way no one else is. This will require something more.

"Given you have company, I thought you might be a little more . . . aware. That's all."

My shoulders slump as she successfully plants a cluster of paranoid thoughts in my head with one simple comment.

I'm not good enough. I look rubbish. Cole will find someone better— more refined—less . . . me.

You can know my mother's game, but remaining unaffected is an entirely different challenge. One I'm yet to conquer.

"I'll shower and change soon," I say, scanning over my hoodie to ensure it's at least stain-free. It is.

Mum chuckles a breathy laugh. "Well, at least they match your hair, I suppose."

Strike two. In the space of ten minutes. I think she's gotten better at this. Or I've grown accustomed to not facing criticism every day. Either way, tension knots in my chest. I rub my fist against it, trying to ease the ache, but it's no use. Mum doesn't just get under my skin; she seeps into every organ, muscle, and cell of my body like a lethal poison. A vaccine against inner peace.

I set Mum's steaming teacup down on the side table next to her. She mutters a thank-you as I drop to the sofa opposite and assume my default *Mum* position—arms crossed over my heart, leaning back as far as the cushions will allow. I arch a brow. "*Mrs. Wilson?*"

Mum swallows a sip of tea and tightens her lips.

Silence.

I narrow my gaze. "You aren't going to tell me? It sounds like I have a new stepdad. Surely I should know."

She laughs at the ceiling. "Oh, Avery Lee, forever the drama queen." Her hand swats away vacant air. "Don't worry, it didn't work out anyway."

"It's over already? How long were you married?" I scramble to do the maths. She's been gone for what, seven months? That's usually the maximum length of her relationships, sure. But marriage? This is extreme, even for her.

"We're still married. Just not together," she clarifies.

"Is that why you're here?"

She swallows another sip of tea, her pinkie poised in the air as she grips the ornate handle. Shit. I do that too. "If you must know, I need a place to stay until my divorce is finalised. Are you happy now? It's difficult to talk about, you know? My heart is irreparably broken." Mum presses a hand to her chest and knits her over-plucked brows, but I'm not buying it. Her eyes are filled with cunning—not hurt. Her gaze is sharp—not soft.

"Who is he?"

"He . . . is a bastard," she says with the passion of a Broadway star.

I shake my head. The woman is exasperating. "What's his name? What does he do? How did you meet? When were you married?"

She rolls her eyes and sighs. "Dr. Henry Wilson. I met him on the internet. We married in February. Are you happy now?"

"February . . . but that's a few weeks after you left. How?"

Mum's chin nudges higher. It's a defence reflex, one of her favourites. "I met him before I left. I'll have you know we chatted for months."

My heart free-falls into my Ugg boots. "He's why you left?" Why she moved to the middle of fucking nowhere? It's all starting to make sense.

"I wanted my life back, Avery Lee. You were done with school. It was time to stand up and fend for yourself. You weren't easy, you know? Always so . . ." She looks to the heavens for the right word, circling her hand like a waving royal. "Needy," she settles on, meeting my eyes. The amused spark in hers is subtle but glints like a tiny shard of glass. The comment is intended to hurt, and it succeeded. My stomach turns in a sickly somersault.

Scanning my memory, I try to find examples of needing more than a typical child would. I went to school without protest. Brought home good grades. Skipped a year ahead and caught up to Jen. I didn't insist on fancy clothes or shoes. I imposed my own curfews and made my way around the place as soon as I was old enough.

I furrow my brows. If anything, she was the needy one. Always wanting more. Nothing ever good enough. Appease her on one front and twenty more demands arise.

She clears her throat and breaks my daze. "Have you finished interrogating me?"

I stare at her silently while her words circle my head and drop into place. *Dr.* Wilson. "Is he rich?"

The teacup halts halfway to her mouth as she stiffens with a scowl. "How dare you. I will not justify myself to you, Avery Lee. This conversation is over."

And just like that, I know in my heart of hearts Dr. Wilson—*stepdaddy dearest*—is loaded, and Mum's awaiting payday. She never used to be like this. Before . . . Dad. At least, I don't think so. But in the right conditions, rot breeds.

I rub my forehead with the palm of my hand and pray for the ability to travel back in time so I can phone Beth and beg her not to let Mum stay. This is a disaster.

Footsteps sound on the stairs. Cole appears like a guiding light on rough dark seas, dressed in yesterday's jeans and soft grey tee. Despite that, he looks as fresh as morning dew, and his mere presence unknots my muscles. With him by my side, I'm stronger—better—no longer that pathetic girl. I can handle this. "Hey, you." I smile as the memory of the promise he made last night twirls around my heart.

I'm not going anywhere, Avery.

His eyes glint, and his dimple deepens as he strides over and drops a kiss to the top of my head. "Morning, Angel."

Angel.

The name that turns me to goo. Sparkly glitter goo.

I take a deep breath to recentre. What Mum and I need is a fresh start. We've had time apart. I'm an adult now. Surely things have changed. It's time we re-established our relationship in a healthier way—with respectable boundaries, courtesy, and common decency. I'm sure if I'm willing to try, I can make it work. After all, Beth manages.

With a deep breath, I rally my politest tone. "Mum, this is Cole. He's my . . ." Hesitating, I crane my neck to meet Cole's curious smile. He offers an encouraging nod. "Boyfriend," I finish, scrunching my nose. The word sounds as giddy as I prayed it wouldn't. *Boy-*

friend feels inadequate and juvenile, but what other option is there? "And, Cole, this is my mother, Sheila Wilson." I struggle to keep my voice even over Mum's new last name but manage it. Just.

Holding his hand out to shake, Cole approaches Mum. "Nice to meet you, Mrs. Wilson. I apologise for our earlier state."

Mum's hand rises, palm side down and bent at the wrist, in a silent request he kiss it. Her eyes sparkle when Cole obliges, and I ignore the acid building in my veins and keep my smile plastered on. I've never seen her do this. Not once in my life.

As Cole's lips land, Mum's smile grows seductive. Her hooded eyes smoulder, and her voice comes extra breathy. "Call me Sheila, please."

I mentally facepalm. She's one second away from pulling Cole to the floor and riding him like a bull at a rodeo. I wonder if he sees it. Or is it just me? Is it always just me?

Cole takes a seat next to me, his warm arm coming to rest around my shoulders. The weight is welcome. There's less chance I'll jump over the coffee table to strangle Mum if I'm pinned. Her earlier words pop into my head. I look like hell, and now Cole's here to see it. I rake my fingers through my hair, but they catch in knots. Oh God, Mum's right. It's ready to nest a family of birds.

"Leave it. You're beautiful," Cole whispers in my ear, his warm breath tickling my neck. "Freshly fucked looks good on you." My hand drops to my lap like a duck shot from the sky, and I snap my eyes to Mum, but her expression offers no hint she heard. Relieved, I sink against Cole with my heart pulsing bigger—greater—soon it won't fit in my chest.

"It sounded like you needed saving," Cole adds under his breath, and I grimace.

Great. He heard everything.

"So, Cole, what do you do for a living?" Mum asks.

He offers a modest smile. "I'm a lawyer."

"He isn't just a lawyer," I say. "He's the managing partner of a prestigious firm."

Mum's brows shoot high. "Well then, perhaps you could represent me in my divorce. I imagine the fact you're sleeping with my daughter affords me a significant discount."

"Mum," I gasp. "What the hell?"

Cole laughs and squeezes my shoulder—a silent instruction to relax. "I'm sorry, Sheila, but I don't handle divorce cases, and the one who does isn't taking new clients."

Smooth as satin, Cole shuts her down with a falsehood. One divorce lawyer, my arse. My spine straightens with pride.

"Oh," she says, "I guess I'll have to keep looking, then. You'd think having a lawyer for a daughter, one wouldn't have to search far, but apparently you'd be wrong."

Huh. It seems Beth refused her call for help too—at least in the legal sense. *Good*.

Mum takes the last sip of tea, then rests her cup on the table beside her with a delicate chink. "So how did you two meet?"

I stiffen. Cole could divulge the entire sorry story, since he might not see the harm. I guess most mothers would know if their then seventeen-year-old was arrested, but it's one weapon I couldn't gift her. Swallowing, I throw Cole a panicked look, but he squeezes my shoulder again.

"We met at work," he says. "Avery works in our child care centre."

My muscles relax, but something stirs in the pit of my stomach. He's lied twice in as many minutes, and the easy way they slid from his mouth unsettles me. I would believe him if I didn't know the truth, but hell, I'm grateful.

Shaking away the thought, I look back to Mum and re-engage my polite tone. "I've been there for six weeks now."

"Hmm," she says, skimming her gaze over her fingernails. "It's not law, but I guess child care is better than all that starving artist rubbish, at least."

My mouth drops open, and the flickering flame in my belly extinguishes in a gust of icy wind. Cole stiffens but then clears his throat. "Avery is incredibly talented. She could forge a well-respected career if she so desired." His words are laced with a coldness I've only heard directed at Slade.

Mum chuckles. "You seem like an intelligent man, Cole. Sculpting will never return a liveable income. Surely you see that?"

"With mediocre talent, perhaps, but your daughter is . . . breathtaking." He stares at me, and the frosty bite in his voice melts on the last word. "I'm sure she could find a way."

Goo. Sparkly rainbow glitter goo.

"How adorable young love is. As blind as it is new." Mum's patronising gaze finds mine. She picks up her teacup and holds it out in my direction. "I need a refill."

Clearing my throat, I glance at Cole. "Would you like anything?"

He shakes his head but retrieves his arm and stands to take the cup from Mum. "Allow me." His tight smile doesn't reach his eyes.

Seizing the opportunity, I follow him to the kitchen. "I'm sorry about her," I whisper.

He flicks the kettle on to a boil. Still warm, it rumbles to life, providing us with some privacy. "Stop apologising. It's not your fault." Tenderly, he tucks my hair behind my ear and kisses my forehead.

Stepping in closer, I press my hands to his chest and sigh. "I'm glad you're here, at least."

Cole winces. "Actually, I need to get back to work." My heart sinks, but I hide it. Cavalry lost. "Will you be okay?"

"I've survived eighteen years so far."

Cole flashes me an apologetic smile as he refills Mum's teacup. "I'm not sure how."

His grumbled validation makes me smile. "I'll walk you out while it brews. Queen Sheila will request a replacement if it's too weak." Come to think of it, maybe her dislike of me follows the same logic. Perhaps my weakness renders me unpalatable too.

Connecting our hands by monkey grip, Cole leads us back into the living room and stops short of Mum. She stares up at him expectantly.

"I'm afraid I must be going, Sheila. It was . . . enlightening to meet you," he says.

I hide my smile at Cole's carefully chosen word, but it bursts free regardless when he turns Mum's outstretched hand to the side, opting to shake rather than kiss it.

"So soon?" she asks. "We were just getting to know each other."

"Work calls," he says.

"Of course. An important man such as yourself." Mum bats her eyelashes, flashing a flirty smile, and I wonder if she realises how she presents. Does she choose this behaviour, having considered all options and consequences, or simply lack awareness?

I clear my throat and follow Cole through the gallery. Three hot-pink suitcases stand at attention outside Beth's open bedroom door. Funny, that. "Where would you like these?" Cole asks, halting at their feet.

"On a plane?" I suggest, and he smirks. "But in here will have to do, I guess." I walk into Beth's room and gesture towards her bed. One at a time, Cole lays each case at the end of the mattress, ready to unpack. The sight makes me shudder. I still can't believe Mum's here. "Thank you."

When I click the bedroom door shut, Cole pulls me into his arms. "I feel terrible leaving. Are you sure you'll be okay?"

I nod. "I'll lock myself in my studio for the day and crank up the music."

"Good idea," he says. "You were wrong, by the way."

"About what?"

Cole crinkles his nose. "She's pretty bad."

My shoulders slump. "I'm so glad you see it."

"It's hardly subtle," Cole scoffs. He strokes the back of my neck with warm fingers, and my gaze drops to our feet as Mum's opinion of my art sweeps through my bones, turning them black and crumbly.

"Hey," Cole says, lifting my chin. "Don't let her get to you."

I huff out a hopeless laugh. "Believe me, I try. It's harder than you think."

He catches my eyes with his. "You are exceptional. Don't let anyone tell you otherwise."

A smile tugs at my lips. I hold my fingers up an inch apart. "I think you may be a tad biased."

"Bollocks," Cole says, but I grimace and drag in a breath.

"My mum doesn't actually like me, just so you know. She's told me more than once and knows me better than anyone. So consider yourself warned."

Cole seems stunned as he silently takes me in. The disbelief is there—after all, mums are biologically built to like their offspring, right?—but then his frown returns, almost angrily. "Then there's something wrong with her, or she doesn't know you at all." He presses his hand to my sternum. "It's my job to read people, and I see you. The real you. In here, and she's kind—brave—honest. *Very* likeable."

I can't help but shudder. Is it possible I've fooled him too?

As if reading my thoughts, Cole sighs, then cups my cheeks. "No one else smiles and greets Bernie every morning, let alone helps him pack away. Unlikeable people don't do that. And did you know Hannah is your number one fan and forever warning me not to screw things up?" He shakes his head. "You're a good person, Aves. Your friends see it. I see it. It's time you did too."

"Wait . . ." I frown. "You see me with Bernie? How?"

Cole sighs and drops his arms. "That's what you took away from everything I just said?" He rolls his eyes, then lowers his lips to mine, but I turn my head.

"Not so fast, Mister. Tell me how you know about Bernie." A rosy blush blossoms across Cole's jaw, and I narrow my eyes, calculating possibilities. "Do you watch me on the surveillance cameras like a creepy stalker?"

He grins. "I'm afraid I can't answer any further questions without my lawyer present."

I throw my head back and laugh. "That tells me everything I need to know." With a crooked grin, I shrug. "I guess that shouldn't surprise me. You do have somewhat of a history." Closing in on his lips, I wind my fingers through his hair. "Should I do a show for you tomorrow morning? Flash a little flesh and brighten your day?"

He bites my bottom lip, sending shivers south. "You should. I'm sure Joe in the security office would love it."

I feign sincerity. "Well, in that case, I'll do it."

Cole growls against my mouth and squeezes my bum cheek. "You do and I'll spank this pretty arse."

"Is that meant to deter or encourage me?"

Cole laughs under his breath, but then his gaze turns molten, and he rests his forehead against mine. "The only eyes I want on you are mine. Are we clear?"

"Crystal." I wink with a grin. I love being wanted. Protected. Desired. *Owned*.

After a final scorching kiss filled with everything from last night, Cole bops me on the nose with his index finger and opens the front door. "I'll see you tomorrow. Good luck."

My heart twists. Tomorrow feels like a week away. "See you then."

I lock the door behind him and slump against its back, listening as his car fades into the distance. I'd give anything to snuggle up in front of his fireplace tonight rather than be here. I don't want to go back into that room, but what choice do I have?

"I must say, I was appalled to hear you lost the apartment. I went to great lengths to get that for you," Mum says as I slump to the sofa.

Staring at my knees, I pluck at the stretchy fabric of my yoga pants. "I know. I had trouble paying the rent after Mia left."

Mum arches a brow. "She seemed a nice young girl. Why did she leave?"

I don't bother to explain Mia bailed the minute the quarterly bills arrived. Or that getting her share of the rent was harder than quantum physics. Mum would insist I act, then possibly discover the action I took. "She missed her family," I lie.

"Well, you should have found another housemate, then. I mean, really, to let it get to the point of eviction." Mum shakes her head, then takes another sip of well-brewed tea. "Although, I can't say I'm surprised. Supporting yourself is hard. Much easier to freeload off Bethany, I suppose."

Shame emerges from its shallow grave, but I bite the inside of my cheek and find solace in the metallic tang of blood. "I pay my way here," I say. Well, at least, I try. Glen Iris is out of reach for many.

"But you must realise what an inconvenience it is for Bethany. She worked hard to build this house for herself—not you."

The magical mirage of being wanted here wavers, and nausea swirls up my throat. "Beth said I can stay until I find my feet. We get along great. And I'm house-sitting now."

"I'm sure she did. Her saviour complex well in action—forever pitying the weak. She has a big heart, your sister. Sometimes, to her detriment."

If Mum loathed Beth as much as she loathes me, I'd know it's just the way she is. But she doesn't, and that fact leaves one terrifying question dangling in the air like a giant Filipino fruit bat. Is it my fault or hers?

With a pained smile, I resolve not to take Mum's bait. "Beth is the best."

Silence falls, and Mum eyes me with cool curiosity. She isn't used to my composure and doesn't quite know what to make of it. She'd rather I lose my shit. She craves it—needs it—like a junkie needs their fix. Because at the point when I scream and cry, it's clearly me who's rotten—not her.

See! Avery Lee is awful. Avery Lee treats me terribly. The disrespect after everything I've done for the child. What did I do to deserve such horror?

I shudder as I remember all the phone calls I overheard saying as much and worse.

In classic form, Mum would turn up the heat, wait for the boiling point, then twist and turn every fact on its head until the truth lay shredded and veiled by a noxious fog. It was in there somewhere . . . *I think* . . . but beyond rescue. Or maybe it wasn't, and Mum was right.

She was the victim, and I the monster.

The breathy laugh returns like puffs of toxic gas, and the teacup chinks against the saucer as they meet the side table.

God, I hate tea.

"I see," Mum says, adjusting the fall of her sunshine dress so it spills evenly over her crossed knees. "You think you're all mature now you're screwing your wealthy boss? Well, you can delude yourself all you like, Avery Lee, but we both know this fling with Cole is temporary. I imagine you're merely flavour of the month. Every successful man slums it at least once, and a leopard doesn't change her spots."

A gasp bursts free from my mouth as her words reach into my torso and steal my essence. I bolt to my feet with clenched fists as tears spring to my eyes, blurring Mum's face. She's zeroed in on my weak spot like a skilled assassin does their mark, and she knows it.

Satisfaction curls up the corners of her mouth, causing fire to rise up my spine. My heart thumps violently but traps my voice. There's so much I want to say. Perfect, witty, biting words that will form and haunt me later. But right now, my throat is seized, and my mind is frozen.

For a beautiful second, I imagine smashing that flipping teacup to the floor at her feet. But it's Beth's teacup and Beth's floor—Beth's velvet sofa—and I don't want to prove Mum right. So, instead, with a quivering bottom lip clamped between my teeth, I charge for the studio, slam the door shut, flip the lock, and slide down the wall like splattered slime.

My breaths heave. In, out. In, out. In, out. Faster. Faster. Faster. And bony knees cradle my forehead as I grip my tangled hair, choking on tears. The emotional tornado is too much to contain, too confusing to sort, and too fast to process. I'm at its complete mercy and can only hang on for the ride as it rips through me and pray it passes—pray I survive.

I crawl across the studio floor, drag my patchwork cushion closer, and bury my face. Tears bleed into the silk, and my hip bone protests as it digs into the hard floor, but I don't care. Pain that makes sense is my friend.

I fight for steady breaths, and eventually, they slow down until nothing remains but eerie silence and an empty shell. I slide my phone out of my hoodie pocket and shoot Beth a text. Only three words long but perfect in their truth.

I hate her.

But guilt drowns me as soon as I hit send, and every kind thing Mum's ever done for me flashes through the ether—pink-tinged and blurry at the edges like a vintage Hallmark film.

Fuck. She's right. I am the monster.

Hours later, the flopped vase spins around and round, parading its derangement as if to taunt me. I growl at the pottery wheel and hit the off switch. It's my seventh failed attempt, but my head and heart simply aren't in it. How can they be when they're sifting through every conflicting childhood memory?

"It's meant to be like riding a fucking bike," I grumble as I slice the mangled clay from the wheel and launch it across the room with a frustrated grunt. It thuds against the door, then splats to the floor.

There. Perfect. I'll pop it in the kiln like that as a representation of what Mum does to people. Hopefully, it explodes. That'll capture it even better.

With a deep inhale, I close my eyes and do what the school counsellor once taught me: I imagine a safe place in nature where I can calm down. I choose a tranquil teal lagoon surrounded by rainforest and rocks. A gentle breeze kisses my skin, and dappled sunlight warms it. I step into the water and visualise it dissolving all my worries. It doesn't work, but the long-awaited sound of the bathroom door latching brings a wave of relief, and I bolt from the studio, starving. I was starting to think the woman had a catheter inserted.

Raiding the fridge, I grab a bottle of water and the tub of yoghurt, then race back to my studio unseen. Fuck the spoon. A carving tool will work. While I love the mezzanine, it's times like this I wish I had a bedroom door like most people. One with a lock.

The toilet flushes next door, and I hold my breath, waiting for Mum's footsteps to pass by and fade, but they stop too soon. A knock sounds on my door. "Avery, can I speak to you?"

There's no pretending I'm not in here. I could ignore her, but that would only antagonise. Why didn't I crank the music like I told Cole

I would? That would have provided plausible deniability. Dumb. Dumb. Dumb.

Begrudgingly, I walk to the door and open it to the width of my Ugg boot. She doesn't deserve to see my sanctuary. "What is it?"

"Can I come in?" Before I respond, Mum pushes against the door, but I hold it steady.

"No."

Mum sighs. "I obviously upset you earlier."

I raise a brow without a word. She doesn't need me to confirm that for her.

"I apologise," she says, and as the foreign words pass through her lips, I fight to keep my eyes from boggling. I scan her face with a frown, looking for the catch. Averting her gaze, she smooths the back of her beehive with one hand. "I'm tired from my trip. Things haven't been easy the past few weeks, and I forgot how sensitive you are."

Me. Sensitive. Of course, it's my sensitivity—not her words.

"I'm not upset because I'm sensitive," I say quietly. "I'm upset because you were mean."

Her chin nudges higher, and her sharp eyes dart back to mine. "You are too sensitive, Avery Lee. You can't deny that. Anyway, I've apologised, and whether or not you like it, we'll be living together for months, so we must reach—"

I cut her off. "*Months?* That long?" My life force fades.

Please, no.

"Yes. So we'll have to learn how to get along."

I stare at her while my perfect new world crumbles before my eyes and my old one rises from the dead. "I can't do this," I whisper more to myself and the floor than her.

"Well, if you don't like it, you can always leave." I look up to see Mum smugly pointing to the front door.

I don't like it. Not one bit. But I'm not leaving my home, even if it is temporary, or imposing on Cole or Jen. I can't afford a hotel for months. And my studio's here. But what's more, Mum is struggling, and I want to be her daughter—not a monster. I should be here for her, at the very least. That's what family does. But what if you're poison to each other? When is enough, enough?

Ripped in two, my heart continues to war. Memories of Mum's smile when I was little—when she was happy—appear again. She gave me life. I survived because of her. She endured the pain, the sleepless nights, every scraped knee and school drop-off. But somewhere along the line, things deteriorated. Dad . . . *vanished*, and I grew a personality. My malleability dissolved.

My shoulders slump in a defeated sigh. "We'll make it work."

I shut the door as Mum opens her mouth to speak. I don't want to hear it. And if I look at her again, I risk seeing the scared little girl behind her venom, and guilt will strangle me whole. That's what our relationship is—a fillet of premium quality guilt, topped with mixed spite, and finished with a healthy dose of resentment on the side.

I need time to process, and I have work to do. Lots and lots of work. That will be my escape.

Eighteen

"This frown is becoming permanent," Cole says as we lie naked in his bed, our legs entangled. He rubs his thumb between my brows, easing the tension, but I continue to stare at his cedar-clad ceiling, lost.

This week has been hell. *Mum* has been hell, and I can't rid her from my thoughts for long. It's like she has me in a psychic choke-hold.

Cole strokes his fingertips up and down my arm. "I'd hate for the wind to change—you'd be stuck like that forever."

His words penetrate the dark daze, causing a smile to prick my lips. I glance up at him. "My dad used to say that."

His grin tilts. "So did my mum."

It's the first time he's mentioned his mum unprompted, so I tread carefully. "Can you tell me about her?" I soften my voice, giving him an out if he needs it, but instead Cole shifts to his back with a sigh, tucking his technicolour arm under his head.

The white sheets twist low around his waist like they would a classical Greek statue, and his light-honey skin gleams as it hugs every chiselled muscle.

God, he's gorgeous.

"My mum was beautiful," he says, "and not only on the outside. Love radiated through her skin—through her smile—like she was filled with light. Her hips swayed whenever music played, and she would sing whenever a paintbrush touched her hand. There was a gentle strength about her. I was fifteen when she died, and after that"—Cole swallows as his eyes squeeze shut—"nothing was the same."

Fifteen. That's rough. At least when Dad . . . *went*, I wasn't yet hormonal or lost in the throes of adolescence, and Beth had already left her teens.

"I'm sorry," I whisper, kneading his shoulder. When you rip the keystone from an arch, everything can crumble. Dad was my family's keystone. Cole's mum was likely theirs. I want to know more—every bend and break and bump in the path that led him here—but I won't push. Instead, I sweep my fingers through his hair, press a kiss to his forehead, and whisper, "She sounds as incredible as her son."

Sad eyes meet mine, staring intently. "You remind me of her, you know? You have that same light. It has to fight its way through sometimes, but it's there—in your eyes, in your smile. Maybe it's an artist thing."

A rush of warmth floods my chest, and I can't help but smile.

"Like now," he says, brushing his thumb over my cheek, wearing a grin of his own. "You're glowing." He chuckles. "And now blushing too."

I avert my gaze and will my cheeks to cool. "What was her name?"

"Charlene," he rasps.

Charlene. Ella's middle name. "That's lovely."

He folds me into his arms, tucking me against his chest, but while my heart aches for him, guilt gnaws at my insides too. Here he mourns his mother while I detest mine.

"You must hate how I treat my mum," I say, circling his belly button with my finger, tracing the fine line of dark hair headed south.

A long silence falls, but Cole's heartbeat remains steady beneath my ear. "On the contrary," he says. "If this is Sheila's MO, I've been wondering why you keep her in your life."

I climb to my elbow with my brows in a twist. "She's my *mum*."

"And?"

"I don't have a choice."

Cole cocks his head. "Don't you?"

His question circles my brain. It's one I've never considered. What's he suggesting I do? Cut off my own mother? What kind of person does that? Besides, I don't have the visible scars or stolen innocence—the solid reasons people might understand. "No, I don't."

Silence erupts again, but the idea lingers, spinning like a shiny pinwheel at a fair. The rainbow foil glimmers with possibility, but I crush it in my fist. No. I could never do that.

"You deserve better," Cole says gently.

I shake my head. In my quest to purge frustration, I've misled him. It takes two to tango, after all. "You haven't seen everything. I give as good as I get. I'm no angel, trust me."

Cole huffs a soft laugh and pulls me back against him. "We'll have to agree to disagree on that."

My mind races for a solid minute before I rein it in. "How's your case going?" I ask, taking the spotlight off me.

Cole sighs heavily. "It's over, thank Christ. I wouldn't have survived another week. It was a nightmare."

I gathered as much. The man practically slept at Benedict's all week, his sweet goodnight texts creeping closer to dawn with every day that passed.

"Are you okay?" I ask, glancing up to assess the pallor I've noticed of late.

He looks at me like no one's ever asked him that. "What do you mean?"

"You seem heavier, that's all, even for you. So I'm wondering if you're okay?"

Cole swallows as pain fills his eyes. The same pain that gripped his voice when he talked about wanting to leave Benedict's, I'll bet, but quickly it's contained. "I'm okay," he says. "I've found a trick to get me through."

"Oh yeah?" I mirror his smile.

He touches my temple, then skims his fingertips down my jaw. "I pretend you're my client in every case so I can actually care."

Wow. That's flattering but concerning. I prop back up to one elbow, resting my head in my hand. "In your position, you get to pick cases, right?"

Grimly, Cole turns his focus to the ceiling. "The firm has certain clients it can't say no to."

"Like Miss Blue Satin Sparkles—*Vivian*?" I tease.

That earns me a brief smirk. "She's one of them, but there are plenty more."

"And why can't you say no to them?"

Again, Cole sighs as if every question dumps another weight on his chest. "They're important people and friends of the firm with too much sway over high society and much of our client base to enrage. I need to protect Benedict's. It's the least I can do. I owe Gerard . . . everything." Cole's voice cracks on that last word, and he continues to glare at the ceiling, seeming to drift away.

I want to ask what Gerard actually did—why he's owed so much. I'd assumed he'd merely boosted Cole's career—left him an inheritance—but now I'm not so sure. Would that equate to owing someone *everything*? Everything is a lot. But I sense my question limit for the day has been exhausted.

"Well, I missed you," I say to gently coax him back. After spending most nights with him the first week Mum was here, five in a row alone at home was torture.

"Me too," he says. "You survived Sheila though. You're tough."

"Barely," I groan. "And I have twenty bowls, a dozen vases, and two jugs to prove it."

Cole squeezes my breast. "Two jugs, you say?"

I laugh but then engage a haughty tone and lift my nose to match. "I would have thought jug jokes were beneath both your intellect and maturity, Mr. Benedict."

He grins. "Inside every man is a pimple-faced boy who still loves boob jokes." He drops his mouth to my breasts, kissing and sucking them with fervour.

"Ouch!" I say, elbowing him away.

Cole's eyes glint with mischief as he comes back up, and I take in the purply-pink circle marring one boob. My blood heats, and I squirm.

He marked me.

"You're bad," I whisper seductively. I drag my hand across his chest and head south, over his abs and down the valley of his *V*, ready for round four. But abruptly, he rolls off the bed and stands, offering out his hand.

"Come. You've made us late enough already."

"*I've* made us late?" I scoff. "I was dressed—almost ready to go—thank you very much."

"Yes, but you knew that dress would end up on the floor when I saw you in it. That was your evil little plan. No one dresses like that to babysit." He winks with a devilish smirk. "Now hurry up. Hannah will have my balls if we keep her waiting any longer. This was your idea, don't forget."

I roll my eyes but give him my hand to help me up. He's half-right. I knew he'd love the dress, just not that much. And in defence of the tiny hemline, I intended to tame it with tights and boots, only I didn't get the chance. As soon as I slinked it over my head, Cole strolled out of the bathroom all wet and warm with a towel hung around his hips, rubbing his glistening skin dry with another. We both froze, our eyes roaming each other before meeting again. And that was it. Goodbye, dress. Goodbye, towels. Hello, bedroom wall. Then floor. Then bed. We're ridiculous, and that knowledge makes me giddy.

I re-fix my dress, then pull on my tights. "Do you mind dropping me home afterwards? You're welcome to stay. I just want to get a full day in the studio tomorrow, since Mum will be out." She has new friends. I'm not sure how.

"Whatever you want," he says. "It seems you're becoming quite the workaholic."

As I wrestle on my sparkly boots, I smile. I guess I am. I wasn't lying when I said the studio would be my escape. That's where I am every night I'm home until Mum's bedroom door clicks shut. "Maybe I've learnt from the best."

"Or maybe you're just avoiding your mum," Cole says, shuffling into his jeans.

"Well, duh. But maybe I've also emailed photos of my work to galleries. Maybe I want to be ready in case anything comes from it. Not that it ever will."

I look up to find Cole has stopped dressing. Over a brilliant smile, his brows are high. "That's incredible. Why didn't you tell me?"

I shrug. "Like I said, it's unlikely anything will come from it."

"Bollocks," he says. "I've seen your work."

"Well, I haven't heard anything back, and it's been a couple of weeks."

"You have the talent, baby. Now you need the connections."

I glance up as I tie my laces. "Connections?"

"Yeah. People in the industry. People who know people. Ones to help get your foot in the door."

I scan my brain. "Other than my old art teacher, I don't know any-one."

"Have you asked anyone else? Old friends? Family?"

"That seems sleazy. I can't use people like that."

Buttoning his jeans, Cole shakes his head. "Only you would think of networking as a moral abomination." The mattress dips as he sits next to me and tucks my hair behind my ear. I'll never tire of him doing that. "How about asking your man friend, then? Surely he sup-ports your dreams."

I arch a brow and smirk. "Man friend? That is the cheesiest thing you've ever said."

His eyes darken. "Well, I think we've established I'm no boy."

That we have. Many fucking times. "Well then," I say, "do you know anyone with connections like that, *man friend*?"

His dimple sparkles. "I do. Forward me your email and photos, and I'll make a few calls."

"You'd do that?"

He drops his mouth to my ear. "I'd do anything for you, Miss Mas-ters." He catches my earlobe between his teeth, his hot breath feath-ering my neck, and I shiver as warmth curls down to my core, but then he retreats. *Tease*.

As he walks to the closet, his lean, muscular back is on full display, but I'm too busy dissecting his offer to appreciate the sight. Images of fancy gallery openings carousel through my mind in a spin of satin and champagne, but I'm jumping the gun. It'll probably never hap-pen, and even if it does, do I want it credited to screwing the right man?

Dressed, Cole returns, carrying my jacket. He holds it up, prompt-ing me to slide in my arms. I oblige. Forever the gentleman, except in bed, where I'm glad he's not. He turns me to face him. "What's going on? Your thoughts are practically screaming."

I bite my bottom lip, wrestling over whether to say anything. Who am I to impose conditions on his generous offer? But this is important. This is *mine*. Wincing, I lift my gaze to meet his. "My work needs to stand on its own. I don't want special treatment just because they owe you a favour or something. That would be humiliating, and I'd feel like a fraud."

Cole's lips twitch. "I'll make it clear there are no expectations. The merit of your work alone should be the focus. But, in my opinion, they'd be lucky to have you."

His certainty, the reverence in his stare, the tenderness in his smile—they all fill my chest and threaten to explode like a grade-six science experiment. I throw my arms around his neck and kiss his cheek. "Thank you," I say, but in those two words swims so much more.

Hannah's interior style can only be described as hippie boho. Macramé wall hangings with beaded tassels cloak her apartment walls. Mismatched painted furniture fills the lounge room, showcasing stacks of colourful books, tie-dye doilies, and more babushka dolls than I've ever seen. A bronze couch loaded with mandala cushions faces the television, and a hint of lavender lingers in the air.

It's 2:00 a.m., and Cole disappeared ten minutes ago to check on Ella. I rise from the couch to search for him and find him standing at the end of the hall, leaning against Ella's door frame, lost in a trance. I tiptoe towards him as quietly as boots allow, then slide my hand over his shoulder and peek inside. Tiny and cherubic, Ella lies fast asleep under frilly pink covers. Her little breaths float across the room, and I sigh at her sweetness.

She was a bundle of energy tonight. She clapped her pudgy hands, bounced on the couch, spilt spaghetti everywhere, and made us dance with Dorothy the Dinosaur no less than a dozen times. And let me tell you, Cole has *moves*. It's official, he'd make an excellent Wiggle. An excellent father too.

"She's angelic," I whisper, glancing up at him. The light from the muted television bounces down the hall, painting Cole's profile blue, and I spot moisture in his eyes.

He clears his throat. "That she is." Stepping back, he slowly clicks her bedroom door shut, then turns to face me. His thumbs graze my cheekbones as he cradles my face. "She means the world to me."

"I know," I say. That was more than evident tonight, but still, sadness seems to ooze from him, thickening the air and clogging my throat. I swallow it down. "Where's Ella's dad?" I gently ask.

Cole's jaw tightens, his hands drop away, and immediately, I regret prying. He delivers four hard words: "Where despicable creatures belong." Then turns away and charges down the hall.

I trace his steps. "Sorry. I didn't mean to pry."

"No, you never do," he snaps.

The icy words Taser my heart and shock me still. *What just happened?*

Cole halts at the end of the hallway with a heavy sigh, hangs his head, then turns back to face me. "I'm sorry. That was unfair."

I swallow the rocks in my throat. "It's okay." But is it really? He seems to guard a circus tent full of secrets while knowing every humiliating one of mine. But what's worse is feeling so incredibly close to him one minute and shut out the next. Smacking face first into an invisible shield is disorienting.

He grips the back of his neck with an agonised expression. "No, it's not. Come here."

Tentatively, I close the space between us, and the second I'm within reach, he wraps me in his arms. I rest my forehead against his collarbone, willing the panic to wash away.

He kisses the top of my head. "I can't talk about it," he says in a strangled voice. "But my reaction was shitty. Forgive me?"

Pulling back, I nod, my wide eyes glued to his. The air buzzes around us, dense and electric, as though a dark storm looms nearby. A hundred questions zip through my head, and his pain grips my heart, but it's none of my business. He said as much. Not everyone can open up on my command, and why should they?

The sudden slam of a door makes us flinch.

"Oh, *looove*birds. Where are you?" The slurred singsong voice drifts from the entrance, followed by a clang, rattle, smash, and, "Whoopsie."

Cole and I look at each other. "She's tanked," I say.

"She doesn't hold liquor well. One of the many reasons she's safer at home on Saturday nights." Cole rolls his eyes, but his lips twitch with a smile.

Thankful for the atmospheric change, I take his hand and tug him along. "Let's stop her before she wakes Ella."

As we approach the front door, Hannah stands in a sexy silver mini dress. Her glossy black heels lie askew, and her bare feet, covered in black thigh-high stockings, rest perilously close to ceramic shards scattered all over the floor. She grips the wall with one hand and leans into the mirror, fogging the glass with her breath. Sparkly fingernails drag down the side of her face as she admires her reflection. "Oh, fizzle sticks. I look like a zombie."

She doesn't. Even in her state—with her cinnamon waves nested in knots and mascara smudged under her eyes—lives dishevelled beauty.

Cole curses and runs a hand through his hair. "Don't move." He grumbles about a dustpan, then disappears to the kitchen.

Hannah drops her gaze to the pale timber floorboards. "Oh crap, that was my favourite one." Pouting at the broken orange vase, she tries to finger-comb her hair with no success. Her fingers catch in the tangles, so she gives up and instead pats the top of her head with both hands. It does zilch to fix her hair, and I bite back a laugh.

"Where's my baby girl?" she asks with a floaty smile.

"She's in bed, fast asleep. She had a great night. How about you?"

Hannah takes a moment to process my question, then her face lights up. She throws her arms in the air and spins in a wobbly circle, narrowly missing the hazard on the floor. I rush towards her, zigzagging between the pieces, to clutch her shoulders still. "Careful. You'll cut yourself."

Cole returns and crouches at Hannah's feet with the dustpan and a pair of thongs. He taps her ankle. "Lift."

Hannah listens, raising one foot as she digs her fingernails into my arms. Cole slides a thong on over her stockings while I hold her steady. He does the same with her other foot, and we both sigh when she's out of danger.

Pointing to her feet, Hannah erupts into laughter and cradles her stomach. "I'm a sloth. Look, I'm a sloth!" She keels over, hyperventilating as tears run down her cheeks, cutting white valleys through her bronzer.

It shouldn't be so funny, but for some reason, it really is. Cole and I look at each other with loaded smirks, then down to Hannah's two-toed, black hot-pink-thonged feet. The dam bursts, and we lose it. Leaning on each other, we dissolve into wild belly-aching laughter, re-erupting every time we glance back to Hannah's feet.

Eventually, we regain a semblance of composure. Hannah's ragged breaths calm, and her eyes sparkle with joy. For once, she looks her age, and that thrills me. "I had the best night, Aves. The *bestest* best. Thank you so much." She plants a wet kiss on my cheek.

"Any time," I say, amused.

Cole shakes his head, then lobs Hannah's arm around his shoulders to help her walk. She almost falls over anyway. "Hell, I'll just carry you," he says. "Come on, trouble. Let's get you to bed."

Taking over clean-up duty, I squat to the ground and gather the dustpan and broom. Hannah sags in Cole's arms, limp and loose, like a sack of potatoes. "Christ," he grits, stumbling backwards. Ceramic cracks under his shoe. "Help me out here, would you?"

Hannah giggles before throwing her arms around his neck. Gaining balance, Cole heads for the hall. Halfway across the dining room, Hannah throws her head upside down to look at me. "*Psst*, Aves, I met a sexy man. See?" She releases one arm from Cole's neck, and it flops down, dangling like a dead snake. Black digits scroll across the pale skin of her forearm, messy and jagged. "He's so hot. You'll love him." Her eyebrows jump up and down, or rather down and up from this angle.

"No, she damn well won't," Cole growls.

Hannah snickers, slogs her head back upright, then pinches Cole's cheeks and shakes his head from side to side. His steps falter. "Aw, you're so cute when you're jealous, Dribbles."

I quirk a brow at Cole's back. "Dribbles?"

"Ignore her, she's drunk," he deadpans before disappearing down the hall.

I smile at the dirt and shards as they collect in the dustpan. *Okay, then.*

Nineteen

On Monday morning, I stroll into the Mini-Bees staffroom to find Hannah leaning over the kitchenette bench, cradling her head in her delicate hands. She peers up at me, moving as little as possible, then groans and looks away. "You're early."

I bite back a smile as I hang my satchel and jacket, then saunter towards her. "So tell me about this sexy man."

Her cheeks fume red, and she shakes her head. "I'm so embarrassed."

"Don't be. You got drunk, big deal."

Hannah stands up with a sigh and leans her hip against the benchtop, folding her arms. "It's not only that. I wish it was."

"Why, what happened?" She shakes her head again and mashes her lips into a hard line. I huff out a laugh. "C'mon, it can't be that bad, surely?"

Wincing, she drops her chin. "I had sex with him, Aves. In a dirty nightclub toilet, of all places."

My shoulders relax. "That's not so bad. People do that. You're only young once."

Her jaw clenches. "That's not all."

I quirk a brow. "What else?"

She clasps a hand over her mouth. "Nope, I can't even say it."

I nudge her. "Just tell me."

Disgust darkens her delicate features, stirring dread in the pit of my stomach.

God, it must be bad.

She steps closer, plants her hands on my shoulders, suspiciously scans the room, then stares at me, horrified. "I can't remember his name," she says, annunciating each word through gritted teeth.

I erupt in laughter. "Jesus, Hannah. I thought you were going to tell me someone hurt you, or after him, you did the rest of the queue."

She whacks my arm. "Avery, you're terrible!"

"Huh," I retort, "I'm not the one who screwed a stranger in a public toilet, am I?" I flash her a wink. It's completely true. Cole most certainly wasn't a stranger.

Hannah's cheeks reignite.

"I'm joking," I say. "Seriously, don't beat yourself up. You've done nothing wrong. Did you use protection?"

Her arms flop to her sides, and her gaze hits the floor. "That I do remember." She crinkles her nose. "I sang 'The Condom Song.'"

"'The Condom Song'?" My eyes gape, but I can't stop a shit-eating grin from engulfing my face.

She shudders. "Please don't make me repeat myself. It was a grade-seven sex-ed thing."

Laughter threatens to explode from my mouth, but I breathe through it. She sang a *condom* song? Oh lordy Lord, this girl is gold.

Her nostrils flare as she inhales. "I don't do things like this. What kind of mother am I? What got into me?"

"Tequila, by the sounds of it." I jiggle my brows. "Amongst other things."

Hannah drops a hand to her stomach, and her face further pales. "Please don't mention alcohol. I'm never drinking again."

If she's still suffering this bad today, yesterday must have been hell.

"Why don't you just phone him and ask for his name?" I suggest.

She looks at me, dumbfounded, but doesn't deny having kept his number. "Are you serious? I can't do that."

"You never know, he might answer the phone and say it. Or better yet, if he doesn't answer, his voicemail might tell you."

"And what if he answers but doesn't say it?" She shakes her head. "No, no, no, no. I am not doing that."

"Does he have your number, then?"

She facepalms. "I don't remember that either."

The poor girl is two minutes away from crawling into a dark hole for the rest of her days. I squeeze her elbow. "Hey, don't worry. We've all done crazy things, trust me." If only she knew.

"Well, I don't do crazy things, Aves. Not typically. I also don't do men with tattoos and earrings typically. They're not my type." Her words say one thing, but the flush of her cheeks and sheepish smile say something else entirely.

I grin. "Well, they do say once you go tat, you never go back."

Hannah huffs. "That's not the saying."

Staring wistfully at the ceiling, I force a dreamy expression. "No, but it really should be."

"Ugh, please don't torture me with details of my brother. Then I really will throw up."

Snickering, I spy two suited-up parents through the window, entering Mini-Bees. "We're up. I'll change the nappies today because that's what kind of awesome friend I am."

"Thank you," she says. "If I saw one stinky . . . oh, shizzle, I can't even say it." Hannah clasps her mouth and takes a few seconds to gather herself, then looks at me pleadingly. "Please don't tell Cole about this. He still thinks I'm sixteen."

I offer a reassuring smile. "Your secret's safe with me."

"Thanks." Hannah sighs, then turns to leave the room, but I call out her name. She spins back around, her brows high in question.

"You know, I could always phone mystery man. Pretend I have the wrong number. Ask who I'm speaking to." After all, one phone call won't kill me.

She stares at me, her brain ticking behind narrowed eyes. "You think that'd work?"

"It might. In any case, we have nothing to lose."

Her eyes glimmer like sapphires when she smiles. "Tonight?"

I nod and grin. "Tonight."

One greasy chow mein noodle slops against my chin, and another splats to the dusty studio floor where I sit cross-legged. The rest, by some sweet miracle, land in my mouth. Discreetly, I clean up my mess, hoping it went unnoticed, but Cole lets out a wheezy snort. "You eat like a tornado. You know that?"

I do. It's a symptom of a mind always elsewhere. I tilt my head to the side and look up. "Can't you pretend not to notice for once and leave me with some dignity?" I twirl my plastic fork in his direction. "We can't all exude grace and show off our dexterity as we eat."

Sitting on the workbench stool, Cole cocks a thick brow, then frowns at the chopsticks perched in his fingers. Sculptures surround him, along with drip-stained buckets of glaze, crimped silver letters, and busy shelves. The top few buttons of his white shirt lie undone, offering a glimpse of pale-caramel skin and a dusting of dark hair. Oxford shoes rest on the chrome foot ring, and his black suit pants stretch over splayed knees. It's yet another magazine-worthy scene. "They're just chopsticks," he says. "Sometimes I prefer them, but not to show off."

I roll my eyes and dig back into my noodles. "Uh-*huh*."

His amused stare twinkles in the last bands of sunset pushing through the shutters. "What?"

I can't help but grin. "Why?"

"Why what?" Eyeing me quizzically, he grins too.

God, we're adorable.

"Why do you prefer chopsticks? Explain yourself." I suspect why, but I want to watch him squirm. I've been to Chinese restaurants with Beth, and you can taste the palpable pride wafting from that one white dude who's mastered chopsticks and wants everyone to know. How do you spell . . . *smug?*

"Well, for one, they improve coordination. Secondly, they increase mindfulness while you eat, and lastly, it's tradition with this cuisine."

Damn it, I didn't expect him to have sound reasoning, but of course he does—he's Cole. I opt to mess with him anyway because it's fun. "Oh, I believe you."

He narrows his eyes. "What exactly are you implying?"

I swallow my last bite, then enclose my boring fork inside the small white box and close the lid. "You can't tell me eating with chopsticks is preferable to a fork, even with all those alleged benefits. There's another reason, you just don't want to admit it."

"Proven benefits—not alleged," he corrects. "They become second nature. It's really no big deal."

I hold up my thumb and forefinger an inch apart. "You don't even feel a teensy bit clever? Are you telling me chopsticks don't feed your ego at all?"

He rumbles a beautiful, deep laugh. "That's ridiculous." But a rosy tinge flushes his cheeks.

"Ha, I knew it!"

He slaps the chopsticks down on the workbench. "Please pass me my fork."

I eye the plastic takeaway bag next to me but think better of it. "Oh no, I might be mad jealous, but I also find chopsticks in your manly hands sexy as fuck. No fork for you." I wink at him, and his mouth tugs into a dirty smile.

"Language, Miss Masters."

His low, gravelly voice tingles at the apex of my thighs, causing me to wriggle. I pretend I'm merely adjusting my position for comfort, but Cole knows better. His gaze darkens, and he winks back, fuelling my urge to crawl across the studio floor, Marilyn-style, and straddle his lap. But my phone vibrates against the wire rack and steals the spotlight. I check it.

Hannah:
Let me know the second it's done!

It's the fifth panicky DM Hannah's sent since I left work. "Your sister's a little nutty. You know that?" I rest my phone back down.

Cole's chopsticks re-emerge, loaded with a tidy mouthful of Singapore noodles. "I do." They find his mouth with ease. No slops on the chin. No splats on his shirt. God, I really need to at least master a fork.

My phone buzzes again, and it's Hannah *again*. Cole and I only have an hour before he returns to work, at which time Mum will be home from her new divorce support group full of rich lonely men. I wanted to wait, but it's time to put poor Hannah out of her misery. "Can you give me a minute? I need to make a call for your sister real quick."

"What for?" Cole asks, tilting his noodle box to catch the scraps.

With a smile, I climb to my feet, rubbish and phone in hand. "Secret girls' business."

"Is that right?" He looks amused, and his face shines with that extra glimmer of joy he gets whenever he watches me and Hannah mess around. Anyone would love Hannah, but I can tell it means something more to him that I do.

I peck his cheek as I saunter past to the corner bin. "Mm-hmm."

"You can't tell me anything?"

I consider his question and figure the bare basics will do no harm. Pretty sure it's the sex in the toilet part Hannah doesn't want him to know. Without that tidbit, forgetting someone's name is no big deal. I turn back around with a shrug. "She can't remember sexy man's name. I offered to fake a wrong number and find out."

Cole glances skyward. "Christ almighty. Why doesn't that surprise me?" He stands up, throws his empty box and chopsticks into the bin, then collects our empty glasses. "I'll be back in a minute."

I nod, then look at my phone. Here goes nothing, I guess. Plonking down, I steal Cole's stool, scroll up to Hannah's first message, and press sexy man's phone number. It rings, and my hands tingle. With a shaky smile, I glance up as Cole returns with two bottles of spring water and leans against the door frame. He is an exceptionally attractive leaner. Especially against door frames.

"Hello?" a raspy, half-asleep male voice answers.

Crap. I've woken sexy man up. He's probably a shift worker, and I've probably ruined his day. I clear my throat, formalise my tone, then launch into my over-rehearsed dribble. "Hello, can I please speak with Adam?" It's a relatively common name. I might even get lucky and have it right. In that case, I'll add a random surname to throw him off, then apologise for having the wrong number and hang up. Simple.

There's a beat of silence before sexy man clears his throat. "Aves, is that you?"

My stomach free-falls as the familiar voice turns my bones to ice. I rip the phone away from my ear and glare at the screen. No. It's not even his number. I slam the phone back to my ear. "Who is this?"

A dark, husky chuckle rattles through the line. "Thought you never wanted to speak to me again?"

Wooziness crashes over me, and the room wobbles. I stare up at Cole. *This* I wasn't prepared for. "I'm sorry. I think I have the wrong number." Immediately, I end the call and drop the phone like it burnt my hand. It thuds to the workbench, then dims.

Cole's shoulders stiffen as he takes me in. "What just happened?"

My heartbeat thumps in my ears, fuelling the chaos circling between them, and my lips move, but no words form. Cole crosses the room to squat in front of me, gripping my thighs. "Aves, what's going on?"

I meet his eyes and swallow the melon in my throat. "It was Slade," I whisper, and it sounds as unbelievable out loud as it did in my head.

Cole tightens his grip. "What?"

"It was Slade."

His face pales. He shoots to his feet, fisting one hand at his side, carving the other through his hair.

Hannah and *Slade*. Holy shit. "What do I say to her?"

Cole stops pacing and turns to face me. "Tell her it was an old lady. Pretend the arsehole duped her." His voice comes low and choked— *pained.*

I stare at my lap. "But she'll be devastated," I say, more to myself than him. How the hell is this even happening?

I glance up to witness an eerie composure settle over Cole's face. His nostrils flare, and he tilts his chin ever so slightly to the left. "Devastated. Why will she be devastated?" His shrewd eyes narrow, but his voice remains calm—calm but tight, like a rubber band about to snap. "What exactly happened between them?"

I squeeze my eyes shut. Goddamn lawyers. Forever reading every word unsaid. I can't lie to him, but I don't want to betray Hannah either. I lower my chin and stay silent.

"Don't make me ask again," he says.

With a deep breath, I look up to find Cole warring with rage. My vision turns watery. "Please don't ask me that. I promised Hannah."

The band snaps, and his eyes grow wild. "I'll bloody kill him." He charges out of the studio towards the kitchen.

"No!" I jump to my feet and follow him. "Please don't. This is a fucked-up coincidence, I'll give you that, but don't do anything dumb."

He stills at the island as if my words doused the fire, and for a sweet second, I'm relieved. But slowly Cole turns to face me, his jaw slack. Rapidly, he blinks. "You actually think this is a coincidence?"

"Of course. What else would it be?"

He stares at me like I've fallen off an imaginary pedestal. "I never considered you that naïve."

His words sting, and I flinch. Crossing my arms, I frown. "You think Slade planned this? He's not that calculated—or smart."

Cole whips his wallet and keys up from the island, then rips his suit jacket from where it hangs on the dining room chair. "He's a career criminal who's only spent thirty days in an adult prison. That indicates some strategic competence. He certainly doesn't have the damn money to buy his way out of trouble."

Cole grips the back of his neck and stares at the island for a tense moment, but his arm soon falls limp at his side, and he looks at me again. "You know, at least you're not the only one you underestimate, I guess." And with that, he takes off.

The air seems to part in his wake, rippling an icy breeze across my skin. "Cole, wait." My phone sounds again from the studio, but I ignore it and give chase. I picture him in jail—or worse yet, hurt—in hospital—*dead*. I don't imagine Slade plays fair. Going after him is a bad idea.

My bare feet slap against the cold tiles as I sprint through the gallery. "Please, I'm begging you, don't go."

Cole yanks open the front door, then stills with a sigh, scrubbing a hand down the side of his face. Our eyes meet, and I latch onto the glimmer of softness still in them. "I don't expect you to understand, but Hannah is my responsibility. If I don't look after her, no one will." He holds my gaze for a few beats with sad eyes and then severs our connection. The door slams shut, and half my soul leaves with him. The other half slides down the gallery wall and slumps to the tiles. Tears tumble down my cheeks, painting spots on my jeans, while angry tyres screech, then fade.

Shit. Could I lose him over this?

Dread thrashes through my body like a werewolf in chains, but there's nothing to be done. My happiness rests in Cole's livid hands, and I have zero control.

God, I need to hit something—throw something. *Hurt. Fucking. Something.*

I drag myself to my feet and head for my studio but stop dead at the laser-cut sign on the door. The fragile spark of worth that lives inside my heart begs me not to go in there. *Don't ruin everything good you've created*, it says.

I heed its wisdom and instead snatch up my phone and stomp to my bedroom. The bed springs squeak when I land face down and even more when I kick, scream, and throttle the pillows until every ounce of helpless frustration leaves my bones. Then I inhale Cole's heady scent from the covers, grab my phone, and do the only thing I can. I call him. As expected, he doesn't answer. I hang up and stare at my phone, willing him to call back. He doesn't, but Hannah's messages persist.

Hannah:
Have you done it yet? You're killing me here.

Hannah:
I wonder if he likes kids. Can you tell by someone's voice?

Hannah:
Grrr. Why are you leaving me on read? It's
rude!

Hannah:
Oh no. It's bad, isn't it? What happened?
Just tell me. I'm wearing my big girl panties.
I can take it.

Fuck.

My thumbs fly over the keyboard, and I do the only thing I can.
Lie.

Me:
Sorry for the delay. No answer. No voicemail.
I'll try again later xx

The jingling sound of keys drifts up the stairs. Mum's home early.
Double fuck.

I wipe my eyes, then dart from my bed to the mirror, but hiding evidence of this clusterfuck is impossible. My eyes are bloodshot, my face puffy and pale. I'm a goddamn mess. A mess who'd give anything to fall into loving arms and sob until there's nothing left. But Mum's arms are full of razor-sharp strings and soul-destroying expectations. They haven't been a soft place to fall since I was ten. And even then, Dad's were where I typically fell. He was my safe haven—a solid, tranquil refuge to Mum's perpetual storm. My sage, protector, and soul mate all melded into one.

Heels clack up the steps, and I cringe. God, I wish I had a fucking door.

"Avery Lee?"

With a deep breath, I turn to face her, wishing I could rally a fake smile—*the smile*—but I can't.

"I was wondering if you could do me a favour?" Mum says as she reaches the landing. When she looks up, she arches an eyebrow. "Trouble in paradise already?"

I grit my teeth. I'm not telling her shit.

"Listen, I was wondering if you could be home tomorrow? I'm expecting an important delivery."

Irritation crawls up my back. "I have to work. You know that."

Her cunning smile ripens. "Well, you know"—she shrugs, twirling her hand—"as the boss's little pet, I figured one tiny day off wouldn't hurt."

My mouth falls open. "Are you serious?"

"I'm just asking, Avery Lee. Gosh, you don't need to be so rude."

"I can't skip work to wait for a parcel. Why can't you be here?"

She fluffs her buttery blonde locks. "I have a hair appointment with Phillipe. I really don't want to cancel."

I stare at her, gobsmacked.

"Don't look at me like that," she snaps. "Normal daughters help their mothers, do you know that? Yet you refuse to do anything for me."

With a breath of composure, I shake my head. "I tolerate you. That's exhausting enough."

The fall of her face spears guilt through my stomach. With laser eyes, she scans me from head to toe, causing that thick, tar-like feeling of shame and disgust to rise and bubble. "You're so cruel, Avery Lee. It's amazing you have anyone at all." With glossy eyes and a manicured hand clutching her heart, Mum turns away and dashes down the stairs, her heels clacking double time, long, floaty dress wafting dramatically.

She'll phone someone now to tell them about my latest atrocity. How horrible I am. Her friends hate me, as did every boyfriend that ever came along. Always pitted against me from the get-go.

The air turns syrupy, and my throat narrows. The mezzanine walls seem to be closing in on me. Desperate for escape, I scan the room. I need to go—get out of here—but it's dark and cold, and I have nowhere to run. Soft moonlight glows through the window, beckoning me outside. I shove on my Chucks—this time doing up the laces—then mount the sill and ease down onto the roof. The frosty air fogs my breath, and Cole's warning flits through my head as I shuffle down low enough to lie, but screw him. I need this small act of defiance right now. It's the only control I have.

The stars twinkle away, singing their cosmic song, and a pang of longing hits my stomach. I want to be like them—higher than all this earthbound sludge. I want to shine amid chaos and be unaffected by the storms. But that's not what life is. Life is a string of hurricanes, and any peace is merely the eye—a cruel glimpse of sweetness so you can grasp the gravity of sour.

A star shoots across the sky, rubbing its freedom in my face, but I make a wish. The same wish I've made every night since our first kiss.

Please keep Cole safe. Please don't take him away too.

Twenty

Hannah beams when I enter Mini-Bees the following morning, but I feign interest in my phone and make a beeline for the staffroom. My hands tremble, my thoughts spin, and the fatigue, courtesy of a restless night, only amplifies every fear. I'm wired, tired, and millimetres from losing it. I need to know if Cole's okay. He hasn't replied to my texts. He hasn't returned my calls. And he won't answer his fucking phone.

From the corner of my eye, I spot Hannah scruff Alex's hair as he rolls out a Play-Doh snake, then stand to follow me.

Fuck. What will I say?

I hang my satchel on the hook and stare at the spotless floor. The antiseptic lemon scent from Bernie's morning clean still lingers. I'm a mess, and I don't do mess discreetly. There's no dignity in panic. Maybe I should've stayed home and waited for Mum's stupid delivery after all.

Hannah's flower-print Keds soon enter my peripheral vision, bouncing from heel to ball and back again. "So how'd it go? Did you try again? I'm sorry for hassling you all night. I was just excited, you know?" Her innocence turns my stomach. Reluctantly, I unglue my eyes from the floor and meet hers. Her smile drops away. "Oh God, what's wrong?" Frowning, she steps in to squeeze my elbow.

I swallow and shake my head, but tears fill my eyes, then spill over, and I hate how convenient they are. Hannah won't press me for more information on Slade if I'm upset. That brings relief and makes me want to puke at the same time. "I'm sorry. I have some stuff going on—" Worry lines set hard on Hannah's face. Shit. Cole wouldn't want her to know about this. I clear my throat. "—at home. There's stuff going on at home. With my mum." There. Not a complete lie.

Hannah's relief is palpable, but she tries to hide it. "I'm sorry to hear that." She opens her slender arms out towards me. "You look like you really need a hug."

I do. I do need a hug.

Gratefully, I step into Hannah's arms, but the affection rips me open. The tears come hard and heavy, and I sob uncontrollably on her shoulder while cursing my lack of control.

"Is there anything I can do?" she asks. "Do you want to talk about it?"

Unable to speak, I shake my head.

She tightens the hug, rubbing small circles high on my back with her dainty hand, and it triggers a bittersweet memory. Dad used to do that, every night before I went to sleep, only his hand was huge. Then he'd script imaginary letters that said "I love you" with his fingertip.

God, I miss him. Why does Mum only seem to make that worse?

Hannah holds me until I calm down, and I let her, despite knowing I don't deserve it. I've betrayed her trust, snitched to her brother, and lied to her too. I'm a horrible person.

Giggles drift in from the playroom, reminding me where I am. At work. Sobbing like a goddamn child on my supervisor's shoulder, whose brother I happen to be fucking.

Well done, Avery. Top job.

Grimacing, I detangle myself from Hannah's embrace, then scrounge up a mangled tissue from the bottom of my satchel to dry my eyes. "I'm sorry."

"Don't be," Hannah says gently. "We all have bad days." But awkwardness hangs in the air, thickening the silence between us. I feel her discomfort and her need to eliminate it. "Have you seen my brother today?"

Pain stabs my heart. "No."

Hannah sighs. "Me neither, but I'm sure he'll be here soon." The notion sparks hope and nausea simultaneously. Hannah chews her bottom lip, then her brows jump as she holds up a finger. "Wait, I have an idea. Stay here. I'll be right back." She snatches her phone from the kitchenette bench, then scurries off, only to return a few minutes later with a triumphant smile that matches the one her mum wore in the portrait at Cole's house. "You, my love, are taking the day off. Marla will be here in an hour to take over. Meanwhile, I want you to sit and chill. Tej and I have it handled."

My tears start again. She's such a beautiful girl. How dare Slade touch her. And to think Cole could be right. I shudder. If this isn't a coincidence, it's my fault. First, I dragged Jen, Liam, and Beth into this bullshit. Then Cole. Now maybe Hannah too. The list just keeps growing.

It's amazing you have anyone at all, Avery Lee.

Mum's right.

And Hannah likes Slade. She stepped out of her comfort zone at my insistence, only to be stung. And if anything happens to Cole . . . A chill rolls down my spine. I can't even finish the thought.

"Hey, breathe, okay?" Hannah says.

Oh no. It's happening.

I drop to sit on a nearby chair, then silently count my breaths. In, two, three, four. Out, two, three, four.

Fuck. Why now, in front of Hannah?

Several long, stormy minutes pass before I regain control. And when it's over, Hannah steps closer to rest a hand on my shoulder, tentatively, like I might bite. "Jeez, Aves," she whispers. "Do you get them often?"

I don't reply or look up, wishing I could dissolve. Great. Now she knows her brother's dating a nutjob. How fond of me could she possibly be now?

Hannah retreats, the kitchen tap sounds, then a glass of water appears in front of me. I take it from Hannah's hand, and she squats at my feet, making eye contact unavoidable. "Listen, I need to check on the kids. I'll shut the door, but I'm right outside if you need me, okay?" Her smile is gentle and sweet, but alarm still hijacks her gaze.

Yeah, back away carefully and quietly from the freak.

I rally a shaky smile. "Thanks. I owe you one." Damn it. In Hannah's eyes, I wanted to stay shiny and normal forever. *Cole-worthy.*

The door clicks shut, and I slump in my seat. But by some sweet miracle, by the time Marla arrives, I've got my shit together and devised a plan.

When I phone upstairs, Cole's assistant informs me he called in sick overnight, and fourteen hours of dread deflates from my chest. He's alive—able to communicate. That's something, at least.

But why hasn't he called me?

I thank her and hang up, then pull up Google Maps and pinpoint the windy road to Cole's house. I book an Uber and throw on my satchel, say my goodbyes and one last apology to Hannah, and then head outside into the fittingly grey and gloomy day.

The Audi sits on a furious angle millimetres from a deck post, its tyres having gouged out dirty valleys in the quartz gravel. That's my first clue something's wrong.

Thanking the Uber driver, I dash from the back seat and run up the stairs to bang on Cole's front door. I peer inside with cupped hands, pressing my forehead to the cold glass. The cavernous living room is empty and still, but near the dining table I spy Cole's suit jacket, shoes, and car keys scattered across the shiny concrete floor.

Thankfully, the door handle turns when I try it. I wouldn't have had the balls to literally break in. The windows are all high up and louvred, and I doubt Cole keeps a stupid thief beacon in his garden like Beth.

I cross the threshold with a deep breath, all too aware I'm intruding. "Cole?" I close the door gently behind me. "Hello?"

No answer comes.

Like a burglar, I tiptoe past the leather sofas. The irony isn't lost on me, but I guess Cole knew what he was signing up for from the start. The fireplace hovers above the ground asleep, its scorched wood scent still tingeing the cool air. I eye the bank of portraits and smile at Ella, wince at Hannah, then shudder when Cole's mum seems to follow my every step. "I'm sorry," I whisper to her. "I'm not a thief. I just need to make sure he's all right." Hell knows he'd do the same in reverse. She doesn't reply—if she did, I'd commit myself—but I swear her dimple presses a smidge deeper, and her eyes twinkle that spark brighter. I'll bet she was so lovely. The kind of mum love heart mugs and Mother's Day cards are made for.

When I reach the dining room, I pick up Cole's keys and rumpled jacket, shaking out the latter. His phone thuds to the floor. "Fuck." I pick it up, accidentally mashing the power button, but nothing happens. It's as dead as Elvis, and that pretty fact dials down the blender in my belly a welcome notch, since it justifies at least some of the ghosting. I chuck it on the river table with his keys, hang his jacket on the chair, and shove his shoes clear of the walkway as if righting this mess will undo the clusterfuck that caused it. "Cole? It's me."

The continued silence Red-Bulls my nerves. He could be ignoring me. Shit. After everything, he might have finally realised I'm not worth the trouble. What if he never wanted to see me again and I didn't take the hint? What if he and Slade somehow bonded, then rubbished me over beers, chinking together their bottles to seal a never-again vow?

God, Avery Lee. It's always about you, you, you, isn't it?

I cringe. No. Today it's about Cole's welfare—*Hannah's virtue*—not me and my perpetual list of insecurities. Fuck, I hate myself sometimes.

I reach the hallway and rush towards Cole's bedroom door standing open at the end. The king bed is made, but the light-grey woven covers are crumpled and dirty—the en suite pristine but empty. The faintest hint of music registers then, and I follow it back into the hallway. Cole's house might be an architect's wet dream, but it isn't big. Two bedrooms, two bathrooms, and one insanely gorgeous man.

I head for the second bedroom—Cole's home office—and knock twice on the door. "Cole?" It brushes the plush carpet as I push it open, and the wave of relief that sweeps out has me steadying myself against the architrave. Cole sits slouched in a buttoned leather chair near the window, staring at the gum trees glittering outside. A near-empty bottle of amber liquid dangles from his hand, glowing artfully in the mid-morning sun like stained glass, and Kings of Leon sing about walls coming down softly in the background. Cole rolls his head towards me, then smiles, reopening a split in his swollen bottom lip. "Angel." The melt-worthy moniker comes slurred at the edges, and the blood on his lip glistens as mine drains.

"Oh my God." I race towards him and drop to my knees at his feet, gripping his hard thighs. "Are you okay?" I scan him for further damage while adrenaline whips my heart. One beautiful cheekbone shines purple and blue. Blood and mud Pollock his white shirt. The pocket is torn, and several buttons are missing, leaving frayed cotton in their place. The right side of his chest shows through, grazed red and raw. I reach out to trace around the rash of tiny cuts. "Holy shit."

"You should see the other guy." Cole throws his head back with a morbid laugh. It falls back down a second later, bobbing as if too heavy for his neck.

"What happened?" I ask.

His smile fades, and unsteady, bourbon-glazed eyes lock on mine. "He laughed."

"What?"

"When he found out Hannah was my sister. He laughed. He knew she was a friend of yours, but I guess he hit the jackpot." Cole holds up the Wild Turkey bottle in salute and swirls it near my head. "Saw you both on *Schmace*book." He takes a hearty swig, then swallows. "Seems my sister had to tell the world about her big night out."

As his words hit home, queasiness takes root. Oh no. Hannah was excited, and she did post about it, tagging me as her beloved babysitter and new best friend. But who could blame her? It was her first night out in forever, and everyone posts everything everywhere these days. Squeezing my eyes shut, I rest my forehead on Cole's knee. *Fuck.* He was right. This was no coincidence.

He strokes the nape of my neck, sending shivers down my back. "You really should update your privacy settings. You never know where evil lurks."

My eyes pop open. *Double fuck.* My privacy settings. Or more aptly, lack thereof. I rarely use my account, but had I simply been careful, none of this would have happened. Bile burns the back of my throat, and I groan. It's all my fault. Slade wanted revenge, and poor Hannah was caught in the crossfire. God, he's an arsehole. A conniving, slimy, vengeful arsehole. I snap my chin back up. "What did you do to him?" Part of me hopes the worst. The rest fears it.

"I should have killed the prick, but I called him an ambulance instead because I'm a nice guy, really I am."

"An *ambulance*? How bad is it?"

Cole arches a dark brow. "Do you even care?"

I guess I do. "I don't like seeing anyone hurt. Arseholes included." I shrug.

Cole's jaw ticks as he searches my face. "Broken nose, rib, and concussion at worst. He'll live. Unfortunately." The last word comes grumbled.

"But he could press charges. Your reputation . . . Benedict's . . ." As the next possibility sprouts, I stiffen. "You could go to jail!"

Chuckling, Cole fumbles a lock of hair behind my ear. "Don't worry, I have friends in jail. I saved those guilty fuckers years. I'll be a hero. Hell, it will be a holiday, away from all the corruption and lies." He takes another swig from the bottle, then flops his arm back down, narrowly missing the floor.

My stomach pretzels, and my knees buckle. I think I might actually puke.

Cole tsks, then leans forward to erase the worry from my brow with his thumb. He almost pokes my eye out, and his breath is flammable. He doesn't usually drink. Or swear.

God, what have I created?

"I'm joking, Angel. Don't worry. I'm no idiot. He hit me first. I made sure of it."

My frown doesn't dissipate. Soon I'll have a permanent line like him. "How?"

Cole flashes a shit-eating grin, and his emerald eyes sparkle. "I told him how sweet your pussy tastes when you come on my tongue." Fire engulfs my face, and Cole dissolves into laughter. "There they are. My favourite hyper-colour cheeks."

Savouring the break in tension, I shake my head and reluctantly smile, but Cole's laughter soon dies off. His long limbs slump heavy, and the air turns sombre and funeral thick. He's an emotional roller coaster. The Wild Turkey Express.

He stares over my shoulder in silence with a pained expression, sadness seeping from his skin. "I failed her again. I always fail her. I try to protect her. I try my best, but people always hurt her." A tear runs down his bruised cheek, disappearing into the maze of dark stubble, and mine flood in response.

I want to ask a million questions—now's the time I'd get answers—but I won't take advantage of him. He's broken. A gleaming skyscraper reduced to rubble, and in some ways, I was the bomb.

Wincing, I climb into his lap and kiss his forehead. "I'm so sorry this happened."

Filled with warmth, Cole's pale gaze finds mine. "I don't deserve you, Miss Masters."

I roll my eyes. "It's the other way around. Why can't you see that? You see everything else with those X-ray eyes." I playfully poke his shoulder and smirk, desperate to bring back levity, but he doesn't follow my lead. Instead, Cole frowns.

"No. I'm going to lose you. It's only a matter of time. There are things I can't change." He cups my neck with his free hand, stroking my bottom lip with his thumb, then shakes his head. "I should have walked away."

The drunken words settle like an anchor in the pit of my stomach. He should have walked away? From what exactly? *Me*? I ignore my own questions and the flourishing doubt. He's drunk. Unlikely to have slept a wink. In this state, nothing he says should be taken seriously.

"My uncle screwed me," he sighs, flopping back against the headrest. "He left me everything, including his shit. He was meant to be all good. He saved us. But there's no such thing. Everyone has a dark side. Some just hide it really well." The bottle drops to the ground, and a splash hits the carpet before soaking in.

I shake away his ominous words and climb to my feet, coaxing his heavy arm over my shoulders. "You need to sleep this off. Let's get you to bed."

His dark chuckle rattles through the room. "Think you can carry my weight, Angel? You can't. You're too innocent. You'll break, and it will be all my fault."

Swallowing the billiard ball now lodged in my throat, I hoist him up. "I'm already broken, remember?" I mumble the words to my chest, quiet enough for him not to hear.

Step by stumbling step, I guide us through the hallway and into Cole's bedroom. My stomach churns like it's stuck in a wash cycle, or as though I'm the one who's downed a bottle of bourbon. This man is so far from the one I know—the one I feel safe with. Why do I seem to poison those I love?

Love.

The thought flows effortlessly like only truth can. I love this man. I love him when he's shiny and tall and when he's messy and small. I love him whether he's safe or not, and that paints a target on my damaged heart and hands him a bow and arrow.

Cole falls onto the mattress, taking me with him. The springs squeak as we land on our backs, panting at the ceiling. I roll to my side, weave my legs through his, and press my lips to the undamaged side of his mouth, breathing in the heady cocktail of bourbon, mud, and blood yet somehow finding comfort.

When I pull back, Cole's face is grim. He catches my hand, threads our fingers together, and frowns. "Promise you won't leave me. No matter what. *Please.*" The plea rides an undercurrent of doom with rippling red sails, and I stop breathing.

What the actual fuck?

Untangling myself, I sit up off the side of the bed to gather my wits. That's it. This cryptic bullshit needs to end. I whip my head around to look down at him. "Why are you worried about that?"

Cole groans and rolls to press his face into the dirty covers. I wait for his answer, despite an army of questions wanting to charge from my mouth, but one doesn't come. Instead, his breaths even out, and a soft snore caresses the air.

Damn it.

I stare at my knees, wringing my hands, as his words stir up a whirlpool of panic.

He's drunk, Avery. Let it go. Not everything is about you, remember?

With a heavy sigh, I rub my stinging eyes with the heels of my palms. My bones ache from the twenty-hour drama marathon. I've reached that bittersweet point where even I'm too exhausted to ana-lyse and dissect. And to be honest, I don't want to. Cole might hold a bow and arrow, but I won't help him aim or watch him shoot. At least not until I've slept.

Twenty-One

Warm fingers feather through my hair, prompting my eyes to flicker open.

"Hey," Cole says, appearing like an apparition sitting at the edge of the bed. The bruising to his cheek is angrier, and the delicate skin of his rosy lip strains to hold the split together.

As the memories flood back, I jolt upright. "Are you okay? How are you feeling?" I scan him up and down, taking inventory. His hair is wet and slicked back, light-caramel skin marred but clean. Pale-grey sweats sit low on his hips beneath ripples of muscle and jungle ink, and the sharp scent of antiseptic wafts from the nasty graze across his chest. He must have showered, then treated it. Shit, I should have done that for him last night. A decent girlfriend would have.

Wait . . . I look out the bedroom window. Vivid smears of orange and pink paint the horizon and silhouette the trees as the sun bids goodnight. *. . . This morning.* I should have done that for him this morning. How long was I out?

Cole offers a crooked smile, favouring his undamaged side. "Apart from someone forging steel in my head, better than I look or deserve."

He looks amazing. He always does. "Have you taken something for the pain?"

He shakes his head and shrugs. "Physical pain never much bothered me. It's the most tolerable kind."

I stare at him, understanding exactly what he means. *Pain that makes sense.*

"I'm sorry about last night. And this morning," he says, brushing his knuckles down my jaw. The gentle touch awakens my body. "You must have been worried."

"Worried" is a gross understatement. "Freaking the absolute fuck out" barely falls in the vicinity. "Why didn't you reply or phone me back?"

Cole winces. "At first, I couldn't. Too angry. Then my phone died, and I was too drunk. I really am sorry."

Scrubbing the sleep from my eyes, I sigh. "It's okay. You're safe. That's all that matters." But my tone doesn't quite match the sentiment, and he notices.

"It's not okay, but forgive me anyway? *Please*." With prayer hands and a tilt of his chin, Cole crumples his brows into adorable fuzzy caterpillars.

"Seriously?" I tsk. "You're using scrunchy brows?" They're a worthy rival to Jen's puppy-dog eyes and pout. "You don't play fair at all."

Cole grins. "They always seem to work for Hannah. I've never had a reason to try them before. You're my first."

Smiling, I roll my eyes. "At least I'm your first something." I climb to straddle his lap, then cup his stubbly cheeks and press a kiss to his forehead.

"You're my first lots of things," he says when our eyes reconnect, all humour gone. My cheeks flush in response, and he squeezes my shoulders. "I truly am sorry."

Dropping my gaze, I fiddle with the frayed ends of his drawstring. "My shitty judgement brought Slade into your lives. I'm the one who's sorry."

Cole tenses. "Don't blame yourself for *his* actions. I let him off the hook once, but I won't this time. You need to know that."

Glancing up, I frown. "What does that even mean?"

"I've pressed charges." Cole studies my face, awaiting a reaction. I remain impassive, so he continues. "He was on parole. Assault charges will land him back behind bars straight out of hospital."

I swallow, waiting for the familiar rush of dread to come. It doesn't. "He's going back to jail?"

Cole offers a curt nod. "It was only a matter of time. For men like him, prison is a lifestyle."

Men. Calling Slade a man is an undeserved compliment.

Cole's hands dwarf my hips. "Are you upset?"

That question is more layered than Nerikomi pottery. I could simply say no, but instead, I consider the crux of the question—what Cole really wants to know. *Do I still have romantic feelings for Slade?*

I search every corner of my heart. No. But is there a microscopic part of me thrilled by Slade's need for revenge? If the question even arises, there must be an element of truth.

Sheepishly, I meet Cole's gaze. "A teeny part of me is flattered and relieved Slade cares enough to cause trouble. I didn't think I ever meant that much, and I probably don't. His bruised ego's fuelled most of this, I'm guessing. But I hate what he's done. I won't miss him. I don't blame you for what you did. I'm relieved he's gone—that he can't hurt anyone else. And there's only one man I have feelings for."

Colossal, transformative feelings.

The tension in Cole's frame melts, and with a soft smile, he tucks away a wisp of my hair. His eyes flicker to my lips, then his inch towards mine, landing in a soft and languid kiss. Three small words long to fly from my mouth, but I clip their wings. It's too soon.

Cole catches my bottom lip between his teeth as we part, but his post-kiss serenity slowly evaporates and morphs into a frown. "We need to tell Hannah the truth."

I groan and drag a hand down the side of my face. "But she'll be hurt, and I lied to her. She'll hate me."

"No, she won't. I'll take care of it."

Wincing, I drop my forehead to rest on Cole's shoulder, then bang it three times.

He chuckles and winds a hand through my hair but then freezes, his body stiffening. "Christ, I hope she used protection."

"She did," I immediately say. "That you don't need to worry about." Secretly, I grin. Whoever wrote that crazy condom song will never know the good they've done.

Cole lets out a hefty sigh. "I don't want to know how you know that, but good." He resumes stroking my hair, then a quiet moment later, whispers, "I need to protect my three girls."

Tiny fireworks explode around my heart, and I lift my head to study his face. *His three girls.* Have I joined that exclusive club? I trace my thumb lightly across the bruise on Cole's cheekbone. He doesn't flinch, only returns my stare with possessive conviction. It's divine to feel wanted and cherished—protected and secure. It fills the numb black hole in my soul that once sucked all the goodness away.

Maybe he really isn't going anywhere.

The notion is too fantastical to believe, and my destructive brain agrees. It swoops in on those optimistic flourishes and stamps them out like spot fires, leaving only the memory of Cole's less coherent ramblings from this morning alive.

I should have walked away.

The small voice inside begs me to ask my laundry list of questions. I know I shouldn't, but words bungee from my mouth without permission. "This morning, you said some stuff."

Cole narrows his gaze. "Like?"

I bite my top lip, fighting back the words. Trust me to let my insecurities ruin a perfect moment.

Cole grimaces. "That bad, huh?" With a hopeless chuckle, he flips me onto my back and covers me with his delicious weight. The thin fabric of his track pants does little to buffer the hardness growing between his legs. He drops a tender kiss to my neck, then whispers in my ear, "Don't listen to drunk people, Angel. They're generally full of shit."

I leap onto his dismissal like it's a runaway horse and seize the opportunity to change course. I tilt my mouth into a half smile that mirrors his. "Even the part about using my pussy as punch bait?"

Cole's eyes glimmer. "Well, that part was true."

I shake my head with a smirk. "You're an arsehole."

"And you're beautiful when you blush."

Hannah hates me.

She's too polite to say it. Too kind to show it. But it's there in the lack of chit-chat, fewer smiles, and painful silences.

Wincing, I shift Ella from my lap and plop her down on the floor with Alex and Lily. We need to talk. Alone. But three tense hours pass before the milk-moustached munchkins fall asleep on their gym mats and Tej disappears for lunch.

I tiptoe my way through the maze of little arms and legs to confront Hannah in the staffroom. She sits on the window seat with her legs crossed, staring vacantly at the kettle as it rumbles to a boil. "Hannah?" I lean against the kitchenette bench, cradling my elbows. Here goes nothing. "I'm really sorry about yesterday. About Slade."

Hannah drops her chin, then shakes her head. Glitter-tipped fingers grapple in her lap. "What's done is done. Just forget about it." She refuses to look at me, and I die inside.

"I never wanted to jeopardise our friendship. I should have told you the truth. It's just . . . I was torn between you and Cole."

She glances up. "And you chose him?"

I frown but slowly nod. "Yeah, I did."

"Good. He deserves someone who chooses him." She looks back down and clenches the ornate architrave either side of her knees, her posture stooped like a wilted weed. "I'm not angry with you, Aves. I know my brother. I understand the spot you were in." She looks up again, and her eyes shine with unshed tears as vulnerability weeps from her pores. "But tell me, do I have 'use me' tattooed on my face?" Two fat tears slide down her cheeks, taking mascara with them.

I drop to sit next to her and squeeze her denim knee. "Slade's not worth your tears. Trust me."

Hannah wipes her nose with the back of her hand and sniffles. "What is it with men? Are Cole and Tej the only good ones alive? I felt sexy for the first time in forever. I thought Slade at least wanted me for that. Not that I want someone like him to want me, but you know. *Ugh*." She scrubs a hand down the side of her face. "It hurts. He probably hated every sordid second. I'm so stupid."

Speechless, I stare at her glistening blue eyes, prettier than a Caribbean sea. How the heck could she think so little of herself? I square my shoulders. This situation calls for sassy Aves. "First up, you are so far out of Slade's league in the sexy stakes, it's unlikely he'll ever touch such beauty again." Hannah opens her mouth to argue, but I raise my finger to shush her. "Secondly, he's a scumbag, and that is wholly a reflection on him—not you. And thirdly, deception is his superpower. I don't know if Cole told you, but I dated him for two whole months before discovering he had a girlfriend he'd been with for years."

She shakes her head and wipes her cheeks with her palms. I rise to pluck a tissue from a nearby box and pass it to her before resuming my seat. "Cole didn't mention that," she says.

I quietly sigh, thankful Cole was sparse on detail. The last thing Hannah needs to know is how we met, why I'm really here, and the dumb choices I made. That was a different girl. Someone I no longer recognise but who still scares me nonetheless. "And what's worse . . ." I hesitate as my voice cracks. "I gave him my virginity the night before I found out, then still took him back. Girl, on the fool meter, you don't even rate." I throw her a half smile, trying in vain to lighten my confession. Only Jen knows about that.

"Ugh, I'm so sorry that happened to you." Hannah's empathy melts my heart. Even in pain, she still feels for others.

I nudge her with my shoulder. "I'm only telling you so you don't feel so alone. Don't let him break your spirit. He's not worth it. I'm sorry you were dragged into this. You deserved better."

Hannah lets out a heavy sigh. "It's just, if I can't find a guy who wants no-strings sex, how will I find someone who wants more? Someone to love both me and Ella. I'm worried we'll be alone forever, and Ella deserves more. She deserves a dad who loves her. A two-parent family. Stability. She deserves it all."

The depth of Hannah's loneliness and maternal love chokes me. I clear my throat and cover her hand with mine. "Ella has all the love she'll ever need. She has a wonderful mum, a doting uncle, and a safe home. Your person will come. Aim high. Dream him into existence. You know, like the law of attraction and all that."

She chuckles through tears. "I've tried. Believe me. Maybe I should make a vision board. Cut and paste different body parts from a magazine to make my perfect man. Yeah," she huffs, "that won't be creepy at all." Hannah rolls her eyes, and I laugh, grateful to see her light rekindling.

"Aves, about yesterday." She pauses for a pregnant moment, then sucks in a deep breath. "I'm worried about you."

"*Me?*" I frown over the top of my smile but retrieve my hand. "Why?"

"You had a panic attack, and when I asked if you get them often, you didn't answer. So do you . . . get them often?" Her brows draw together, and my heart plummets like it's suddenly made of iron.

I'd forgotten. She *saw*.

I swallow hard. Should I be honest? Will she run? What constitutes *often*?

As I stare at my knees, questions and feelings war in my head, but I don't have time to sort through them all. So instead, I rally my nerve, choose not to pretend Alex called my name, and hesitantly answer. "Once a week, maybe. Usually for a reason, but sometimes they come out of nowhere, and I don't know why." The admission feels like I've stripped off all my clothes and now sit here nude awaiting critique.

God, please kill me.

"Have you thought about getting help?"

Oh no. She isn't suggesting what I think she's suggesting, is she? "What do you mean?"

"A psychologist. They can help."

As my face flames, I laugh off her suggestion. "I'm just too sensitive and a little dramatic, always have been. I need to toughen up, that's all. No need to waste anyone's time."

"Aves." Hannah's tone softens, but her baby blues pin me with a ferocity that rivals her brother's. "There's no shame in seeking help for mental illness."

Mental. Illness.

Oh. My. God. She really thinks I'm insane. Maybe I am. The floor wavers as faintness washes over me.

"I see someone," Hannah says, and I dart my eyes to hers.

"What?" I whisper. But Hannah's so . . . perfect. Nothing's wrong with her.

"I have PTSD. I see someone. And she helps me."

"Oh," I stammer, "I . . . I didn't know."

"How would you?" Hannah smiles ruefully. "It's not something I advertise. Most people don't."

An invisible shield pulsates between us, begging me not to pry, so I don't. "But I've been like this since I was ten." Since . . . *Dad*. "It's just the way I'm wired."

Hannah gently nudges my shoulder with hers. "You could still try. Life can be easier, and you deserve that. You're a good person, Aves. I can see why my brother loves you."

Her words steal my breath, and I stare at her, bug-eyed. Blood rushes to my cheeks, forcing me to look away. "We haven't . . . uh . . . It's only been six weeks—not even. You're getting ahead of yourself." Silence ensues until I build the courage to glance up. A knowing smirk pulls at Hannah's lips, and my cheeks reignite. "It's too soon for that."

Her smile grows as she stares straight through me. X-ray eyes. They must be genetic. "It's nice to see his feelings are reciprocated." I open my mouth to refute that assumption, but she presses a finger to my lips. "Uh-uh. Don't lie to me again, Avery Masters." She winks and then leans forward to whisper, "And don't worry, this time your secret really is safe with me."

Twenty-Two

The email of my dreams chimes my phone at 10:05 a.m. the following Monday, and I squeal louder than the little ones as they dance to Tej's cool-arse rendition of "Baby Shark." Gloria Browne—*the* Gloria Browne of Green Bird Gallery—wants to meet and view my work. *Tonight*.

I hit reply and accept her request, tee up a time when Mum will be at her support group, then pinch my wrist throughout my shift to check I am in fact awake, since the toddler chaos doesn't convince me enough.

Every kilometre of the shivering tram ride home knots my throat tighter. Gloria Browne. Green Bird Gallery. Two names I stumbled across during my research but two names I dismissed. The studio was too swish—the website too professional. They deal in high-end art and established artists way beyond the likes of me. I didn't dare bother them.

My keys tumble to the porch twice before I manage to unlock the front door. I would be no less nervous meeting Michelangelo himself. But on the plus side, by the time the studio is visitor ready, I've reached grandmaster level on the Beth breath. I could teach the shit.

A knock sounds at the front door, and I leap from my stool onto jelly legs, which barely survive the gallery dash. Before opening it, I take a final Beth breath and straighten my jumper, then plaster on a professional smile.

Calm and confident. You got this, Aves.

The cold night air hits me like a snowball to the face, and Gloria Browne appears, illuminated by the porch downlight, looking mildly futuristic and runway ready. She wears a sharp red blazer with a giant pointy collar rimmed in faux zebra fur. Her red pencil skirt and stripy stilettos match. By comparison, I'm a slob. But Gloria flashes a contagious smile, and a kind voice choirs from her mouth, both of which loosen my knots. "You must be Avery Lee," she says. The scarlet fingertips of one hand touch her chin as she studies me. "I didn't expect you'd be as stunning as your art."

My cheeks burn, and I nervously chuckle. "Call me Avery, please. Only my mother calls me Avery Lee." I try but fail to keep the bitter tinge from my voice at Mum's mention and beckon Gloria inside.

She offers out her hand to shake, and I accept. Her warm handshake is firm and sincere, so I try to copy it. "Gloria Browne. It's delightful to meet you, Avery."

"Likewise. Come on in. I'll show you to the studio."

The snappy click of Gloria's heels on the gallery tiles triggers a pang of longing for Beth, as does her expensive perfume. But I push down that feeling and stop at the studio door to usher Gloria inside. She drags her gaze away from Beth's paintings and politely smiles. "Very nice."

"My sister's a lawyer," I say before mentally cringing. I often feel the need to brag about Beth's success and to clarify that I'm not the wealthy one who can afford five-figure paintings. "This is her house."

"Speaking of lawyers," Gloria says as she glides into the studio. She cheapens everything around her, especially the dusty lino covering the floor. I should have at least mopped. "Mine put me onto you. He sang the praises of a talented young artist working at Benedict Kane. When I received the photos, I was surprised to see he was right." She scans the studio in a gentle spin, then her intelligent eyes land on mine before sweeping me from head to toe. Not in a judgy, Miss Blue Satin Sparkles way, but like one would if they were admiring a sculpture. Fitting, I guess, though my hands still join forces to wring, and my smile quivers.

I clear my throat. "Well, this is it." I motion to the recent work lined up across the bench. "These are the pieces from the photos." I pivot and gesture to the shelving unit. "Those are my recent thrown bowls and vases. Some of them are finished. I paint unique designs on each one. They're all mini canvases, really."

Gloria nods once, then approaches the workbench. "Hmmm," she says with a tilted chin and finger tapping her top lip. Silence ensues before she speaks again. "The scale is impressive, larger than I thought. Quite the feature pieces." She then meanders to the shelves and seeks silent permission to pick up a bowl, then a vase. Gently, she places it back down. "I understand you're looking for a debut showing?"

I swallow. "Yes, I am."

When she turns around, her eyes catch the top shelf where my early work from high school sits. Embarrassment flusters me. I forgot about them. I step forward, and it takes all my restraint not to jump in front of Gloria to block her view. "Those are old pieces from school. I . . . I was still learning. Just ignore them."

She's silent for a torturous beat before gesturing towards the centre piece—the blue-ribbon winner from the state junior art competition. The same piece that won me entry into a summer retreat working with an Aussie clay legend nearly two years ago. "May I?" Gloria asks.

I hide my sigh. "Sure."

She picks up the piece to admire. "Are you willing to part with this collection too?"

I frown. "You'd actually want them?" The question flies out of my mouth before I can stop it, and I grimace. So much for confidence.

Gloria turns to face me, her brows high. "The prices will be a little more conservative, but yes, they'll do fine."

God, is she saying what I think she's saying?

Gloria leaves my side to take a final loop of the room, then leans her hip against the bench, facing me with folded arms. "I have a collective exhibition running in two and a half weeks. It's short notice, but I have the space, and I want you in it. Are you interested?"

I resist the urge to pinch my wrist for the fiftieth time today. I already have a bruise developing. "Absolutely."

Clapping her hands together, Gloria grins. "Excellent."

We discuss logistics, commissions, insurance, and endless other details I never considered related to being an artist, but none quite spin my head as much as the price Gloria sets on each piece. Who the hell would pay thousands for *my* work?

I give Gloria a sceptical once over. While I might not be dreaming, this could be a joke. Maybe there are hidden cameras filming me for some prankster's YouTube channel. Maybe Cole waived Gloria's bill in exchange for blowing smoke up my arse. No. He promised. And Gloria seems genuine enough. She walks the walk and talks the talk, but doom smothers me regardless. Even if she is for real, I can see it now: a gallery full of unsolds, or even worse, buyer's remorse and post-show refund requests.

Lawsuits lodged against me for being a fraud.

I rub my sternum. *Breathe, Avery. You are mature and professional and able to discuss business in an assertive composed manner, remember?* But, as usual, my loose lips betray me, and my flawed essence exposes itself like a trench-coat flasher. "Are you sure I'm worth that much?"

Likely not used to being questioned, Gloria flinches but recovers in a nanosecond and warmly smiles. She cradles my elbow reassuringly. "Avery, I have an exceptional eye, a top-notch reputation, and extremely wealthy clientele who won't bat an eyelid at handing over that kind of money if they love a piece. You'll be my shiny new breakthrough artist—the one to watch and invest in now. The question is, are *you* ready, my dear?"

I stare at her as I search my insides. They scream in terror, but I ignore them. No one and nothing will cost me this opportunity. "You bet I am."

"Who was that?"

Mum's voice Tasers me as I close the front door behind Gloria, and I spin to face her, clutching my chest. "Shit, you scared the crap out of me. I didn't hear you come home."

Draped against Beth's bedroom door frame, Mum arches a brow. "Well?" She taps impatient fingernails against the glossy paint, but not even she can wipe the grin from my face. I can't wait to tell Cole.

"Gloria Browne," I reply. "Owner of Green Bird Gallery."

I glide past Mum towards the kitchen. Her footsteps patter behind. "And what did she want?"

Hesitant to answer, I open the freezer door in search of dinner, but the excitement is too damn much. I want to tell the world. Mum included. "I just booked my first ever exhibition. It opens in two and a half weeks."

"Oh," Mum says as I close the freezer door, frosty box in hand.

I rip open the cardboard and shove the plastic tray of chicken risotto into the microwave, then turn around. "Just 'oh'?"

Mum rolls her eyes and drops to sit on a barstool at the island, sliding a gossip magazine closer to her. "Well, what would you have me say?" She flips open the busy cover, flaunting the latest celebrity fail.

"Um, maybe 'congratulations,' 'way to go,' 'that's wonderful.' It's kind of a big deal, you know."

Mum sighs. "Well, congratulations, then. Is that better?"

I return her eye roll, shaking off her apathy. It's unfair to expect everyone to be as excited as me, but I hope Cole is, at least. And Beth too. Jen will be for sure.

The microwave beeps, and steam sizzles from the bubbling risotto when I open the door. I slide the plastic tray onto a dinner plate.

"Will lover boy be dropping by tonight?" Mum asks.

Grabbing a fork from the drawer, I glance over my shoulder. Mum licks her index finger and flips another page. "Later," I reply, settling down on a barstool opposite. Mum will be asleep by the time Cole comes and not awake until after we leave for work. Crazy hours bring some perks, at least.

"He works late a lot, doesn't he?" She flips another page, casually eyeing me before looking back down.

I swallow a mouthful of gluggy risotto, trying not to gag. It's like eating Clag glue, and yes, I've tasted it. Hazard of the job. I shrug. "He has a firm to run. Law is notorious for horrific hours. Beth works the same."

"Well, you're braver than me," Mum says, and I frown.

"What's that meant to mean?"

Mum hitches her dainty shoulder. "If my man worked late every night, I'd assume he was having an affair."

My heart stutters, and my fork clatters to the granite. Had the thought occurred to me? Sure. Most terrible thoughts do, but that's one I quickly dismissed. However, now that Mum's mentioned it too, maybe I shouldn't have.

I pick my fork back up and force nonchalance. No. She's just trying to rattle me. "Cole's not like that."

Mum chuckles her breathy laugh. The one that makes my skin itch. "That's what all the wives and girlfriends think. None of us believe it will happen to us until, of course, it does." She shrugs. "Men are men. Expecting them to look but not touch is like asking a toddler not to eat their candy."

I shake my head, but knots bind my chest. "Men have more self-control than toddlers, Mum. They don't all cheat, and Cole wouldn't do that to me." The words sound more confident than I feel, but I believe them. Mostly. I take another bite of Clag risotto and find it still tastes better than this conversation.

Mum traces a nude fingernail across her pouty bottom lip, staring at the two-page spread of Ariana's gorgeous beach bod. "Hmm, I wonder how many female colleagues stay late with him?"

This time, I deliberately slam down my fork and glare at her. "What are you doing?"

Her head jolts up. "Whatever do you mean?" But beneath feigned innocence, turquoise sparkles in her eyes, and my skin grows hot.

I've been strong all week. Refused every bait. Fulfilled her requests, kept my distance, and ignored her veiled comments. But, alas, she's finally cracked my armour and achieved her goal. I was in a good mood, goddamn it. "Why do you play these games? Do you want me miserable, is that it? Do you get some sick satisfaction from breaking me bit by bit?"

Mum throws her head back and laughs at the ceiling. "Oh, here we go. I've been waiting for it—the inevitable theatrics. It's like walking on eggshells around you, Avery Lee." Mum slaps the magazine closed and shoves it away. She squares her shoulders and plants her elbows on the island. "Do you know what your problem is? You think everything is about you. No one can merely make a passing comment without you finding the worst meaning possible."

I grind my teeth. "You implied my boyfriend is screwing his colleagues and lying to me. Is there a better meaning I missed?"

Mum opens her mouth to speak, but I hold up my hand, itching to slap the smirk from her face with go-go gadget arms. "Don't. Just don't. I'm done with this conversation." Proud of my restraint, I hop off my stool and abandon my dinner to head for the stairs.

If I stay, everything will twist and warp. This is when the swarm of screams, denial, and chaos typically descends to hollow out my heart and fuck with my head. Mum's spiteful words will brand my brain—a fragment of my soul will be lost. And in the end, I'll forget how it all started. If it was me or her. How it escalated to take the hellish path it took. I'll retrace our words in search of sense, but all I'll find is a pit of tangled razor wire. It's futile. "I'm going to bed," I say as I take the first step. "I'll get the door when Cole comes."

"No need. It was unlocked."

Startled, I turn around to find Cole standing in the kitchen doorway, his eyes locked on Mum and blacker than his suit.

Mum visibly gulps, then plasters on a smile. "Cole, I didn't hear you come in. Lovely to see you."

His jaw ticks, and he flickers his eyes to mine. "Hey," I whisper. *How much did he hear?*

He forces a tight smile. "I did knock." Then looks back to Mum. "Sheila, I am not screwing around, and I resent any implication I would."

Mum jolts from his words as if a cattle prod found her butthole. Her pale face flames Tabasco. "I . . . I didn't—"

"I'm not done." Cole's sternness samurais the room, and Mum's mouth flaps shut.

Frozen to the bottom step, I stare on in shock. No one has ever gone to bat for me against Mum before, and it feels like I've tripled in size—like I'm made of gold. Is this really happening?

Glowering, Cole continues. "Without direct experience, I'm not surprised you don't understand the value of hard work. But know this: I will never cheat on your daughter, and I can't believe you'd put that idea into her head. I suggest you stay the hell out of our business from this point forth. Are we clear?"

Mum shrinks in her seat, but her submission is short-lived. She soon mashes her lips into a hard line, re-straightens her spine, and nudges up her chin. "How dare you speak to me like that, young man. You're a guest in this house. Don't forget it." I wait for the rest of her vitriol, but it never comes. Instead, Mum rises from the stool on slightly wobbly knees and scurries from the room like a scared rabbit.

Guilt snakes around my chest, but I sever its head. No. I refuse to feel bad for her.

Cole doesn't look away until Mum disappears, but then he drops his chin, closes his eyes, and winces. "Sorry. I just . . . lost it."

I unglue my feet from the bottom step and go to him, cupping his cheeks, forcing his eyes to mine. They're filled with a sickly remorse that curdles my stomach. "Don't apologise. That was actually the most amazing thing anyone's ever done for me. And Beth built me a studio—you saved me from juvie—so that's saying something."

The tightness in his jaw eases, but a doubtful frown persists. I slide my hand over the back of his and lift it to press over my heart. "For nearly a decade, I've dreamt someone would fly in and defend me during an argument with Mum. Not only that, but witness what happens so they can tell me I'm not crazy. You just did that, and it means a lot." Tears wet my cheeks, and I swipe them away.

God, this man is . . . *everything*.

"You know I'd never do that, right? Mess around on you. I'm a lot of things, but a cheater isn't one of them." The ferocity in his words washes away Mum's.

I press my index finger to his lips. "*Shhh*, I know. I'm sorry she said those things about you." He kisses my fingertip, then moves my palm to press against his heart. No words are spoken, but silent ones dance in our eyes. Climbing to my tiptoes, I plant a long, tender kiss to his soft mouth and then opt to change the subject. "You're early."

"Surprise," he deadpans.

We both sigh but then laugh. I bury my head against his chest and breathe him in. "It's so good to see you."

He leans back, prompting me to look up. Beneath an arched brow, a knowing spark glistens in those pretty green eyes. "Do you have something to tell me?"

I narrow mine. "You already know, don't you?"

He surrenders his palms to the air. "All I know is I got a call today and saw Gloria's Jag leave as I arrived."

The butterflies reawaken in my stomach, and I grin. "My first show is in two and a half weeks."

"Congratulations. That's amazing." Cole's smile glows snow bright. He lifts me off the ground and spins me in a circle, then slides me down the front of his hard body until my feet find the floor. My mind descends to the gutter. "See, you did it," he says.

"With your help."

Cole laughs. "Trust me, Lady Browne was on that phone with a hundred questions as soon as she got my email. Had you contacted her yourself, it would have happened anyway."

"Thank you," I whisper. "A million times over."

"Don't mention it." Cole nods towards the microwaved risotto on the island. "Did you have your heart set on that, or can I whisk you away for dinner at my place to celebrate?"

I rub my chin, pretending it's a tough choice. "Well, I don't know. That's gourmet cuisine right there. Not to mention the company here is outstanding."

Cole's smile fades, and he rests his hands on my shoulders, hardening his stare. "Come stay with me for a week or two. Let things cool down here. I can drop you back whenever you need studio time."

I refrain from breaking into a dorky, happy dance and instead kiss his cheek. The light stubble on his jaw scratches my lips. He doesn't need to ask twice. "I'll get my stuff."

Twenty-Three

Ten hours and nineteen minutes before the exhibition opens, my rib cage feels like a stadium full of gremlins devouring a stash of speed. And by the time we glide up to the kerb outside Green Bird Gallery, they're peaking.

Cole squeezes my goosebumped knee. "Are you okay?"

I grip the leather seat like it will keep me safe. "Nope. This was a huge mistake. What the hell was I thinking?"

His laughter fills the car. "You'll be fine. Trust me."

Tonight, Cole smells like a cosy evening of shiraz and roses in front of an expensive fireplace and looks so damn fine in a tux it almost hijacks my panic. *Almost.* "Hundred bucks says everyone will laugh at me. Or worse yet, nothing will sell." Not that I care about the money. I just want someone to love my work enough to pay for it.

Cole flashes his dimple and holds out a hand. "You're on. But fair warning, I intend to collect my winnings in more unconventional ways."

As he raises a suggestive brow, I press my thighs together.

Oh hell yes.

"We have a deal." I surrender my hand, which Cole promptly shakes, only he doesn't let go. Rather, he leans across the centre console to whisper in my ear.

"That dress is insanely sexy." The gravelly words zing between my legs, and his hot breath tickles my neck. He sure knows how to distract a girl, I'll give him that, but now isn't the time.

I retrieve my hand, nixing the temptation to climb across his lap, then I douse the ill-timed fire with a bucket of ice. "Shame about Hannah not being able to come."

The mention of Hannah has the desired effect, and Cole winces, straightening back up in his seat. He cuts the engine. "Ella and late nights equal pandemonium. And there's probably a 'break it, you bought it' policy. I'd rather not go broke or have to dance to 'Dorothy the Dinosaur' all night."

Chuckling, I open my door. "Do you know why God makes toddlers so cute?"

We both climb out, resuming the conversation in the chilly night with frosty words. "Enlighten me," Cole says.

"So you don't kill them."

Cole laughs as he makes his way around the car and up onto the footpath. "Doesn't the cuteness wear off when you're surrounded by them every day?"

"Actually, they only get cuter." I shrug.

"I'll have to take your word for it. I only have patience for Ella."

I grin. "That's pretty normal, and she is pretty special."

Cole's face softens like it always does at Ella's mention. He tucks my hand inside his and lifts it to his mouth, planting a kiss to my knuckles. "That she is."

Green Bird Gallery is a quaint cottage, tucked back from the main road and surrounded by leafy trees frosted in fairy lights. Laser-cut stainless-steel letters gleam across its vintage red bricks, and the mammoth front windows glow gold from the galleries alight inside.

Cole holds open the ornate entry door and winks at me. "You've got this."

But I'm not so sure I do.

Heat and the faint scent of jasmine hit me as I step over the scuffed threshold and into the first massive gallery. Paintings fill the lily-white walls with squares and rectangles of colour, and rows of black spotlights track across the ceiling to illuminate them. The space is calm and sophisticated, yet nausea swirls in my stomach. In twenty minutes, my soul will lie bare for strangers to judge. My intimate thoughts and feelings will be shared like a Christmas feast. My bleeding carcass may well be eaten by vultures.

I wander to a standstill centre of the room, dizzied by the thought. Creativity whips the air like cream, and every breath infuses the visual feast into my blood. Abstract art, pop art, realism, romanticism—all the *isms*—surround me, big and small, while soft jazz music curls around my ears.

I float over to the biggest painting on the south wall.

The Reckoning
Artist: Leila Lockhart
Medium: Oil on canvas

"Wow," I whisper, picturing my meagre work next to this. I glance up at Cole, who's equally mesmerised. "I am so screwed."

He gives my sweaty hand a squeeze, and it's then I realise I've gripped his this whole time. His mouth tugs into a filthy smirk. "Later you will be."

I swat him. "Stop it. I'm trying to be anxious here." But that's what two weeks of earth-shattering shacking-up sex does. I thought it would satiate, but we only want more. More skin to skin. More late-night chats. More deconstructing each other's innermost thoughts without exchanging a word. More . . . *everything*.

His pale-green eyes glimmer. "What can I say? Being here to witness my girlfriend step into art scene stardom does it for me." He leans down, dragging his nose up from the nape of my neck to my ear. "And then there's this dress."

I shiver all the way down to my ruby-painted toes but abandon his hand to smooth out the satin and calm the fuck down. I know what he's doing—trying to smother my nerves with desire—and I love him for it. But my fight-or-flight response is the strongest thing about me. It's Muhammad Ali in his prime. I'd need to be knocked out or die for it to ever dim before it's good and damn well ready, and adding a layer of lust only frazzles me more.

"Avery, Cole, you're here!" Gloria sweeps into the room, her energy as vibrant as the art. She ushers us over with a frantic hand. "Come, come, you must see the display." Then dashes off into the next room, her high heels echoing against the polished pine floorboards. Mine do the same as I follow, my steps shaky despite my having finally conquered them. This is it. The night I'll know if I fit anywhere in this crazy world.

Gloria steps aside as she enters gallery two, and my breath hitches. I take a few tentative steps into the room, then stop to drink up the magical scene. Each one of my clay babies stands on a pedestal behind scarlet rope, with uplights and downlights accentuating each line, press, and crevice. And the *glaze* . . . Brilliant rainbow colours shine through tendrils of clay hair. Kissed by light, copper and stainless-steel glimmer. Banners and plaques, displaying *my* name, hang everywhere. I dig my nails into my palm, searching for pain. "Am I dreaming?" I ask Cole.

One corner of his mouth tilts up. "No, Angel, you're not."

I turn to Gloria. "This is incredible. How can I ever thank you?"

She picks up my hands and kisses each of my cheeks. "You just did. And by the end of the night, I'll be thanking you." Gloria winks.

"Now, if you'll excuse me, I have guests to schmooze and wallets to pry open."

I laugh. Right now, I don't even care if nothing sells. Seeing this—my work on professional display—is all the hope I'll ever need.

I move slowly from piece to piece, stepping out of my familiar perception to see my work in the light others will. Discreet silver plaques request I do not touch, but I'm tempted, if only to check they're real. They sit in sequence from *Girl, Crushed* to *Shattered Mind* to *The Cowered Child*, to *Child, Joy*, and *Wonder* respectively, followed by *Girl, Take Me*. And then there's *High Heart Symphony*: the centre-piece of the collection. The one that hugs my heart. Cole and me, our copper hearts and bodies entwined. It was a premonition in the end, as if creativity from its unearthly realm knew what would become.

God, what if it does sell? That didn't seem like a real possibility until now. My stomach cramps. It's like selling a piece of me, albeit for stupidly good money. That's what I have to remember. If tonight pans out, I can start my life.

We float through the school collection, finishing at the hand-painted bowls and vases, and I'm lost for words. Cole slips an arm around my waist and tugs me into his side. "Whatever happens, I'm proud of you. I know this wasn't easy."

I turn to face him and slink my arms around his neck. In heels, I'm only two inches shorter. Our sparkling eyes connect and do that silent thing they do, as if our souls are the ones who talk. We're the only two people in the universe . . . until hands cover my eyes from behind. I freeze.

"Boo," says the familiar voice.

Grinning, I yank down Jen's hands and pull her into a big hug. "You're here. Thanks for coming."

"As if I wouldn't," she says.

Scarlet curls nest at the top of her head, pinned in a loose bun, while a slinky black dress skims her curves. Then there are her cherry-red eight-hole boots. Classic Jen.

"Hey, Liam," I say with a smile. He ducks in for a hug. Without much fat on his bones, it's kind of like hugging a spindly tree. But Liam is a tree I love.

"Been a while, little lady. Too busy for us now?" He cocks an accusing brow as he lets me go, but a lazy grin counters it.

"I'm sorry. I've missed you guys."

Tonight, his glasses are neon blue, and black trousers graze his ankles, showing off pineapple-print socks that match his suspenders. Yep, suspenders. "Sure you have." He winks, then looks at Cole. "Hey, man. You must be the smokin' hot lawyer I've heard about." He looks him up and down, exaggerating awe. "God, they weren't wrong. You're beautiful."

Cole laughs. We all do. "And you must be Liam. The car enthusiast."

"The one and only."

They shake hands, then Cole moves in to kiss Jen's cheek. "Nice to see you again, Jen."

"You too," she says before glancing back to me. "So Beth's flying in all rock-star style?"

I nod. "Yep. We have her for three glorious hours." I can't wait.

Jen scans the gallery. "She here yet?"

"Soon. She's coming with Mum."

"You invited *Sheila*?" Jen hisses, and I glance around to see if anyone heard. A spattering of people now mill about gallery one with champagne in hand.

"She's my mum," I whisper. "I couldn't exactly exclude her. Besides, Beth promised to keep her in check." In truth, I did wrestle with inviting her. Especially after what happened. But Beth wants to see Mum too in the little time she has, which is fair enough. And if I know anything about Mum, it's that appearance is everything. Risking a public scene isn't her style. So all I have to do is keep my distance to avoid her more subtle thorns.

"But she—" Noticing me stiffen, Jen sighs. "Never mind. Now's not the time. I mean, check out all this." Her face relights as her hands showcase the room.

"What do you think?" I ask tentatively.

She bumps her hip against mine. "I think you'll kill it tonight." She pulls me in for a side hug, then kisses my cheek. "Now, I don't mean to be rude, but where is the free booze?"

"Ah, that's my woman right there," Liam says, clutching his chest. "My throat's as dry as a nun's cunt."

"Liam!" Jen gasps, whacking his arm.

Cole's eyes practically leap from their sockets, and I struggle to contain my laughter. Failing, I snort. "Gallery one, in the corner. Help yourself."

"Don't mind if we do," Liam says, throwing a nod Cole's way.

Jen rolls her eyes. "Sorry, Cole. Liam grew up in the country. He speaks fluent bogan. Just ignore him."

"Aw, you're just jealous you're not bilingual, babe," Liam quips before clasping her wrist. "Let's go before they run out."

Jen shakes her head, but humour dances in her eyes. She winks at me as she lets Liam drag her away. "Good luck. We'll be around if you need us."

When they leave, I glimpse up at Cole. His expression is quizzical. "Well then," he says, rocking back on his heels, hands tucked into his pockets. "I guess you grew up in the country too?"

Huffing, I plant my hands on my hips. "Liam makes me look like Mary fucking Poppins, thank you very much." Cole throws his head back and laughs, then drags me in for a sneaky kiss.

Guests soon filter into gallery two, and my heart backflips. Cole squeezes my shoulder. "Let me get you a drink. I'll be right back."

"Thanks," I manage to say instead of screaming, "No! Don't leave me here alone." That would be unprofessional and waste the ridiculous amount of time I've spent preparing to talk to people. Tonight, I need to sell myself. Divulge the sources of my inspiration. Metaphorically strip down to my undies and yell "look at me." I'm terrified, and liquid courage is definitely required.

Still, me being prepared or not, when murmured conversations start humming next to my sculptures, those gremlins from earlier try to claw their way out of my chest. Oh God, what are they saying? What are they thinking? Is that man with the spiral notepad and pen frowning in contemplation or horror? And why does he have a notepad and pen? As if hearing my thoughts, he looks up and nods his chin my way. Warily, I return the gesture.

Someone nudges my shoulder then. "Hey, stranger."

I turn to see Beth and gasp. Backlit by golden light, she's my angel of salvation. "Beth." I pull her into a hug that lasts too long, basking in her warmth and familiar Chanel scent. "God, I've missed you. I can't believe you're here."

"Surreal, isn't it?" she says.

We break apart but hold hands and look each other up and down. Her cheeks glow a healthy pink, and the shadows beneath her eyes have faded. Sydney must agree with her.

"You look great," we both say, then laugh.

"Nice dress," she says.

"You too." I spot Mum hovering behind Beth and summon a breath. "Hey, Mum."

"Avery Lee." She dips her chin in acknowledgement, offering me a tight smile. The knots in my stomach loosen some. I never know if Mum will match my dread or not. Tonight, it seems she won't, which is a relief. Hell, if all goes well, she might see me in a new light. Concede this "starving artist rubbish" has merit. Treat me like she treats Beth. That's my secret hope, anyway.

Cole returns with three flutes of champagne, obviously having spotted Beth and Mum arrive. "Champagne, ladies?"

I observe Mum's reaction. She and Cole haven't seen each other since *the confrontation*. But to my surprise, Mum bats her lashes and takes the crystal flute between her French-manicured fingertips like nothing ever happened. "Thank you, Cole," she says, all flowers and honey.

He stiffens a smidge but fast recovers. "Sheila." He nods. "Nice to see you."

With a kiss to my temple, Cole hands me a flute, then offers Beth hers.

"Thanks," Beth says, taking it. "I gotta say, it's nice to finally put a face to a voice." She darts her gaze between us with curious delight.

"Likewise," Cole says, holding out his hand. "Nice to finally meet you, Beth. I've heard a lot about you."

Their hands shake. "And I haven't heard nearly enough about you, it seems." Beth throws me an arched brow and leans in. "That needs to be rectified ASAP," she whispers behind a cupped hand.

I grin. While Beth is lacking in the juicy detail department, I have no intention of over-sharing. Cole is different. *This* is different. It only belongs to us.

Gloria reappears. "Sorry to interrupt, but people are asking about you, darling. I'll introduce you shortly, then it's time to mingle and share your magic, okay?"

A wave of nausea rushes over me, and I gulp down the rest of my champagne. It floats straight to my head, only worsening matters. Cole takes my empty glass, locking his eyes on mine. "You've got this, okay?" His conviction strengthens my spine, and the eye contact grounds me back to earth.

With a deep breath, I turn to face Gloria. "Okay," I sigh. The gremlins grip my vocal cords and swing like Tarzan wannabes, but it's now or never. Time to sink or swim. At least I can take comfort in the fact artists are known to be eccentric. If I mumble high-pitched incoherency, then puke into one of my bowls, it might only fulfil expectations. "I'm ready," I say.

But oh God, who am I kidding?

Two hours fly by in a blur of bubbles, jazz, cash, and colour. The feared criticism never comes, and my ability to network smooths. As wingman, Cole interjects with intelligent wit whenever required, and together we charm the pants off potential buyers as if we've practised for years. It's a glimpse of how our future could be, and I want to wrestle it to the ground and never let go.

Countless times, I catch Beth watching us with a smile ghosting her lips. And before she leaves, I soak up every precious minute I can with her.

When the first red sale dot appears on *Girl, Crushed*, I want to cartwheel across the gallery, dance in circles, and squeal. I want to drag Cole to the toilets, strip that sexy tux from his ripped body, and sin my dirty little heart out. Judging by the ever-growing fire in his eyes, he feels the same. But I remain composed. And continue to do so as every. Single. Piece. Sells.

It's midnight when we arrive back at Cole's house, high on success with the escalating hum of sexual tension threatening to explode. The car engine shudders silent, and our twinkling eyes lock. Cole tilts his mouth into a glistening smirk full of dirty promises. Mine follows suit, and in silent agreement, we hotfoot it out of the car and race up the stairs.

Our mouths collide as we reach the deck. Cole blindly fumbles with his keys but somehow unlocks the front door. We stumble in through the dining room with needy breaths and frantic hands tearing off each other's coats. Shoes tumble to the ground, and Cole's socks follow.

"Can you believe everything sold?" I ask. Our mouths rejoin as I whip off Cole's bow tie, then fumble open the buttons of his dress shirt. Courtesy of my impatience, the bottom two ping free and roll across the polished concrete. Cole chuckles as he plucks bobby pins from my hair and rustles it free, but I don't. After spending a night in an art gallery without seeing the best there is to see, I'm antsy—*desperate*.

"It was inevitable," he says, undoing his cuff links to slide off his shirt. He scrunches it into a loose ball, then tosses it away. "You're brilliant." It lands, dangling haphazardly from a chair, and I bite my bottom lip as I admire the resulting view.

He is the brilliant one.

Cole stands barefoot in black suit pants, lit only by the fireplace's crackling amber glow. His muscular chest rises with each loaded breath, causing the lush jungle to sway as if alive. Abs ripple through the shadows and crest in firelight. *V* muscles plunge from his hips into his pants, teasing the way to ecstasy. But eclipsing it all are his intense pale-green eyes—prettier than the Emerald City—holding me captive. Desire slickens the insides of my thighs.

"So how does it feel to make more in one night than four months?" he asks.

"Screw the money." I lick my lips. "All I want is you."

Cole stalks forward, closing the space between us. He presses one hand to the centre of my back and jerks me closer, landing me hard against his chest. "This dress," he murmurs against my jaw, dragging rough stubble across my skin. He slides the long zipper slowly down my spine, then nudges each strap from my shoulders. The dress slumps to my feet in a shiny pool of ruby satin, leaving a lacy black

G-string and nothing else. Cole steps back, allowing his eyes to drink me in. Goosebumps flourish across my skin under the scorch of his gaze, and his throat bobs as he swallows. "I need inside you."

"I need that too," I whisper.

We eye the giant tan ottoman squatting in front of the fireplace—one of the few surfaces we have left here to christen—and I squeal as he tosses me atop the soft, oiled leather. I land with a thud, sinking into feather fill that deflates with a sigh.

The fire-kissed leather is warm against my back as Cole's body covers mine. He grinds his erection between us, and I spread my legs wider to allow him better access—*lower* access. We moan into each other's mouths as we kiss, swallowing each other's pleasure. I drag my fingernails across his silky back, hard enough to leave parallel pink lines that will mark him mine for the rest of the night.

The retaliatory pinch to my nipple makes me yelp, and Cole's low chuckle reverberates through his chest. "You want to mark me, Angel?" His greedy hands continue to roam my body, leaving delicious, tingly trails. "Well, two can play at that game." He bites down low on my neck, sending a flash of lightning to my nethers, and I clench and shudder, growing ridiculously wet as he sucks on the delicate skin. As if he knows, Cole slips his hand south. He moves the crotch of my panties to one side and then plunges fingers deep into my core. My gasp melts into a mindless wail as Cole raggedly groans. "You're soaked."

Once upon a time, that would have embarrassed me—yet another humiliating thing out of my control—but not anymore. Not with him. To him, everything about my body is beautiful. Every part he worships as if sacred. "That's what you do to me," I say, undoing his pants to slide my hand beneath the monogrammed band of his briefs. I grip his rock-hard length and squeeze, causing a sharp breath to hiss past his teeth. "Take them off," I whisper. "I need you."

He listens but not before removing my sodden scrap of lace to level our nudity score.

I try to sit up, desperate to take him in my mouth, inhale his manly musk, and taste the bead of salty goodness glistening at the tip of his beautiful cock. But he pushes me back down with one bossy palm to my sternum. "Not so fast, young lady." He circles my nipple with his thumb, causing it to tighten. "Tonight's about you."

A devilish smirk flickers in his eyes as he hooks his hands under my knees. In one smooth motion, he pushes them up to my shoulders, effectively pinning me down and securing an all-access pass.

Nibbling my bottom lip, I stare at the cedar ceiling, jittering with anticipation, but I don't have long to wait. Cole grumbles a few rough words, then descends. His tongue, lips, and stubble tickle and tease the edges of my pussy and the delicate inner seam of my thighs, but he deliberately denies me the touch I truly need.

The restless ache inside my core grows until it fucking screams. "Tease," I gasp in a breathy mess.

I feel him smile against my upper thigh. "Whatever do you mean?" His fingers join in now, feathering over my clit way too softly. I groan a strangled groan.

Cole's laugh is hot against my skin. "You know what to say."

"*Please*," I whine.

"Please, what?"

This is our new thing. The thing that turns me raspberry red every single time. I might have mastered body confidence, but dirty talk is next level, and Cole knows it. I swallow hard, then inhale. "Please eat me, Mr. Benedict. Savour every last drip of my sweet little pussy."

A low, evil chuckle vibrates through my thigh. But then . . . Then comes heaven. Cole's hot, wet mouth. Cole's skilful, slick tongue. Cole's girthy fucking fingers. Two sink back deep inside me, and I cry out, bucking against his hand. "Oh God."

He circles my clit with his tongue as he plunges in and out, curling his fingers to hit my G-spot with practised precision. "You really do have the sweetest little pussy."

"I'm going to come." Embarrassingly fast. The second the words leave my lips, I shatter, and my screams echo through the house. My back arches off the ottoman as I buck from the charge of ecstasy, but Cole holds down my hips and continues his feast, determined to wring out every blissful bite.

Panting, I float back to earth, barely landing before he slams his length inside me. My head falls back, grinding into the leather, and I cry out a helpless, wrangled sound. With every nerve ending buzzing from release, I sink into nirvana, worshipping every desperate thrust. "Oh God," I repeat.

Cole fucks me deep and hard with my leg hitched over his elbow, stretching me open. "Look at me, Angel." The gritty words come stilted between rough breaths, and I open my eyes to find his locked on mine, mere inches away. Intense silver-jade eyes. Eyes that both devour and destroy me—inspire and adore me. Eyes that promise realms beyond this superficial plane where he is me and I am him. The place where our souls once planned to meet on earth.

He cups my face and tenderly strokes my cheek with his thumb, easing his pace. "It feels like my zenith to be yours."

"Ditto," I rasp.

"Turn over for me," Cole says as he pulls out. I comply and roll onto my stomach to perch off the edge of the ottoman, the fluffy rug soft under my knees. But then I click. There's another reason everything feels so damn good tonight—amplified—*connected*. "Condom!" I gasp.

Cole doesn't flinch, probably because he knows I'm on the pill and never forget to take it. Rather, he reaches for a bolster cushion two feet away, then covers my back, bracing himself on one elbow as he draws invisible spirals on my hand with a fingertip. "I forgot, but I also want nothing between us. I need all of you. Is that okay?"

He knows it is. With clean tests, we already agreed the current box of condoms would be our last. I nod. "More than okay."

He kisses my temple, coaxing my hips to rise. "Lift," he says, sliding the bolster cushion under me as I do. My arse tilts up to an obscene angle, leaving me on full, wide, and intimate display. The air is chilly against my soaked bits, and my face burns. I rescind what I said earlier. This I'm not quite ready for. Any number of forest critters could be peeping through the curtainless windows, but Cole groans. "Christ, you should see yourself like this."

I glance back over my shoulder to catch Cole licking his lips and biting the bottom one, his eyes ablaze. His expression is one of a hungry, desperate man wrestling with an impossible choice—to prolong the experience and savour the desire, or to consume and drown in pleasure, knowing that only promises the end.

The emptiness inside me grows unbearable. "Please, I need you."

Caving, he runs his tongue and chin up the length of my spine, then fills me as he reaches my ear. "Better?"

The pace has calmed, but the angle hasn't, and I mewl and moan like a cat in fucking heat. One hand grips my hair, and his other finds my clit. Fingers perfectly stroke, making the sensitive nub buzz as if shrouded in a delicious fog of feathery current. He blankets my back with his weight and whispers in my ear, "You're so beautiful, Avery Masters."

"So are you, Cole Benedict," I breathe.

He catches my mouth in a messy diagonal kiss infused with our words, and we trade moans and hungry gasps as we inhale each other's souls. Fuck. Only Cole could make doggy-style this intimate.

He continues the wanted assault, thrusting deep and hard while I clench the ottoman's piped edges, anchoring myself to meet his demand. Pleasure wraps every hypersensitive cell in electric bliss. Foreign sounds fly from my mouth and spin through the room, colliding with Cole's. The orgasm, building low in my pelvis, gathers power like it's sucking energy from the sun. But as its ferocity grows, fear jolts the hell awake. "It's too much," I gasp. "Cole. Oh God. Oh God. Oh God."

Cole rests his sweaty forehead against my temple. "Let go. I've got you." His teeth sink into my shoulder then, and I explode—screaming, clenching, bucking. I escape the suffocating confines of my body to glimpse a magical plane where I am free.

"Christ," Cole grits through clenched teeth as I strangle his cock. The primal roar of his release vibrates through the ottoman and enters my bloodstream, branding every cell with his name.

Sated and boneless, I slump against the ottoman, and Cole slumps over me, our lungs scrambling for oxygen. I manage to catch my breath, but then a strange, twisted, oily sensation orbs low in my belly. It swells and rises past my stomach, strangling my heart on the way through. Then it hits my throat and explodes.

I catch the first loud sob in my hand and bury my face in the ottoman. My shoulders shake uncontrollably as tears patter to the leather. "I'm so sorry," I say, mortified and confused.

Panicked, Cole pulls out of me and grips my shoulders. "Are you hurt? Did I hurt you?"

Unable to speak, I shake my head.

What the fuck is happening?

Oh God, am I that girl now? The weird, overemotional one who cries after she comes?

Just kill me.

Cole drags me onto his lap and tucks my head under his chin, pressing the side of my face to his heart. The tears continue to stream, mingling with the sweat sheened across his skin, but he simply waits and holds me, rocking us back and forth while I purge whatever the fuck this is. Buried pain. Repressed emotions. *Grief.*

Several long, cringeworthy minutes pass before I manage to calm down. I leave Cole's chest to sit up in his lap, then dry my face with my fingers, too humiliated to dare look up. "Sorry. I don't know what's wrong with me."

Everything, Avery Lee. Remember?

It was careless to forget.

Cole rubs between my shoulder blades. "Nothing is wrong with you, you hear me?"

Every muscle in my body recoils against that lie, and I huff a sad chuckle. Cole lifts my chin, forcing my eyes to his. He searches my face with knitted brows. "Nothing is wrong with you." His tone verges on anger now, and I squirm, averting my gaze to stare at my bony knees.

"Well, I've done my best to hide those parts," I say, hitching a shoulder.

Laughter booms through his chest. "Well, you did a lousy job. You hide nothing. You're the woman who sculpts her feelings for the world to see. The one whose face conveys her every thought. From that cute scowl to those hyper-colour cheeks, to the kaleidoscope of little smiles with a hundred different meanings. Long story short, baby, you'd suck at poker."

I huff again, but Cole skims his warm knuckles down my cheek. "Look at me, Angel." I do, letting him read every ugly secret inside me. "Don't tell me the woman I love is anything less than perfectly her or you'll have me to contend with."

My heart freezes a beat, then pirouettes through my rib cage, clearly finding sense before my head can. "You love me?"

"I don't just love you, I *like* you. Have since the first moment I saw you sitting in that court foyer."

My head spins. He likes me. He likes me *and* he loves me. My heart dissolves into a glittery explosion of effervescent mush—the gooey kind—the Sunkist-and-sherbet kind—the I'll-never-be-alone-again kind. A crooked smile tugs at my lips as tears of a different sort fill my eyes. I push Cole down onto his back, straddle his waist, and cup his stubbly cheeks, hovering my mouth an inch above his. I inhale his breath as he does mine. "I like you too. So, so, so much."

He cocks an amused brow. "And . . . ?"

I smirk. "And I might even love you, Mr. Benedict. But you knew that already. You know everything."

"I know you," he says, sweeping away the strands of hair hanging between us. Our chests kiss with every breath as gravity fills his expression. "And you are *everything*."

And just like that, I'm finally whole.

Twenty-Four

It turns out Mr. Spiral Notebook Man is a somebody: Jack Larson, esteemed art critic and blogger extraordinaire. And while Cole and I were still lost in each other's orbits the morning after the show, he published a gushing review.

Traffic to my website then skyrocketed, my social media following tripled, and a stream of commission enquiries has flowed in ever since. I have work to do. The only drawback to selling out is having nothing left to sell. But that's okay. The thought of endless studio time makes me buzz with glee.

I slip my phone into my satchel, climb the bullnose steps two at a time, and enter Benedict Kane. Today, the cloudless sky is a brilliant blue, spring kisses the air, and everyone bustling through Collins Street has a bounce in their step. Either that or the world's new rosy hue is dazzling my perception.

Cole left my bed at the crack of dawn for an early meeting, but even the discarded bubble gum stuck to the tram's seat had its charms today. It was pink and shaped like a unicorn. If that's not a fortuitous sign on a Monday morning, I don't know what is. Add that to the fact Mum's actually been nicer to me since the show, and everything feels . . . right.

Chantel silently greets me with a smile, talking into her headset as I stride past the reception desk. I smile back, then resume looking ahead, only to spy a change of scenery in the distance. One that slows my steps to a halt and causes my heart to trip over itself.

Oh my God.

Forcing my feet to move, I float over to the granite pedestal standing against the back wall beneath the shiny brass letters of "Benedict Kane." But the pedestal isn't alone. On top stands an intimately familiar sculpture, and below sits a placard embossed with golden words.

High Heart Symphony
Artist: Avery Masters
Medium: Terracotta, glaze, and copper

He didn't.

The "Lee" from my name is missing, and for that tiny but potent detail, I could kiss Cole's feet. I can't believe he did this. As if I'm not enamoured enough.

I'm still glued to the terrazzo, staring in wonder, when firm hands slide over my shoulders from behind. Immediately, I relax into the familiar touch. "You bought it," I say without looking away.

"Of course I did."

"Why?"

"*Why?*" Cole's tone implies it's the stupidest question I've ever asked. "It's us—an excellent investment—I'm madly in love with the artist. Should I continue?"

I twist to face him and find his dimple in full bloom. With a smile, I shake my head and silently resume admiring my clay baby. The one I feared long gone. "And you put it here . . . in the foyer?"

"Everyone should see how talented you are."

"You realise we're naked, right? And possibly engaged in . . ." I tilt my head to better assess the connecting points of our bodies and feel my cheeks flame.

Cole's deep laughter bounces through the foyer. "No one knows it's us."

Arching a brow, I glance up at him. "It wouldn't take a genius to figure out. My name's there, and thanks to your insistence on public displays of affection . . . Not that I'm complaining."

Cole leans in, dragging his lips along the shell of my ear. "They know nothing," he says, and the hot, gritty words shiver down my body. My toes curl, and a bubble of joy rises from my belly, bursting free as a giggle.

This is what happy feels like.

I turn to face Cole and slink my arms around his neck. "I never thought I'd see it again."

"It was never going anywhere," he says. "I bought it before the show even started."

My mouth falls open. "But there was no sticker until the end of the night."

"As requested. I didn't want you to think it prompted the other sales. It would have sold three times, by the way."

"Really?"

He nods, then bops my nose. "Really."

I press up onto my tippy-toes to level our height. When I say the next words, I want him to feel their sincerity. "Thank you. I love you so much." I plant a gentle kiss on his cheek, conscious of Chantel and whoever else has wandered in, but Cole threads his fingers through my hair and crushes my lips to his.

"Pride looks good on you," he says once we part.

I smile. "It feels good." In fact, it feels like a whole new fucking world. I nudge my chin back towards *High Heart Symphony*. "When did it get here?"

"First thing this morning."

I narrow my eyes. "Huh, the early meeting. Liar."

Cole winks. "Sometimes lies are for the greater good."

Secret smiles and silent words pass between us, and my heart swells so huge it could hang in the middle of Federation Square on Valentine's Day. But Cole soon breaks our trance with a smack to my bum. "You'd better get to work now, Angel, before I have to reprimand you in my office."

I flash him dark don't-tempt-me eyes, then release him with a smirk. "See you after work?"

He nods once, trailing fingertips down my arm. "My place this weekend?"

"Sounds perfect."

As I hike home from the tram, the postman buzzes to a stop at Beth's letterbox on his motorbike, hovering like a fluorescent wasp as he drops mail through the slot. He's typically long gone by the time I arrive from work, but I clock the anomaly as a positive sign.

The cheque from Green Bird Gallery is due any day. Then I can count my chickens and start making plans. I could pay for uni—rent my own place when Beth returns—restock studio supplies. God knows I need them now.

The postman scoots away before I reach the box, but sure enough, the sole letter he left is addressed to me.

I dash inside and upstairs with my stomach in flutters, taking a seat at the end of my bed. The envelope is thin and crisp in my hands as I stare at my name and memorise this moment. With a Beth breath, I rip it open and then fall onto my back with a goofy grin, holding the cheque up high. Yellow light from the pendant above streams through the paper, turning it translucent with shadows of pulp, but the dollar amount remains, and it's everything I'd hoped for.

Twenty-two thousand, five hundred and thirty-two dollars.

The fruits of my labour. The product of all my hard work. But more than that, it's proof. Proof I have something to offer the world, and that I might belong here. Proof that things *can* go right. Multiple things. All at once. I drum my feet against the floor and squeal.

This is what happy feels like.

I stare for a good ten minutes before heading downstairs to start dinner. Not ready to let go, I bring the cheque with me and devise a plan to copy and frame it, along with Jack Larson's review. They can hang pride of place on my studio wall and nudge me along whenever I doubt myself or life again.

The sweet aroma of puree pumpkin saturates the air thirty minutes later, and Mum appears in the kitchen. "Do you have enough for two?"

Throwing a glance back over my shoulder from the cooktop, I nod. "Sure."

Mum's civility still jars me. At first, her one-eighty was suspect, but it's growing on me. In fact, I think my wish materialised. After Green Bird Gallery, I think she finally sees me differently—better—worthy of her respect and love.

A tight smile flattens her lips as she climbs onto an island stool and adjusts her floaty dress to cover her crossed knees. "How was your day?"

"Fine, thanks. Yours?" I swap the wooden spoon out for a ladle and kill the gas burner.

Clasping her hands on the granite, Mum shrugs. "Pleasant enough." She nudges her chin towards the bowls I'm filling. "Smells nice."

I slide a steaming bowl of bright-orange soup towards her, then hitch up onto a barstool opposite with my own. We haven't eaten together once since she arrived back from the middle of fucking nowhere, and it triggers memories of my early childhood—ones with fuzzy edges and a pinkish hue. Once upon a time, this was the norm; only, four of us sat at a rustic pine table and Mum still bothered to cook.

Mum sips her first bite from the edge of the silver spoon, and I eagerly await her reaction—praying it meets her lofty standards. I'm no master chef, but my pumpkin soup slaps harder than she ever did. Trust me, I remember. Mum says nothing but takes another mouthful. An encouraging sign. "You like?"

She nods. "Not bad. Thank you."

Relief finds me, and I taste my own. "Yum," I hum before noticing my cheque lying in the centre of the island. Discreetly, I drag it closer, then flip it face down. Not that I think Mum would steal from me, but I prefer to keep my business private.

We eat in silence, the occasional polite smile drifting over the island. So far as meals go, this one is superficial and awkward as fuck, but we need to start somewhere. When finished, Mum stands and offers to clear the island. I thank her and watch curiously as she loads the dishwasher and wipes the granite until it gleams. Again, memories surface and hope shimmers.

"Would you like some dessert?"

The offer almost knocks me off my stool, but I clamber to keep the shock from my face. *Now she's feeding me.* "Ah . . . yes, please."

Mum smiles again, removes two fresh bowls from the cupboard, loads them with cookie-dough ice cream, hands me mine, and resumes her seat.

"Thanks." The little girl stuck inside my heart jumps up and down with glee, clapping her small hands. But to hide my smile, I quickly stuff my mouth full.

"I'm proud of you," Mum suddenly blurts, and my eyes snap to hers. She continues with one graceful hand animating her words. "The show. Your success." Discomfort swims in the shadows beneath her compliment, but I choke up nonetheless.

Tears sting as I clear my throat. "Thanks, Mum," I rasp. "That means so much to me." Mum dips her chin like a curtsey, then takes another bite.

I should be next to break the silence. She's extended an olive branch. Now I should do the same. "How are things going for you?"

"Oh," Mum says with a dismissive wave. "You don't want to hear about that."

I shake my head. "No, I do." And lo and behold, it's somewhat true.

She meets my eyes, then rapid-fire blinks as she drops her gaze, absently stabbing her ice cream. "Well, it seems my husband has excellent stalling skills. He's determined to see me destitute."

Mixed emotions bubble inside my rib cage like a sweet-and-sour stew. I don't condone Mum's methods or manipulation, and I don't know what she's trying to leech out of Dr. Wilson. But I know she left Melbourne with a modest amount of money after selling our family home. Surely he won't deny leaving her with that?

The questions I long to ask will ruffle Mum's feathers, so I choose a different route. One more befitting of this strangely pleasant occasion. "I'm sorry to hear that," I say.

Her shoulders rise and fall on a feathery sigh. "I thought I loved him. I truly did." I meet her pained blue eyes and feel my armour melt. She glances heavenward, pressing a palm to her chest. "Everything's just been so hard since your father. I never signed up to be a single mum. I suppose marrying Henry was my attempt to recreate what I lost, you know?"

Pity strangles my intestines while grief takes out my heart. *Oh, Dad.* That would explain the rotating door of boyfriends that swept in and out every six months the past seven years. I swallow down a horrible feeling as I stare at the fragile woman slouched in front of me. Why is it the second I don't hate Mum, guilt drowns me?

"Why not stay man-free a while?" I suggest. "Find your own groove and enjoy the perks of singledom?"

Mum smiles sadly. "That's all I'm trying to do. I came back to start fresh alone. I planned to buy a little house and start a beauty salon from home."

Well, I never. "That's a great idea. You're qualified with a good eye. Clients will love you."

"So now you understand why I need the settlement," she says, her voice wobbling. "But at this rate, I'll sooner be dead." Mum chokes on a sob and buries her face in her weathered hands, and I freeze up.

Awkwardness hangs in the air like a smelly fart in an elevator. I should comfort her, but my wounds and resentments are far too raw. I don't want to hug, console, or let Mum cry on my shoulder—the very thought makes my skin crawl—but if I want our relationship to heal, sacrifices must be made.

I slip off my stool and make my way around the kitchen island to squeeze Mum's shoulder. It's the best I can do. "Don't worry, everything will be okay."

Mum shudders as tears tumble into her bowl. "If only there were a spare room here. I could start my business now and save up to move. But it's already taken."

Warning sirens scream as I glance towards my studio. That quaint room is my haven—an extension of my soul—not to mention a treasured gift from Beth that I need now more than ever. I won't part with it.

I stroke Mum's shoulder while her powdery, sweet perfume curdles my stomach. "Just relax. It will all work out. You have a safe place to stay and food to eat while you wait. That's the main thing."

Mum withers further into despair but ever so slowly collects herself. I hand her a tissue and clear away our half-eaten bowls. It turns out this was not an ice cream kind of conversation. "Thanks for listening," she says, patting her cheeks dry. "Sometimes one just needs to vent, you know?"

"Any time," I reply, pressing start on the dishwasher with an unexpected sigh. Suddenly I feel drained—as if my jovial mood has died—but it's been a long day and a crazy week and a half. All the excitement was bound to hit me eventually. Raking fingers through my hair, I turn to face Mum. "I'm exhausted. I'm going up to bed. Will you be okay?"

"Actually, darling." The endearment jolts me. "Do you have another five minutes? I need to ask you something."

I wrinkle my brows but slide back onto my stool. "What is it?"

Blotchy-cheeked, Mum releases a small, breathy laugh. "This is quite embarrassing, really, but I've been thinking. Just hear me out, okay?"

A smidge of dread swirls in my gut, but I nod. "Fire away."

"There's a small two-bedroom house available for rent ten minutes away. It's darling and perfect for my salon. I might even buy it from the landlord once my settlement arrives. The only thing is, without an income right now, I can only secure the lease by paying six months ahead. Then I'll need funds to set up my business and survive until clients pick up."

I raise an eyebrow, interested to see where this is heading. It all sounds like a reasonable plan. "Maybe a bank loan could help? You could present a business plan . . ." I shrug.

"I've tried that. They said no."

My eyes widen. "You wrote a business plan?"

Mum straightens her spine, lifting her chin. "Yes, I did."

"Wow, can I check it out?"

"Oh . . . it's packed away somewhere. I'd have to find it," Mum stammers. "Anyway, the bank said no." She looks at me expectantly, and I stare, confused. "All I need is twenty thousand dollars to make this work. I know you did well from the exhibition, and I assume you have no immediate use for the money, since you live here and work full-time. I'm wondering if you'd loan it to me, just for a year?"

I flinch as an invisible hand clamps around my throat. "What?"

"I hate to ask, but family should look after family when they need help. Lord knows, raising you and your sister wasn't cheap."

I suddenly feel foggy—a little dizzy—and disconnected from my body, but somehow I manage to speak. "But I haven't even banked the cheque yet."

"Don't answer right away." Mum slides off her stool, preens the fall of her dress, and approaches me with a flowery smile. Her willowy arm snakes around my shoulders, and then she does the unthinkable. She hugs me. "Just think about it, okay?"

And with that, Mum bids goodnight.

The night drips by painfully slow as Mum's loan request pecks at my brain like a vicious hen. I toss and turn in bed, failing to find comfort, so check the time on my phone—3:00 a.m. God, I wish Cole were here. He'd know what to do.

I picture him hunched over his desk, tired and pale. The poor guy. These big cases are brutal. But thinking about him instead of Mum for one glorious minute brings relief. Until the cycle restarts.

Twenty. Thousand. Dollars.

My chest aches, and bitterness rises like Poseidon from a stormy sea, his trident on fire with rage. Yet the anger can't burn for long, since guilt swoops in and douses out the flames. Then comes the overwhelming grief. Mum's kindness this past week was manufactured purely to aid her request. She wanted something. She *needed* something. I've been used—played—buttered up like a dumb bread roll.

Or have I?

Maybe the timing is coincidental—her request reasonable. Maybe it's a test, and if I agree, things will be good between us forevermore. After all, Mum raised me. She ensured I had food, shelter, clothes, and an education. Maybe I owe her, and family *should* help family.

Imagine the bad karma if I say no. *Imagine the guilt.* Will Mum hate me? Will our progress evaporate?

I kick my quilt and growl at the ceiling. Damn it, I had dreams for that money. I worked hard. I'm at the start of my adult life, still sponging off Beth, but at the cusp of launching a career.

Will Mum pay me back? *Can I trust her?*

Only broken, shallow sleep comes, but by sunrise, my decision is made.

Mum's sitting on the velvet sofa, sipping a tall glass of lemon water, when I plod downstairs with my satchel. My tram comes in twenty-five minutes, and I was hoping she'd still be asleep like usual, but no. Wide, expectant eyes follow my every step, giving me the distinct impression my think-about-it deadline has expired.

"Good morning, dear," Mum says with a sugary smile.

Another endearment. Oh yeah—she definitely wants an answer now. Fuck it, I may as well deliver. I inhale a deep, weary breath and reply on the exhale as I make my way over. "Morning."

Dumping my bag on the rug, I sink to the sofa opposite Mum and rub my knobbly knees while I mentally rehearse my speech one last time. Then I clear my throat. Here goes nothing. "I've had the chance to think about the loan."

Mum's face brightens, and she straightens her posture as if excellent deportment might favourably influence the outcome. "Yes, and?"

"Mum, I don't want to jeopardise this new thing we have going on." I motion between us. "But I also need to think of my plans and future. I'm really sorry, but I can't lend you the money."

Her expression drops along with her gaze. "You mean you *won't* lend me the money."

I shake my head, trying to ignore her catty tone. "I'm sorry."

She releases an Oscar-worthy sigh. "I knew you'd say no. I don't know why I bothered to ask, frankly."

"Don't be like that. Please."

"Like what, Avery Lee?" Her chin snaps up, revealing laser-sharp eyes. "Like a mother who, Lord forbid, expects not to be left in the lurch by her own children?"

"Mum," I groan. "You're asking to borrow twenty grand, not a hundred bucks."

She scoffs. "I doubt it would make a difference. You've always been about one person only, Avery Lee, and that's you."

I curl my hands into fists, but hurt punches me in the stomach. "Don't start attacking me just because you didn't get your way." I wrench my glare away before Mum sees too much. Fuck this. Fuck her. I collect my bag and stand, hooking the strap over my shoulder. I guess it was good while it lasted. "I'm going to work."

But Mum isn't done. She jumps up from the sofa to block my escape route and, with gritted teeth, stabs her pointer finger towards me. "I have a right to be angry. I gave up everything to raise you, you hear me? Everything!"

I throw my hands in the air. "You chose to have children. That doesn't make us indebted to you for the rest of our lives."

Disgust sours Mum's face, but she casually strides closer, shortening the gap between us. "Do you know what you are, Avery Lee? A self-absorbed, cruel, and heartless bitch. There, I said it. It's about time someone did."

My heart wails in agony, and a yelp bursts from my mouth like someone kicked a dog. Tears flood my eyes, but my blood simmers to a raging boil. "How can you say that to me? It's not normal to say that to your own kid. Why do you hate me so much? Are you jealous? Is that it?"

"How dare you," she seethes.

"How dare *you*! I was doing fine before you returned. I was making progress—building a life for myself—and you've waltzed back in to fuck everything up."

Her eyes spit venom, and a low, patronising chuckle rattles through her chest. "You found a rich dick to ride, and now you think you're all grown up. It will end soon enough. Mark my words."

Her cruelty steals my breath as her words obliterate my soul. Only adrenaline keeps me upright—mentally, I'm dying on the floor. As tears fall from my chin, slowly I shake my head. "No wonder Dad killed himself. I would too if I was married to you."

The slap comes in the blink of an eye, and I gasp, cupping my stinging cheek. It was a low blow on my part, one I immediately regret. That is, until Mum delivers worse. "You're the reason he killed himself, you entitled brat. Not me. He *loved* me. He *forgave* me. It's you who broke his heart."

My brows screw up. "What the fuck are you talking about?"

Mum's eyes widen for a beat, and a flicker of panic washes over her face, but her combat mask swiftly returns, and she clenches her jaw. "Forget it."

I take one step closer and glare down at her, feeling the power Sergeant Nile must have felt when he towered over me that night. "No." A humourless laugh leaves my throat. "You tell me how a ten-year-old girl is the reason her dad committed suicide." It's a dare. I want her to say it out loud and hear the flaws in her fucked-up logic.

Mum's shoulders rise and fall with rapid, shallow breaths, but she meets my fiery gaze with ice. "I suppose it's time you knew the truth."

"What are you talking about?" A sense of doom seeps into the room like poisonous gas, and I clench my trembling hands into fists to control them. Every primal instinct tells me to flee—now—and fast. If I did, I'd still make the tram to work. But for some reason, my feet won't fucking move. They're frozen.

Mum must sense it too, because she shifts back to the sofa and resumes her seat, smoothing out her frazzled hair. Leaning back, she crosses her legs and perches her hands on her knee, one above the other. Then her chin does that defiant little nudge. "Nineteen years ago, I had an affair. It was the biggest mistake of my life, and you are the result."

My feet unglue without warning, and I stumble back a few steps as if I've been shot, colliding with the arm of the sofa. My mind spins on hyperdrive, trying to make sense of what she said, but only one logical conclusion appears. "Bullshit." Dad loved me. Dad was kind to me. He read me passages of poetry and sang me to sleep every night. I was his. I was more his than I've ever been anyone's. Until Cole.

"Why would I lie?" Mum asks.

"To hurt me. Why else?"

"Think, Avery Lee. You look nothing like him."

"I look like you." My voice comes out squeaky and pathetic, but as the words leave my lips, I remember the oddities. My cherry chin to their clefts. My Nordic-pale hair. Sans bleach, Mum's a dirty blonde, and Dad was dark as midnight. Why am I so fair? And my hairline is flat. I always wanted a cool vampire-esque widow's peak like the three of them.

"Same with Bethany. You two hardly pass as sisters."

Beth resembles Dad. I look like Mum. That makes sense, goddamn it.

I shuffle around the arm of the sofa, using it to keep my jellified body upright, then sit back down. It feels like planet earth was just thrown off its axis, and the cells in my body shriek as they're flung into walls, scrambling to find purchase. And my head . . . A gazillion thoughts and questions cram towards the exit, causing them all to get stuck in one almighty jam.

God, is this really happening?

I pinch my wrist hard, praying I don't feel the sting. But I do. Loud and clear. This is real. As real as it fucking gets.

Tears flow down my cheeks, bleeding into the fabric of my jeans. I swipe them away and shake my head. Even if this tragic bombshell is true—one thing definitely isn't. I glance up at Mum. "Dad adored me. I never broke his heart. He didn't—" I swallow "—*leave* because of me." Until today, I've never uttered Dad's official cause of death aloud, and I never want to again. It's too grimy and black for a gentle giant who smiled like he was made of sunshine.

"At least he waited until Bethany was an adult," Mum points out. "Face it, Avery Lee, he couldn't stand to look at you. Every time he did, he felt pain. How could he not?"

My throat catches as I swallow, feeling like it's full of sticky, hot marbles. "In what backwards world is that my fault and not yours?"

"He forgave me!" Mum says, poking her chest. The finger turns. "But *you* wouldn't let him forget. *You* were a walking reminder that tortured him every day."

Holy fucking shit. Can this woman hear herself? Does she actually believe that's true? Do I? I wish Beth were here to intervene with clarity and common sense.

I stiffen. *Beth*.

My head snaps up. "Does Beth know?"

Mum's chin rises again, and the urge to squeeze the life from her elegant neck tingles in my fingertips. "She knows."

Vomit surges up my throat, and I slam my hand over my mouth as I run for the kitchen sink, déjà vu swamping me as acrid yellow slime splashes against stainless steel. I heave, over and over, as the idyllic relationship I thought Beth and I shared shatters into a million pieces. It was all a lie. She's my mentor—my best friend—my idol. How could she keep this from me?

Pain slams through my chest like nothing I've ever felt. I ache, throb, and burn. Every muscle screams like my blood is acid and eating me from the inside out, aiming to leave an empty husk—a *numb* husk. One that'll blow away and never be missed.

Braced against the sink, I work to calm my panic, then wipe my mouth with the back of my hand, clearing away the vomit. I rinse the sink and watch beads of water trickle into the drain, all the while feeling my devastation return to rage. "Who is he?" I don't turn around or even raise my hanging head, but I speak loud enough for Sheila to hear. Fuck her—she's Sheila now—no longer is she Mum.

"*He* was a nasty, manipulative arsehole."

I release a heavy sigh. This old gem. More bullshit. More everyone else is to blame. I don't want to hear it. Sheila was a married woman who cheated and fell pregnant. Period. "His name. What's his name?" I grit through clenched teeth.

"Thomas."

That's only half the answer. I spin around, my glare shooting razors at her face. I've never felt a stronger need to be violent, and I'm not sure I'm in control.

Sheila's throat bobs. "Thomas Nilsen. He's a . . . politician."

"Does he know about me?"

"Yes," she whispers, eyeing her lap, at least having the sense to finally adopt a smidge of humility.

This man knows I exist. He knows and, evidently, wants no part of my life.

I survey the big, open room around me, which suddenly seems fuzzy and fake. Why am I here? Why do I subject myself to Sheila's toxicity now that I have a choice? Because of blood? Because she's my mother? Mothers are sacred and universally adored for a hundred reasons missing from mine. There's no soft place to fall—unconditional love—or trust my best interests even rate. On the contrary, my mother seeks to hurt and destroy me like a missile disguised as a shooting star. So again, I ask, why am I here?

And why the hell is she?

I meet Sheila's gaze, hoping I'm wrong—hoping I'll see a glimmer of reason to close my eyes again. But beneath her splotchy cheeks and the speck of genuine fright swims everything I feared. Satisfaction. Excitement. Victory—dancing in the depths of her pupils, the glow of her cheeks, and at the up-ticked side of her smug mouth. She's enjoying the goddamn show—the psychological horror she creates. *She's enjoying my pain.*

Hellfire shoots up my spine, and something snaps inside my brain. The final fucking straw. "Get out of this house," I seethe under weighted breaths.

Sheila gasps. "You don't have the right—"

"Get the fuck out!" I growl, my voice unrecognisable with feral rage. I charge to the sofa and grab her under the armpits, yanking her upright.

"Let me go! You're hurting me."

I let go only when Sheila complies and stands up in her piss-coloured dress. Then, stealing a page from her bitch-face handbook, I scan her from head to toe, spraying my contempt like Roundup on weeds. Her face is ghostly pale, and her veined feet wobble inside their expensive metallic heels. She's terrified, and that fact makes me smile a crazy Joker smile. She wants to pretend I'm a monster? Well, wish fucking granted. "You have ten minutes to pack your shit and get the fuck out of this house, or I'll remove you myself."

Wide, panicked eyes skitter across my face, scanning for sincerity, but a shaky nod is granted, and Sheila turns away, then rushes from the room.

The lock latches on Beth's bedroom door, followed by the thump of suitcases being dragged down from the closet shelf.

I sit in numb silence as the front door squeaks open. I count down the seconds as suitcases roll through the gallery. And I fist my hair and scream at the top of my lungs when the door slams shut.

Twenty-Five

I lie in bed, numb and devoid of presence, staring at the roof windows as the sun climbs the blanket of grey, then disappears from frame. Apart from calling in sick, I've not spoken to a soul, nor answered my phone the half dozen times it's rung. I know who it is. Sheila wouldn't have wasted any time relaying my monstrosity to Beth. No, with the zeal of a tween on speed, Mother dearest would've painted a glowing halo above her head and blood-red horns on mine.

I should phone Beth back—explain why I took such liberties in her house—but I don't want to. That'll make it real, and right now there's still hope. Hope that Sheila's full of shit and I'm still Dad's treasured girl. Hope that Beth didn't lie to me all these fucking years.

Wincing, I rub the ache in my chest. Beth's betrayal swims like hot sewerage, drowning every good deed she's ever done. Right or wrong—fair or not—I'm gutted. She kept the source of my existence a secret yet still looked me in the eye. She let me envy her—idolise and trust her. And what's worse, Beth knows about me. About my perpetual unsteadiness—the mental tightrope I walk. The fact I crumble like cake when hurt. Most people are built on a slab of reinforced concrete, and betrayal merely causes a crack. But me, I stand on a Jenga tower forever missing half its blocks.

My phone rattles against the bedside table again, and my eyes fall shut.

Answer it, you coward.

I do without speaking.

"I'm flying home," Beth says, all flustered and breathless. Car horns blare and engines sing in the background. It sounds like she's speed-walking through the heart of Sydney.

I release a heavy breath. "Don't do that."

"Aves, I'm not losing my sister over this. Please hear me out. I need you to understand why I played along with this shit. Jesus, I hate Mum right now. If she intended to finally tell you, she could've done so with tenderness—not during a bloody fight." Beth sighs. "Are you still there? Tell me you're still there."

I nod, even though she can't see me. "How long have you known?" I swallow the boulder in my throat and brace for the answer.

"Not even a year, and I found out by accident."

"By accident?" My voice cracks.

"Do you remember when you were in hospital after you broke your arm?"

How could I forget? Rollerblading, age eight. My elbow still bears the faint silvery scars from surgery. Like my sculptures, I have a few metal parts. "Hard to forget."

Automatic doors whirr through the receiver, then the city bustle dies, and Beth continues. "Well, being the nosey girl I am, I peeked at your medical chart. Your blood type stuck with me, but silly details often did when I was at uni cramming for exams. Anyway, I thought little more of it, just mentally filed it away next to mine, Mum's, and Dad's. That is, until I helped with a divorce case last year. Our client's son needed a blood transfusion, but our client was neither a match nor biological possibility, and it turned out the child wasn't his. I learnt a few things about genetics as a result. But then, that night, I jolted awake with your blood type flashing in my head. Google confirmed the incompatibility between you and Dad straightaway. At first, I thought I remembered wrong, but I did some digging, then confronted Mum, and she broke down in tears."

I stay quiet, processing everything Beth confessed, and that last spark of hope regarding Dad fizzles to black.

"Aves, are you there?"

I clear my throat. "I'm here." Silence stretches between us. Beth's known for a year—*only a year*—but still. "Why didn't you tell me?" I ask but immediately suspect the answer.

"You were prepping for exams. It was your final year of high school. It wasn't the time. A bombshell like that could have screwed up everything for you. Then Mum left, and that wasn't the time. Then you were arrested, and that wasn't the time. Then I had to leave for five months—you get the gist. I intended to tell you the minute I got back, when I could be there to support you."

My limbs turn to spaghetti as relief rushes through my blood like morphine. Beth's explanation makes sense. I haven't lost my sister. My Jenga tower is safe.

Thank fucking God.

I put Beth on speaker and lay my phone on the pillow next to my head. "I thought you lied to me for years. It made me question everything I thought we were. I was shattered."

"Aves." Beth's voice breaks. "You're not only my little sister, you're my best friend—a powerful combo. Your best interests live in my heart along with my own. You can always bank on that."

Oh God. I'm crying again, blubbering like a hormonal fool. It doesn't help that my period is due and my pelvis feels like it's full of wet concrete. "Sheila said Dad . . . died . . . because I broke his heart. That he couldn't stand to look at me."

"She said *what*?" Beth's voice screeches through the speaker, and I flinch. "You're kidding me?"

"Afraid not."

"Oh, Aves, I'm so sorry. Mum failed to mention that part. Jesus, what the hell is wrong with her?"

"Everything, Beth. Everything."

"No wonder you kicked her out. You know that's garbage, right?"

"Maybe?"

Beth huffs. "Dad loved you so much. Please never doubt that. Besides, kids are supernatural sensers. You would have felt any resentment aimed at you. Did you ever feel anything but love?"

I fiddle with the quilt cover as I flick through my carousel of childhood memories. "No. Not at all. Dad was all fluffy rabbits and rainbows."

"See? Hold on to that. I know we never talk about it, Aves, but Dad battled severe depression. You were too young to know, and he hid it well, but I wasn't. I saw it. He struggled daily. The curse of a creative mind, one might say. Mum's antics wouldn't have helped, of course, but it wasn't anyone's fault. You were his little princess. So much so at times I was jealous."

I frown at the phone. Dad had depression? Beth was jealous . . . *of me*? What else didn't I know?

Beth snorts. "Jesus, I can't believe Mum said that."

"Really? You can't?" Beth doesn't answer, but her silence speaks volumes, as does the weary sigh that follows. "You know I'm done with her, right?" I ask.

"Yeah," she whispers, "and you know I'm not. But I get it. Do what you need to do."

I wish Beth were with me on this, but I get it too. If I had the side of Sheila Beth gets, or even her resilience, I mightn't be done either. I roll onto my back and stare at the ceiling. "Did she tell you about him? My sperm donor?"

"Not much. Only that she waitressed at a café he frequented near Parliament House, and he wooed her. Honestly, I'm not all that interested in someone who isn't interested in you. Nor someone who sleeps with married women behind their husbands' backs. Stuff him."

I huff a laugh. "You never even Googled him?"

"Nope. That's for you to do if or when you feel the need."

My heart launches into a sprint. Googling Thomas Nilsen myself isn't something I've considered doing until now.

"Do you need me to come home, Aves?" Beth asks. "Say the word and I will."

I shake my head. "Please don't. I'll be fine. Truly." It's a shaky promise, but I want to hold Beth's highest good in my heart too, and that starts by not jeopardising her beloved career.

A knock sounds at the front door. "Uh, Beth, I gotta go."

"Righto, then." She sounds hesitant. "Are we . . . okay?"

"We're fine." Her stealth exhale triggers a flash of guilt. "I love your guts, sis."

"Love yours more," she singsongs. "Check in later, okay?"

"Will do." I end the call and sit up in bed, hoping whoever's at the door will bugger off. Unfortunately, the knock sounds again, but so does the door handle.

"Hello? Aves, are you home?" Cole's voice floats up the stairs and wraps a soft bandage around my heart in a pretty bow.

"Up here," I call out, my voice suddenly Marge Simpson hoarse. Shit, I probably look rubbish too, but I barely have the energy to care. *Suck on that, Sheila.*

Cole bounds up the steps, making them dong like a bell. "Hannah said you're sick." He reaches the landing, looking fifty shades of fine in yet another slimline suit. "Are you okay? Why didn't you call me?"

Ah, because I was a catatonic zombie after being told I killed my dad, who actually isn't my dad?

That concise summary doesn't transfer to voice. Instead, I'm struck mute, staring. Where do I start? I'm tempted to downplay the whole debacle now that Beth and I are cool, but Cole's crinkled forehead and worried X-ray eyes dig for truth and fast dismantle my walls. He softens his expression then, as if he feels my pain, and his mere acknowledgement triggers another tidal wave of tears. So I do what any self-respecting girlfriend would. I bury my face in a pillow and hide as sobs wrack my body.

The mattress dips as Cole climbs on to spoon me. "Tell me what's happened, Angel." I shake my head, choking on snot. Delightful. "Take your time," he says, kneading my shoulder and pressing his thumb into the painful knots.

Fuck. Apparently, tears never run out. I could have filled an ice cube tray by now. But when they finally do ease, I recount the whole sorry tale, thankful I don't need to look Cole in the eye. I might see pity or judgement. Or worse yet, annoyance. Hell knows, if I were him, I'd be sick of the incessant teen drama and my gross deviation from normal by now. I'm *not* him, and I'm sick of it. But this is endlessly tolerant Cole we're talking about, and as I delve through the details, he doesn't interrupt. The ever-increasing tension in his muscles the only clue to his thoughts.

He stays silent a beat after I finish but then clears his throat. "Wow. That's a lot."

I nod into my pillow. "If I could turn back time, I'd just loan her the stinking money if it meant I'd never have to know."

Cole hugs me harder. "*Shhh*," he whispers. "Calm down. I've got you." And it's then I realise I'm hyperventilating. But the weight of Cole's body grounds me, and those words soothe my soul.

He waits until my breaths slow before speaking again. "You were right to say no to Sheila—and to sever that toxic relationship. I know she's your mum, but I've seen how she treats you, and it's far from okay." He draws small circles on the back of my neck, and I sigh. "As for this dad revelation, I'm sorry you're hurting. I'm sorry they lied, and I'm sorry the news was delivered the way it was. You deserved better. So much better, Angel." The empathy in Cole's voice is so potent and raw I regret saddling him with my pain.

I roll to face him. "How do you do that?"

"Do what?" he asks, his eyes clearly sheened.

"Stop the war that rages inside me with a few meaningful words?"

Cole searches my face and tentatively caresses my cheek. "My heart just seems to know what yours needs to hear, I think."

God, this man.

He brushes fingers through my hair, but they fast get tangled in knots, forcing him to implement a careful extraction op. I wince but also seize the opportunity to lighten him up. Cole seems as wrecked as I am about this whole ordeal, which is beautiful but also bad for him. "I gotta look worse than my mugshot right now, huh?"

"Bollocks," he says. "Trust me when I say that worse than your mugshot doesn't actually exist." He delivers the dig dryly but cracks a smile that grows as I swat his arm and laugh.

I press my lips to his, then tuck myself under his arm, resting my head on his chest, inhaling that woodsy cologne. An easier silence follows, but Sheila's barbs soon hook me again. Cole must sense it too. "Did Sheila say who he is?" The mere mention of my mother's name seems to tighten him back up.

"Thomas Nilsen," I whisper as strange old men parade through my mind.

Cole stops breathing, and his heartbeat scatters beneath my ear. I prop up on my elbow to look at him. "Do you know him?"

"No." He frowns. "I know a few other Nilsens though."

"Maybe they're related?"

"I doubt it."

"Apparently he's a politician." Cole shifts to sit up off the side of my bed, so I crawl up next to him. "Are you okay?"

He covers my hand on his thigh with his, threads our fingers, and stares at them. "Listen, take the rest of the week off. I'll talk to Marla. I'm sure she'll happily cover a few more days."

"Today's enough," I say, and I mean it. Now that he's here, I feel stronger. Less broken. Like I've levelled up on the resilience meter.

"No." Cole squeezes my hand. "I insist. This is a big deal. You need time to process, and I imagine a dozen screaming toddlers will render that impossible."

I chuckle. He's not wrong. "Thank you," I say, dragging my thumb over the deep concern etched between his brows to erase it. "What would I do without you?"

I expect a witty comeback or at the very least a smirk, but Cole just stares at me, his eyes thunder-cloud bleak. "Aves," he says with a heaviness that sinks my stomach.

My smile evaporates. "What?"

Cole swallows, and my heart bolts, but then he closes his eyes, shakes away the thought, and flashes me a weak smile. "Nothing. We'll talk soon."

In Loving Memory
Matthew Sean Masters
July 28, 1971 – January 20, 2016
Beloved Husband, Father & Son
With You in Spirit, Always & Forever

I lay a long-stemmed yellow rose atop a copy of today's *Herald Sun* newspaper at the foot of Dad's honed granite headstone, then drop to lie down on the manicured grass next to his plot, staring up at the glowing cotton clouds.

With you in spirit, always and forever. That was the second-to-last sentence Dad wrote before he climbed into his candy-red sedan, drove to a quiet beachfront car park two hours south, and downed a bottle of sleeping pills. As the sun bid farewell, so too did he. Always and forever.

"I'm sorry" was his last sentence. I know because I found the note and coroner's report boxed up with his belongings in the garage when I packed before Sheila left. It was an unwanted Christmas gift and yet another heartache that precipitated my derailment. One that will be *always and forever* tattooed to my brain.

The rose's sweet scent rides the spring breeze and fills my nostrils as the mid-morning sun heats my skin, but I wince. Such pleasantness only serves up a cruel contrast to the pain that's crippled me for two whole days. Still, I ignore it and begin our favourite game. "I see a giant crocodile's head with its jaw open," I tell Dad as a reptilian-shaped cloud floats past. Once upon a time, it would be his turn now, but these days I do all the spotting and just pretend he makes the shapes.

Another cloud transforms. "I see it. A wizard with a bulbous nose, beard, and pointy hat, right?" No answer comes, and it occurs to me that anyone might be watching me lying in a graveyard, talking to the sky. But a graveyard is a special place. One that rouses empathy and compassion from passers-by, rather than judgement. Here, in the quiet, amongst the dead and grieving, I can be me.

Besides, it's not my first time. I visit Dad to cloud-watch whenever the reality of his death smacks me in the face so hard I can no longer pretend it didn't happen. Plus, I needed to escape the house. There's only so much solace clay can provide. And there are only so many times hurt can circulate, screaming its pain story to the empty theatre in my soul, before I go mad. What's more, the temptation to Google Thomas Nilsen hasn't let up. It's itched at my fingertips and lured me to my phone over and over again. The curiosity is killing me, but to open Pandora's box, I need Dad by my side. It feels like less of a betrayal to him that way.

"Dad, are you still here?" A butterfly flutters down to land on my nose, and her tiny feet tickle as she bats her lemon-yellow wings before flying away. In my book, that's a universal yes. "There's stuff I need to tell you." So I do. I tell Dad about the showdown with Sheila and apologise for estranging his one true love. I tell him about Cole—how quintessentially good he is. I tell him about Beth taking the legal world by storm—about Green Bird Gallery and my sell-out show. But then I address the elephant. I tell him about Thomas and my desperate need to know more.

No butterfly lands on my nose when I request Dad's Google blessing. But no trees crack and fall—no thunder rumbles—so I take that as silent permission and suck in a deep breath. My phone shakes as I unlock it, and my thumbs fumble as they type in four pivotal words. *Thomas Nilsen. Politician. Australia.*

Strange faces swamp the image results, but one more so than the rest. A man in his fifties, dressed in a navy suit and lilac tie with short white hair, ice-blue eyes, and a dazzling smile. I scrutinise his features, and an eerie familiarity slides up my spine. No widow's peak. Nordic pale. Chin cherry proud. My heart hammers. God, this is weird.

I blink a few times to re-water my eyes, then click on an image of Thomas in a tux, standing with his arm locked around a middle-aged brunette who looks gorgeous in gold. And then I tumble down a rabbit hole like Alice, learning all there is to know.

Thomas Nilsen—my sperm donor and biological father—is a well-known individual with power and wealth. One with an impeccable reputation for being forthright and fair. A proud family man, with a wife of twenty-three years, who grew up in Melbourne before moving to Canberra to pursue his career. He's political dynamite and leader of the Australian Centrists. The first genuine threat to the two-party duopoly that's doomed us to date. The guy is borderline famous.

And . . . he has two sons. One my age, the other twenty-one. My half brothers, handsome and whole, who look more like me than Beth ever will.

Holy shit.

I swipe back to Thomas and stare into his eyes, trying to picture this shiny man cheating on his beautiful wife, but I can't see it. They're a picture-perfect family, all bursting with pride. Sheila must have been Thomas's one slip-up—his biggest regret. I wonder if the wife knows or if I'm a dirty little secret he's kept buried in the dark. It wouldn't be my first time there.

I run my fingertips down the pale face on my screen and shake my head. Thomas presents like one of the good ones. Is it possible he doesn't know about me? Maybe Sheila lied. I'm his child, after all—his own flesh and blood. How could he pretend I don't exist? But maybe Sheila designed it that way, wielding threats and scorn. Maybe Thomas had no choice.

The thought jolts me upright. "Dad, I've gotta go. I love you." I climb to my feet and plant a kiss atop his cold headstone, then dash for the vintage gates.

A silver lining to this clusterfuck shimmers for the first time. I have two brothers and the possibility of a whole new family. For all I know, the wife is aware of Thomas's indiscretion and forgave him long ago. Images of meeting, befriending, and bonding with these people sashay through my mind in a Hallmark-worthy montage, complete with piano.

Maybe one day I could be in their family photo too.

A voice in my head snorts. *Yeah, I'm sure the fruit of an affair would poll epically in the court of public opinion,* she snarks, but my hope stomps her out, and excitement bubbles.

I need to tell Cole, and now.

When I reach the tram stop, I sit and dial his number, but it diverts to voicemail. My heel bounces against the pavement, and I drum my fingers on the bench as I chew my bottom lip. Fuck it, I'll tram it to Benedict's instead of home. This is news I need to share.

Eyes prickle the back of my neck as I press the up button next to Benedict's golden elevator. I was hoping to sneak by unnoticed given I'm technically on sick leave, but alas, Mini-Bees is virtually a fish tank and standing directly behind me, which has been a bonus until now. Biting the bullet, I turn around with an awkward smile, and sure enough, Hannah and Tej are staring at me, a sea of toddlers asleep at their feet.

Hannah folds her arms with a smirk and arches an accusing brow, tapping her foot as if to say, "So much for being sick."

"I'm sorry," I mouth before pointing upstairs. "Blame your brother." Hannah rolls her eyes and shoos me away with a light-hearted wave.

Tej, however, is beaming. He radiates light as if he's swallowed the sun. He excuses himself and dashes towards me, soon barrelling out the glass door. "Aves, I'm so glad you're here. I have some news."

His electric excitement startles my frayed nerves. "What is it?" He holds me out at arm's length, squeezing my shoulders. The elevator dings, and the doors glide open, but I ignore them. "Did you win Powerball or something?"

"Close." Grinning, Tej inhales a deep breath and puffs out his chest. "Last night, Riot of the Ruby Soul signed a record deal."

I gasp and grip his forearms. "Oh my God. You're kidding me?"

He shakes his head. "Nuh-uh. We did it, baby."

I jump up and down, squealing like a loon, then yank him in for a hug. "Congratulations. I knew you would. You guys are amazing."

Over Tej's shoulder through the glass wall, I spot Hannah playing air guitar, spasming one leg dramatically in the air. I laugh.

"I still think I'm dreaming," Tej says as we break apart.

I shake my head. "You get to *live* the dream now." Tears fill my eyes, primed and looking for any excuse to fall. "I'm so happy for you."

Tej hitches a shoulder and jerks his chin towards the elevator. "Looks like both our fantasies came true, hey?" My cheeks flush, and Tej chuckles, play-punching my arm. "Hey, I had you figured out before anyone." He winks, and I nod.

"That you did."

"I gotta get back," he says, hitching a thumb over his shoulder. "Marla's on lunch. When are you back with us?"

"Monday," I say. "Will you still be here?"

"Sure will. See you then." He grins, then leans past me to smack the up button on the elevator once more. "Give my regards to Mr. B."

I smirk. "Will do."

When I exit the elevator, I scan the fourth floor. Inside glass offices, pristine staff meet with clients, stare at their laptop screens, or eat at their designer oak desks while flipping through papers. Cole's assistant is notably absent. Her Eames replica chair sits tucked behind her desk, and no jacket hangs from its back. She must be at lunch.

I glance towards Cole's office. Daylight glows through the glossy white glass, and his door sits an inch ajar. I should probably phone him again, but that feels stupid when I'm five metres away. Besides, what's the worst that could happen? If he's busy with a client, I'll simply apologise for interrupting and be on my merry way.

A rush of jittery excitement returns as I traverse the hall, my Chucks quiet against the chevron timber floors. I have three siblings. How surreal. I raise my fist to knock, but halt when the growly, bitter version of Cole's voice torpedoes out. "I'm out. I've done everything I agreed to do."

I should walk away. Clearly, this isn't a good time, but as I turn to go, a sardonic laugh erupts, and curiosity wins out. Sheepishly, I peek left and right to ensure no one's here to witness me snoop. Then I brace myself against the aluminium architrave and hover in close, careful to avoid the see-through letters on the door.

"And then some," a deep voice spits. "No one said to hire her. That you took upon yourself for some godforsaken reason."

"And it's proved wise," Cole says. "Now you have advanced warning—time to prepare your family."

"I'm not preparing anyone." The man's voice drops to a formidable octave. "This isn't going to happen, you hear me? Bury it."

"Bury it?" Cole says, exasperated. "Everything was done to prepare in case this happened."

"As a very last resort. But as you said, we've been forewarned, and it hasn't yet leaked to the press. If you think I'm going to roll over so easily in the final hour—cause my family unnecessary upheaval—then you're sadly mistaken. Money's worked to date. I assume the apple doesn't fall far from the tree. Talk to her. Name her price."

Silence ensues, and my heart jackhammers in my ears. Sheesh, this is intense. I wrongly assumed the arguments only occurred in court.

Cole's chair squeaks, and then I hear him sigh. "She's beautiful, you know. Inside and out. Talented and bright. Not knowing her will be your loss." The intimate way Cole cradles those words strikes a chord within my soul, but dread coils around my ribs too.

Is he . . . talking about *me*?

God, Avery Lee, you think everything is about you.

Ain't that the truth. I shrug away the notion.

"She's a mistake, plain and simple. Don't risk everything your uncle built, boy. Do your damn job. Fix this shit and let me know when it's done. I fly home Sunday night."

Footsteps charge towards me, but I don't have time to move. The door flies open, and I stumble back to hit the wall, my face flushing hot.

Busted.

The man stops dead in his tracks, and familiar pale-blue eyes lock on mine, causing the flustered apology I had ready to die on the tip of my tongue. My brows furrow. "T . . . Thomas? Thomas Nilsen?"

There's no ember of doubt I'm right. He has the same white hair, cherry chin, round, shiny cheeks, and pale complexion that graced every photo online. The only things amiss are the friendly sparkle and easy smile. He's taller than I imagined. On the grasshopper side of thin too.

Thomas narrows his cold eyes to match the sharp lines of his pin-stripe suit as he scans me up and down. "Good Lord, the resemblance is uncanny. You're practically your mother."

So he does know about me.

I square my shoulders and lengthen my spine. "I am nothing like my mother," I say, nudging my chin high in the air. Just like my mother.

God, kill me.

One side of Thomas's mouth curls up. "Is that so?"

"Aves?" Cole appears in the doorway behind Thomas, his face drained of colour. "You're meant to be at home. What are you doing here?"

"Eavesdropping, it seems," Thomas snarks, sliding his knobbly hands into his pant pockets.

Denial springs to my lips, but I mash them shut. I'm not the one who should be explaining myself. "What's going on?" I ask Cole, cautiously—reluctantly—acutely aware I may not want or like the answer.

Thomas scoffs. "Do all the minions question you like that?" His gaze darts from Cole to the ceiling. "Gerard would roll in his grave."

Cole clenches his jaw but doesn't respond, and my limbs tingle like I'm drowning in effervescent slime. The conversation I overheard screams through the goo, fighting to replay in my head, but I block it out.

Not. Everything. Is. About. Me.

I grip that truth like a tree in a tornado and hang on for dear life.

Thomas nods his chin towards Cole's office. "Do come in, then, Avery. Since you're here, we can end this now." Thomas saunters back inside with cocky nonchalance, deliberately shouldering Cole on the way past. Cole recovers quickly, raking fingers through his mussed hair, but the act of dominance doesn't go unnoticed. Thomas is top dog here.

My stupid visions of ever being welcomed or loved by this man and his family deflate like a hot-air balloon. Counter to the pristine public image created online, the guy's a dick. Or maybe I have that effect on people. I'm the common denominator, after all.

Cole stays mute as I enter, his gaze downcast and locked on his shoes like that of a boy stuck in timeout. Never have I seen him so rattled or small. As he shrinks, so does the room. I stop in front of him. "You do know him," I say as my grip on the tree falters. It's a statement, not a question, but the acid swirling in the pit of my stomach tells me it's true. "You lied."

Cole winces, then lifts his eyes to meet mine. A cocktail of remorse, guilt, and fear swim in their jade-coloured depths. They speak of a betrayal far worse than one measly lie, but I refuse to process or connect the jumble of clues. Ignorance will sustain our bliss—denial our last shred of happiness—for one more minute, at least.

I float past him as if I'm levitating through the ether and no longer connected to my body.

Cole tugs on the hem of my daisy-dotted blouse. "Aves," he whispers desperately.

Self-preservation begs me to resist his plea, but Cole's touch is my oxygen, his warmth a firelit cave in a blizzard, and his love the lush green earth beneath my feet. Without him, I'll evaporate—dissolve into perpetual darkness, untethered. So I fall into his arms and melt like chocolate, longing to hide in his soul. He holds me against his chest fiercely with one hand locked in my hair, planting kisses on my crown, and I breathe him in, allowing his scent to soothe the agony he's caused. "I'm so sorry, Angel. I wanted to tell you. Please forgive me. I had no choice."

"Don't speak," I whisper. "It hurts."

Cole's admission of guilt is a guillotine blade hanging above our heads like mistletoe, but still, I cling to denial, desperate to stop it from falling.

"Well, well. This is starting to make more sense." Thomas tuts. "Hell, Cole, I didn't pay you to fuck her."

The blade drops between us, severing our connection in the blink of an eye like it had no roots or resilience to begin with. My breath hitches as my heart implodes and sucks my essence into a dead black hole. In the space between seconds, I disappear.

Cole's shoulders slump and his arms fall away as he squeezes his eyes shut. I slowly back away from him as tears stream down my cheeks. The ache, throb, and burn I felt after Beth's perceived betrayal is magnified by ten. I'm not an empty husk—there is no husk—and the Jenga tower has gone.

Horrified, I dart my gaze between the man I love and the one who created me. Both are the reason I breathe; now both are the reason I can't.

Thomas reclines in Cole's chair, stretches out his legs on top of the desk, and crosses his feet at the ankles. He wears pointy tan leather oxfords with fun polka-dot socks. Another lie. There's nothing fun about him.

"Can someone tell me what the hell is going on?" My voice quivers and doesn't register as mine. It's like I'm listening from afar or watching a play from the sky about some dumb girl's imminent demise.

"Don't look to Cole for answers," Thomas says, clasping hands behind his head. "You won't get any. Client-attorney privilege and all that."

I stare at Thomas. "You enlighten me, then."

The side of his mouth kicks up, but not in a friendly way. "Well, it's really quite simple. Gerard and I had this little situation"—he nods his chin towards me—"well under control, until he went and died, and you went and got arrested. I might be able to spin a love child if it ever came to light, but a criminal love child is another beast. I enlisted Cole to quash the charges and keep you squeaky clean. You can thank me now if you like."

I snap my gaze to Cole. "Is that true?"

Cole's jaw clenches as he wrestles to loosen his favourite emerald tie. His face is clammy, his breathing harsh, and it's all the confirmation I need. "No," I whisper as pain slices through my chest like I've been dissected with a machete. "This isn't you."

Seemingly unaffected, Thomas continues, but his words are muffled like they're travelling through fog en route to my ringing ears. But I hear enough. Every vomit-worthy claim.

One.

Sheila's been paid handsome hush money every year since my birth, right up until I finished high school late last year.

Two.

Cole didn't appear thanks to Beth's connections—it was no fortuitous twist of fate. Cole was paid to intervene, and Beth was his way in. But he took it even further. He hired and fucked me too.

Three.

An eye was kept on me since I was old enough to cause Thomas any trouble, courtesy of Benedict Kane and their band of merry PIs . . . until Cole essentially took their place.

And four.

Thomas *is* a nasty, manipulative arsehole, just like Sheila said. In fact, they seem perfect for each other.

I sink to the zigzag chevron floor as my knees buckle. I guess it all makes sense. Sheila never wanted me to skip year ten at school, since it meant less money for her. And Cole—his help wasn't free at all.

My throat constricts as if locked in a noose, and I can't breathe. I've been played again. Tricked. Used. Deceived like the clueless, stupid, naïve little girl I am. How could I believe out of all the women on earth, Cole would choose *me*—love *me*? I was a job, a pay cheque with benefits, and a gullible pawn in a sadistic game. And what's worse, that little voice in my gut tried to warn me our lopsided pairing made no sense. Yet I ignored it.

I gasp for air as a tsunami of doom hurls me away. Footsteps smack against the floor, charging towards me. "Aves."

I shoot my hand out and shake my head. "Don't come near me!" I scream, gripping the ground as I try to hold on to my stomach contents and consciousness. Cole's shiny black size-twelve shoes halt at the outskirts of my vision.

"I see she has Sheila's flair for dramatics," Thomas says. The chair creaks as he rises, and soon his shoes appear too.

"Leave her alone," Cole growls.

"Or what?"

I lift my gaze, silently begging Cole to get this vile man away from me. It's all too much.

"Don't look at him, sweetheart. He won't do jack. Cole knows his place and what's good for the firm."

Cole's face turns a crimson shade of red. White-knuckled fists shake at his sides. But still, he does nothing.

I look at Thomas, panting. "You're a bastard."

Thomas rocks back on his heels with an ironic chuckle. "No. Technically, you are."

The words have barely kissed the air when Cole snaps. He grabs Thomas by his jacket and slams him up against the brick wall facing Collins Street. "One more fucking word and I'll kill you." Cole's voice is demonic, but Thomas's mouth twists into a goading smile, and he stares Cole down with missile eyes, daring him to take a swing. Instead, Cole releases him and walks away, scrubbing a hand over his face.

Thomas recovers, peeling himself off the wall, then straightens his suit and tie, his nostrils flaring. "You've made a grave mistake, boy. Gerard might have been a fat son of a bitch, but at least he wasn't stupid. I'll ruin you. You can kiss your whale clients goodbye."

Cole's eyes squeeze shut as his chin meets his chest. "Get out of here," he says, deflated.

Thomas looks down at me. "Will fifty thousand do it?"

"Do what?" I ask.

"Make you forget I exist."

I cringe. "I don't want your money."

"That's too bad." Thomas rubs his chin. "I've tried to play nice with your mother over the years, Avery, but I would strongly advise you not to back me into a corner. You don't know what I'm capable of. I want this over, once and for all. So name your price and let me know. This could be the start of a very prosperous future for you."

A business card flutters to the ground at my knees, and I close my eyes as Thomas walks away, then flinch as he slams the office door shut. Ignoring the card, I gather myself up from the floor. I need to get out of here. Cole swoops in to help, but I jerk away and hiss, "Don't fucking touch me."

Cole drops to his knees, circling his arms around my hips. "Please, Aves. Let me explain."

His teary eyes shoot arrows into my heart, but I have no blood left to bleed. "What's there to explain?" I ask as my tears christen him. "Please accept my resignation, effective immediately, and let me the fuck go."

Cole's arms fall limp, and their absence leaves me hollow and cold. "I love you. That wasn't a lie," he whispers.

I swallow the clump of fleece in my throat. "Deception renders love null and void, Mr. Benedict." And with those last words, I leave.

Twenty-Six

Jen:

Why give me your new number and then ignore
my calls? Are you trying to worry me to death?

Me:

I'm fine. Just can't talk right now.

Jen:

Biggest load of bull I've ever heard. It's been two
freaking weeks. I'm coming over, and if you
don't answer that door, I'm calling the cops.

sigh as my leaden arms flop back down, sending my new Cole-memory-free phone skittering across the dusty studio floor. Great. I probably broke the fucking screen already, but what's another disaster? I'm the disaster queen. My life is a stream of shit—one Jen shouldn't want to swim through again. But nevertheless, twenty minutes later, her muffled voice tumbles down the hall as she thumps on the front door. "Avery Masters, I swear to God if you don't let me in, I'll make good on my promise."

At least I know it's her. I've ignored all other knocks the past two weeks. Especially those preceded by the expensive purr of a euro engine. The stupid fake rock now sits pride of place on the kitchen island. If Cole wants in, he'll have to break something. But I know he won't.

He pounded the door, calling out my name every night last week, but I curled up into a ball on my studio floor and cried until he left. By day six, I couldn't take it anymore, so I taped a ragged-edged note to the glass that read, "If you genuinely care for me, you'll respect the space I need." After that, he only came once more and never knocked. Instead, he slipped a puffy envelope under the door with "Angel" looped in blue cursive across the front.

My thumb traced the beautiful endearment as it wrung more tears from my soul, but I couldn't bring myself to open it. I still can't. What good will it do? Nothing can undo the damage or restore my trust. And what if his letter—assuming it is a letter—only says goodbye? I'm surviving on the fumes of his want. If they vanish, I'm done.

I plod through the gallery, my shoulders stooped and concrete heavy, then unlock the door and yank it open.

Jen's plum-stained lips gape, and her bright eyes bug, forming three perfect Os a bowling ball would envy. "Holy shit. What the hell happened to you?"

Despite me thinking I had no tears left, my eyes refill as my chin slumps. I step back, allowing Jen entry, and she slips inside, clicking the door shut before turning to scan me up and down, her face tensing into crisis delta mode. I don't miss the crinkle of her pale, freckled nose either. I probably smell awful. I can't remember when I last showered or changed. Dried clay is my second skin, shielding me from the bitter, cruel world.

"Aves," Jen whispers, lifting a clump of my hair up between her thumb and index finger before letting it go. The lock thuds back down like it's made of mud, and I shrink a little. I haven't seen a mirror in weeks. I haven't wanted to look into my eyes and face the damage. My hair is probably matted, but really, who the fuck cares? This world is full of superficial bullshit, and I, for one, am sick of it.

"What's happened?" Jen asks, her ginger brows crumpled in concern.

Biting my trembling top lip, I shake my head. "I can't . . ." I swallow. ". . . talk about it."

"Oh, chicky." Jen's eyes soften as if all at once she *knows*. Immediately, she locks me in a power hug, and I ugly cry against her lacy white dress as the horror scene at Cole's office replays in my head for the gazillionth time. Usually what then follows is the exclusive screening of our entire relationship—every word Cole ever uttered, every action he ever took—forcing me to sew all the heartbreaking clues together, one by one, like a patchwork quilt devoid of any warmth. In hindsight, it was all so painfully obvious.

Cole seldom queried my past. He lacked the typical amount of curiosity one should have about the person they're dating, probably because he already knew everything about me from the time I was bastard-born. He fled to Canberra too—Thomas's home base—the day after we first kissed. Coincidence? I think not. His true motivation for saving me from the stolen car is crystal clear now too—Cole was driven by money, not affection. And the drunken ramblings that night he fought Slade weren't nothing at all. In fact, they were likely the most truth Cole ever shared. After all, the lies started five minutes after we met when he claimed Beth had friends in high places to justify his free help. God, how dumb am I? And the job at Mini-Bees, working alongside his very own sister. All the better to keep tabs on me, I guess—ensure I didn't breach my bond and cause Thomas further grief.

I've wondered if Hannah knew about this—if she was in on it too. I hope not. It would be nice if at least she was real, but I have my doubts. She and Cole are close—it's them against the world—and I can't face more betrayal, so I deleted my Facebook too.

And Sheila. Fucking Sheila. Screenings of our relationship have featured too. She left so soon after graduation—announced her departure at my celebratory dinner, for fuck's sake—and now I know she'd planned it for months, maybe years, knowing full well Thomas's money would dry up. It all makes me physically ill, but one thing more than the rest.

If Cole knew we were a lie and I'd inevitably be hurt, why be so cruel as to show me the full depth of everything we could be? Why the sweet, whispered promises—the relentless support? Why capture my heart—entangle our souls—and tease a glittering future I never could have fathomed? I would have been smitten with a song, yet he gave me a symphony, and now there's no going back. I know the symphony exists. I've tasted the miracle of colour, then had it ripped away. And a miracle it was. No other man will ever come close. I'm condemned to a future in greyscale. If I survive, that is. This much pain should kill a person. It would be far more humane.

Stifling a cringe, Jen pats my hair. "Let's get you into the shower, then we'll talk, okay?"

I nod, and we head for the bathroom. That is, until Jen halts outside my studio with a gasp. I follow her line of sight into what's now my hidey hellhole. There's crap everywhere. Rubbish and dirty dishes on the floor. Mouldy food. Clay offcuts and dust. Tools strewn far and wide, and a distinct pungent, fruity odour smothering the air. In fairness, given my usual tidiness, it does look like I've had a psychotic episode. Maybe I have.

The guest quilt and pillow Beth kept in the linen press lie rumpled on the ground next to the pottery wheel. I haven't been able to go upstairs, let alone sleep in my bed, nor Beth's, since Sheila contaminated hers.

Clean sheets won't cover Cole's scent, which now lives in my mattress, and I can't so much as glance at the roof windows without pain ripping through my body. The corner armchair, where his jacket always hung, triggers nausea. And the stars in the night sky? Well, fuck them too. Everything reminds me of him—how impossible it feels to let him go—and the fact my heart was so horribly wrong when it all felt so real. I didn't only lose trust in Cole—I lost trust in me. The little I had.

Jen zigzags her way to the middle of the studio, tiptoeing through the mess, then slowly spins on the spot once she finds a clearing. "What is all this?"

"I'll clean it later," I say with the enthusiasm of a sloth.

"No," she says, stepping over the remnants of last night's microwave dinner. At least I ate. Her diamanté sandal clips the end of my fork, and it catapults over her foot, then clambers to the floor. "*This*," Jen emphasises, motioning down the long span of my workbench where a dozen new pieces sit.

I hitch a shoulder. "Therapy."

"They're fucking horrible."

"Thanks," I deadpan. "Made them myself."

Twisting towards me, Jen cocks a brow. "Is there some kind of satanic exhibition coming up?"

My jaw clenches. I know they're dark and twisty and barely fit for a bogan bong shop, but it's all I can do right now. "The collection's called Decimation of the Soul," I offer.

Jen plants fists on her hips. "Jesus. If he hurt you half as much as these . . . *things* imply, I'll kill him."

She bores her pissy I've-got-your-back-girl eyes into mine, but my lips tremble and tears threaten again. "I can't—" A horrendous sob escapes my throat, and I keel over, bracing my hands on my knees. "Jen, I can't do this anymore. I think I'm actually dying."

In a blink, Jen's back in front of me, holding out her arms. "Oh, chicky. Come here."

I shake my head. "I stink. You don't want to hug me again."

"I don't care," she says, but I don't budge. "Let's sit down, then."

Jen walks over to my makeshift bed and plonks down on the quilt, proving she's as brave as she is caring. That quilt is covered in snot, sweat, and sadness. I wince on her behalf before shuffling down beside her, resting my right shoulder against her left as we lean against the wall. She threads our hands together, giving mine a little squeeze, then pins me with soft yet determined eyes. "Now tell me everything."

I take a deep breath and stare at the scraps of purple nail polish left on my toes, then relay every single horrible detail of the forty-eight hours that broke me.

Jen cries when I cry—my pain her own—and I apologise for dumping on her, but every time I do, she insists that's what friends are for. She doesn't proclaim Cole a bastard or Sheila a psychotic shrew. Nor suggest I hear Cole out or chastise me for quitting my job. She doesn't even get angry. Jen simply holds space while she holds me and promises everything will be all right. And when the well of tears has finally drained, I'm ushered to the shower.

Jen gifts me fresh clothes from my room, saving me the brutality of going up there, then makes us hot chocolates and cheese toasties.

I curl up on the sofa with my knees guarding my chest and nibble at the corner of my lunch. My hair paints wet patches on my Adele concert tee, but some of the tension in my muscles has gone along with a morsel of despair—washed down the drain with the dirt and stench of my rotting heart.

"Do you remember when we met?" Jen asks from the other end of the sofa, cradling a jumbo geometric mug in her hands.

"Of course," I reply. It was at the start of grade four. I went to wash my hands at the end of recess and heard small, huffy sobs echoing from a toilet cubicle. I knocked on the door, asking if she was okay, but no answer came, yet the sobs continued, leaving me only one choice. I dropped to the filthy wet floor and wormed my way under the door to find the new girl from my composite class. She had tear-stained cheeks, frizzy copper braids, and a cute spatter of freckles across a heart-shaped face. Instantly, we were friends.

"You saved me that day."

I scoff. "I didn't save you."

"Yes, you did."

I roll my eyes.

"Don't do that." Jen frowns at me. "Don't discount that experience for me."

Her words slap me in the face. "I . . . I'm sorry. I didn't mean it that way."

Her expression softens. "I wanted to die that day. For the first time in my life, I questioned if I should be here."

I close my eyes and shudder. "I didn't know." I mean, tiny Jen was super sad, sure—but contemplating death at age ten? No. That wasn't on my radar. It might have been a year later, thanks to Dad, but certainly not then.

"That's just it," Jen smiles wistfully. "I didn't feel that way for long. A fierce heroine charged in on her white horse and dragged me to safety, forever changing my life."

My cheeks heat, but a smile cracks through the sorrow. "They were idiots for saying those things to you."

Jen chuckles. "And boy, did you let them know it."

Recalling my tirade, I smirk. "They had it coming."

Jen beams as she shakes her head. "I'd never met such a ballsy nine-year-old. What did you say to them? That if they dared taunt me again, your sister would sue them so bad they'd be homeless and their family would starve to death."

I shrug. "Beth was almost a lawyer. We could have made it happen."

Jen smiles. "You made them apologise, take back every cruel word they ever said in front of the whole canteen. And then," Jen chuckles, "well I don't have to remind you about that."

I smile to myself. It wasn't easy getting all the seat posts out of their BMX bikes, but filling them with sardines was one of the most satisfying experiences of my young life—well worth having fishy fingers for a day. No one messes with my bestie.

"You saved me that day in so many ways. By believing in me. By defending me. By showing me a truth I couldn't see: that I was worth fighting for. Now I'm going to repay the favour."

My stomach twists as a teardrop splats to my plate. "This is so different, Jen."

"No, it's not. Someone's been bullying my best friend for years, and it's time it stopped."

"Sheila's long gone," I say.

Jen shakes her head. "I'm not talking about your mum. I'm talking about *you*."

I almost choke on my toastie. "*Me?*"

As I plonk my plate on the coffee table, Jen raises her brows. "Yes, you. When you told me what happened earlier, beyond Cole's deceit, Sheila's barbarity, and your broken heart, there was one big problem." I frown, and Jen continues. "Do you realise how many awful names you called yourself? The horrible things you said about *my* best friend?" Jen counts her fingers. "You claimed you're stupid, trashy, naïve, delusional, unlovable, fatally flawed, and worthless. You are your own worst enemy, Avery Masters. You wouldn't let anyone speak to me or anyone you care about the way you talk to yourself. Am I right, or am I right?"

I rapidly blink, momentarily speechless. *Fuck.* "I . . . uh—"

Jen cuts me off. "I admired the girl I met when I was ten. I loved her. She was feisty, witty, and strong—unapologetically comfortable in her own skin and forever chasing her passions, whatever they were for the week." Jen laughs, but her smile quickly drops. "But slowly, piece by piece, year by year, I've had to watch her confidence erode, her spine flop, and the spark in her bright blue eyes fade."

Sniffling, I wipe my nose with the back of my hand. Damn these never-ending tears. "Everything changed after Dad," I whisper.

Jen nods. "I know. Your mum turned into a crazy bitch."

I huff a sad laugh. Three weeks ago, I would've hated Jen saying that. Blood-born loyalty and guilt would've crushed my stomach, summoning me to Sheila's defence, hypocritical as it seems. But not anymore.

"There's nothing wrong with you, Aves."

I close my eyes and nod, pretending to agree, but *pfft*. Cole once claimed that too.

"No," Jen says, "I need you to look at me." I lift my gaze to meet hers. "There is nothing wrong with you," she repeats.

Her conviction ploughs into the centre of my chest, shining a spotlight on that deep-rooted belief I've long held dear. Even more tears slide down my cheeks. God, who needed a shower?

"There is nothing wrong with you," Jen says again. "You are not flawed, less than, stupid, or unworthy of love. Say it."

I try to swallow through the knot of muscle lodged in my throat. "You want me to say it?"

"Yep. I want to hear it from your mouth. Repeat after me: there is nothing wrong with me. I am not flawed, less than, stupid, or unworthy of love."

I repeat her words, shaking my head. "This is dumb."

"Again. This time louder and prouder."

I roll my eyes. "This won't work, you know that, right?"

Jen ditches her mug and sits taller in her seat, rubbing her hands together. "I'm only just getting started. Now say it again with gusto."

A smile tugs at my lips. She's cute when she's bossy.

I repeat her words with extra vigour and volume, and shockingly, they make a dent. I've never tried to disarm that belief from the inside before. I've relied on other people for that.

"Better. Now listen here. For years, I've had to watch you beat yourself up, doubt your abilities, and believe you're somehow defective. And all that time, I've prayed that one day you'll see yourself as the smart, loyal, and loving person I see. But more than all that, Aves, you're strong. You're a fighter. That nasty voice in your head that says all those horrible things to you—please fight it, ignore it, or recognise it for what it is . . . fucking lies. *Your mum's lies.*"

Jen's clarity cracks something open deep inside my chest, and I clench my T-shirt, mutilating Adele's pretty face. There's a release—a realisation—some kind of beautiful epiphany that unchains my lungs and lets me fucking breathe easier than I ever thought possible. It's akin to dropping a boulder I never knew I carried.

Sheila's lies.

"Your mum planted toxic seeds in your head, and events here and there helped them sprout, but babe, you've been fertilising and watering them for years—and torturing yourself in the process. It's time to set that field on fire and reclaim your power. You're worth it." Jen thumps her chest. "*My* best friend is worth it. So be broken-hearted and feel that pain, but don't use it to rip yourself apart, and don't let a few arseholes ruin your hope for the future. Cole included."

His name on Jen's lips makes my body scream, but she continues.

"When you met Cole, I caught a glimpse of the girl I once knew. Your spark was back, and I was thrilled. But now I see the mistake you made: you built your self-worth on Cole's opinion of you when it can only survive on yours. So plant new seeds, Aves—kind, self-compassionate ones—and nurture that field instead. Stand there. It needs to come from within, and only you can do it."

I drop my drenched face into my palms, my shoulders shuddering with heavy sobs, as what feels like a decade of angst pours free. She's right. So fucking right. I've worn shame and self-doubt like a second skin and tortured myself every day. It's complete madness. The old me would use this realisation to add more weight and self-loathing to my mountain of shame, but I'm done. So fucking done.

I look up at Jen's beautiful face. "You're right. I'm sorry."

She shakes her head. "You don't need to apologise."

"Yes. Yes, I do. Your best friend deserves better, and so does mine."

Jen smiles a victorious smile, rising from one end of the sofa to plop right down next to me. She throws her arm around my shoulders and pulls me in for a hug. "So what now?"

I inhale a deep breath through the new space inside my lungs. "I'm going to stand up, dust myself off, and fight my way through this. I'm going to set that motherfucking field on fire and start again."

Squeezing me tighter, Jen grins. "There's the girl I fell in love with."

Twenty-Seven

Three Months Later

Through the all-consuming agony of heartbreak lives a secret land of peace. But access to this land requires an action counter to my every instinct—surrender. Rather than resist, I must let the pain stampede through me unobstructed, but when it's done, there I find myself, floating in merciful serenity. Until the next caustic wave rolls in.

The cycle is gruelling yet cathartic, and every day, I feel a smidge lighter. Whether that's thanks to healing or mere adaptation, I don't know, but it also doesn't matter. I now have the kind of support I've always craved—an ever-present friend that will never leave. *Me.* And as a result, everything is bearable, and the ground upon which I stand is solid.

The broom knocks against the skirting boards as I sweep the studio floor, gliding in time to Sam Smith's soulful croon.

"Are you sure about this?" Beth asks, wrapping up the gilt-framed photo of me and Jen in bubble wrap.

I throw her a half smile. "The lease is signed. It's a done deal." Truth be told, I'm as nervous as I am excited.

"I know, but I can get you out if you want. There's always a loop-hole."

Don't tempt me.

I stack my hands and chin on the end of the broom handle and look at Beth. "I need to do this. I want to do this."

She nods once and then resumes taping up a cardboard box. "I know you'll make it work."

"I'd better, or I'll be flat broke and back here." With a wink, I lean the broom against the wall and take the box from Beth's arms to stack on top of the others lining the gallery wall. The amount of crap I've accumulated since moving in is ridiculous.

"That wouldn't be so bad," Beth calls out.

"No offence, but yeah, it would." To pull this off, I've had to pledge every cent I own and ditch my spot at uni. I'm all in with six months to make it work, so failure isn't an option, and I'll be dead before ever taking a cent from Thomas. It's a shame going to the press and destroying that fucker would drag me through the mud and hurt my brothers. If only there were another way. A man like him should never be in power.

A deep horn blasts from out front as I return, prompting Beth to clap. "It's showtime, baby."

With a deep breath, I scan the barren studio, memorising its smell and the way the plantation shutters slice up the sun and paint glow-ing stripes on the floor. If it weren't for this inspiring space—and beautiful Beth—none of this would be happening. The muse might never have returned. A pang of sadness and pre-emptive nostalgia clutches my chest, and I catch Beth wearing an expression to match. "Have I ever told you you're the best sister in the world?" I ask.

Her watery smile tilts. "A few times."

Closing the space between us, I pull her in for a hug, squeezing her like a sauce sachet. "I'm going to miss the crap out of you, sis. If you hadn't brought home a stray from Sydney, I'd feel terrible. But now you won't be alone or sex-deprived, so that's good, right?"

Beth whacks my arm, huffs, and pulls away with scarlet cheeks but soon scrunches up her nose. "Do you think it's too soon to live together?"

"I think you should do whatever the hell you want. You only live once. Besides, *Desmond* seems nice."

She rolls her eyes. "Stop saying his name like that."

"Like what?" I jiggle my eyebrows. "How else should I say *Desmond*?"

Beth cocks a brow. "You dated a criminal called *Slade*. Are you truly one to talk?"

Slade. Now there's a name I haven't heard in forever. I chuckle. "Touché." But the mention of any former flame triggers memories of Cole, and another wave of pain crashes through me.

Breathe, Aves. Just breathe. You've got this.

I do—I do got this—but fuck, I miss him. His resonant laugh, our meaningful talks, the smile that's just for me. The way he stares into my eyes and reads my soul. *Stared*. The way he *stared* into my eyes—past tense. My heart spasms, hitching my breath. This was so much easier before the initial anger washed away. It should be illegal to miss someone this much.

The horn bellows again, but I'm thankful for the distraction. I plod to the front door and step out onto the porch to find a grimy truck reversed up the driveway, idling. Gaudy fluoro paint advertising the hire company blankets one side as black smoke putters out the exhaust pipe. I plant my hands on my hips. "Are you two going to sit there pounding the horn all day or come in to help?"

Liam's boofhead pops out the driver's side window. Today his glasses are sleek and black—way too sophisticated for him. I frown. He almost looks . . . normal—*mature*. Weird.

"Think I'll just stay here," he yells. "Might even buy one of these fuckers. My balls tripled in size the second I cranked the engine."

"Betsy would be jealous as hell," I call back. A notion Liam seems to seriously consider as he rubs his scruffy chin with a frown.

The passenger door sounds, and Jen appears, grinning as she skips towards me. "Let's get loaded."

I smirk. "Thanks for your help."

"Don't mention it." Jen scans my face, her smile fading some. "Are you okay?"

I nod. "I'm hanging in there." No longer do I mask up or play pretend.

"Good," Jen says. "Now show me to the stuff. Last time, I missed out. Is it weird that I'm excited?"

I lead her to the garage. "Definitely. Moving house sucks."

"Soon I'll find out for myself," Jen says.

I stop and turn around. "Come again?"

An epic grin plays on her lips. "I'm moving out with Liam."

My mouth falls open. "Oh my God. When? Where? Shit, what'd your dad say?"

Jen laughs, then counts off her fingers. "We're looking now, near uni, and let's just say I learnt a dozen Scottish Gaelic swear words. Anyway"—Jen hitches a shoulder—"I'm an adult now, so Dad will just have to deal."

I hug Jen, knowing how hard that conversation would have been. "I'm so proud of you."

"Ditto," she says. "Who would have thought two crazy gals like us would ever grow up?"

I laugh. "Weird, isn't it?"

Jen and I duck under the half-open garage door to assess the box pyramid and my abandoned furniture—the wonky red dining table and peeling vinyl couch. My rusty wrought-iron queen bed. It will be a step down from the unearned luxury I've been living in, but at least it's all mine.

I open the garage door the rest of the way, and Liam strolls in, furrowing his brow. "Think I'm having déjà fucking vu. Didn't I move all this junk seven months ago?"

Indeed, he did. "You know I love you for it though, right?" I offer with a shrug.

"Yeah, right." Liam snorts as he shoulders past me and grabs the top box from the stack.

Jen bops the bandana tied around my hair, then eyes me up and down, tugging at the frayed bib of my faded denim overalls. "Cute. Very 'I run an art studio, can't you tell?'"

I smile. "Thought I'd look the part."

"It suits you," Jen says. "This whole idea does."

"C'mon, you two. Don't expect special treatment just because you have vaginas."

Jen shakes her head and grabs a box. I copy her but eyeball Liam. "I'm surprised you can still walk normal with triple-sized balls. They must have been small to begin with."

Liam belts out a laugh. "Tiny," he agrees. "Jen neutered me long ago."

"Hey," Jen objects. "Not nice. You love being my bitch."

Amongst the four of us, we're loaded one hour later and ready to go. Jen waves out the truck window as it wheezes to life. "See you there."

I salute her, then look at Beth, joining my hands in prayer with a sugary smile. "Pretty please, can I drive?"

Beth inhales through her nose but throws me the car keys with a sigh. "Please don't kill me. I've finally found great sex."

I smirk at her uncharacteristic admission, but just like that, a new nickname is born. Beth's new beau shall henceforth be known as Des

Diggler. "I'll do my best," I say. Beth glances heavenward, mumbling, then crosses her heart before climbing into the passenger seat.

If I'm honest, driving isn't my strong suit. Slow and steady is my motto, much to the annoyance of fellow motorists. It's funny how everyone seems to morph into an aggressive shithead behind the wheel. Apparently, sitting in a tin box on four wheels makes such behaviour acceptable. Who knew?

Within five minutes, impatience vibrates off Beth in sonic waves. "Aves, put some lead on it, would you?"

"Do you want me to crash?" I ask.

Beth scoffs. "Fat chance, you're going too slow for that. Everyone's overtaking you. Hit the accelerator and move away from the gutter. They think you're pulling over."

I grit my teeth and do as I'm told, slowly picking up speed. "This better?"

When no answer comes, I glance in Beth's direction to find her staring at me.

"What?" I hiss, refocusing on the road.

"The speed limit is sixty kilometres per hour. You're doing forty. Do you want me to phone Jen and tell her we'll be twenty minutes late?"

I shake my head. "Don't bother. She knows how I drive. They'll wait."

Beth chuckles at that and drops her head back against the headrest. "I'm impressed, you know," she says a few moments later. "You're very brave."

I throw her a smile, knowing she definitely isn't referring to my driving. "Thanks, sis." I only hope she's still impressed when she sees the place. "Rundown" is a generous description, but it's the best I could afford this close to the city with living quarters and studio space. Besides, I have free rein to renovate, money set aside, and a vision. One that will embrace and capitalise on the local hipster vibe.

I've connected with a few home-grown artists—a modernist painter, a welder who creates amazing abstract sculptures from scrap metal, and an eccentric restorer who turns mid-century furniture into one-off masterpieces. They all fit the vision, and they've all agreed to consign their work into my shop. So along with my own, opening stock is sorted. All I need to do now is arrange the fit-out, order signage, finalise the website, beg the *Herald Sun* to feature us, and a million other things. I'm in way over my head, but every morning, I spring from bed with purpose pumping through my veins. I promised Jen I'd fight, and I am. I'm fighting for my future and against the endless loop of negativity that plagues my head. I'm planting new fucking seeds if it's the last thing I do.

Thirty minutes later, I carefully park a few shops down from mine. *My* shop. I never thought I'd be able to say that. I cut the engine and gather my wits as a whirlwind of butterflies and glitter dances in my chest. "Now I gotta warn you—"

"I know, I know." Beth waves me off. "Look beyond aesthetics. See the vision. Blah, blah, blah. Don't worry, the way you've been carrying on, if the building doesn't collapse on our heads, I'll be impressed."

It very well might, but it's her reaction to the cockroaches, peeling paint, and antique dirt that truly worries me. Beth is the epitome of pristine. The fact she's wearing four-inch stilettos to help me move says it all, really.

I climb out of the car and throw Beth her keys, then dig mine out my pocket as we reach the red brick footpath lined with wonky vintage shops and frilly bullnose verandahs with fancy posts.

"Did you detour through Adelaide to get here or somethin'?" Liam yells up the street.

Jen elbows him. "Leave her alone. She's *learning*."

I huff a laugh at Jen. "You can talk. You were only too happy to give me endless shit after my lesson last week."

"Ha!" Liam says. "Hypocrite."

Hypocrite.

That singular word is enough for Cole's smile and section 3.1 of Benedict's dumb company manual to resurface, but I bury it deep down in the dark to deal with later when I'm in bed all alone. Nothing is ruining this moment, and tonight, the demons will descend no matter what. They always do.

Jen rubs her hands together as we approach, and I jingle my keys in the air, stopping outside the grubby white roller shutter. The shop frontage is narrower than a one-way street, but the building runs deep, comprising two long rooms, a retro kitchen, a teeny bathroom, and a creaky staircase that leads up to my new bedroom. It's perfect, and my home for the next six months. If all goes well—longer.

I unbolt the roller shutter and hoist it up, then turn to face my three favourite people on earth. They all grin with genuine excitement, and I silently thank the universe for their presence in my life. Holding out my hand towards the entrance, I take a small bow. "Ladies and gentlemen, welcome to Mud Mash Studio."

Beth flashes a megawatt smile. "Love the name. It's perfect."

I throw her a wink. We lay on her bed for hours, throwing around ideas. The suggestions grew funnier the more champagne that flowed, and in the end, we were in hysterics, rolling around cry-laughing. "Yeah, as much as I liked Shitbox Studio, this sounds a smidge more professional," I say, holding up my thumb and finger an inch apart.

Liam shakes his head. "Oh, Shitbox would've had my vote, for sure."

"No surprises there." Smirking, I unlock the glazed timber door and eye the big Georgian-style window attached with its grid of glass panes and chipped cream paint. *Black.* The whole lot will be painted gloss black by next week, and it'll look amazing. The frames will disappear into the view rather than obscure it, and by the time I'm done window dressing, the view inside will be enticing as fuck.

A tarnished brass bell chimes when the door opens. I step over the battered timber threshold and usher everyone in. The damp, musty scent hits the back of my throat, and I shudder, mentally adding bleach and scented candles to my endless list.

Beth stops in the centre of the first long room and twirls on her heels. "This is great." I side-eye her, scanning for sarcasm, but she doubles down and taps her foot. "The old hardwood floors, high ceilings, and decorative mouldings—it oozes character. I like it."

Relieved, I grin. She can see the vision. Excitement swirls in my belly, but Liam gags. "What colour paint do they call this? Baby-shit green?"

"Actually, I think it's army excrement," I say. "But don't worry, by next week all the walls and ceilings will be bright white." The final reveal of my very own fixer-upper appears in my mind with crystal clarity, causing adrenaline to fizz through my veins and my feet to move. "An electrician will install downlights through here and spotlight tracks across there." I stomp my foot against the hardwood. "These will be cleaned and waxed, left rustic-style, and paintings will cover each side wall, with shelves lining the back. Then sculptures and furniture will fill the floor."

Jen wanders around as I speak, nodding. "Where's the counter going?"

I skip to the exact spot. "Right here. I found a cheap one on Gumtree. It's being delivered tomorrow."

"Wow," Beth says. "Sounds like you've thought of everything."

Thankfully, some perks come with an anxious mind. I lead them into the next room, the one set to guarantee cash flow and fill the only hole left inside me unrelated to Cole. I miss Mini-Bees, or more aptly, the kids. I miss their chubby-cheeked grins and bright-eyed optimism—their energy, honesty, and joy. Alex and Ella especially. And whenever I miss them, I miss Hannah, which inevitably leads me back to Cole. Argh. My heart hurts.

Later, Aves. Save it all for later.

I take a deep, fortifying breath and present the space. "This is my new studio and where I'll be teaching kids' pottery classes. I'll be distributing flyers and hitting up local schools next week."

"Oooh," Jen says. "Can I help sometime? I love kids."

"Sure, whenever you want. I could definitely use your help at the grand opening in three weeks."

Jen claps. "Count me in."

I catch Beth finally wince at the state of the kitchen and bathroom, but she quickly hides it with an overenthusiastic smile. "Nothing some elbow grease can't fix."

"And a hazmat suit," I add, to which she laughs.

I lead them up the narrow staircase next. The steep, old, rickety steps creak in protest but hold our weight. I'm not sure how much life they have left in them. It's lucky I'm light, more so now than ever. Grief is appetite's enemy, I've discovered. "And this is my bed slash living room," I announce as we cram into the dingy space.

Liam's head almost hits the angular ceiling, and he laughs. "Hell, Aves, lucky you only own four pieces of furniture."

I shrug. "I happen to like cosy."

"So what's the plan for up here?" Beth asks.

"Nothing yet. The shop takes priority."

Beth nods. "Good thinking."

Jen walks over to the lone window and peers out over the street. "Oh my. You didn't tell me there's a male strip club upstairs across the road. That view will be delightful. I'm surprised they didn't black out their windows."

"What?" I gasp, racing to the window.

Beth and Liam follow, but Jen bursts out laughing. "You guys are either perverted, gullible, or both."

I hip-check her. "You suck."

She pats me on the shoulder. "Aw, you sound disappointed. Don't worry, I'll take you to a strip club."

Liam huffs. "No, you bloody hell won't."

"Children, children," Beth says. "I'm not sure this knotty old floor will survive my shoes much longer, so how about we go downstairs and unload this truck?"

Our eyes all drop to Beth's shiny devil-red stilettos. They could poke holes in concrete, so she's probably right.

Jen elbows me. "Was she born wearing high heels? I'd like to see her baby photos."

I crack up as we hit the stairs, but Beth clears her throat. "Jen, I'll have you know these are the most comfortable shoes I own. Looks can be deceiving."

Beth remains poker-faced when we look back to scrutinise her sincerity, but then her smile cracks. "I'm joking." She shrugs. "They look hot as hell, and I can't feel my feet anymore, so it's a win-win."

My quilt smells of mothballs and cardboard, my bed is lumpier than I remember, and in the cloak of darkness, my tiny new timber bedroom feels like a cold, cavernous void. And right on cue, when I close my eyes, demons come to dance on the grave of my heart, pelting me with raw red memories and pain.

Me and Cole. Snuggled in puffy jackets and blankets beneath a million stars. Fire crackling. Secrets shared. *You won't crash, Angel. You'll fly.*

Me. In smiley-faced pyjama pants, safe in Cole's arms, as he carries me inside and up to my room.

Desperate sex. Against walls, in restrooms, on benchtops and clay-dusted floors.

Making love. On beds, warm leather, and soft, woven rugs. Sweaty foreheads kissing over shallow, frantic breaths. Greedy mouths, clenching hands, and synchronised hearts. Feeling each other's thoughts.

Declarations of love and forever.

I groan in pain.

Breathe, Aves. It'll pass. Just let it on through. You know the drill.

I do. But holy fuck, will this ever end? I'm suffocating in sadness. For me. For *him.*

The desperate plea in Cole's eyes, him on his knees, arms wrapped around my hips as he begged. *Begged.* And I walked away. After everything.

He deserved it, Aves. Slade and Sheila taught you nothing if not to never put up with shit. Lessons unlearnt will only repeat.

Then why do I still feel so bad?

Maybe if Beth hadn't insisted we watch *The Lincoln Lawyer* last week, then take the opportunity to unsubtly explain the rigid confines of client-attorney privilege, I'd feel more resolute. Whose side is Beth—

A sharp bang severs that thought, and I freeze.

What the hell was that?

It sounded like it came from the shop downstairs. The tiny hairs on my arms stand up, glowing petrified in the moonlight as adrenaline floods my bloodstream. I try to listen, but my heart gallops so loud I can't hear anything else, and the fact I could be missing the warning sounds of my imminent murder only makes it thump harder.

Five minutes later, I'm still alive so try to talk myself down. Every house has its unique sounds, right? And this building is old. So old . . . there might be ghosts.

Maybe I should call Ghostbusters. The last thing I need is to become possessed and destroy the building after all the effort and money already spent. At the apartment, my neighbours slept on the other side of the walls. If the worst happened, they'd hear me scream and call the cops or rush in to help. But here, I'm all alone. As alone as one can be. Unless, of course, there *are* ghosts. Then I'm not alone at all.

I pull my quilt up around my face, shivering. Maybe this was a mistake. Shops get broken into all the time. And fires. Fires happen more often in shops too. How the hell would I get out?

Oh God. Why did I ever think I could do this?

My pillow grows damp from tears. I itch to phone Beth or Jen, but it's my first night here and that would be epically pathetic. So instead, I take ten deep breaths, channel Liam's triple-sized balls, and resolve to calm the fuck down. Daylight will bring relief. It always does. And the vision taking shape downstairs will drive me through another day.

I can do this.

So, with wet cheeks and a deep-rooted ache, I fight my way to sleep, grasping a vision of silver-green eyes in the last whispers of wakefulness, and a dazzling smile that promises I'm safe. "I love you," I murmur.

Twenty-Eight

Beth insisted I frame the colourful newspaper article promoting Mud Mash's opening and hang it over the counter, even though in it, I'm wearing the cheesiest grin with cheeks so shiny and full I look ready to burst. But I can't complain. Along with the flyers, social media posts, plumes of gold helium balloons standing out front, and the glittering grand-opening banner draped over the window, the article worked.

People have flowed in all day, milling about the shop, admiring the sculptures and paintings, and chatting to Sadie, Bex, and Leo, my trio of local artist consignees, while they were here. Even now, the studio is full of pint-sized bottoms on mini blue stools with parents watching on as they create snakes and snowmen and smother themselves in terracotta. Jen loves her temporary teaching gig, but not as much as Liam seems to enjoy distributing flyers out front to entice people in. He's been moonwalking back and forth all day.

"Restock," he calls out, performing an impressive Michael Jackson spin.

I wink at Beth as I grab another small stack of flyers from behind the counter and deliver them outside to Liam. "Here you go."

"Thank you, milady," Liam says with a slight bow and tilt of an imaginary hat. His mouth and manners have been as clean as Gwyneth Paltrow's diet so far today, thank fuck.

Modern piano music floats in the background as I return inside, smiling once again at a middle-aged couple as they ponder one of Sadie's paintings. "If you need any help, sing out," I say, not wanting to hover. The shop's musty smell is gone, replaced by soft vanilla, fresh paint, and rich, earthy clay. My stomach still flutters every time I walk in. The place is hella hip and a vibrant visual feast I can't believe is real, let alone mine.

"Who was that woman before with the gorgeous black curls?" Beth asks as I return to the counter.

"My year-twelve art teacher, Mrs. Donovan. She saw me in the paper." I hitch a shoulder as my cheeks heat. I don't think I'll ever get used to that level of exposure.

"Ah," Beth says. "That explains it. She seemed thrilled to see you."

That she was. She snuck up on me and whispered in my ear, "I knew you'd make it," before clutching me in a pudding-soft hug.

"She invited me to talk to her senior students at my old school."

"Are you going to do it?"

"Absolutely. I owe her. I even offered to showcase some of their work here. She *loved* that idea."

"I'll bet."

To be honest, since Mrs. Donovan rocked up and it hit home people I know actually saw me in the paper, I've wondered if Cole will show too. I've seen him in the crowd several times today already, mistaking a graze of stubble here, a tailored suit there, and even Bex's tattooed arm once. My heart jumped every single time but then plunged back into a misery made all the more glib by the sparks of false hope. What would I even say to him, anyway? And here I am assuming I ever still cross his mind all these months later.

Jen pokes her curly red head out of the studio and taps the top of her wrist. "Do you want me to wrap things up?"

"I'll do it," I say, glancing at Leo's starburst clock on the wall. It's come in handy. I want to promote the lesson timetable one more time to squeeze out every sign-up possible. Two sheets are already full, and at this rate, the lessons alone will pay the rent.

See, I can do this.

The kids sigh a collective groan when I ring the five-minute warning bell, but most then jump up and down in front of their parents' legs, begging to come back. It might be a little unfair I mentioned the lessons in front of them—even more unfair I told them to ask their mum or dad—but hell, I'm a small fish with bills to pay. And they'll love it. In a world dominated by tech, real, hands-on creativity is more vital than ever.

Twenty minutes, several tiny hugs, and a dozen thank-yous later, the shop is empty.

Jen and Liam lean against the counter, looking a little frazzled and tired but smiling. "That was wild," Jen says.

I plop down on the chair behind it with a sigh. "Totally, but it went way better than I'd hoped."

"The feedback was great," Beth agrees, leaning against the wall next to me. "And nothing was broken, which is a miracle."

"Yeah," I say. "Sure is."

"I think it was my smooth-arse dance moves that really saved the day," Liam says, raising his collar with a wink.

"Definitely," I agree.

Jen glances at Liam, and I catch her giving him that silent "are you ready to go now?" look that couples master, but I raise my index finger.

"Wait one sec. Before you go, I have something for you." Renovations aren't the only thing I've been working on the past three weeks.

I rise from my chair, squeeze past Beth, and duck into the studio to grab the two clay pieces I hid in my second-hand storage locker. Then I return, pausing as I reach the doorway. "Close your eyes and tell me when they're shut."

"They're shut," Liam calls out.

"What are you up to?" Jen asks, her eyelids fluttering behind her red fingernails.

I tiptoe to the counter without answering and gently place each piece down in front of them. Beth smiles when she sees what I've done. "Okay, open."

They do, and Jen gasps. "Is that for me?"

"Yup. I believe you requested a purple bowl with elephants, right?"

"Oh my God. You remembered." She gently picks it up. "It's awesome. And huge. And they're so cute, all the little trunks are up. That's meant to be lucky, you know."

"I know." I grin.

Jen sets the bowl back down and throws her arms around me. "Thank you. I love it."

"Good. It's my thank-you to you. For everything. Not that a bowl will ever be enough, but you know what I mean. I love you."

Jen pulls back and meets my eyes. "Ditto," she says, giving my hands a squeeze. "Always." She kisses my cheek, then lets me go.

We both turn to face Liam. He stands before the counter quieter than ever before, staring at his gift with a lone tear rolling down his cheek. Roughly, he brushes it away.

"You like?" I ask.

His Adam's apple bobs. "It's the most beautiful fucking thing I've ever seen." His voice comes thick and raspy.

"I grabbed some photos of Betsy from your Insta and modelled her from that."

He runs his fingers over the tiny tin bumpers, shaking his head. "You nailed all her chrome parts just right."

"I tried my best."

Liam looks at me, his face furrowed with emotion. I've never seen him so serious. "If you ever need help to move again, Aves, you just let me know, all right?"

"Will do," I say with a smile. And then, after two more hugs, I walk my best friends outside.

When their truck disappears, I grab Beth's hand and drag her to the studio. "Your turn."

"Oooh," she coos. "Do I get a bowl covered in tiny barrister wigs?"

I laugh at the visual. "Um, not exactly."

We stop next to the pack of tables where the kids played, and I fan my hand, silently requesting she shut her eyes too. "You know the drill." Beth's present is big. She wanted a gallery-worthy piece to live alongside her Hesters and Boyds, and I've done my best to deliver. I rest it down on the table, my arms straining under its weight. This piece has been months in the making and was inspired by everything Beth. "You can open them now."

She does, and her pouty mouth drops open, her wide eyes flickering to mine. "Aves," she whispers, clutching her chest. But that hand slowly reaches out, and she traces her fingertips down the edge of one rippled wing. "It's stunning."

"That's what you are to me," I say. "My earth angel."

Her eyes glisten, and she reaches out her slender arms. "Come here this instant." I tilt my mouth into a smile as I step inside her petite embrace. She sniffs back tears and shakes her head. "Well done. You've successfully made me into a blubbering mess." I chuckle. "Thank you," Beth says. "I'll treasure it forever."

I pull back, holding out her shoulders. "I love your guts, sis."

"Love yours more," Beth says, drying her tears with the heels of her palms. She does her best to rally composure but then pins me with big-sister sincerity. "Congrats on today, and promise me, tonight when you fall asleep, do so with a smile on your face. You should be so proud."

"I will," I whisper.

And that night, for the first time since . . . everything, I snuggle up in bed fear-free and no longer wracked with pain. A Cole-shaped ache remains, cookie-cut out of my heart, and it likely always will, but it's one I can learn to live with.

The weekend replays in my head, which makes me smile. And that's exactly how I fall asleep.

Twenty-Nine

On Monday morning, the shop's deserted, but that's okay. I'll probably stay closed on Mondays anyway. I settle in behind the counter with my laptop to finish watching a free book-keeping tutorial.

The brass bell above the door finally jingles an hour later, and I glance up to see a ghost. A pretty ghost with wavy cinnamon-brown hair and a cherub perched on one hip. My muscles jellify, but I rise, screeching my chair against the waxed hardwood. "Hannah."

A tight smile pulls at her plump mouth. "Hello, Aves." There's frostiness in her tone, subtle, but it packs a punch in contrast to her usual easy warmth.

Cringing, I scramble to find words. "You're not working today?" is all I've got, and it comes out fast and jittery with a strong urge to explain myself and make excuses in a rush of verbal diarrhoea. The urge surprises me, but it also tells me something. It tells me I never truly believed Hannah was involved in any of this. But hell, I've been wrong and burnt before, so who the fuck knows?

Hannah shrugs. "I took the day off."

Right. While that might be normal for most people, it's not for her. She has the immune system of an alligator and a work ethic like her brother's, but I guess there's a first time for everything.

I give Ella a little wave and smile, which she returns with those glowing, chubby cheeks I've missed so damn much. She's noticeably taller too, dressed in lilac frills and slipping down Hannah's hip. Hannah hitches her back up. "Can we sit and talk a minute?"

"Sure," I say, stepping out from behind the counter, cursing myself. A kinder person would have already offered instead of standing here frozen like an idiot. I motion towards the studio. "Come through here." They do. I cut off a lump of clay from yesterday's scrap pile for Ella and smack it down on the table. "Do you mind her getting dirty?"

Hannah shakes her head, then glances down to Ella. "Do you want to play with Avery's special Play-Doh, cookie?" Ella nods but eyes the clay suspiciously. In fairness, Play-Doh has way better colours, and she probably doesn't remember making the monsters at Mini-Bees.

While Hannah sets her up on a stool, I gather a bundle of kid-safe modelling tools and lay them out in front of Ella, then grab an apron from the folded stack and squat down to her height. Ella searches my face with that innocent curiosity kids seem to have, and I bop the end of her nose with my finger. "Hey, princess. I've missed you. Have you been doing lots of dancing lately?"

She nods enthusiastically. "Yep. With my friends."

"Oooh," I say, hooking the tiny apron over her head and shiny pigtails. "And what are your friends' names?" I tie it around her little pot belly.

"Isabella and Alex."

Alex I know, but Isabella is new. I look up at Hannah. "You have a new one?"

"Yeah," Hannah says, sliding her hands into the pockets of her soft pale jeans. "A lot has changed."

Right. For some reason, that information makes my stomach curdle. I pick up a plastic cutting tool and carve a few lines into Ella's clay, then hand it to her. "Here you go. You can make snails and caterpillars or even a unicorn. Do you like unicorns?"

She crinkles her nose. "No, they're not real. I'll make a fairy."

That makes me laugh. "Good idea." Jeez, she's talking way more. To be honest, I'd rather keep chatting with her than face her mum, but I'm no coward. Kind of. . . . Well, I'm working on it.

Standing up, I look at Hannah. Hurt and confusion float in her ocean-blue eyes like an oil spill. Oh *fuck*. That look alone confirms it. She had nothing to do with Cole's shitshow, and from her perspective, I abandoned our friendship without a word like she meant nothing. But what else was I meant to do? Everything was so huge and dark and muddled. And there was so much hurt. Nuclear-level hurt.

"Nice place you have here," Hannah says, forever polite even though she's clearly stricken.

Double fuck.

"Thanks." I smile sadly and motion to the adult-sized stools at the workbench Beth let me steal. "It's all pretty new."

"I know." Hannah takes a seat at one end. "I saw you in the paper."

"You read the paper?" I hop up on the stool adjacent.

"No, but Marla does. She showed me."

Marla. I hope that poor woman wasn't forced out of retirement just because of me. But Tej was leaving too, and it was all so abrupt, so maybe she was. I drop my gaze to the bench and pick at my fingernails, wishing I had a lump of clay to play with like Ella.

"How was opening weekend?" Hannah asks.

"Delightfully busy." I smile.

"Good," she says.

Silence ensues, and it's hard to breathe when the air is thick with unspoken words. An elephant may as well be tap-dancing around the studio in a pink tutu at this point. A minute later, we move to speak at the same time, then both stop, apologise, and awkwardly chuckle.

"You go first," I say, abandoning all bravery. Chicken noises cluck in my head.

"Well," Hannah sighs, "Cole won't tell me what happened with the two of you."

I flinch, and tears immediately fill my eyes. As if staring at his female clone wasn't hard enough, she just had to say his name aloud. Since Jen's pep talk, no one else has, and I'm used to people tiptoeing around the crime scene of my heart.

"And you," she continues, "cut me off like a gangrene limb."

My gaze snaps to hers, finding tears wetting her cheeks too. I stare at my broken friend and gulp. As usual, she deserved better. "Hannah, I'm so sorry. When everything happened . . . Well, I didn't know if you were in on it." Her brows furrow as I suspected they might. "I was in shock—devastated. I didn't know what else to do but run."

"We were friends, Aves. Or at least, I thought we were." Her voice wobbles. "You could have come to me. Whatever it was."

"I'm sorry, but I just . . . couldn't."

She reaches out to cover my hand with hers. "Did Cole hurt you . . . I mean physically?"

"What?" I stiffen. "No. Of course not."

She blows out a breath. "I had to ask. You have no idea what nutso scenarios have been playing through my head."

I can imagine. It must have been awful.

"Did he cheat on you?"

The very thought makes me shudder. "Not that I know of."

She nods once, as if she knew that already. "And he didn't abuse you in any way?"

"No, nothing like that," I say, deflated, but the urge to spill my guts and defend myself itches like crazy. Abuse or not, what Cole did was totally fucked.

"Well, in that case, I need you to hear me out," she says. My molars clench. "*Please.*"

This time, I nod once, but my heart pounds and pain throbs around it. I don't usually have to deal with this shit during the day. Daylight is my safe place, goddamn it. Not to mention I thought I was through the worst of this, but obviously fucking not.

Hannah folds her arms on the bench, tilting her chin. "How much do you know about my family?"

I hitch a shoulder and think back. "I know your mum passed away and that she was beautiful." I say the words tenderly, and Hannah's lips twitch up in one corner. "Cole said little else, but I know he was close to your uncle."

God, now *I'm* saying his name out loud.

Hannah huffs. "That's an understatement." Then she wriggles on her stool, making herself comfortable. We could be here a while, it seems. "I know you might not believe it to look at him, but Cole hasn't had it easy. *We* haven't had it easy," she corrects. "And I think you deserve the full picture before you let him go."

"I've already let him go," I whisper.

Hannah's brows jump behind her fringe. "Have you?"

No. Who am I kidding? But I'm trying, goddamn it, and I don't need a sob story derailing my mission. But once upon a time, the full picture is what I wanted. I wanted to climb into Cole's past and be by his side. I wanted to experience his plights and joys—understand the rich layers that made him and who he is beneath them all. I wanted to *know* him. How can you trust someone you don't? Now's my chance to finish the puzzle even if I'll never admire it again. Closure.

I drag in a deep breath. "Okay. Spill."

Hannah seems relieved. She eyes Ella, who's in her own little world of clay, happily making the strangest fairy I've ever seen, then with a faint smile, looks away from her daughter and gathers her hands together in a prayer-like ball on the bench. She stares at them for a quiet moment as if rallying strength. Despite forging this path, evidently Hannah won't find this tale easy to tell, and that makes me nervous.

"My mum's death destroyed our world," she starts, and I stay quiet, knowing that flavour of destruction all too well. "My father—" She pauses, shuts her eyes, then swallows. "He took it the worst. He started drinking. Got angry. Cole was fifteen at the time. I was nine."

"Tough ages," I say. Not that there's ever a good time to lose a beloved parent. A not so beloved one? Who knows?

"Yeah, for Cole especially. He was impressionable. Combative like most teens. It wasn't long before he was our father's first victim."

Victim. I stiffen as icy dread melts over my skin.

"He resented Cole. Cole took care of Mum in her final months. He nursed her, read to her, and was there when she took her last breath. We both were. Father, on the other hand, dived into his work to escape and missed it all. He simply wouldn't accept reality."

Hannah's nail beds whiten as she presses them into her knuckles. "The first time Father hit Cole, he scored a black eye. The second, broken ribs. The third time put him in hospital for two days, and after that, Cole spiralled. He was sixteen by then."

Oh God.

I picture Cole as a sweet, sensitive, and lanky sixteen-year-old boy wrestling with his mother's death and catch a sob in my hand, feeling physically ill. How could anyone hurt him like that, let alone his own dad? "And you had to witness all that?" I ask.

"I only heard it," she says. "Cole would order me to my room, and I'd hide under my bed."

But she still would have seen the damage. "Oh, Hannah." An avalanche of sadness crushes me, and I bury my face in my palms, not wanting Ella to see or hear me cry. That precious girl's world should remain magical and pure for as long as possible. "I'm so sorry you both went through that. It's beyond awful."

"It was a long time ago," Hannah says, giving me a moment to get my shit together. *Fuck.* Why do I feel everything as if it's mine? Sheila would *love* to answer that question.

Hannah continues. "But it hardened Cole. Broke something inside him that even Mum's death didn't. He went from open to closed—easy to uptight. Soft to hard. He fell in with the drop-kicks at school, started ditching and doing other bad things. He even spent a night in jail. Would have been longer had Uncle Gerard not stepped in."

Holy fuck. This story sounds eerily familiar, and here I thought Cole and I were worlds apart. Me—a messy nest of scribble. Him—a perfectly sketched cube.

"After getting him out of there, Uncle Ger and Cole had a long chat. Cole told him everything about our father, and within an hour, Uncle Ger had him slammed up against our kitchen wall. He told Father if he ever touched a hair on our heads again, he'd kill him, and it worked. The drinking continued, but Cole was safe."

I shake my head. "I had no idea."

"I don't think Cole's told anyone what happened. I don't think he can," Hannah says airily, as if she's floated far away. A few long seconds pass before she returns and finally disconnects her poor hands. "Uncle Ger took Cole under his wing after that. Steered him back on track. Helped him finish school, find a part-time job, then guided him into law and paid for his degree so he could come work at Benedict's. Cole was Uncle Ger's protégé, and Uncle Ger was Cole's idol—his saviour." Hannah smirks a little now, in that riling sibling kind of way. "It was a little pathetic, to be honest. Cole was like his lapdog."

I huff out a laugh. "I cannot imagine that."

"Exactly," she says. "It was creepy. Uncle Ger said jump, Cole said how high. I mean, I get it. We both owed Ger a lot, but it's like Cole connected his own survival to pleasing him or something."

My belly knots. Survival mode is one I know well.

"Uncle Ger was a force. No one could believe death had the audacity to take him at fifty-five, and Cole was in a tailspin at first. He didn't count on having to take over Benedict's for another decade. But," Hannah sighs, "he soon pulled himself together, grabbed the reins, and set out to do what he was groomed to do—continue Uncle Ger's legacy."

"Wow," I whisper on the crest of an exhale. "That's a lot."

"My uncle created the man you see today. The fancy suits. The sharp legal skills. The workaholism. Cole wouldn't be that without him. In fact, he wanted to pursue photography."

"Really?" I ask.

Hannah smiles crookedly. "Mum even bought him a fancy camera for his thirteenth birthday and set up a darkroom in our basement. She was an artist, so she was all for it."

My brain ticks over, sorting out all this new information and slotting it into various memories to see if the picture morphs—if the colours change. I feel for Cole. I'd assumed a man with his success must stand on solid ground and come from relative ease. I'd assumed any decisions he made, and actions he took, were chosen from the helm of his chariot, not while being dragged behind it.

"How is he?" I blurt out, no longer able to repress my need to know.

Hannah's frown deepens from tense to troubled, and it's a knife to my chest. "He's not himself."

I swallow. Hard.

"I'd hoped he'd pull himself together, and he has to an extent. But his eyes have this . . . emptiness, and for the first time in years, I'm worried."

Oh fuck.

"He'd kill me if he knew I was here, but I had to do something. He was happy with you. It's like you relit the candle inside his soul and brought the old Cole back. Do you know he left Benedict's three weeks after you?"

"What?" I gasp.

"I know. We were all shocked. I can only assume your breakup had something to do with it."

I wither on my stool like a dying flower. Cole left Benedict's? He seemed so far away from that I feared he never would. But maybe, after sticking up for me, he had no choice. Maybe Thomas's threat to destroy him was real, thereby forcing his hand. Maybe I cost him his career.

"Aves." I snap out of my reverie and look back at Hannah to find a consoling smile. "I won't ask you what happened. You would have told me by now if you wanted to. But please think about everything I've said. My brother might not be perfect, but he's a good man, and I know he loves you. I know you loved him. What you guys had was special and real, and if you can't make it, we're all screwed."

I let myself laugh a little, despite the fact my entrails are now twisted into pretzels. Everything I thought I knew has been flipped on its head. And my resolve—my certainty that I've done the right thing—is crumbling.

"Just think on it," she says.

And I will. I already am. Every sentence she spoke replays in my head. One in particular catches. "You said Cole was your dad's *first* victim."

Hannah visibly flinches, and her face pales to porcelain. She shifts back and cradles her elbows, curling in on herself like a dead spider.

Oh shit. I open my mouth to retract the question, but Hannah beats me.

"There's more," she says, flickering her gaze to Ella again before sinking it to her lap. Oblivious to the dark storm suddenly circling her mum, Ella quietly babbles while rolling out a worm to join her growing pile. "I look like my mum," Hannah says. "A carbon copy, most people say."

Join the club. I smile. "I saw the portraits at Cole's place. You sure do."

"I always treasured that fact. It made me feel closer to her. But"—she gulps—"it also triggered a nightmare."

If it were possible for a human body to spontaneously rot into a sticky black puddle, that's what Hannah's would do right now. Bleakness radiates from her.

"Hey," I say. "You don't need to tell me this."

She swallows again, still hugging herself. "No, I want to. It's time I confided in someone other than Cole or my therapist. But you can't tell anyone ever. Promise me."

I give her my sincerest expression. "I won't. No matter what."

Chewing her top lip, Hannah nods. "Like I said, our father never stopped drinking, but I was invisible mostly. He barely looked my way, which suited me just fine. He'd stumble through the front door blind drunk most nights, if he made it that far. Sometimes, we'd find him asleep on our fancy front porch covered in his own vomit."

I wince. "I'm so sorry."

Hannah shoots Ella another quick glance but then leans in and lowers her voice. "When I was eighteen, one night I woke up to him staggering into my room. He climbed into my bed, and I scooted back, asking him what the hell he was doing. But he was sobbing—shushing me—mumbling Mum's name and trying to stroke my hair. The stench of vodka burnt my nostrils." Hannah stares past my shoulder vacantly as tears bleed into her steel-blue T-shirt like splotches of ink. "He pinned me down, and I was so confused and terrified I froze. It all happened so fast, and I . . ." She takes a shaky breath. "Well, I couldn't stop him."

My stomach free-falls and splats to the timber floor. "Hannah," I rasp. "Oh my God."

Hannah's chin meets her chest. "I fell pregnant. I didn't know until I was four months along, and I didn't tell anyone until it was impossible to hide."

I shut my mouth the second I realise it's hanging open and then snap my gaze to Ella.

Her eyes. She has her grandfather's eyes.

Family resemblance. Nothing more.

When I look back at Hannah, she offers a soft nod. "Holy shit," I whisper. I don't know what else to say. *What the fuck do I say?*

"You don't have to say anything," Hannah says, as if reading my mind. "She's healthy, happy, and the love of my life. How can I wish it never happened when it gave me my world? I grapple with that truth every day."

Hannah stretches out a hand to touch mine. "Don't," she pleads. "Don't picture it. I can sense when people do that, and it makes me want to disappear. And please don't look at me like I'm irreparably broken, because I'm not."

"Okay." I give her hand a squeeze. A full minute's silence stretches between us before I let her go. "Where's your dad now?"

Where despicable creatures belong. Cole's livid words smack into my awareness. *Fuck.* No wonder he reacted like that when I asked about Ella's dad.

"Prison," Hannah replies. "When I finally told Cole, he was going to kill him, but Uncle Ger stopped him. Cole had only moved out a few months earlier, but he blamed himself for not making me go with him. For not being there. He begged me to go to the police, but I couldn't. Can you imagine having to relay every detail of that? The possibility of press coverage thanks to the Benedict name? The articles Ella or the kids at her school might one day read? At that point, mere whispers would have killed me."

"I get it," I say. And now I get why she goes by Beaufort instead of Benedict too.

"Uncle Ger came up with a plan to placate Cole, protect me, and ensure our father paid one way or another. Ger had connections he wasn't afraid to use. He was a little shady like that. But, three weeks later, our father was caught with a car full of crack and firearms. He's serving fifteen years."

"Good," I say.

"Yep." Hannah forces a smile, but it's empty. Dead. "After that, things did get better. Uncle Ger built Mini-Bees just for me. Bought my apartment and everything for Ella. Cole moved in and stayed until I found my feet as a mum. He helped with Ella at night and still worked all day. I don't know how he did it, but I sure as hell couldn't have without those two men. Like I said"—she hitches a shoulder—"we owe Uncle Ger a lot. Cole just took it to the nth degree."

I ache for them both. That's some big-*T* trauma right there. The kind that's always made me feel like a weak and whiny brat for daring to complain about Sheila, let alone be this screwed up. But I guess abuse inflicts damage even in its emotional forms, and at the end of the day, it's not a competition. "That's why you have PTSD?" I gently ask.

"Yeah," she whispers. "But I've come a long way. EMDR has helped a stack. I rate it five stars. Can highly recommend." Hannah winks, trying to lighten the mood.

"I've heard of that," I say, and it's true. EMDR therapy is advertised on the front window of the psychology rooms two shops down from me, along with a few other fancy-sounding acronyms.

We both fall quiet again—processing. No wonder Cole clammed up whenever I pried into his past. It's now crystal clear why he's so protective of Hannah and Ella too. He lost his mum. His little sister was raped. Bad things happen to the women he loves. And maybe, just maybe, rather than money or Thomas or Gerard's sacred legacy, that's why he protected me too.

"Hannah, if Cole's not at Benedict's anymore, where is he?" All this time, I've pictured him in his office. I knew what he was doing and where to find him, even if I had no intention of doing so. That brought me comfort. This feels icky and unsafe—like someone's cut my string and I'm floating away.

"He's opened a firm in Brighton, but it's the polar opposite of Benedict's—small, humble, and full of pure intentions. He's flying solo but gets to help people that deserve it now. He even donates his time to domestic violence victims and does pro bono."

A rush of sparkly glitter goo wraps me in a hug. *Hello, old friend. It's been a while.* "That's amazing," I concede.

Hannah rolls her eyes. "I think he's vying for sainthood or something. Oh"—she slaps the bench, clearly having perked back up—"and he's taking photos again. I pestered him until he dusted off that old camera just to shut me up."

I chuckle. "He'll do anything for you, won't he?"

Hannah grins. "He'll do the same for you if you let him."

The doorbell rings. "Excuse me a sec." I hop off my stool and return to the shop to find two hipster dudes, complete with man buns and baggy stonewash denim jackets, checking out Leo's furniture. I flash them a friendly smile. "Hi, welcome. Feel free to have a look around and sing out if you need any help." They thank me and continue perusing.

Hannah appears with Ella perched back on her hip, Ella's small, chubby hands now damp but clean. "You're busy, so we'll get out of your hair," Hannah says with a lopsided smile, her earlier frostiness a distant memory. "It was great to see you, Aves. No matter what, don't be a stranger, okay?"

I wrap them both in a hug. "I'm sorry I ever was." Releasing them, I swipe a business card from the counter and pass it to Hannah so she has my new mobile number. I debate whether to ask she keep it hidden from Cole, but the words don't come. Instead, I say, "We should do lunch sometime."

She winks. "I'm holding you to that."

"Good." I kiss Ella on the top of her head, curling a feather-soft pigtail around my finger before letting it go. "Bye-bye, princess. I'll take care of your fairy for you." By "take care," I mean I'll cook it in a fiery kiln and hope it doesn't explode from the air bubbles undoubtably trapped inside it, but I can't exactly tell her that.

Ella's face lights up. "It's for you. For your birthday party."

"Oh." I hold back a laugh. My birthday's still five months away, and there will be no party—no court will be special enough—but Ella's birthday was last month if I remember right, and obviously it left an impression. "Thank you. I love it."

She grins a mini Hannah grin while her mum flashes the full-sized version, and I watch as they walk out the door and past my front window, trying to ignore the gaping hole I'm left with. It weeps a fuddle of pain, conflict, and confusion.

What the fuck am I meant to do now?

And that's the question that consumes me for the rest of the never-ending day as I try in vain to distract myself by starting a new piece. Trust is a fundamental building block of any good relationship, and Cole lied to me. It might have started small and vague and more of an omission, but boy did it snowball. Why didn't he just tell me? I don't buy this client-privilege, legacy bullshit. It's not reason enough.

He tried to, Aves. Even with everything at stake.

The dull, watery memory sharpens. Oh God. He did too. That night we snuggled at the foot of the fire, blanketed by stars. But when I sensed his turmoil, I hushed him. I convinced him, as well as myself, that I only needed to know his now. Guess I lied too. Still, he should have persisted—gagged me if necessary. Then again, I probably would have enjoyed that. And, if I'm being honest, I'm glad I got that magical time before my life blew up.

As evening peak hour descends, the traffic builds, and the sun drops behind the parapet rooftops across the road. I drag my open sign in from the footpath, smiling at the florist next door who's doing the same. The psychology rooms still have their sign out, I notice, but it calls to me stronger now than ever. I guess my conversation with Hannah was the last nudge needed.

I lock up my shop, leaving the lights on and the roller shutter up to capitalise on the traffic jam, and ten minutes later, I've booked in my first therapy session with a Dr. Rachel Carmichael. No longer do I see getting help as weak. God knows Hannah is anything but that. And why should mental illness be treated any differently from the physical? When I broke my arm, I didn't debate whether to see a doctor. I wasn't ashamed my bones cracked or that I fell. If anything, seeking help takes guts, and I'm ready to work through my baggage. Dad's death. Sheila's toxicity. Thomas's arseholery. But ultimately my fear—the ever-present tyrant that loves to captain my ship. I want to heal and be able to love without anything contaminating the flow.

Again, I think of Cole. Maybe he needs to heal too. Maybe his trauma contaminated his flow. Maybe he deserves a second chance. Doesn't everyone? He was adamant I did.

As that last thought marinates, I'm pulled towards the stairs by some invisible but persistent force. I frown but then swallow when I remember.

His letter. *I need to find Cole's letter.*

Thirty

Rumpled clothes and empty cardboard boxes cover my bedroom floor, bed, and sad-arse vinyl couch squished in the corner, leaving me cursing all previous thrift shop adventures, but I know the letter's here somewhere. I remember slipping it down the side of a box, only I didn't bother noting its label or size. A fact I now regret, since I'm down to the last one and my room's a bomb site. A knot forms in my throat. Panic. Desperation. Please be in here. *Please*.

I plonk the last box on the end of my bed, rip open the flaps, and tip it upside down. The contents clatter to the mattress in a jumbled mess, but I don't care because I spot the envelope, thank God. I inhale a sharp breath, grab it with greedy hands, then sit on the edge of my lumpy mattress, staring at it—holding it like it contains the sole key to my future, and maybe it does. It's certainly thick enough.

The word *Angel* still graces the front, looped in blue cursive prettier than any man should have, but now the thought of actually opening it freaks me the fuck out. I still don't know if I can do this. What if it's more bad news—more deception—or, even worse, a goodbye? My old fears return in a rush, along with a shiny new one.

What if I'm faced with forgiveness?

I shake my head. I'm jumping the gun. For all I know, this envelope contains papers related to my former employment or good behaviour bond and nothing more. A tear splats on the front, blurring the letter *A*. I wipe it away, but only smudge it worse.

You've got this, Aves. You're strong. Independent. Planted in a field of flowers now, remember?

I close my eyes, feeling a warm flourish of gratitude for that new, kind little voice that always has my back. She's right. I'm all those things now. So I rip out the pages and read.

Angel,

I have so much to say. Things I should have told you from the start. Things I'm finally ready to share, albeit too late. But first, know that I love you. That was real. It hasn't changed. It won't ever change. And second, I'm SO sorry. I screwed up, royally. There's no excuse for what I did—what I hid. It was wrong, and I was selfish. Unfortunately, I still am, for a better man might've left you free to move on, but if I don't fight for you, I'll hate myself forever.

You see, I didn't expect to find you sitting alone and scared in court that day and feel like gravity suddenly weighed a tonne. I didn't expect your eyes to be so deep and blue or a strange familiarity to swallow my heart. I didn't expect your cheeks to flush or your breath to hitch—your nervous smile, fuck-me hair, or faint vanilla scent. I didn't expect to look at you and see a whole new world that instantly felt like home.

Something deep and dire flared inside me that day. A need to protect you. To save you. To hold you in my arms and know you. Yet I was meant to let you go—spare you a conviction and be on my merry way. But I couldn't do it, even when I tried.

You see, some people feel things deeper and live gripped by their past. And that kind of pain recognises itself. It recognises the opportunity to be understood. That kind of pain forges kindred spirits and forever. It binds together lost souls who need each other to heal. You are the other half of my broken soul, Avery Masters, and I need you just to breathe.

I'm sorry for lying to you, deceiving you, holding back a truth you deserved to know. I'm sorry for destroying your trust, holding your heart under false pretences, and then shattering it.

I should have come clean the second I knew what we were. Many times, I almost did. The words sat on my tongue while you were naked in my arms, but I was weak. Scared. Conflicted. I didn't want to lose you, nor destroy your world. And the harder I fell, the messier it got. Then there was Benedict's to consider, Thomas's client privilege, and my career. After a decade of hard work, I'd been at the helm for five whole minutes and was already on the edge of screwing it up. Gerard would have crawled out of his grave just to kill me.

He died five months ago today. I was in a meeting with him one minute; the next, he was dead at my knees. I was gutted, but the truth is, I didn't fully know that man until he died and left me his subpar ethics and den of shady clients. Thomas included.

That day you came to my office, I was trying to make things right. I wanted Thomas to meet you, see how incredible you are, come clean to his family, and bring everything to light because that's what I intended to do, no matter the cost, that night. I was done, and it was time you knew the truth, only I wanted it delivered as painlessly as possible. I wanted you to hear it from my mouth, in my words, while I looked you square in the eye. But that's not what happened, and instead, I froze.

I froze because for the third time in my life, I had to watch my world die, only this time it was all my fault. I froze because I felt every piece of you breaking inside my bones. I froze because when faced with Thomas's malice, I was again sixteen years old—small, weak, too dumb to know my place—and it wasn't Thomas in that room but my father, who I hate.

But when you fell to your knees, Angel, and struggled to breathe, I woke up from what felt like a ten-year trance. I'd put you there, and I wondered how I could do that to someone I cherished. What kind of man had I become? When did work and a stupid law firm start trumping all else? My morals. Common decency. Love.

My mother's head would have hung in shame. This. Isn't. You. That's what you said to me. That's what she would have said too.

Angel, I was a fool, but I woke up. I realised when compared to my father, Gerard was a saint, but the bar was in hell to begin with. I realised the grass might be greener yet still full of beetles—that greener than dead doesn't always mean good. I realised I let myself be moulded like your clay into someone I wasn't. Did things that felt wrong because I didn't trust myself. My uncle gave me everything. He even saved my life. But he also tried to extend his by hijacking mine.

I'm so sorry. My actions don't speak to the man I am, nor the one I want to be. Please know I'll respect whatever path you choose and forever wish you well, but I'll also be waiting for as long as it takes in case you ever gift me a second chance.

Come back to me, Angel, so I can spend eternity making amends, love you like you deserve to be loved, show you everything I am, and never lie to you again. Gerard's ghost has gone, and I'd like you to meet the man I truly am while I get to know him too. But fair warning, I actually hate suits and I'm leaving Benedict's (I hope that's not a deal-breaker for you). I still love, like, and adore you though. Always and forever.

—Cole

PS. Get him.

Fat tears are rolling down my face as sobs quake my shoulders. Always and forever. Of all the words Cole could use, he chose two of Dad's. Maybe it's a sign. *It feels like a sign.* But regardless, one thing's for sure: Cole's letter is everything I could have hoped for. Genuine. Apologetic. Insightful and raw. *Beautiful.* And now I get it—I get *him.* A whole facet of him I couldn't see because I plonked him on a pedestal, then knelt self-loathing at its feet. That was unfair to us both. Cole's been in a messy, grief-stricken place for nine long months. And while he is older than me, successful, and super smart, he's still young and human. And humans make mistakes and bad decisions no matter how perfect or clever they seem. That realisation comes as a relief, to be honest, on many levels.

I inhale a deep breath and sigh, flopping back on the bed, clutching the letter on my belly as I stare at the light bulb dangling from the ceiling on a dirty cream cord.

I'm now faced with that bittersweet fear from before. I feel lighter. Like I'm filled with foamy bubbles in lieu of lead—like I'm the colour pink instead of grey. I forgive Cole—completely and with compassion—and I believe what we had was real. But forgiveness is one thing—trust is another. And in that respect, I'm nowhere near close. If I go back, that little voice of doubt will linger and whisper in my ear. It will be far from nice and test me every single day. But Cole deserves a second chance. Of that, I'm sure. And maybe it's not about if I can trust Cole to never hurt me again because that's beyond my control. Maybe the golden question is, Can I trust myself to cope if he does?

Can I be hurt again without crumbling or wanting to die?

Can I love him and stay whole?

Yes. I think I finally can. If he'll still have me, that is.

I read his letter again and cry again. But this time, I'm tingly all over, and those two curious little words in the postscript, plus the extra pages, actually register.

Get him.

Frowning, I flip to the next page, unsure of what I'm reading. It's a document. Multiple documents. Confidential-looking ones with Thomas Nilsen's name littered throughout. An email too, linking Thomas to a shell company in the Cayman Islands operating under an alias. References to a foreign law firm and bank account. Financial statements with sporadic activity involving big dollars. Evidence of what appears to be . . . Tax evasion. Money laundering.

"Holy shit," I whisper, holding the documents tight in my hands. Cole has gone and gifted me the key to killing Thomas's career. He knew. Somehow, Cole knew I'd want revenge without risking the spotlight. He's also trusted me with this, even though betraying a client could kill his own career too. Even though he knew I was angry and hurt—a probable loose cannon.

Right now, I could kiss him. I could climb him like a gum tree and never let go. I check the time on my phone. It's late—near ten— and this needs to be done in person if it's to be done at all. But short of Ubering to his house, which is a full hour away, I can't do anything tonight. Nor should I. I'm now Avery 2.0—a newer, better, less impulsive, more mature, patient version of the previous. Thus, I'll sleep on it to be 100 percent sure. Even though my heart is already halfway up that hill.

I look over the documents again, shaking my head. Sadly, I'm not surprised Thomas is a criminal in addition to a ginormous dick. But am I this vindictive? Not typically, but maybe I could be. Maybe this situation warrants it, and maybe Thomas Nilsen shouldn't have been so fucking nasty. God knows Australia would be better off without him—we need less corruption in power, not more. In fact, outing this arsehole might do the whole country a giant favour and benefit the greater good, my brothers included. Guess I'll think on that too. But just in case, I whip out my phone and shoot a text to Liam, who's pretty tech-savvy for a car-crazed chippy.

> **Me:**
> Do you know much about VPNs? I might
> need to leak something anonymously online.

His reply comes immediately.

> **Liam:**
> Sure do, little lady. Happy to help whenever
> you want.

Good to know.

The dignity and restraint I had last night that stopped me from Ubering to Cole's house has dwindled to naught over the last 1,076 minutes, and I'm itching. Itching with a kaleidoscope of emotions, desperate to see him, but I have a business to run, and that's in part what keeps me whole.

From behind my counter, I glare at Leo's starburst clock, waiting for that pointy gold hand to click that last minute to the top. Four p.m. That's the deal I cut with myself, and that's when Operation Find Cole will commence.

I hold my breath, jackhammering my knee up and down, until . . . Bingo. Then I grab my satchel, race out the front to collect my sign, and lock up the shop in time to make the first train.

Forty-three jittery minutes and two more letter reads later, I disembark the second, one block south of Cole's new firm, and run. I run as fast as I can, turning heads as I tear through the sunny street, sidestepping prams and school kids, shoppers and dog walkers.

The cream brick terrace Google showed me soon appears, the number seventy-five standing proud on a glazed front door. There's no other hint of the building's purpose, but a sign greets me upon entry, promising legal help, with an arrow pointing up a flight of tan carpeted stairs. There's no receptionist when I reach the top either, only an empty desk and acrylic sign asking clients to please knock twice on the red door, then take a seat.

I stare at that shiny red door, swiping my sweaty brow as my chest heaves. Cole's name hangs printed on more plastic adjacent, which feels strange because in my mind, his name should be stamped into solid gold or at least circled by lights. I scan my shagadelic surroundings: the stripy beige wallpaper, the tan carpet that didn't stop at the stairs, the splashes of retro orange and red, the old brown air conditioner wheezing away on the wall. This office is worlds away from the gold, glitz, and shiny terrazzo of Benedict Kane, but it's cosy—relaxed—and I like it.

Willing courage, I step towards the door and knock twice. "Come in." Cole's reply is immediate, and those two tiny words are enough to make my racing heart trip over itself like a clumsy puppy, hysterical to hear its owner return.

God, that voice.

With trembling fingers, I open the door and step inside. The sight of Cole in the flesh after four long months steals my ability to breathe, but our eyes lock, exchanging a hundred words before a single one is uttered.

Cole stands from his chair. "Angel."

God, that name.

I swallow. "Hi." Then continue to stare, utterly Cole-struck. Despite rehearsing everything I intended to say, I'd forgotten what it's like to be in this man's presence—the magnetism that swirls between us and the power Cole effortlessly emits. The room smells like him too. That heady, woodsy, sophisticated scent that feels like home. It's dizzying, but I manage to nudge myself lucid and clear my throat. "The letter . . . ," I say, choked by a level of emotion even I didn't predict. "Tell me it's all—" My voice trails off as I notice an elderly lady seated in front of Cole's desk, her eyes and feathery smile sparkling with curious delight. She gives me the teensiest of nods as if to say, "Carry on. Don't mind me."

Cole steps out from behind his desk and strides towards me, but I startle and back away. Immediately, he halts, studying me with that signature WTF line pressed into his frown. "It's okay," he says, surrendering his hands in the air. He resumes his approach cautiously as if I might bolt, and he's right to be wary, because for whatever reason, my flight instinct has kicked in full gear.

"Your letter," I say, trying to override it. "Is it true? Everything you wrote?" I need to see it—honesty in the depths of his eyes—from where I stand in my flowery field on the very same level as him.

"Yes," he grits out, his voice low and severe as he stops two metres away, and it's there in abundance, the honesty. Clear as motherfucking day. Cole thuds his fist against his chest. "Every. Single. Word." Pained but pretty eyes bore into mine.

His face is weary—devoid of the light it once had—and to know I had anything to do with that kills me. I never let him explain, and I refused to read his letter. When I consider what that must have been like for him, I feel sick to my bones. One strike and he was out.

I scan him from head to toe. Gone are the shiny shoes and designer suit he claims to hate. Gone is the manicured stubble and short, product-preened hair. In their place are well-worn jeans and trusty Chucks—a sea-green polo shirt that matches his eyes. More scruff, and longer locks. He's wilder and softer, like the jungle that covers his sinewy arm. Like a regular man with feelings, who carries a past, and just wants to be loved like everyone else.

"Please don't run," he says. The desperation in his voice glues my feet to the floor. I shake my head, almost imperceptibly, but Cole relaxes his shoulders a smidge.

He glances back to the dear old lady who's completely enthralled, watching us like she might a favourite daytime soap opera. "Mrs. Taylor, would you mind terribly if—"

With a sweet smile, she huddles to her feet and gathers up her Glomesh purse before he can finish. "I must be off now anyway. The girls are waiting for me at the club. We're having shots before bingo." Mrs. Taylor winks, and Cole mouths his thanks.

On her way to the door, she stops at his side, patting his arm with one brittle hand. "That's her, isn't it? Good luck, dear." But her attempt to whisper fails from a foot below Cole's ear, prompting his cheeks to flush.

Biting back a smile, I avert my gaze to the shaggy carpet, watching Mrs. Taylor in my peripheral vision as she hobbles out the door. Cole closes it behind her, pausing for a beat before turning to face me.

Once again, our eyes lock and speak a thousand silent words. The ocean of tenderness in his wraps me in a sunshine hug, but I also see fear, and Cole stays in front of that door.

"You talk about me to your clients?" I ask, rubbing tiny circles on the inside of my wrist with my thumb.

He shrugs with a half smile. "Mrs. Taylor isn't exactly a client. She's a . . . well . . . I guess you could say she's my wise old friend."

"That's nice," I say, meaning it.

His Adam's apple bobs. "Would you like to, uh, sit down?" He motions to a settee and duo of armchairs sitting in the corner of his office, but I shake my head. Right now, the adrenaline won't let me sit.

Cole nods but stiffens a little, causing guilt to tighten my chest. I never realised how easy this man is to read, or perhaps I couldn't see clearly through the faulty lenses I wore. "I won't run," I say, dumping my satchel on the floor. "I'm here to talk."

Releasing a hefty sigh, Cole steps away from the door and walks over to the half-open window. There's a slice of ocean visible behind the buildings across the road, at which Cole seems to stare while kneading the back of his neck. "Christ, I've missed you."

"Me too," I whisper as tears surge.

He turns to face me. "Aves, I—" Then squeezes his eyes shut beneath a tortured frown. "I screwed up." He glances back up. "*Please*—" But then presses his mouth shut and shakes his head. "Sorry. I shouldn't put that on you. I've caused enough damage as it is." Defeated, he flops his arm back down.

"No," I say, "I should've given you a chance to explain." The flash of hurt on his face seems to glow in the late sun as it streams through the window, catching dust motes around him. "Hannah came to see me," I add.

Cole's jaw ticks. "She was under strict orders to leave you alone."

"It's okay. I read your letter last night. I wouldn't have if she hadn't come."

Cole's face pales. "You only read it last night?"

Sheepishly, I nod.

"I thought—" He shakes his head, then sighs. "Never mind."

I know what he thought. He thought I'd read it long ago and didn't care. He thought his heartfelt honesty and revelations made no fucking difference to me. And honestly, they might not have had I read them too soon, but now things are different. *I'm different*. I know more about him, myself, and this crazy, fucked-up world. I know I can survive on my own. But I also know I don't want to, because I, too, love, like, and adore every luminous spark of this man's soul. "Do you still feel the way you said in the letter?"

Cole's gaze locks onto mine with warrior-fierce resolve. "My feelings aren't fleeting. I thought I made that abundantly clear. You own my heart, Aves. Whether you want it or not."

God, those words. That conviction.

My feet override any pride or doubt left in my mind, and I float towards Cole as my body begs to reconnect with his—as it begs to go home. I halt toe to toe with him—Chuck Taylor to Chuck Taylor—and our chests rise and fall in synchrony as we silently stare. Tentatively, I reach for his hand, where it hangs clenched at his side, and slip my thumb inside his grip, cradling his knuckles. The tingles I felt the first time we touched in the court's foyer return with a vengeance, fizzing up my arm like a galaxy of tiny shooting stars. I shudder, and Cole sucks in a sharp breath. Again, his eyes fall shut, but this time, there's serenity.

Home.

I slide my other hand up his lean, muscular arm, over the tropical jungle of tattoos, and watch as his throat bobs and his eyes flutter open to reveal pupils huge and hungry. "I need to touch you," he says in that deep, gravelly voice that seems to vibrate along an energy cord tethered to my core.

"Do it," I whisper, and then I'm hard against his chest, wrapped in strong arms with fingers threaded through my hair. Cole grips me like I might dissolve—like I'm merely an apparition born of his desperation—and then inhales me like I do him. A waterfall of tears erupts, purging tension from my bones as the weight of us being apart finally lifts, leaving in its wake a deep sense of peace and rightness.

Home.

"Say you forgive me," Cole mutters against my hair. "Say this isn't the last time I'll hold you."

Still choked with tears, I pull back, just far enough to look at him. "I forgive you. I want you in my life. Always and forever."

Cole's whole body appears to relax, and light fills up his face, making his glassy eyes glitter like silver-green gems. He cradles my wet cheeks, stroking away the tears with his thumbs. "Thank fucking Christ."

A smile tugs at my lips as I cock a cheeky brow. "Language, Mr. Benedict."

His laugh is a symphony. "Touché, Miss Masters."

We smile at each other, exchanging the kind of jubilant, soul-deep, sparkly smiles that meld together hearts, and then he presses his forehead to mine, and we share each other's air. "I'm going to kiss you now, Angel, and I can't promise I'll ever stop."

I reach up onto my tippy-toes, licking my strawberry-glossed lips as I close in on his. "Do it."

So he does. He crashes his peppermint-tinged mouth to mine, forcing my feet to shuffle backwards until my back hits the door. His weight presses against me, caging me in, and he continues to devour my mouth as if I'm the water he prayed for while lost in an endless blazing desert. We both groan.

God, his taste. His intensity.

We swallow each other's shallow breaths and hungry whimpers as our tongues glide and our teeth nip. The fresh sea-salt breeze blowing in through the window tickles my bare skin as Cole lifts the hem of my top, splaying a warm hand low on my back. I love the way he holds me—how his firm hands dwarf my body and make me feel small, fragile, and completely his.

Desire pools between my legs as his arousal presses against my belly, low and hard but not low enough, and I need more. I'll always need more.

I hook my leg around his hip, and Cole slides a hand under my knee, hitching me up to wrap my legs around him, granting friction where I need it. The rush of syrupy tingles that flourish through my body trigger a mess of breathy moans, but denim still separates us, and that simply will not do. I need Cole naked, free in my arms, and hot against my skin.

He kisses up my neck like he kissed my mouth, leaving a trail of goosebumps, and my head falls against the door while I scratch my nails down his back. "You smell so damn good," he whispers at the shell of my ear with singeing hot breath that tickles and makes me shiver right down to my pointed toes. I kiss and lick down to his collarbone, relishing his salted-candy taste, and he grinds harder against my core, catching my earlobe between his teeth, biting down hard and soft enough to drive me fucking wild.

Reaching between us, I flick open the button on his jeans, then tug at the hem of his polo shirt. "Please," I say. "I need you naked."

Cole's smirk is equal parts triumph and filth, and his eyes glimmer like black diamonds as he gently sets me down. In one smooth motion, he grasps his shirt from the back of his collar and pulls it over his head, then steps back, kicks off his shoes, and gets rid of his socks and jeans.

The head of his hard cock teases the waistband of his black trunks, but it's him in his wholeness that stills me in awe. My memory did not do this man justice—it was too blurred by heartbreak and tears. I drag my gaze up from his bare feet to his sculpted thighs, then over every golden ridge and valley of his stomach and chest, licking my lips as I envisage tasting and worshipping every square inch of him. It could be the hazy slant of summer light coursing through the window, or the orange hue it throws, but Cole, this very minute, appears radiant and surrounded by gold. The lush jungle on his arm vibrantly beckons while the tiger dares me near, and I swallow. "You're stunning," I say, meeting his eyes. "Just so you know."

Cole smiles gently this time and closes the space between us. "So are you," he whispers in my ear, tucking away my hair. Reaching past my waist, he flips the lock on the door, then slides my billowy top up my raised arms and over my fingertips, letting it float to the floor as he unhooks my pink bra and disposes of that too. He greets my breasts and tight nipples with a greedy mouth and hands before peppering kisses down the centre of my stomach as he drops to his knees. Cole stares up at me then, his gaze heavy and hooded while he unbuttons my frayed denim shorts and slips off each shoe. I watch him, steadying myself on his strong shoulders, as he shimmies down my shorts and lace panties until they fall clean to the floor. And I stay watching as he hooks my leg over his shoulder and bites his plump bottom lip. "Christ, you're even more perfect than I remember."

He dives in to feast without wasting a second, causing my breath to hitch and shudder. His scorching, wet mouth is soft on my sex—his stubble scratching my inner thighs—and the combined feeling is ecstasy.

"Oh God." I grip Cole's hair, thankful there's more there to grab, as he sucks down on my clit and pushes two fingers inside me, plunging them in and out. I'm ridiculously soaked—that much is clear to the ear—but I don't give a fuck. I'm way beyond that.

His gluttonous murmurs vibrate through me, setting every cell ablaze, and I melt into him on weak and trembling knees. Fuck. I'd forgotten how attuned Cole is to my body—how he plays me like a fine violin. A bespoke one built just for him that cherishes every stroke and responds precisely to his needs.

Long-dormant pleasure surges through me, strong and fast. "I'm going to come," I gasp.

Again, Cole's fingers plunge into me. Once, twice, three more times before he bites the inside of my thigh, then gently nips my clit and resumes soothing it with a sinfully skilled tongue. I explode. God, how I explode. Rapture slams through me, arching my back and liquifying my legs. Cole holds me upright, anchoring me hard against his mouth, while I rock against his tongue and surrender to wave after wave of potent bliss.

I'm still in fuzzy la-la land when Cole stands and shoves down his trunks, wrenches my legs around his hips, and slams his long length inside me. A rough groan tears from his throat, sopranoed by one of my own as my freshly fired nerve endings ache in the most beautifully painful way.

"Fuck," Cole grits as he thrusts in and out. Now isn't the time for slow or sweet—now is the time to purge four long months of torture—four months of desire and pain. To sinter our souls together and melt in sweet relief.

My hands find his chest, and I relish the contrast of satin-smooth skin over his flexing muscles. Again, Cole finds my neck and grazes a line of kisses down to my breasts where he sucks so damn hard I yelp and spiral into another orgasm. He follows my lead and roars his release but stays deep inside me once done.

Our eyes lock, and sweat glistens on his forehead as his cock pulses inside me. Our chests heave as we struggle to catch our breath and make sense of the alchemy we create. "Holy shit," I breathe.

A smile tugs at Cole's kiss-stained mouth, and a giggle bursts free from somewhere deep inside me. "Sorry. I don't know why I'm laughing. It's just, I forgot how—" I shake my head.

"Incredible we are together?" he finishes.

"Um, yeah."

Cole tightens his hands on my arse and drags his forehead across mine. "Promise me you won't wake up tomorrow and regret this."

I skate my fingers through his damp hair and rub the tip of my nose against his. "That won't happen." How could it? My heart hasn't just dropped anchor here; it's welded itself to Cole's. "But I need complete honesty. I need you to confide in me—to trust me with your secrets. I want us on the same team from now on."

Cole pulls us away from the door and carries me to the settee. The cushions are soft against my back as he lays me down and slides out his cock. With one knee planted on the floor and the other between mine, he hovers over me, stroking my hair. "Do you have anywhere to be tonight?"

"Other than with you?" I ask.

That answer earns me a crooked smile. "Well, then." Cole climbs to his feet and grabs a box of tissues from his desk, then returns to clean us both up. "This place might be ragged, but cum stains on the couch are still beneath it."

I snort a laugh as I glance around the room, trying to ignore the resurgence of heat rushing to my core in response to his gentle but thorough cleaning skills. Like the reception, Cole's office is cosy and retro. The striped wallpaper continues on through here but is broken up by copper wall art and mid-century furniture. "Did Mrs. Taylor do your decorating?" I poke.

Dumping the dirty tissues in the mesh bin under his desk, Cole chuckles. "No, but she approves. I did this. Salvos-chic, I believe it's called."

My jaw drops. "*You* went thrifting?"

"I did." He grins, standing there naked and proud. "You made it sound like wonderland, and I thought it'd fit the space."

I prop up on one elbow to take in all the cute details. The small rocket lamp on the table nest behind me, and the colourful West Ger-man pottery scattered across the sideboard. "It's lovely," I say, spotting *High Heart Symphony* perched on its pedestal in the corner behind his desk. My heart sings. He kept it. He not only kept it but put it in his office to stare at every day. What a masochist.

"*You're* lovely," Cole says, re-garnering my attention. I look up to find him staring down at me with pure adoration, and my cheeks flush, prompting him to snicker. "Can I photograph you?" he asks.

"Huh?" I frown but then remember what Hannah said. "Oh. Now?" I cock an amused brow and pretend to fluff my hair. "Like one of your French girls?"

Cole laughs. "You're my only French girl, and you look spectacular right now. Draped across my couch in the misty sun with bed hair and the dewy afterglow of sex on your skin."

Usually, I'd think hard before posing for nudes—in fact, until now I've had no requests—but I simply nod, struck mute by Cole's reverence.

It only takes him ten minutes to capture what he wants, and once he returns that fancy camera to the bottom desk drawer, he climbs onto the couch behind me, arranging us so that he's lying on his back and I'm tucked under his arm with my ear pressed to his chest. He takes a deep breath, then exhales a ragged sigh. "Okay, it's time for all that naked honesty you wanted. Are you ready?"

I glance up at him with a smirk. Naked indeed—just like us. But the ocean breeze is balmy and warm with a salty scent that perfectly complements his, and there's nowhere else I want to be. Naked, on all levels, is perfect. "I'm ready."

I trace meandering circles over his chest and stomach while he talks. His heartbeat is strong and steady, just like his voice, as he relays the story Hannah barely scratched the surface of.

He conveys the depths of his grief after his mum died, and the gut-wrenching betrayal he felt when his dad first raised a fist. How he found solace in self-destruction and landed in trouble he was lucky to escape.

He speaks of Gerard as his white knight of salvation and then crumbles into tears about Hannah. About his failure to protect her and his profound love for Ella—his profound hate for his father.

Tears of my own trickle onto his chest as I bleed along with him. If only I'd known. If only I'd considered someone else's struggle in addition to my own.

Cole explains his inability to see Gerard as anything but good. How his perception was skewed by gratitude and how that led him down paths he never should have taken.

And then he talks about Thomas—my sperm donor and shitbag extraordinaire. Cole details their every encounter. Mr. Nilsen's long history with the firm. And the threats that proved worthless in the end, since Benedict Kane continues to thrive without his business or that of his cronies. Cole explains more about *those* documents too, and by the time he's done, I know exactly what *vindictive Aves* will do.

At times, Cole speaks distantly, like it all happened to someone else, but I just lie here listening—reassuring him—stroking his skin as I lock myself inside his world and learn what it's like to be him. And by the time he's done, I feel like there's no space left between us. Like the universe that lives inside him has swallowed my very own, and alone no longer exists, nor will it ever again. I feel like I *know* him.

I glance up, worried I've forced Cole back down roads he wasn't ready to take—worried I've caused him harm. But despite his cheeks being damp and his eyes rimmed red and raw, there's a weightlessness to him. Like he finally dropped a boulder and dissolved some of his shame.

I wriggle up his body and press our damp lips together, then place a kiss in the centre of his forehead, infusing it with as much love and strength as I can. "I wish I'd been there for you. I'm so sorry."

"Me too," he rasps, looking deep into my eyes. A moment's silence passes before he clenches his jaw. "I almost killed my father."

"I know," I whisper, caressing his cheek as he does mine.

His brows gather. "I don't mean figuratively. I literally almost killed the man with my bare hands. I'm capable of that. Can you accept that reality?"

I hitch a shoulder. "Under the circumstances, I'd think less of you if you hadn't."

A spark shines in Cole's eyes, and it's like the sun breaking through black clouds. "You'd think less of me if I hadn't?" he repeats almost whimsically, with a smile itching at the corner of his mouth. He shakes his head, and a laugh bursts free from his throat, one mostly fuelled by tension and relief, but I laugh too because what else can you do? This world is a messy place, but I want to experience all that mess with him.

Twilight and the twinkling of street lights seep into the room, prompting Cole to reach behind his head to flip on the rocket lamp. "Do you miss it?" I ask.

"What, Benedict's?"

I nod.

"No," Cole says. "Is that bad? I finally feel like myself, and I never realised the willpower it took to be there every day. I mean, I can't begrudge what I achieved, nor the money, but I'm looking forward to more balance—a life that better fits me. And besides, Benedict's is in good hands. Perverted hands perhaps, but Mike Reynolds knows what he's doing."

"Alex's Dad? He's running Benedict's?"

"That's who the partners committee appointed." Cole shrugs. "It's okay. He became a little more tolerable when he finally stopped eye-fucking you." I roll my eyes with a smirk, and Cole's dimple shines. "It's your turn now," he says a moment later. "Time to tell me your sorry tale."

"You mean the one in the file? The one you already know?" I quip.

Cole winces. "It's briefer than you imagine. Clinical and nondescript. I want to hear it from you. From here." He presses his palm to my heart, and any inklings of annoyance simply wash away.

"Do you still have it?" I ask. I hate the thought of anyone else seeing that file, Mike Reynolds included.

Cole nudges his chin towards his desk. "It's locked in the filing cabinet right over there."

I prop up a little. "Can I see it?"

"You can have it. The key's in the top drawer. Do whatever you want with it, but personally, I'd burn the damn thing."

That's exactly what I plan to do, but I guess it can wait until our next bonfire. I flop back down with a sigh. "Later. I have a story to tell."

So I do. I tell Cole everything he probably knew and everything he doesn't, earning myself a smack on the bum when I confess what happened that fateful night that led me to him. But I just cheekily grin. "I have no regrets."

Cole's brows jump. "No? You spent your eighteenth birthday trembling in court."

"And I met you." I grin. "As someone told me not so long ago, how can I wish it never happened when it gave me my world?"

Cole looks at me with a sad smile. "Hannah."

I nod. "Our circumstances are wildly different, but her words ring profoundly true. Your sister is extremely wise. Brave and beautiful too."

Cole stares at me. He stares at me like I'm magic and he can't believe his luck. Like there's beauty in even my shadow and clarity in all my mud. Like he sees me—*all of me*—and marvels nonetheless. "I love you, Angel," he says. "Just when I think my heart is full, you somehow double its size."

I melt into goo—sparkly, unicorn, rainbow glitter goo. *I melt into him*. "Ditto" is all I can say, because what combination of words could ever top the sentiment in those or aptly convey my love? Instead, I'll try to show him.

Between kisses, I climb to straddle Cole's lap. And this time, drenched in the lamp's amber glow, with the urgency gone and our truth laid open and bare, we make love.

Slow. Smooth. Sweet and fervent love.

Love that cosmically binds us together.

Love that takes me home.

The End

Thank you for reading *Muddy Messy Love*!
If you enjoyed this book, please tell your friends and consider
leaving a review on Goodreads, Amazon, or anywhere else.
Your support is truly appreciated.

Author's Note and Acknowledgements

I remember the exact moment I decided to write this book. I was standing in my kitchen at age thirty-four, having just received an invasive melanoma diagnosis. To my supremely anxious brain, it didn't matter that it was caught early and my survival odds were excellent—I was absolutely terrified and, for the first time in my life, felt the truth of my mortality. I realised things like that could, in fact, happen to me. That it wasn't always someone else. And in that moment, I knew I could never unknow that. Such blissful ignorance was forever gone, along with any ability to completely relax again . . . Not that I was ever good at that.

It was then I also had the jarring realisation that, apart from wife- and motherhood, I'd hardly done anything I wanted to do. I hadn't travelled. I hadn't tried to revive my love of art. I hadn't yet written a novel! So I made a mental bucket list and, the following year, started writing *Muddy Messy Love*. I tried a term of pottery too, but it wasn't for me. It did, however, inspire Avery's talent!

I'd like to tell romantic tales from that point on. A shiny new lease on life. Sunlit mornings spent tapping away at a laptop with my hair in a topknot and music humming in the background. But the best I can say is that I obviously didn't die from melanoma. The wide excision was successful, and I've been in the clear ever since. What I can also tell you is despite that, over the next few years, I slowly became sicker and sicker, until by 2020, what I was having to endure every day had me thinking death was the kinder option and actually considering it countless times.

I had developed what they (inadequately) call chronic fatigue syndrome, or ME/CFS, and I was categorised as severe. Which meant I was an avid reader who could no longer read books. I couldn't sit or stand without feeling horribly ill. I was constantly breathless, frequently nauseous, and dizzy. I was in constant pain. Walking to my front door could tip me into a brutal "crash" for days, as could even one phone call, any stress, lights, smells, noise, talking or listening too much. *Thinking too much.* Music was gone. TV was out. I could barely shower on my own and once a week at most. Even lying on a couch was too much. My body felt like it was full of wet concrete and as though a mild acid now ran through my veins instead of blood. My head and the base of my skull near constantly ached. I felt like I'd been poisoned.

On my bad days, I spent over twenty-three hours lying flat in bed in a dim room, praying for it to end but not knowing if it ever would. On my good days (if you can call them that), I had about three to four hours in total where I could sit up in bed in short stints, walk to the kitchen to get my own food. Sit outside for ten minutes. Attend a health appointment if I was desperate and sufficiently prepared. And . . . I could continue writing this book—even though I had to email scenes to my phone to rewrite and edit flat on my back. Even though my symptoms would flare after just thirty minutes, thanks to the mental exertion, and I'd always pay harshly for the privilege. But it was one of the few things that gave me hope. And that was my life for two and a half grim years, until some kind of switch flipped in 2022 and slowly I started to improve. It's an ongoing battle, but I'm now at least well enough to publish! And my perspective on life has forever changed.

Needless to say, this book is more than merely a novel to me. It buoyed me through hell and back, and I'd first like to thank it. Because without the meaning it gave me and the little bursts of excitement and joy along the way, I don't know if I'd still be here. So (though I hope it is) whether it's a *good* book or a success is irrelevant. It's already given me everything. And my bucket list now has one item fewer.

The second thanks I'd like to give is to the kindest person I know and my best friend—my husband. He undoubtedly deserved first mention, but I also wanted him acknowledged for sticking by me through all that. For taking care of me. He's my hero. He is the reason I know what true love is and why I can write about it. So thank you, honey. For *everything*. I love, like, and adore every luminous spark of your beautiful soul. ;-)

To my daughter. Thank you for being my greatest fan, for rekindling my love of reading romance with your fanatical *Twilight* phase, and for tolerating my obsession with Avery and Cole. But mostly, thank you for being so beautifully you.

To my Jay. Thank you for your eagle eyes, the helpful tips, and your unflappable assumption this book will succeed. If you're still this adorable now, I can't ever imagine you won't be.

To Isabella. When you arrived six years ago, I discovered the purest love of all. Thank you for being everything good in this world and for inspiring Ella and Mini-Bees. And thank you to Mason for only compounding all that.

To my beta readers, Kaycee, Dimitra, and Tara. I hit the jackpot with you guys. You were all so helpful in uniquely different ways— the perfect beta team—so thank you again. And thank you also to Sarah for reading act one in the early days.

To my copyeditor, Lyss from Lyss Em Editing. Thank you for your efficiency, your knowledge, and for making working with an editor a friendly and undaunting task! It was truly a pleasure.

To my proofreader, Laura Boon from It's All Write. Thank you for jumping in on a moment's notice, for your skill and encouragement, and for believing in this book. I'm touched and deeply grateful.

To my cover designer, Sarah Hansen from Okay Creations. Thank you for creating such a gorgeous cover. I feel so fortunate to have your incredible talent connected to this story.

To all the ME/CFS (and now Long Covid) patients—especially those severe or worse—know that recovery *is* possible, and please don't lose hope. To all the crusaders—many of whom have recovered themselves or have a loved one battling the illness—thank you for spreading awareness. Thank you for giving us hope when we're often told there is no cure. And thank you for helping us through recovery.

And finally, to you, dear reader. Thank you for taking a chance on a newbie indie author. I hope this story expanded your heart, made you smile, and gave you all the feels you desired.

Love always,

Emme xo

About the Author

Emme Spire was born and raised in the charming city of Adelaide, South Australia, and discovered a passion for romantic fiction at age eleven thanks to Judy Blume's *Forever*. Unfortunately, Emme's primary school didn't appreciate her sharing that particular book amongst her friends, but the risqué story and trouble she experienced as a result perhaps sparked her path to writing *Muddy Messy Love*. So thank you, Judy. (And Ralph.)

When Emme isn't writing or grappling her way through chronic fatigue syndrome, she's enjoying her beautiful little family or pondering existence and spiritual teachings in her Nepalese socks while drinking tea.

For more information or to keep in touch, visit Emme's website:
www.emmespire.com